SPIRE CLIMBERS

TITAN HOPPERS
BOOK 2

ROB J. HAYES

PREVIOUSLY ON TITAN HOPPERS

Humanity has survived on a fleet of decrepit spaceships, orbiting giant interstellar titans. The titans themselves are spaceships the size of planetoids, filled with supplies, guarded by vicious monsters and deadly traps. Warriors and explorers known as Hoppers make trips over to the titans to retrieve the needed supplies. Hoppers are born with one of 7 classes:

Paladin - can enhance others, increasing their strength, durability, speed, etc.

Corsair - focus their current through a sword to deliver short range attacks.

Mage - focus their current through a cannon to deliver long range attacks.

Berserker - become stronger the more current they use.

Vanguard - adept at defending others and creating shields.

Surveyor - scouts, medics, used to disarm traps and discover safe passages through the titans.

Mechanist - uses automatons to control battles.

Hoppers can learn to focus their current through a variety of talents unique to each class. The 5 Gates of Power exist within all

Hoppers and it is only through opening those gates that Hoppers can become strong.

Courage Iro was born talentless, yet he always dreamed of being a Hopper. When the titan his fleet is orbiting explodes, killing his Paladin sister, he takes up her broken sword, determined to unlock a talent and follow in her footsteps.

5 years after the death of titan 01, the fleet arrives at a new titan (titan 02). Iro accidentally ends up on the first Hop and manifests a Corsair talent. He is shipped over to live and train on the Eclipse, a Corsair ship.

Meanwhile, Courage Emil, a trainee Paladin, is angry that Iro saved his life aboard the titan. He begins training on his own, determined never to need saving again.

The Corsair trainees from the Eclipse and Paladin trainees from the Courage begin hopping together, working to open their first Gates of Power. On one such Hop they encounter Hoppers from another fleet orbiting titan 02. Before the encounter can lead to violence a couple of deadly warriors wearing black cloaks appear and warn the Hoppers away. The Black Cloaks kill Master Courage Tannow and kidnap one of the trainees.

Iro blames himself for the trainee being kidnapped and makes a promise to find and rescue her. Emil, frustrated at his trainee group disbanding, breaks his own class and turns his talents in on himself so he can enhance himself but not others.

The Corsair trainees from the Eclipse are given a new trainer, Master Alfyn. Alfyn is determined to make Iro open his first Gate of Power no matter the cost. On another Hop, he throws Iro into danger and eventually takes matters into his own hands, threatening to kill Iro unless he opens his gate.

Emil gets in the way, protecting Iro before Alfyn can kill him. Iro opens his first gate to protect Emil, then Emil opens his first gate just moments later to protect Iro. Together, they hold back

Alfyn long enough for the other trainees to flee back to the Eclipse. Alfyn is swamped by monsters and presumed dead.

Before he leaves, Iro encounters a small automaton who claims to be his guide. He names the bot North.

PROLOGUE

Mufar leapt over the charging paragore, spun in midair to avoid its barbed tail, landed into a roll that lost none of his momentum. He couldn't afford to be slowed down. His armor was scrapped, his spear long gone, his current running low. He sprinted on.

The corridor was dark. Flickering lights strobed the metal panels beneath him. The persistent drip and hiss of something far more corrosive than water punctuated the gloom. A howl echoed through the space, bouncing off the bulkheads. They were gaining on him. He had to get to the Spire. The others needed warning.

A snarl warned him the paragore was close. He threw himself to the side, hit the wall hard. The paragore snapped at him, its teeth ripping his already tattered cloak, tearing it from his shoulders.

Before the beast could recover, Mufar cartwheeled onto its scaly back, rolled, grabbed a protruding spine, and flipped the monster over. He slammed it against the metal floor with such force the panels buckled and bent. Mufar raised his fist, drew on what little current he had remaining, and activated his Crestfallen talent. The corridor lit up with a searing yellow light as his crest filled it, arcane symbols written across the walls, the floor, the ceiling, everywhere. Then the light started retracting, rushing towards him, surging up his legs and concentrating in his fist. His hand shone bright as a fire, blazing as a furnace, radiant as a star.

The paragore struggled, tried to right itself. Its tail lashed out, slammed into Mufar's thigh. He grunted. The last of his crest flowed into his fist and a ball of burning plasma burst to life in his hand. He punched it down into the paragore. It burned through the monster's armored chest, melted its flesh, cooked it from the inside. Then it detonated in a blinding flash so bright, Mufar had to shield his closed eyes and still the light burned itself into him. He was thrown back against the far wall of the corridor. He slumped, hands held up before him.

When the light died down, he opened his eyes and blinked away the dancing spots. The paragore was gone. Not just dead. Not just burned. But gone. Half the wall had gone with it, melted slag where once it had been solid bulkhead. Through that hole, Mufar could see the space between the chambers. Darkness, rushing water, fetid air. Beyond the blackness, he saw a small opening in another wall maybe two hundred feet away. It led to a brightly lit room with a flickering green light. That was it! The Spire. So close. But so far away. The space between the titan's walls were too dangerous, even for him.

The howl sounded again. Closer than before.

Mufar stood and his left leg collapsed beneath him. He looked down to see his thigh bleeding from the wound the paragore had dealt him. Worse, it burned like fire. Venom. Of course it was venom.

Mufar groaned. "Next time there's a delivery. Someone else can go. I'm gonna volunteer for guard duty where it's nice and safe."

Another howl.

"Alright. Alright. I'm going."

Mufar activated his crest with his right hand. Dull yellow light fizzed in his palm. "Whoops. Wrong one." He waved the crest away and activated his other crest with his left hand. Bright purple lines flared bright. He gripped hold of his thigh and his crest burned, searing the skin closed. It was a stupid way to use it, but at least it was quick.

Mufar leapt down through the hole he had made into the darkness. He landed on a large pipe, almost slipped on a pile of brown goo. Another howl drifted from behind him. He forged on. The pipe was slippery and it made for slow, treacherous going. Every moment he drew closer to the far hole in the wall and the pulsing green light. So close.

A gust of hot, rancid wind blasted into him. Mufar froze. He half turned to stare out into the oppressive darkness of the space between the walls. He heard a chittering like thousands of teeth grinding against each other. Then six huge, bright orange lights ignited in the dark. Whatever it was, it was massive. A behemothic monster hunting in the null spaces.

Mufar ran. He decided falling to his death was better than being eaten. A huge chitinous claw flashed out and he leapt into the air away from it. It smashed into the pipe, crushed it. Metal screamed and tore away. Steam hissed into the darkness and engulfed him. Mufar activated his purple crest and threw out an ethereal platform. He hit the glowing light and slid to a stop. His current was almost gone again, the platform fading.

The monster lurched out of the darkness for him. Mufar caught sight of twin rasping jaws. He filled the platform below him with as much current as he could, and detonated it, launching himself across the gap and away from the creature. He slammed into the far wall, missing the hole by a few feet, scrabbled, trying to find purchase, and failed. He fell.

His hand caught the lip of the hole and he dug his fingers in. His shoulder wrenched in its socket and he screamed against the pain.

The six orange lights drifted closer again and a huge spiked limb darted out, trying to skewer him against the wall. Mufar shifted to the left, still holding on by his fingertips. The limb speared into the wall, shearing through metal. Mufar swung his feet up onto the limb, jumped off and launched himself through the hole in the wall.

The monster roared behind him. Mufar pushed himself to his feet and stumbled on, clutching at his dislocated shoulder.

Finally, he was almost there. The room before him was brightly lit with soft pearly bulbs on the ceiling. Runnels in the floor let water drain from one side of the room to the other in a hundred sparkling streams. At the bottom of each runnel Mufar saw luminescent lines. The water steamed, giving the place an oppressively warm and humid feel. Above, hundreds of hooks hung down from the ceiling on lengthy chains. He decided he was either in an oven, or a torture chamber, and neither sounded like good options.

The door to the Spire was at the far end of the room. It was huge, twisting the wall. Not a natural feature at all, but one that had grown out of the very metal of the hull. On either side of the door, green lights flared then dimmed, flared then dimmed. The door was unlocked, just waiting for someone to enter it.

Mufar staggered on, limped, cradling his left arm. His current was recharging, and he was wounded in so many places. His leg burned with venom and his chest was tight. But he'd made it. He'd be able to warn the others.

The grand door dwarfed him. Ten of him could have walked through abreast comfortably. He pressed the button to one side and an alarm blared out for a moment. A few seconds later, he heard the clunk and whir of gears starting up. The giant door started to rise.

A cacophonic howl from behind deafened Mufar and he spun about just as a Vhar caster popped into being in front of him. A meaty hand shot out, grabbed him around the neck, lifted him from the ground. He was slammed against the rising door. A second of the Vhar's arms grabbed him by one wrist, and then a third arm grabbed his other wrist. It held him there, three hands pinning him against the door, and two more hands to spare.

The Vhar was a hideous thing of bulging, discoloured muscle it had stolen from other creatures. It grinned at him without lips, its muzzle pressing close, breath rancid enough Mufar gagged.

"Do you mind?" Mufar growled around the hand constricting his throat. "I'd rather not die smelling your breath."

The Vhar pulled him close and slammed him against the rising door again. Its brown tongue flicked out between broken fangs. Mufar brought his knee up, smashed it into the Vhar's jaw, snapping its jaw shut so violently it severed its own tongue. The monster dropped him, staggered away, and screamed in pain, spraying stinking gore all over the bulkheads.

Another howl, followed by another and another. Three more Vhar casters popped into existence in the steamy room. Each one was taller than Mufar, rippling with stolen muscle, too strong for him in his wounded, exhausted state. Still, he grinned at them as they stalked towards him.

"You might wanna…" He raised a hand, pointed to the other end of the room.

One of the Vhar turned, screamed in alarm just as the monster from between the walls, shoved a spiky claw through the hole, snapped it shut around the Vhar. Then all the Vhar were screaming, a noise so loud Mufar could barely think.

He dropped to his side and rolled underneath the opening door into the Spire. Mufar sprang to his feet, slammed a fist against the button on this side of the door. The pulsing lights went from green to red and the door started lowering again.

He backed away, breathing heavily, barely able to stand. The noise from the other side of the door was all screams and clicks and splatters. Mufar sat down, buried his head in his hands and sighed.

One of the Vhar launched itself underneath the door. It snarled at him, reached for him, screamed. Then it was dragged back by the monster outside. The door slammed shut, sealing both it and the monster on the other side.

"Well, you made it, Mufar," he said. "Good job. Go me. Woooo." He stood, turned to face the Spire. "Now all you need to do is climb this scrapping thing all on your own, and hope you can figure out how to activate it. Easy."

CHAPTER 1

IRO LEANED against the training hall doorframe and waited for Bjorn and Arne. Ever since he'd opened his First Gate, the others couldn't keep up with him. He was stronger, faster, didn't tire. He couldn't wait to test the limits of this new power.

North launched off his shoulder and took flight, buzzing around his head. The little automaton followed him everywhere and had a habit of asking intrusive questions of people. Iro had yet to see any benefit of the thing, but it had come from titan 02, so he guessed it must be useful somehow. It flew into the training room and started orbiting the girls as they ran through their pre-training stretches.

Ashvild looked no less severe and domineering than ever as she led the trainees. She'd taken over training and slipped into the role of leader so easily. Iro wondered if she'd have trouble giving up the position when Master Rollo returned. Ylfa followed the routine lazily, never putting more than half effort into anything. Ingrid looked haunted, her eyes always drifting and unfocused. She still hadn't recovered from her brother's death at the hands of Master Alfvin.

And then there was Eir. Tall, reedy, head shaved to stubble.

She never stopped smiling, and when she turned that smile towards Iro his chest tightened. There was something so graceful about her, so fluid. She moved through her stretches like oil; steady and slow and sure.

"Command Query," North buzzed in a tinny version of Iro's own voice. "North has detected elevated heart rate. Do you wish North to scan for threats?"

All the girls turned as one, noticing Iro standing against the doorframe. "Are you staring at us?" Ylfa asked. "That's scrapping creepy, Iro."

"I wasn't," Iro said. "Well, I was. But not like that. I was just..."

"You were mesmerised by our feminine grace," Eir said. She rolled forwards into a handstand and plodded about on her hands.

"Yes, exactly that," Iro said. "Wait. That sounds worse, doesn't it?"

"Much worse," Ashvild said with a look like she wanted to shove Iro out the nearest airlock.

"Commencing threat detection," North buzzed. It flew towards Ylfa and scanned a green beam of light over her.

"Hey!" Ylfa took a swipe at North, but the automaton floated out of the way. "Scrapping stupid thing."

"Threat level: 8."

"Eight?" Ylfa said, grinning. "You hear that, Iro. I'm an eight. Ready to kick your scrapping ass, gate or no."

North buzzed towards Eir. She flowed out of her handstand and back to her feet and peered at North as it scanned her too.

"Threat level: 10."

"What?" Ylfa said, frowning. "Why does she get to be top?"

North turned to fly towards Ingrid, but Eir slipped in front of it again. "North, what does the threat level go up to?"

"Lack of Command: Query not recognised." North flew to the

side, but Eir moved with it, keeping in front of it. She reached out a finger to poke the automaton and it zipped backwards.

"It's alright, North," Iro said. "You can listen to Eir. Answer her questions."

North buzzed without words for a moment. "Sub Command Eir added to directive."

"Ooooh." Eir danced closer to the automaton. "Does that mean you have to answer me?"

"Correct."

"Ah, the power!" Eir grinned, looking even more beautiful. "I'm drunk with it already. Drunk with power." She cackled dramatically. "What does the threat level go up to, North?"

"Maximum threat level: 101."

"Oh." Eir seemed to deflate. "And I'm only a ten?" She pouted at Iro like it was somehow his fault.

"Oi!" Bjorn shouted as he charged down the corridor. "You are not allowed to be that fast, Iro." He thumped Iro on the arm as he jogged past into the training hall. A few weeks ago, a punch from the massive lad would have sent Iro sprawling. Now he barely felt it.

Arne arrived a few seconds later, panting. "You're a junk hole, Iro," he said, smiling. "When I open my First Gate, I'm going to run rings around you."

"That sounds like a lot of effort for you, Arne."

The lanky boy frowned at that, then nodded. "Good point. Well, when I open my First Gate I will sit around and do nothing. But you'll know I *could* run rings around you." He gave Iro a companionable shove as he sauntered into the hall.

Iro followed Arne into the training hall. They were all together, their squad complete. Iro had to admit, he quite liked being the first of them to open a Gate of Power. It made him feel special. He'd never felt special before.

"What are we doing?" Bjorn asked.

"North is detecting threats to Iro," Eir said. She grinned, her eyes wide and bright. "North, do Bjorn. Uh, scan him for threats." North buzzed over and swept its green beam of light over Bjorn. "Threat level: 9."

Eir whooped. "I'm a higher threat level than you. Move over, Bjorn. I'm the new queen of combat."

"What? No. That can't be right." Bjorn frowned. "Wait a second. Let me get pumped up." He rolled his shoulders, dropped to the ground and did a few press ups, leapt back up and bashed a fist against his chest, then cricked his neck. "OK. Scan me again. I'm ready."

"Threat level: 7."

They all burst into laughter. Even Ingrid chuckled.

"That can't be right," Bjorn said. "It's broken."

"Line up, trainees," Master Rollo's voice shouted from outside the training hall.

Iro grinned to hear his voice and got into line with the rest of the trainees even as Master Rollo limped around the corner. He was still using a crutch and favouring his right leg, but at least he didn't need Frigg to help him around anymore.

North buzzed over to Master Rollo and scanned him before Iro could stop the little automaton. "Threat level: 75."

"Wow!" Eir said and poked Iro in the ribs. "I always thought he was pretty threatening."

Iro smiled back at her. "I kind of thought he'd be higher. Seventy-five makes him seem cuddly."

Master Rollo limped over to his usual spot and climbed onto the bench, sighing gratefully as he took the weight off his leg. "Hopper Iro," he said loudly.

Iro stepped forward.

"What the scrap are you doing in my training hall?"

Iro glanced about at the others, but they all looked bemused. "Master?"

Master Rollo sighed. "Idiot. You have opened your First Gate, Iro. You are no longer a trainee and you are no longer in my squad. Get out."

"But what do I do then?"

"Not my problem," Master Rollo said with a dismissive wave of his hand. "Go see Frigg. She's the Lead Hopper now."

Iro trudged from the training hall with North buzzing over his shoulder. As soon as he was round the corner, Master Rollo ordered the others to gather round. Just as he was starting to feel like he fit in, he found himself excluded again.

Iro paused at the door to Frigg's office, his hand held ready to knock. He'd been here before, of course. Many times over the past few weeks. Far too many times. And she always had questions. Ones she'd asked before, new ones, old ones asked in new ways. So many questions.

"Command Query: Why has Command Iro stopped?" North asked, buzzing forward in front of his face. "Is Command low on power?"

Iro waved a hand at North, swatting the automaton away. "I'm not low on energy, North. I don't work that way. And I'm not Command Iro, I'm just Iro. Or Eclipse Iro. Or Courage… it doesn't matter."

North buzzed in front of him for a few seconds. "Command Query: Why has Just Iro stopped?"

Iro sighed. "Because this is Frigg's door. You remember Frigg?"

North buzzed more energetically and landed on Iro's shoulder. "Yes," it said quietly and went deathly still.

Iro straightened his new uniform. Freshly printed, Eclipse blue, a Hopper uniform rather than a trainee's. No emblem yet, though. He'd need to get one designed. Ylfa was arty, perhaps he could ask her.

Stop hesitating. You've faced down monsters, insane Corsairs, and crushing traps. You can face Frigg's questions one more time.

He knocked. Frigg called him in a moment later and he opened the door. It was a busy office, small and filled with clutter. There were tablets everywhere. Back on the Courage, Iro's only tablet had been a tech maintenance screen. Frigg had dozens of them lying around, some displaying walls of text, others with symbols like he'd seen on Hopper's crests. The tablets lay on chairs, desks, shelves, the floor. Wherever there was space. Frigg was behind her desk, not sitting, but pacing, easily picking her way between the clutter surrounding her even without looking.

"Ah, Iro," Frigg said in a warm voice. "Come. Sit."

Iro had to move two tablets from the chair onto the desk, stacking them on a pile of others, so he could sit down. Frigg didn't seem to mind. She kept pacing.

"How are you doing, Iro? Would you like coffee?" She immediately paced towards a row of shelves and pressed a button on a machine that started whirring.

"I've never had coffee before," Iro admitted.

Frigg pulled the mug from beneath the little machine and handed it to Iro. "You still haven't." She said with a smile.

Iro looked down into the mug. It was algae. Hot algae. He wondered if they'd at least tried to flavour the gunk so it didn't taste like old shoe.

"Unfortunately coffee is a non critical resource," Frigg said. "Until we have enough food to permanently feed the fleet, it will remain that way. One day, though, Iro. One day we'll have real coffee again. That burnt, nutty smell. The warm bitterness of the taste." She sighed.

Iro sipped at his warm algae. Somehow, the heat made the taste worse, like boiled snot.

Frigg focused her gaze back on him. "And how are you, North?"

North didn't answer. Didn't so much as buzz. The little automaton almost seemed to slip a little down Iro's back, over his shoulder and out of sight.

"North is... in standby mode," Iro said.

"Oh," Frigg plucked a tablet from the table and made a quick note with a pen. "I didn't know it did that. Conserving energy, I suppose. I wonder how it recharges? Hmm. So how have you been, Iro? How are you feeling with your unlocked First Gate? Any nausea or aching limbs?" She stared at him so intently he tried to shrink into his chair. "You said facing your fears allowed you to open the gate; any dreams? Nightmares? How is your crest?"

She was always like this. A barrage of questions without pause. And when finally she did stop, she expected Iro to remember all the questions and answer them all in order.

"I've been fine, I guess. I'm feeling strong, fast, a little bored. No nausea or aching limbs. Uh... I've dreamt... Of light. A room filled with light. A patch of darkness shaped like a person in the centre, I think. Is that relevant?"

Frigg shrugged, made another note on the tablet.

"My crest is strong, I think."

"Show me."

Iro swallowed a sigh and activated his crest in front of him. It burst into icy blue light, the edges almost fizzing. It was a series of three concentric circles, symbols and arcane lettering dotted around. The centre circle was small and had a design like a triangle formed of sword slashes. The second circle was much larger and Iro recognised the broken slash symbol of his Blink Strike talent, the crossed tusks of a bhurbeast, a hammer. He still couldn't understand what any of the letters or words meant. The third circle was at the top of the second and had the flightless bird symbol of the Courage, his original home ship, in the centre. That was the lock he had opened when he passed through his First Gate. His crest was starting to expand beyond that now, though the edges were faint and faded away to nothing. There was already one symbol in the expanding area; a broken sword. His sister's broken sword. His sword now.

"Strong, consistent glow. Your current is steady," Frigg said as she studied Iro's crest.

"What does the symbol in the centre mean?" Iro asked. "Master Rollo seemed surprised the first time he saw it." He traced a finger through the triangular design, the lines fuzzed and tingled around his skin.

Frigg made a note on her tablet and shrugged. "I don't know. I've spent some time looking into it already, but I've found no references yet. It's new. All Strikers have one of four variant designs at the core of their crest. There's been a few theories as to why there are original designs. Some people suggest that it's relevant to specific bloodlines, but I've found no proof to that. Others think it pre-implies the natural progression of the Hopper, what new talents they will unlock. Again, there's no proof and two Hoppers with the same central design can take entirely different paths, unlocking different talents."

She looked up at Iro. "Have you spent any time considering which talent you want to learn? I understand you manifested with the Blink Strike talent, and your First Gate unlocked the Light Blade talent. With your First Gate unlocked, your crest can support one additional talent, and it's entirely your choice. Though it's important to choose one that will support the style of combat you wish to pursue. You understand there are different ways to fight?"

Iro nodded. He'd come to realise that Blink Strike was not the powerful talent he once thought. It didn't help him hit any harder, but was more of a mobility talent, allowing him to quickly traverse a battlefield. Light Blade allowed him to reforge his sword from his current. It meant he was never truly disarmed as long as his current flowed and he had so much as a stylus to focus through, but again it provided no extra raw power. "I need a talent that will let me deal a decisive blow," he said. "Something with real punch behind it."

Frigg made a note on her tablet. "That's certainly one possibility. Or you could focus on mobility. Rollo uses Blink Strikes and Thread Edge to great effect. Have you ever seen him swing through a room? It's fascinating. Other Corsairs prefer to learn talents that will give them greater range. Alfvin's favourite talent was Arc Blast." Iro had seen it. Arc Blast released a slicing arc of energy from the sword. Alfvin had used an Arc Blast to murder Torben.

"Well," Frigg said. "There's no need to choose right way, but it's worth putting a lot of thought into. You'll also need to find a Corsair who already knows the talent you choose to teach you. Maybe talk to a few of your fellow Hoppers and question them about their talents."

Iro nodded. He'd already given it a lot of thought, and still couldn't make a decision.

"So, why are you here today, Iro?"

"Master Rollo kicked me out of the squad. He said I should come and see you."

"Ahh." Frigg placed her tablet on the desk. "He was right too. You're not a trainee any more, Iro. If we kept you with your old squad, you'd hold them back and they'd hold you back."

"So what do I do now?" Iro asked. He had no idea how to go about finding a new squad.

Frigg smiled at him. "It's alright. This is normal. Eventually I'll add you to the Hopper rotation and send you out on Hops with squads as they request Corsairs. Or you may make contacts from other ships who specifically request you, knowing you work well together. But until then, you'll have a regular squad assigned to you."

"Who?"

"I don't know. The Council of Grands assign new Hoppers squads. They'll make sure there's a balanced group of classes. They haven't sent me your squad listing yet. But when they do, you'll receive word directly from your new squad leader, and it will be up to you to make sure you rendezvous on time. You're a Hopper now, Iro. Not a trainee. You still have a lot to learn, but you can't rely on a master to beat you into line anymore.

"On that note, it's past time." She picked up a tablet and tapped. Iro's own tablet chimed from his pocket. "You're moving. Hoppers get their own private quarters. No more sharing a room with Bjorn."

"Oh. I…" Iro wasn't sure how he felt about that. He'd never lived alone before. On the Courage, there was so little space no one lived alone. "What about training? When I'm not on a Hop?"

"That's also up to you. You can book time in the Power Acceleration Chamber and the off-use training halls. Make friends with your fellow Hoppers and ask them to train with you. There are six other First Gate Hoppers aboard the Eclipse at the moment."

Iro nodded, his head awhirl. He couldn't rely on others to direct him anymore. He had to stand on his own.

Frigg smiled at him. "You'll figure it out, Iro. We all do. I'll let you know as soon as they assign your new squad to you."

CHAPTER 2

EMIL STRODE through the corridors of the Courage with his head held high. Ever since he'd opened his First Gate, and ever since he'd walked out of his father's quarters, he felt different. For the first time, he felt like he belonged to something. That something was a near derelict space ship drifting through the void next to giant titan, but it was something.

He passed a couple of techs welding a new plating to the bulkhead wall. Although new wasn't really right. It was a section of wall stripped from another part of the ship, a section that had since been vented and left to the void of space. The two techs paused as he passed, nodded their respect to him, then went back to securing the panel to the wall. It wasn't an uncommon sight, these days. They had patched more of the Courage over than not. Emil couldn't remember the last wall he had seen that wasn't riddled with rust, fractured from acceleration stress, or coming away from shattered bolts. Again, that wasn't right. He'd seen pristine walls was when he was on the Eclipse. The mid ship was so spotless, it even smelled new.

Even from the corridor outside, the engineering deck sounded like a manufactory. Emil heard thumping, grinding, banging, clashing, whirring. It was a cacophony that made his head hurt. The smell was atrocious, too. Like something, or possibly everything, was burning. He'd never actually been to the main engineering before, and now he knew why.

Emil stepped around the corner into chaos. A tech bumped into him, muttered some insult, scurried away. The Courage's engine housing filled the spacious chamber, a madness of rings spinning and pumping around a central core that glowed orange like fire. The heat hit him like a fist to the gut, and the atmosphere felt so thick he had to wade through it.

"Clear the plasma injection feed, then run a level three diagnostic," bellowed a balding ancient man with more wrinkles on his face than his creased jacket.

"That'll take hours," shouted a little woman with oil smeared across her face.

"Oh?" The ancient man placed a gnarled hand against his chest. "Do you have somewhere else to be? Is it more important than making sure we don't all explode and die?"

"Yes! It's called bed. At least if we all explode, I'll get some rest. I've been working three days straight, Isaak."

"We all have."

The two stared at each other for a few more seconds, then the woman threw up her hands, growled an insult, and stalked away. The ancient man did the same and stalked in a different direction. Emil stood, unsure who to ask. He looked around for other techs, spotted the little one with the big nose who had been friends with Iro.

"Hey!" Emil waved at the little tech, desperately trying to remember his name. "Rory."

The little tech looked up from his work station, startled, then placed one of his tools in his bag and slunk closer. He looked like a spooked rustling about to run. "My name is Roret," the little tech said in a thin voice.

"I'll remember," Emil said and decided to commit the name to memory this time. "Where do I go to request getting new armor printed?"

Roret snorted out a laugh. "Another ship? The printers on the Courage haven't worked for… as long as I can remember. It's part of the reason we can't replace anything, including clothes."

Emil clenched his fists. How was he supposed to Hop to the titan without armor or weapons? "How can I get the printers working again?"

"You?"

Emil set his jaw and nodded. "I'm going to be Hopping now. You need parts to fix them. What should I be looking out for?"

"Oh, you're serious." The little tech rubbed a greasy hand across the back of his neck. "I can send you a list of things to look out for. Best scenario would be getting us access to a manufactory."

Emil winced. He'd tried that. They'd found a manufactory but before they could claim it, a couple of ridiculously strong Hoppers had turned up. They both wore Black Cloaks and had warned them away by killing Master Tannow and kidnapping Mia.

"In the mean time, if you need armor, why don't you ask some of the old Hoppers?" Roret said. "Maybe you can find some bits and pieces and scrounge together a full set?"

Emil smiled and clapped Roret on the shoulder. The little tech stumbled and looked offended. "That's a great idea. Thanks."

Emil turned and strode from the engineering, full of purpose. The tech was right. The Courage only had a few active Hoppers left, but there had to be pieces of armor lying around unused.

Emil heard the young trainees even before he stepped into the training hall. They were Steeling each other, stepping into range of training dummies, getting smacked around. It reminded him of his own squad before the Black Cloaks kidnapped Mia, and Cali quit being a Hopper. Now it was just him. All alone.

He rounded the corner into the training room angry, though he couldn't really decide why. There were three trainees in the now only training group aboard the Courage. They were all young, between nine and eleven years old. Phusone, their trainer, was the only Fourth Gate Hopper left on the ship, but he limped so severely he walked with a cane, and even then he couldn't go far. Some injury he'd taken back aboard titan 01 had crippled him.

Emil watched as a young girl stepped into range of a training dummy. The boy behind her activated his crest. It flared yellow for a second and the girl weathered a weak strike by the dummy. Then the boy's crest vanished and the girl took a hit that knocked her back on her ass. The dummy was on the lowest setting. These kids would not be going anywhere near the titan for a long time yet.

The girl struggled back to her feet and spotted Emil. Her eyes went wide and she gasped. "It's you!"

Emil found himself surrounded on all sides by the three kids. They shouted questions at him as they danced about and pulled on his uniform, trying to get his attention.

"What was the Gate like?"

"How did you enhance yourself?"

"When's your next Hop? Can I go with you?"

Emil had no idea how to handle the children, nor why they were so excited by his presence. He was older than them, sure, but they treated him like a hero or something. He didn't like it. He looked to Phusone for help and the crippled Hopper laughed.

"Trainees," Phusone said loudly, his voice gravelly. "Leave the

Hopper alone. Take a rest over there for a minute, let me talk to Emil."

The kids gave a collective groan and moved away. The dark-haired girl stared up at him for a moment longer, grinning, then ran off to join her squad mates.

Phusone limped over to a chair near one of the walls and lowered himself into it, wincing. He'd been a big man once, but his injury had shrunk him, leaving him soft in the belly and jowls. He wore a thick, dark beard to try to hide it. No wonder he didn't go on Hops anymore. There was a reason not many Hoppers stayed active into their grey years.

"I don't have another chair, I'm afraid," Phusone said as he rubbed hands down his left thigh, massaging the muscle.

"I'm happy to stand," Emil said.

"So I see. Very rigid." He smiled, but it quickly faded. "Sorry about Tannow. He was a good man."

Emil grunted in reply. Everyone said the same thing, and he still had no idea how to respond.

"But I can see you're not here to talk about old men. What can I do for you, Hopper Emil?"

Emil fidgeted a little, tried to think of the best way to approach the request. Direct. He was always best being direct. "I need armor. Weapons, too. Gauntlets. I like to use my fists."

Phusone nodded slowly. "I have a few bits left, but I broke most of mine during my last Hop."

"How did you…" Emil stopped himself. Nobody talked about how Phusone had been injured. It was probably impolite to ask.

"The Vhar," Phusone said. "A zerker got hold of me. The problem with Paladins, we're good at enhancing others, but not so useful in the thick of the fight. Though, from what I hear, that's not the case with you?"

Emil nodded. Paladins' talents enhanced others, made them tougher, stronger, faster. But not Emil. He still didn't understand how, but he had turned his talents inwards. He could enhance himself, but not others. He wondered if that made him an anti-Paladin? Then decided it was a terrible name.

"I had an idea," Emil said. "If ex-Hoppers brought what bits of armor they have left lying around. I might be able to scrounge together a full set. It would be better than nothing."

"An excellent idea. Trainees, you hear that? Of course you did. The only time you're ever quiet is when you're eavesdropping. Go. Run around the ship, talk to every Hopper you know. Tell them to bring whatever armor or weapons they have lying around here. The Courage needs to arm our newest Hopper." He lowered his voice. "Our last Hopper."

Emil had not forgotten that fact. With Tannow dead and Phusone clearly too crippled to Hop. The trainees left were too young and weak. He was the only Hopper the Courage had left. It was up to him to find a manufactory, to secure enough parts to get the ship back in working order. So much pressure. Emil grit his teeth and decided he would just have to be up to the task, no matter what it took.

The trainees whooped and raced off, eager to be running off around the ship. Emil waited for them go, then turned back to Phusone. The crippled Hopper looked at him expectantly.

"If I'm the only one left," Emil said slowly. "Who is the lead Hopper aboard the Courage."

Phusone chuckled. "I am."

Emil breathed a sigh of relief. That was a responsibility he did not want.

"Speaking of which," Phusone continued. "I have your orders. From the Council of Grands themselves. Looks like they've taken an interest in you, Emil. Be careful about that."

Emil started pacing. His next Hop could wait until he was armored and trained up. "I need you to teach me a new talent," he blurted.

Phusone groaned as he pushed off his cane and stood again. "You've decided already? Best put a lot of thought into this, Emil. You won't get to learn another unless you open your Second Gate."

"I know!" Emil snapped. It was rude, but he didn't apologise. It wouldn't mean anything anyway. "I need you to teach me Strength."

Phusone limped past Emil into the centre of the training hall. "A fairly basic talent. Useful for a normal Paladin to know."

"But I'm not normal. I know. I can Steel myself and take a hit, but I need to be able to strike back and hard. The best way I can do that is with Strength."

"The talent has its drawbacks."

"And I'll learn to deal with them. Teach me."

Phusone sighed, then nodded. "Activate your crest."

Emil brought his crest burning to light in front of him. It had a clenched fist gripping a cog in the centre, a bunch of symbols floating around it, some wavy lines, letters. Emil didn't care what any of it meant, only that it let him be a Hopper and get stronger.

Phusone activated his own crest. A cool turquoise maze of lines and symbols filled the space before him, easily five times larger than Emil's crest, and so much brighter.

"This is going to sting a bit," Phusone said. "But keep your crest steady."

The crippled Hopper pushed his crest forward a little. Where the crests met, the air fizzled and popped. Emil winced at a sharp pain inside, like his chest was being torn in two. He grit his teeth and suffered through it. Phusone reached out a hand and placed it before a symbol on his crest, a broken circle with a jagged line zigzagging through it.

"Place your hand against mine."

Emil reached out, touched his palm to Phusone's. The pain in his chest flared to a burning sensation. His crest sizzled and the

23

broken circle symbol burned into fiery orange light, sparks lighting the air between them.

Phusone stepped back and his crest faded away. Emil staggered, panting. He looked up to find the symbol seared into the outer ring of his crest.

"Now you just have to learn to use it," Phusone said. "I can't help you there. You might be a Paladin, but you're not like any other I've known."

Emil took a step back and pushed current into his new talent. He felt suddenly sluggish, swollen. His arms and legs pulsed with new power, but they seemed to grow, his muscles bulging. The right shoulder of his uniform tore at the seams. He swung a punch at the air, overbalanced and stumbled. He felt stronger, for sure, but so much slower.

Phusone watched him with a neutral expression. Emil growled and took a few more swings at nothing. He stalked towards one of the training hall walls and threw a jab against the bulkhead. It dented from the force of his punch.

"Hey now!" Phusone shouted. "Enough. No damaging the ship. I warned you it was a strange talent."

A woman cleared her throat and Emil spun around. He dropped the talent and immediately his arms and legs shrink back down to their normal size. He felt lighter, quicker on his feet.

Iro's mother waited in the doorway to the training hall. She was a small woman, which explained Iro's height, and wore an officer's uniform. She clutched at a piece of metal in her hands.

"It's not much, I know." She stepped into the room and smiled wistfully. Held out the shard of metal to Emil. "My daughter's old vambrace. The clasp is broken and needs fixing, and the flashlight is out of charge. She didn't have time before her last Hop, so left it behind. If you want it, it's yours."

She wasn't the last. One after another, dozens of the Courage's crew appeared with bits of armor. Old Thalia brought a greave from her Hopping days. Viktor brought a pauldron that had belonged to his grandfather. Theofania gave him a titansteel breastplate that had been passed down through four generations of her family before her. Gavril even donated his gauntlets. He was an immense man, seven feet tall and broad as a bhurbeast, but he lost a leg during a hop long ago. His gauntlets were too big for Emil, but they were forged from titansteel. He decided he'd make them work with some padding.

Last of all came Cali. She dragged a bag that clinked with every step. She stopped when she looked down at the pile of armor pieces Emil had collected. Then she dumped her bag down in front of him. She looked tired, dark bags beneath her eyes, and none of the old cheer she used to show.

"I won't be using it anymore," Cali said with a shrug. "It's yours." She turned and strode from the training hall without another word. Emil thought he should maybe go after her, but he had no idea what to say. And nothing he could say would make it any better for her.

He arranged the pieces, tried them on, found some that fit and others that didn't. Eventually, he had almost an entire set of armor. It was mismatched, discoloured, dented, scratched, all of it used and old. It was just like the Courage.

Emil felt ready with a new set of armor, and a new talent. He was eager for his next Hop. Which was good because Phusone had his orders ready and waiting.

CHAPTER 3

IRO SAT IN HIS POD, nervously scrolling through pages on his vambrace-mounted tablet, trying to concentrate on the words. He'd never flown across to the titan on his own before. Always he'd been with a squad and a master looking out for him. Now he was all alone, waiting to meet his new squad. He glanced for the tenth time at the timer. It ticked down to five minutes before he needed to leave.

He was ready. Or at least he thought so. He had new armor, printed onboard the Eclipse. It was lightweight, designed to aid his movement, and painted a deep blue like all the Hoppers from the Eclipse. He'd had Ylfa design him an emblem for the breast-plate; a circular design incorporating the flightless bird of his old ship, the Courage, and his broken sword in the centre. He loved it. It was his emblem and his alone.

He flicked across to the next page on his tablet, still trying to decide what to learn as his third talent. He already knew Blink Strike and Light Blade, so he needed something that compli-mented them. Thread Edge would give him more mobility, able to swing around a battlefield like Master Rollo. Parry would give him a defensive manoeuvre in most combat situations, able to flow around strikes levelled his way. Shadow Blade seemed like a poor choice, making his blade invisible didn't benefit him at all, and it couldn't be combined with Light Blade.

He scrolled to the next page on the tablet. Puppeteer would allow him to connect a thread of his current to a weapon and control it from a distance. It would let him strike with Neya's broken sword from afar, but would also leave him unarmed unless he started carrying a second sword. Then he could attack from two angles at once. Which was good, he could flank an enemy all on his own. But it still wouldn't help him deliver a killing blow to a powerful enemy. He already had mobility and support talents. What he needed was something that gave him raw power.

He flicked to the next page and read about Stutter Strike. It seemed a terrible talent, allowing the Corsair to hit their opponent and delay the damage from the strike, choosing to inflict it at a later time. He supposed he could use it to knock an enemy off guard at the right moment to land another attack. But it didn't lend any extra power to the blow, and you still needed to land the first strike.

He scrolled to the next page and read *Burning Adrenaline.*

"Iro?" Master Rollo called.

Iro shoved his head out of the pod door. Master Rollo was standing by the bay entry, leaning against the wall. He didn't have his crutch with him, which seemed like a good sign.

"Master Rollo," Iro said as he slipped out of the pod and stood to attention.

"You can just call me Rollo now, you know. Or Hopper Rollo. Or whatever the scrap you like."

North buzzed and took to the air, drifting out of the pod behind Iro. It settled on his shoulder. "Command Reminder: 2 minutes until departure time."

"Thank you, North."

"Does Command Iro require further reminders?"

"No. And it's just Iro."

"See," Master Rollo said. "Annoying isn't it." He smiled and pushed away from the wall, limping closer. "Listen, kid. I wanted to give you a warning. Keep your wits sharp and your sword close."

"Of course. I'm a Corsair. My sword is my life."

"I'm serious, you idiot."

"Alright," Iro said. "But that's a bit cryptic, Mast... Rollo." It felt awkward calling him by his name.

Rollo sighed. "You won't have met your new squad leader."

"I have. You were unconscious after the Black Cloaks... Anyway, it was Gadise Samir who found us and escorted us back."

Rollo raised an eyebrow and shoved his hands in his pockets. "That maybe makes a little more sense. But she's still a member of a Legacy family, kid. Upper ships, the real top of the top. More than that. She asked for this role as squad leader. Your squad leader. Every one of you she selected specifically." He shook his head. "Something feels off. She's a Legacy family, but she's assembled a team of a Corsair from a mid ship, a Paladin who can't enhance others, a Surveyor whose got his last two squads killed, and a Mage who... Well, no one else wanted her. It doesn't make sense. I don't trust her and I don't trust her motives."

Iro frowned. It had all made sense to him. He knew little about his new squad, other than Emil, but they were the first to open the First Gates since arriving at titan 02. He guessed the Legacy families and the Upper ships wanted to take control. At least, that's what Bjorn and Arne agreed was happening.

"Is this because you think Gadise Samir is untrustworthy? Or because you trusted Master Alfvin, and he wasn't?" Iro regretted the words the moment they left his mouth.

Rollo sighed and shook his head. "Idiot. Be careful, Iro. You may not be in my squad anymore, but I don't want to lose another trainee. And I can't be there to protect you." He turned and limped from the pod bay.

North floated up off Iro's shoulder. "Departure time in 10, 9, 8..."

"Alright, North." Iro ducked back into the pod. "We're going."

Iro had never flown a pod before. He'd always just pressed the button to follow the leader and let Rollo or Master Alfvin do the navigating. The controls were more complicated than he expected. Luckily, he had received coordinates and punched them into the keypad. The pod's internal systems did the rest. Those systems were another example of technology no one in the fleet actually understood. The ships were riddled with them. Mechanical malfunctions they could repair or replace, but if anything went wrong with the deeper intricacies, no tech aboard any of the ships could help. Iro sometimes wondered when that knowledge had been lost, or if the people living on the Home Fleet had ever even had it. Who built the ships of the fleet? Who built the titans? And if it was humans, then what had happened that no history books recorded it?

It was a long flight. Iro had nothing to do but stare out the little window and watch the skin of the titan pass below him. It was such a massive construct, sailing through the void, that the Hoppers of the fleet had barely explored the surface of the wing they were orbiting. And there were four wings, not to mention the main body of the titan, though the Black Cloaks had warned them off exploring too far or too deep. Iro passed over a garden dome, stared down into the glass and the forest within. The pod banked a little and flew around a Spire. It was massive, easily large enough to dwarf half the fleet. He'd heard there was often loot to be found in the Spires, powerful items that could enhance a Hopper, but that they were also filled with the deadliest of monsters and traps. But the purpose of them was another question zipping around in his head.

"North, do you know the purpose of the Spires?"

North buzzed from his shoulder but didn't take flight. "Query Response: Negative. North is Command Iro's chronicler and guide."

"Guide," Iro said. "Shouldn't you know things? To guide me."

North buzzed again. "Command Request: Information requested is not currently available. North requires data points to access relevant information. Internal data banks at 0.1% of capacity."

"So you don't know anything yet?"

"North is Command Iro's chronicler and guide."

"Which means what exactly?"

North buzzed. Four little legs extended from its chassis and it scuttled from Iro's right shoulder to his left. It buzzed again. "North can learn."

Green light swept over the pod, shining in through the window. The pod's thrusters fired, slowing it to a stop. It landed heavily, shaking Iro, and he pressed the button to open the door. It popped open with a hiss and Iro stepped out into a spacious chamber filled with huge autonomous arms that reminded him of a Surveyor's autodage. Some had a host of tools at the end, others were claws, but all were dormant.

He was not the first to arrive. Emil stood with his arms crossed by one of the autonomous claws. He had new armor, a bulky mismatch of styles and colours. The gauntlets hanging from his belt were massive, easily four times the size of a normal hand and had a rustic look about them. The other boy spared Iro a glance and no more.

North buzzed, took flight from Iro's shoulder and started

zipping about the chamber, scanning things with a beam of light.

Vermillion Gadise Samir stood tall and straight backed by a closed doorway leading from the chamber. Her armour was silver and bulky, a snarling monster head emblem on the breast. Her hair was only a shade darker than her skin and tied into a bun on top of her head, the sides shaved to stubble. She was imposing.

Iro was used to Rollo being in charge and he was lethargic and always slouching, his hands forever buried in his pockets. Gadise Samir was all solid as forged metal. She carried no weapon but had a single round buckler fixed to her right arm.

Courage, Iro. Time to introduce yourself.

He marched over to the Vanguard and stood straight to attention. "Vermillion Gadise Samir, I'm Eclipse Iro. It's, um, nice to meet you."

She stared down at him. "I know who you are, Eclipse. I requested you on my squad."

"Of course. Sorry. We've met."

"I remember." Her voice was empty as the dark between stars.

Iro desperately tried to think of something to say. "Well, thank you for requesting me on your squad. I hope I can, uh, live up to expectations?" He finished with a smile.

Gadise Samir stared down at him, her expression flat. "Is that a question?"

"Uh, no. I don't think so."

"You don't know if you asked a question or not?"

Iro winced. This was not going as he had hoped. "No. I mean, no it wasn't a question. Is that right?"

Gadise Samir drew in a deep, loud breath and turned away from him.

"Hey!" Emil shouted. "Iro. Come here."

Iro took a step back, turned on his heel and all but ran away. "Scrap, that was awkward." North flew down and landed on his shoulder.

"Command Query: North has detected elevated heart rate. Do you wish to scan for threats?"

"Sure. Whatever."

North buzzed and took to the air again.

"I see you got some new armor, too," Iro said as he reached Emil's side. His breast plate was a faded pink color that didn't suit him at all, but it had a new emblem on it, a gauntleted fist clutching a cog. Iro had to admit it was very Emil.

"Scrap you, mid shipper!" Emil snapped. "We can't all have new things printed every time they break."

Iro sighed.

"What?"

"Nothing." He hoped the other two members of his new squad weren't so angry with him for no reason. "Did you pick a new talent yet?"

"Of course," Emil said. "No sense waiting around. I picked Strength so I can get in some good hits. You?"

"I can't decide." He tapped on his vambrace-mounted tablet and brought up the list of Corsair talents again. "Do you ever feel paralysed by choice?"

"No. Scrap it, who cares? The Courage needs working parts to get its printers working again, Iro." Emil tapped at his own tablet. Iro noticed it was strapped to his vambrace with fraying strips of silver tape. Also, the screen was cracked and kept flickering. "Roret gave me a list of things to look out for."

Iro felt a pang of guilt at his friend's name. He still hadn't checked in with him. "How is Roret?"

Emil shrugged. "Fine, I guess. He's a tech. I need these parts." He waved his wrist at Iro. "Will any of these things do?" He gestured at the dormant arms laden with tools.

"Um, maybe," Iro said. "I'd have to take them apart to find out."

"Alright. Let's do that." Emil grabbed hold of the nearest arm and started pulling it down. The servos squealed in protest.

"Courage," Gadise Samir snapped. "You will stop that." She stalked closer, each footstep pounding against the metal flooring.

Emil released the arm and turned to face his squad leader. "Why? I have to find parts to help fix my ship."

"That's not why we're here, Courage."

Emil took another step closer, squaring up to Gadise Samir. "It's why I'm here."

Iro felt ignored. He desperately wanted to diffuse the situation, but Emil seemed to antagonise everyone he talked to.

"Luckily, you aren't squad leader," Gadise Samir snarled. "We have a long way to go on this Hop, and we will not be picking up random scrap along the way. Do you understand, Courage?"

North drifted down from above and swept a beam of light over Emil. The other boy staggered back from it.

"Threat level: 26." North buzzed and spun about in mid air, swept a beam of light over Gadise Samir. "Threat level: 72."

Emil backed up a step, frowning.

"Good work," Iro said to North as the automaton settled back on his shoulder.

Iro heard thrusters firing as another pod rocketed through the crosshatch of green lights. He didn't recognise the symbol on the outside of the pod, an intricate eight-pointed star shape, and had no idea which ship it came from. The door popped open and a young woman stumbled out, shaking her head as if trying to focus.

"Wow! That gets worse every time, doesn't it," she said in a bouncy voice. She was short, even shorter than Iro, and had the lightest suit of armor he'd ever seen, a few pieces of plating covering the vital areas. She wore a green beret over blond hair, and grinned at them all. Then she reached into her pod and pulled out a Mage cannon almost as big as she was. She slung a strap over her shoulder and let the cannon hang at her hip.

"I thought Mage cannons were small things?" Iro said.

Emil shrugged and crossed his arms, staring at the woman.

The woman gasped and leaned forwards, peering at them. She clapped her hands together and rushed towards them. "It's you! It's really you. I'm so happy to meet you." She rushed past Iro without even glancing at him and stopped in front of Emil. Emil took a hasty step back, but the woman closed the distance, all but pinning him against one of the dormant arms.

"Who are you?" Iro asked.

"Huh?" The woman said, glancing at him. "Oh. I'm Toshiko. Uh, that is, Thousand Suns Toshiko. And you're Courage Emil."

Emil tried to back up again, bumped against the dormant arm. "I am. Why do you care?"

"You're the reason I'm here," Toshiko said. "You're the reason I opened my First Gate."

North buzzed from Iro's shoulder and swept Toshiko with a beam of light. "Threat level: 31."

"Scrap, Emil. She's a higher threat than you are," Iro said, grinning.

Toshiko shook her head, her blond hair bouncing around her ears. "I'm not. Not a threat at all."

"I'm Eclipse Iro."

Toshiko glanced at him again. "OK." She went back to staring at Emil.

Iro heard more thruster fire. A fifth pod passed through the barrier of green lights and came to a rest with the others. This one had a circular symbol painted on it, half empty, half filled in black. The door popped open and a head poked out. A young man looked around nervously, then pulled back inside. The door hissed and started closing again.

"Get out of the pod, Justice," Gadise Samir rumbled.

The door stopped closing. "Is that you, cousin?"

Gadise Samir sighed. "Yes. Out of the pod."

The door opened again and the young man slunk out. He was tall and muscular, wearing light armor painted a deep green. He wore a pair of goggles over his eyes and a brown satchel at his hip. Iro spotted a small autodage perched on his shoulder. It was five separate segments and reminded him of kharapid tail, only without the stinger on the end.

"Is it safe?" the Surveyor asked.

Gadise Samir shook her head. "We're on the titan, Justice. It's never safe. But as Surveyor, it's your job to keep us safe."

The Surveyor snorted and pushed his goggles up onto his forehead. "Well, I'm clearly a terrible Surveyor, cousin. Why did you demand I join your squad."

"For your inspiring presence." She walked over to her own pod and reached inside. One after another, she pulled out four heavy backpacks and threw them on the ground. "Everyone take one. Inside are supplies. Everything you'll need for a lengthy Hop. Food, water, bed roll, first aid supplies." The pack she pulled out for herself was considerably larger and clinked with something metallic inside.

Iro raised his hand to ask a question, then realised he wasn't a trainee anymore. "How long will this Hop take?"

"Have somewhere better to be, Eclipse?" Gadise Samir asked. "We'll be on the titan a while. None of you have ever slept here before. We'll be fixing that."

"Exciting," Toshiko said. The smile on her face looked a little forced to Iro.

Emil edged away from the Mage. "Won't monsters find and attack us if we sleep here?"

"Probably," Gadise Samir said flatly. "For most of you, this is your first Hop outside of training. Justice is a special case."

Justice laughed bitterly. "That's putting it nicely, cousin. I think you mean, I'm bad luck and get everyone I Hop with killed."

Gadise Samir glared at Justice for a moment. "This is an exploratory Hop. We're aiming to push deep. Down to the fourth level. I don't know what we'll encounter, but the fleet still needs several vital supplies, including access to a manufactory."

She approached the doorway leading out of the chamber. She reached into her backpack and pulled out a small metal spike with a bulbous top. With a grunt of effort, she drove the spike into the wall next to the door. "We're also planting these at regular intervals. They're signal amplifiers. Most of you, except Justice, are too young to remember titan 01, but we could communicate ship to titan. That was because we had signal amplifiers set up. We don't have many left, and have no way to make more without a manufactory, but we are placing those we have. Questions?"

Justice cleared his throat. "Who is everyone?"

Gadise Samir rolled her eyes and tightened the strap holding her buckler to her arm. "You can all call me Vermillion or squad leader. I'm your Vanguard."

"I'm Flame Horizon Justice. But please just call me Justice. I'll be your doom, if history is any judge." He gave a bitter laugh.

"Justice is our Surveyor," Gadise Samir said.

Iro opened his mouth but Emil barged past him. "Courage Emil, Paladin. Don't ask me to enhance any of you, I'm not that kind of Paladin." He stalked away towards the doorway.

"My turn!" Toshiko said. "I'm Thousand Suns Toshiko. Mage. And this…" She patted the cannon hanging at her hip. "Is Steel Lotus."

"You named your cannon?" Iro asked.

Toshiko gave him a sour look. "She named herself."

"My name is Eclipse Iro. I'm a Corsair. Nice to meet you all." But the others didn't respond. They were already well on their way from the chamber. Iro rushed over to the last backpack and grabbed it, then hurried to follow them all.

CHAPTER 4

THEY MOVED at an infuriatingly slow pace. Their Surveyor, Justice, either had no idea what he was doing, or was too scared to do it. He crept them forward, checking every wall and metal flooring panel. He stopped and took readings with his autodage every ten steps, then spent ages mulling over the results on his tablet. They spent the first hour of their Hop creeping down a corridor that Emil could have jogged across in two minutes.

He ached for some action. He hadn't fought anything since their escape after opening his First Gate. The desire to test himself, to use his new talents was so strong. He needed a monster to fight.

"Well, you have all survived so far," Justice announced when they came to the end of the corridor. He wiped a sheen of sweat from his forehead. His goggles were multifaceted and made him look like a kharapid. "I'm sure it won't be long now."

"Pick up the pace, Justice?" the squad leader said. Emil hadn't decided about her yet. She was Legacy family from the upper ships. No doubt she'd never known a day of hardship in her life. But she was also a Hopper who had opened her Fourth Gate and that demanded respect.

"We can do that, yes." Justice pressed the button to open the door leading to the next chamber. "But you'll die."

The door clunked and opened a hand's width, then froze. Justice recoiled, coughing and holding his nose. The stench engulfed the others a moment later and set all of them coughing. Even the squad leader waved her shield in front of her face, as though she could waft the smell away.

"What is that?" Iro asked.

"Smells like the toilet after my brother has been in it," Toshiko said. She laughed, but no one else joined in.

"Rot," the squad leader said. "There are carrion eaters on the other side of this door."

"Corpse crawlers?" Iro asked. Emil saw him shiver and reach for his oversized, broken sword.

"No. Corpse crawlers devour the dead whole and leave things clean afterwards. This… this is something else."

"Shouldn't you know what's there?" Emil asked. "You're a squad leader. You've opened your Fourth Gate."

She glanced over her shoulder at Emil, and her eyes were dark and hard. "Justice, why don't we know what's on the other side of that door?"

The Surveyor's voice was reedy as he answered, still pinching his nose shut. "New titan, new monsters and traps."

"Be on your guard," the squad leader said. She stepped up to the door, gripped the edge and pulled it all the way open with a rusted squeal of protest. Emil thought he heard yipping noises from the other side.

He slipped his hands into his gauntlets and flexed them a few times, then shouldered Iro aside to be the second through the doorway after the squad leader.

The chamber on the other side was so dark Emil could barely see the squad leader in front of him. She picked her way across the floor. Emil glanced down and saw strange cables running along the metal grating below him. He nudged a cable with his boot, and it was spongy. It also seemed to shy away from him like it was alive and trying to get away.

"Lights on," the squad leader said. They each had flashlights embedded into their left vambraces. Emil flicked his own on and the light stuttered, flickering on and off a few times. He bashed it against his breast plate and the light steadied.

Their lights helped little. There was something in the air like dust, it seemed to catch the light and bounce it back at them. Rather than illuminating the space, the beams blinded them all of everything more than a few feet away.

"This is going to be a new record for me," Justice said from behind Emil.

"Quiet," the squad leader hissed. She was still creeping forwards, and raised her shield before her, shining her flashlight around the edges.

"Barely stepped off the pods and I've killed my squad already."

Emil heard a soft noise, like words whispered far away. There was a soft pink glow coming from behind him as well. He turned to see Toshiko creeping forwards a few steps behind him. Her crest was glowing behind her, a mesmerising swirl of fizzing pink lines and symbols. She nodded at him and said something, her lips moving, the words a whisper. Emil leaned closer.

"At just three hundred feet long, the Infinite Arrow is the smallest ship in the fleet." Emil pulled back. The Mage was reciting the fleet compendium like some sort of mantra. She had her cannon held in both hands. She pressed a button and the front end of the weapon started shifting until it formed two large barrels.

Toshiko stopped and shivered. "I really don't like the dark." She pointed her cannon upwards and pulled the trigger. An enormous ball of burning pink energy shot upwards through the chamber. She pulled the trigger again, and a second ball soared into the air.

The squad leader spun on her heel. "What are you..."

The first ball of energy impacted against the ceiling and exploded into millions of shards of sparkling light, filling the chamber with soft pink luminescence. The second ball hit a moment later and also exploded, showering the entire chamber in the glowing energy. And in the few seconds before the light faded, Emil saw everything.

"I knew it," Justice said. Emil heard him backing up a step. "You're all dead."

The chamber was large and open, with metal walkways above them all leading to a central pillar. Wrapped around that central pillar, infesting it, was a bulbous, pulsating mountain of rotting flesh. Cables of fleshy tentacles spread out from it in all directions, creeping across the floor, the walls, winding around the walkways. There were monsters hiding in the shadows, too. In the moment before Toshiko's lights flickered out, Emil saw rustlings, a kharapid, something that looked human even to the point of wearing armor. The rotting flesh around the central pillar rippled, then belched out a plume of dust that sparkled in the fading light. Toshiko's lights blinked out and bathed them all in darkness again.

"What the scrap was that?" Iro asked.

"A target," Toshiko said. The Mage backed up a step behind Justice. She pressed a button on her cannon and the end whirred into life, shifting from two big barrels into one huge barrel. Her crest flared to life behind her and she started reciting again. "The Alexander's Verdict has a population of seven thousand..."

Emil turned away from her, certain the little Mage was crazy.

"They're coming," the squad leader said from up front. A rustling flew out of the darkness at her. She slammed her shield down on it, crushing it against the floor so hard that bones snapped and blood spurted. Even broken, the thing started moving, crawling forwards. The squad leader raised a boot and stamped down on it.

Emil activated his crest at the same time as Iro. They were standing so close the crests touched, fizzed purple where Iro's icy blue met Emil's fiery red. Emil sent a glare at Iro. "Get away from me."

"I thought Paladins always needed protecting." Azure light ignited in front of Iro as his broken sword became whole again, the top of the blade made of pure current.

"Not this Paladin." Emil Strengthened himself. His muscles bulged with the new power. The clasps holding his armour in place popped and the plates on his biceps fell away to clatter to the grating below. It was the first time he'd used the talent while wearing his new armor.

A diseased-looking kharapid scuttled out of the darkness and reared up in front of Emil. He raised a gauntleted fist to block a couple of bladed limbs, then delivered a thunderous uppercut into its thorax. Chitinous shell exploded from the punch and the force pulverised the flesh beneath. But the kharapid didn't fall. It lurched forward, flailing at him. Emil stepped back too slowly, feeling sluggish. A scythe-like limb smacked into his chest, scratched against the titansteel. He tried to Steel himself, to protect against the blow, but both Steel and Strength slipped away from him. He couldn't hold two enhancements at once.

The kharapid barrelled into him, its weight bearing down on him. But Emil had opened his First Gate and didn't need a Strength enhancement to bear the weight. He growled and gripped the kharapid's thorax in both hands, lifted the monster above his head. Then he activated his crest, called on Strength again, and tore the insectoid in two. A spattering of thick, congealed blood dripped down on him. He threw both halves of the monster to the ground. A fleshy cable retreated from the corpse, slithering away back into the darkness.

Something large and shaggy lumbered out of the gloom towards Iro. It swung a clawed paw at him. He swiped his sword to the side, Blink Striking out of the way of the attack. Then he stabbed upwards, Blink Striking above the monster, and another Blink Strike straight down. The blue light of his blade flared as it connected with the monster's skull, and the force of his momentum carried him straight down. The monster teetered, and fell into two halves, stinking insides spilling out onto the metal floor.

Iro staggered away from the mess, gagging past the smell so rancid he could taste it in his throat. He realised he'd lost everyone else. The dusty particles hanging in the air all but blinded him, even with the sparkling light from his blade. He heard the others though. A grunt sounded like Emil. Metal clashing against metal. The soft cadence of Toshiko muttering something to herself.

Iro spun about, peering into the dusty gloom. One of his squad mates limped towards him. They were injured and dragging something behind them. Iro rushed forward to help.

A heavy blade swept out at him from the dust. Iro brought up his own sword, blocked, was thrown aside by the blow. He rolled back to his feet and held his sword in a cross guard, just as Rollo had taught him, ready to defend. The figure in the gloom limped towards him. The dust eddied and the blade lashed out at him again. Iro ducked underneath the arc and rushed forward.

The wielder of the blade was human, another Hopper but not one of his squad. The woman was tall, pale, glossy eyed and slack jawed, her armor dirty grey, spotted with rust. She staggered about as if drunk.

"What's wrong with you?" Iro said. "We're human."

The woman dragged her arm back, whipping her sword around so fast Iro had to block with the flat of his blade. The swords clanged as they hit, and the woman pushed. Her strength was insane. Iro couldn't hold his defence. It was like fighting against Bjorn.

Fight like Eir.

Iro stopped pushing back and let the woman's strength fling him away. He spun in midair, slashed his sword before he landed, Blink Striking back in front of her. He shifted grip on his sword, thrust the pommel into the woman's face. Her nose cracked and she staggered back, but didn't cry out and didn't go down. She pivoted about, swung her sword up and brought it crashing back down at him. Iro stabbed out to the side, Blink Striking out of the way, then back in again behind the woman.

He stumbled, tripped over a fleshy cable that ran along the ground. In the gloom, he couldn't see where the cable led to, but it was wrapped around one of the woman's legs and disappeared into her armor at her back. He slashed the cable with his sword. A pained squeal sounded from somewhere in the chamber and the cable writhed about and pulled back into the gloom. The woman dropped face first, hit the ground with a thump. Iro dashed forward to check on her.

Her flesh was cold to the touch. He rolled her over, but her chest didn't move with breath and her eyes were still and glassy. There was an old wound in her neck he hadn't put there, still gooey, but with decaying flesh. She was dead. She had been dead for a while. Iro shuddered and staggered back away from the corpse.

"These monsters are already dead," Iro shouted, hoping his

voice reached past the dusty gloom. "I think the big thing in the centre is controlling them."

"We have to kill it," Emil's voice echoed back, sounding strained.

Iro was turned around. Almost blinded by the dust, he didn't know which way led to the centre of the chamber and the monster nestling there.

"Help!" That sounded like Justice, the voice coming from somewhere behind Iro. "Help."

Iro turned toward Justice's voice, and paused. If Justice was in front of him now, then the monster in the centre of the chamber should be directly behind him. He turned around again.

"Help!"

Iro turned back towards the voice. He couldn't decide what to do. To run and help the Surveyor or close on the monster controlling all the others. He didn't know what to do.

The little monster only came up to Emil's knee, but it was so damned quick. It dashed about on all six legs and its teeth and claws were razor sharp. Emil already had a gash in his left arm. He enhanced himself with Strength and jabbed at the creature even as it charged him again. It darted to the side, ran past him. Claws scraped against the metal grating. He spun about, dropped his Strength enhancement and Steeled himself as the monster leapt at him and closed its razor fangs around his elbow. He shouted in pain and anger. His flesh was hard as steel, but the monster's jaws were crushing. He thumped a gauntlet into its side and it let go, darted off into the darkness again.

He couldn't hit the little thing until it was trying to bite him, but he couldn't Strength himself while also Steeling himself. That meant he couldn't hit the scrapping thing hard enough to put it down. But he had one other talent. The talent he'd manifested when he opened his First Gate.

Claws on steel again, this time behind him. Emil spun about and faced the monster's charge. "C'mon, you little void sucker." He held his hands out in front of him, gauntlets open and ready to block.

The monster leapt out of the darkness, closed its jaws around his right hand. Emil grinned as the monster bit down. He used his Retribution talent. Teeth crunched against metal, broke against titansteel. And for every bit of damage the monster tried to deal to him, his talent dealt it right back. One of the monster's feet snapped, buckled. The beast fell to the ground, limping. Slowed. Emil grabbed it by the scruff of his neck and Strengthened himself. He collapsed its skull with a single mighty punch, then tossed the body back into the dark.

Emil stood, waving his hand in the air. Even through his gauntlet that had hurt. His fingers felt crushed. He heard shouting, the Surveyor calling for help. He backed up a step, peering into the gloom, trying to find the Hopper.

Something hit Emil in the back and he spun around, enhanced himself with Strength, swung a wild haymaker. Too late, he realised it was Iro. The Corsair's eyes widened, his own sword glowing blue and swinging towards Emil's neck. No time to block.

The dust swirled between them and metal struck metal with a clang. Emil's fist tugged to a halt. He blinked. The squad leader crouched between them. Her shield was up, blocking Iro's sword. She wrapped her other hand around Emil's wrist, arresting his punch.

"Finally!" Toshiko shouted from somewhere in the chamber. "Capacity charged to forty percent. Ready to fire."

"Enough of this," the squad leader growled. She let go of Emil's wrist and slammed a fist against her own shield. It sounded like a struck gong, so loud Emil winced. A wave of wind rush over him as the shockwave from the squad leader's strike against her own shield blasted the dust away from them all.

With the chamber now cleared of dust, their flashlights and crests lit the room with a ruddy glow. Emil stared at the monster in the centre clinging to the tubular pillar, its body pulsing as fleshy cables writhed out in all directions. Other monsters stalked around the edges of the chamber, closing on the squad.

Justice was over by the wall, staying close to the doorway, wrestling with something that looked half human, but scaly and naked, with claws instead of hands. Beside him, Toshiko grinned maniacally, pointing her cannon directly at them. The single huge barrel was glowing bright white. Her eyes widened when she spotted them.

"Move move move!" she screamed.

The squad leader grabbed both Emil and Iro and pulled them down. Toshiko wrenched on her cannon, tilting the barrel upwards. A deafening zap roared from the barrel and searing white light shot out of the cannon. It tore across the chamber, a burning beam of energy that sheared through the central pillar, the fleshy monster, and half a dozen walkways, slagging metal and charring flesh. Toshiko struggled to control the beam, crying out in panic. It waved left and right in her hands, blasting away half the chamber and punching holes in the titan's walls. Then it was over. The beam of light ran out and Toshiko staggered back-wards and fell on her ass.

The scaly creature wrestling with Justice dropped, the fleshy cable connecting it to the central pillar rotting and deflating in moments. All the remaining puppets dropped. Toshiko's beam of energy had cut straight through the monster at the centre of the chamber. She'd killed it with a single shot from her cannon.

"What the scrap was that, Thousand Suns?" the squad leader said as she stood slowly, wincing as if expecting another attack.

Toshiko smiled apologetically and patted her smoking cannon. "I, uh, call it a Giga Beam."

The squad leader hauled Iro to his feet. "That's not a talent I've ever heard of."

"That's because it's my own variant on the Beam Lancer talent. You see, instead of releasing rapid shots, I store up the power, charging it into one massive blast. Giga Beam."

"Who taught you to do that?"

"No one. I…"

Emil stopped listening to the chatter. He focused on the remains of the monster in the centre of the room. A dozen huge, fleshy sacks all clung to the cylindrical pillar. That same pillar sparked now, arcs of electricity shooting out to strike at everything nearby. Debris scattered about the floor, below the stinking, rotting flesh, and the dead bodies. There were shards of metal that looked a lot like they had once been rings. It reminded him of something.

"Hey," Emil shouted. The central pillar sparked again, the electricity growing more violent. "Does this pillar thing in the centre remind anyone else of the engines aboard our ships?"

"What?" the squad leader said. She turned, saw the sparking pillar. "Scrap!"

The squad leader grabbed Emil by his arm and tossed him as easily as a child. He flew across the room, hit the wall behind Toshiko. Iro hit the wall next to him a second later. Emil fell to the ground and looked up just as the squad leader reached the group. She spun about and raised her shield. Her silver crest flared to dazzling light behind her, massive and so bright it hurt his eyes. A spherical shield of yellow light flashed around them. A second later, the central pillar exploded.

CHAPTER 5

FLAMES RAGED AROUND THEM, kept at bay by Gadise Samir's shield of energy. Debris smashed into it, causing it to flair brighter for a moment wherever the scraps of metal hit.

The shield was formed of glowing golden light, and almost looked like the Vanguard's crest but in miniature and repeated over and over again, interlocking with its other versions. It was fascinating.

Gadise Samir grunted and stood from her crouch. The flames gutted out to patches of fire, charred corpses of monsters, a blaze around the central pillar. Her crest vanished and her golden energy shield shattered like glass, fading away to nothing around them. The heat was the first thing to hit Iro like a punch to the gut. It was oppressive and cloying, made it hard to breathe. And when he sucked in a breath, the smell hit him a moment later. Burning bodies made him gag.

"Huh…" Justice said morosely. "You all survived."

"No thanks to you," Emil said.

Gadise Samir sighed and started picking her way around the fires.

"That was fun. Right?" Toshiko said. She pressed a button on her cannon and the barrel retracted a little. She pushed the device behind her so it was hanging around her back.

Iro shrugged at her. "Apart from the near death. It was a little bit fun."

"Good." Toshiko grinned nervously. "Good. I'm glad." She skipped forward to walk next to Emil. "Hey, that was fun, right?"

Emil grunted, which Iro suspected meant yes, but the other boy wasn't willing to admit it.

Justice stood, rubbing at his elbow and looking miserable. He caught Iro's eye, sighed, started walking. Iro wanted to get along with at least one member of the squad, though Justice seemed an unlikely choice. But maybe that was because no one tried to get along with him.

North launched from Iro's shoulder and buzzed into the air. The little automaton started flying about, scanning the burning corpses with beams of light.

Iro sheathed his sword and rushed forward to join Justice. "Why do you think we're all going to die?"

"History. It repeats itself. I don't know why people keep asking me to join their squads. I'm bad luck, Eclipse Iro. I've been on two other squads and everyone but me has died. It's only a matter of time before you all fall victim to my curse, too." Justice sighed again. "Even cousin Gadise. She should have known better."

Iro moved to the side to dodge around a patch of fire that looked like it might once have been a rustling. "Why did you come then?"

Justice pushed his goggles up onto his forehead. "What?"

"If you're so sure you're bad luck or a curse, and that your entire squad will die, why did you agree to come back to the titan? Why not give up Hopping?"

"Give up Hopping?" Justice laughed. They had to swing

around the central pillar, giving it a wide berth it was so hot. "I don't get to give up, Iro. I'm sure you nobodies aboard the Eclipse can just say '*It's not for me.*' and go be drudges or whatever. My mother was Legacy. I don't get to give up. Ever."

North buzzed forward and started scanning the central pillar. Iro frowned at it, trying to figure out what was strange about the whole chamber. "Why not?"

"Why not?" Justice laughed again, the sound almost manic. "Titans save me from junkers who don't know they're born." He sped his pace and stalked away.

Iro slowed to a stop and turned to study the central pillar. He didn't understand Justice at all. And he didn't understand why the pillar was confusing to him. "Find anything, North?"

North quit scanning the central pillar and flew down to Iro. "Specification request: Anything is too broad a category."

Iro sighed. "What did you find in this chamber?"

North buzzed. "General Classification: Rustling. Status: Deceased. Likely cause of death: Assimilation by unclassified species of monster.

"General Classification: Hornagor. Status: Deceased. Likely cause of death: Assimilation by unclassified species of monster.

"General Classification: Human. Status: Deceased. Likely cause of death: Assimilation by unclassified species of monster."

Gadise Samir waved a hand in the air. "Eclipse. It's time to leave."

Iro waved back. "What about the central pillar, North?"

The automaton buzzed. "The engine core was infested by a currently unclassified species of monster. Command Query: Would you like to provide a classification?"

"Uh, sure." Iro jogged the last few paces to the rest of the squad. "North says the monster around the engine core is unclassified. Does that mean we get to name it?"

Gadise Samir nodded.

"Oooh," Toshiko said. "I know. How about a Rotteteer? Kind of like a puppeteer, but rotting and stuff."

Gadise Samir turned and pressed the button next to the doorway. The door ground open an inch and she pulled it the rest of the way to reveal a bright corridor beyond that had strange tracks running along the floor and ceiling. "Justice, on me."

"Rotteteer, it is," Iro said as he followed them.

"Classification accepted: Rotteteer."

Emil barged past Iro. "Can't you give that thing a different voice? It's creepy that it sounds like you."

Iro clenched his fists. Just once he'd like the other boy not to be so antagonistic. "Sure I can," he said, already knowing it was a bad idea. "North. Change voice settings: Courage Emil."

Emil rounded on him. "Don't you dare…"

"Command alteration: Accepted," North said in a tinny version of Emil's voice.

Emil swatted at North, but the automaton buzzed away. "Change it, Iro. Now!"

Iro stood his ground a few seconds. Emil was more terrifying than half the monsters he'd faced, but Iro refused to show fear. "North. Change voice settings: Master Rollo."

"Command alteration: Accepted," North said in Rollo's voice. It was both somewhat comforting to imagine his old Master was there with him, and also strange.

"Enough," Gadise Samir said from up ahead. "Both of you. Pay attention. Inattentive Hoppers are easy prey."

They all started following her. "How did you know the central pillar in that chamber was an engine core?" Iro asked Emil.

The Paladin shrugged. "I saw it on the Courage the other day. I went to engineering. Spoke with Roret."

"You spoke to Roret?"

"Sure."

Iro decided he needed to find time to visit the Courage and his old friend. "Does the layout of the titan strike anyone else as odd?"

"Yes!" Toshiko said. She was walking a few steps behind Iro and Emil. "It's maddening, isn't it? Doesn't make any sense. They have an engine core this close to the surface of the titan, but nowhere near any of the engines. Why? What possible purpose could an engine core serve there? And how did we survive the explosion?"

"The squad leader shielded us," Emil said.

Toshiko snorted. "That was an engine core, Emil."

"So?"

"So when an engine core explodes, it blows up the entire ship. Well, not on a titan, but it should have torn a hole the size of half the fleet in the side of the wing. We should all be floating in space right now."

Gadise Samir stopped and turned towards them. "Then perhaps you shouldn't have used that oversized beam to shear through the core. We survived because that monster…"

"The rotteteer," Iro said.

Gadise Samir ignored him. "Had syphoned away much of the energy of the core. The broken rings on the floor meant the core was no longer generating energy, and the monster was feeding on the ambient supply."

Toshiko stared at the floor. "We survived, though. It didn't."

Gadise Samir glanced over her shoulder, frowning. "In the future, you will follow orders. I did not tell you to attack. We might have snuck past the monster. If you fail to follow orders again, I will remove you from my squad." She turned back to the corridor. There were a series of doors up ahead.

Toshiko stuck her tongue out and mumbled something that Iro couldn't make out.

"So we should have done things differently?" Emil asked.

"I would have done things differently, yes," Gadise Samir said. Emil waited for more, threw up his hands when the Vanguard didn't elaborate. "How? Tell us how. How are we supposed to learn if you won't teach us?"

Gadise Samir stopped, turned on her heel. Emil wasn't small, but she towered over him. "You appear to be mistaken, Hopper. You are no longer a trainee and I am not your Master. I am not here to dispense praise or criticism, nor coddle you until you feel ready.

"We are a squad. I am your Vanguard and your squad leader. I will defend you from attack, and decide where and when we Hop. If you cannot follow orders or do not live up to your role within the squad, I will replace you." She tightened the straps on her buckler and turned back to the corridor.

"If you desire advice, I will give it," she said as she walked. "Privately. But I will not drag any of you over hot grates in front of the rest of the squad. You are not children anymore. You are Hoppers. You have a responsibility to each other, and to the fleet. Act accordingly.

"Surveyor, check the doors for traps."

"Hmph," Toshiko said. "I think I did fine. I killed the monster. Right?" She looked at Iro as if expecting him to back her up. Then she glanced at Emil. "Right?" The Paladin didn't answer so Toshiko sighed and walked ahead, her shoulders slumped.

Emil stood motionless, staring after Gadise Samir. Iro stepped up beside him. He opened his mouth to say something, though he wasn't sure what. An apology, maybe. He'd been reckless. In the gloom, he'd bumped into Emil, swung at him, almost killed him. It was careless. He was careless.

Iro looked up to find Emil staring at him. The other boy was frowning, his stare so intense. "Sorry." Emil's face twisted as though the word tasted like rotting algae. "For almost hitting you, back there."

"That's what I was going to say."

Emil rolled his eyes, started walking. "Sure."

"No really. I was about to apologise." Iro hurried after him.

"Don't be such a scrapping ass, Iro."

CHAPTER 6

BY THE TIME Gadise Samir called for a stop, they had been exploring the titan for hours. Or possibly days, as far as Iro's feet were concerned. His legs ached, his arms wobbled, his sword needed a good clean, and his current felt drained to the point of exhaustion. He knew it would recharge in an hour or two, but they were struggling to find time to stop between the traps and the monsters. Yet Gadise Samir kept pushing them on, deeper into the titan.

They'd placed eight of the signal amplifiers so far, and had proceeded down to the fifth level of the titan. It was deeper than First Gate Hoppers were meant to push. It was also, Iro couldn't help but remember, further than the Black Cloaks had warned them not to go. No proceeding below the fourth level or they'd break the accords and Mia's life would be forfeit. He couldn't forget that.

The Vanguard pulled them to a halt inside a long room that had a few dozen cubicles lined up along one wall. They almost looked like the cubicles inside the showers back on the Eclipse, but there were no showers heads, nor drainage lines along the floor. Each cubicle had a single large screen in it against the wall.

Many of the screens were cracked and inoperable, but others looked like they could function if only they had a feed leading to them. Perhaps more usefully, if they could detatch them from the walls and taken back to the ships, then the Courage could replace its bridge view screens. His mother had long complained about the dead pixels making the screens all but useless.

Gadise Samir placed her final signal amplifier then walked into the depths of the room, tapping at her vambrace mounted tablet. Iro assumed she was trying to get in touch with the fleet.

Justice was busy doing Surveyor things, which seemed to involve a lot of fiddling with walls, lying on the ground and staring along the floor almost as if he was trying to determine if it was flat, and consulting with his autodage. Much like Burning Ember Franka, Justice seemed to communicate with the little claw without actual words, though it didn't stop him talking to it.

"Must be a Surveyor talent, I guess?" he mused aloud.

North buzzed. "Command Query: Would you like me to scan the Surveyor?"

Justice glanced up at Iro, eyes narrowed behind his fragmented goggles.

Iro grinned. "Sure."

North buzzed into the air and flew towards Justice. The beam of light flashed out at the Surveyor. Justice was on his feet in a moment, his face red. He pushed his goggles up onto his forehead and his little claw started snapping out at North. The automaton flew out of reach.

"Surveyor Request: Reveal your circuitry."

"My what?" Justice snapped. "Iro, tell your little toy to stop bothering me."

North buzzed and flew towards Iro, cutting off the beam of light. "Command Clarification: Circuitry. Pathways of light defining purpose and function."

Emil dumped his bag by a cubicle. "It means your crest."

Iro activated his crest. It burst into icy light before him, blue lines and symbols fizzing in the air. It was growing again, new lines being revealed as though they were always there and he was slowly shedding light on them. The second lock was not visible yet though. He guessed that meant he was far from opening his Second Gate. "This is a crest, North. Not circuitry."

"Clarification accepted." North buzzed down and scanned Iro's crest.

"What's it doing?" asked Toshiko.

"North is Learning," North said.

"It can learn?"

Iro shrugged. "I think so. North, when you make a request of someone, it's polite to say please."

The automaton buzzed, then swept back towards Justice. "Surveyor Request Please: Reveal your crest."

Justice glared at North. "No."

Emil sighed and stood up. He activated his own crest, fiery orange lines burning in the air. It was very different to Iro's. The lines were often sharp angles instead of flowing, and the symbols were different. But there was something else, too. The letters looked different. Iro wasn't sure how he knew that, he couldn't read the lettering on his own crest either, but Emil's letters looked almost like they belonged to another language.

North buzzed towards Emil and spent a few seconds scanning the Paladin's crest.

"You done?" Emil asked when North stopped scanning.

"Affirmative."

"Good. Get out of the way." Emil started punching at thin air. His crest flared a little with each punch, one symbol glowing brighter for a moment, and Iro could swear the other boy's arms kept swelling and shrinking.

"Do you want to scan mine, too?" Toshiko asked. She activated her crest in front of her, soft pink lines that glowed and cast a warm light around her, colouring her blonde hair.

North swept over to Toshiko and scanned her crest.

Toshiko almost seemed to vibrate on the spot she was so excited. As soon as North stopped its scan, the Mage jumped up. "What do you think?"

North buzzed. "Specify query."

Toshiko rolled her eyes. "About my crest. What do you think of my crest?"

North buzzed and turned away, flying towards Justice again. "Insufficient data to form an analysis about Class: Mage.

"Surveyor Request Please: reveal your crest."

Justice stood and faced North. His autodage scuttled forward on stunty mechanical legs and perched on the Surveyor's shoulder, it leaned forward, extending its claw towards North and the two automatons seemed to glare at each other.

"This thing isn't just a construct, is it?" Justice said. "Can you actually learn?"

"North can learn."

Iro shrugged. "As far as I can tell, it's a true automaton, like Mechanists create."

Justice glanced at Iro and rolled his eyes. "Mechanists can't create automatons. Well, some can, but not until they've unlocked their Fourth Gate. I don't know the specifics, you'd have to ask a Mechanist. But mostly they use constructs. A construct is a small device created with a specific and singular purpose. They are not autonomous. The Mechanist controls directly them."

"Autodages," he poked his own little claw with a single finger, "are semi-autonomous devices that we Surveyors can create using parts scavenged from titans. They have a rudimentary AI because that's all we can rip from the titan's sub systems."

"Huh?" Iro barely understood half of what Justice had said.

"You really know nothing about this, do you? Mid shippers, URGH."

"I was raised on the Courage."

"Ahh, a low ship. That explains the ignorance."

Emil stopped punching at thin air and turned, glowering at the Surveyor. "Keep talking, upper ships. Maybe this Hop, you'll be the one not making it back."

Justice laughed. "Very threatening. But you're all already dead, you just don't know it yet. Everyone around me dies."

"Probably because you suck up all the oxygen," Iro said.

Emil chuckled and turned away. His crest flared and he started punching again.

"Very witty," Justice said.

Iro swallowed his pride. He wanted to learn, and Justice seemed to know something about automatons. He was a pompous junkhole, but that didn't mean he was useless. "Why did you say North was a true automaton then? And please just explain it to me without all the insults about my upbringing."

Justice poked a finger at his autodage. "This device has databanks I can interface with on a tablet. I can add information about traps, other devices, anything. Though anything I add has to be useful or it's just clogging up the autodage's memory. It cannot learn.

"But this North of your appears to be a true automaton. It can learn independently of data being specifically added to its memory."

North buzzed. "North can learn."

Justice smiled grimly. "A lot of Surveyors would give one of their own arms to strip this thing down and take the processing unit for their own autodage."

North backed away from the Surveyor as if sensing a threat. Justice smiled and shook his head. "You do not know what you have here, Eclipse Iro."

Justice extended his hand and activated his crest. It lit up before his palm, small and sickly green, the lines almost seeming to drip like oil down a pipe. North buzzed and flew closer, scanning the crest. Then Justice lurched forward, grabbed North, fingers clutching around its chassis. North buzzed, but Justice held on tight. His autodage started waddling down his arm.

Iro drew his sword and took a step forward, levelling the broken blade at Justice. "Let go of North," he growled in a voice that shocked even himself.

Justice glanced at Iro, then his gaze flicked to Emil. Emil stepped up beside Iro, his hands already balled into fists. Toshiko sat, staring at them all wide eyed.

"Fine," Justice said with a sigh. He opened his hand and North flew to Iro and settled on his shoulder. It felt like the little automaton was vibrating. Justice smiled and shrugged.

Gadise Samir strode back to the group. If she'd seen or heard the conflict, she didn't show it. She walked straight to the doorway and poked her head outside, looked both ways, then pulled back inside and pressed the button to close the door. It slid shut without a sound. "Justice, scout the location."

Justice pulled his goggles down over his eyes. He placed a single hand against the wall next to the doorway. His crest bubbled into sickly green light behind him. It was larger than before, as though he was controlling the size of its manifestation. Iro wondered if he could do the same, though the idea of asking the Surveyor to teach him was abhorrent. A symbol in Justice's crest, a cube formed of many lines, glowed a little brighter. The Surveyor's eyes went distant and as Iro peered closer, he thought he could see other places reflected in the man's goggles.

"I'm detecting expansive spaces below us. I would say we have one more floor before the surface levels of the titan end and the interior begins. One chamber is filled with… fluid. Maybe flooded.

I can't see through it. It's very dark." Justice sighed and blinked, and the image reflected in his goggles changed. "Normal power delivery in the immediate area, so no manufactory close by."

"Life signs?" Gadise Samir asked.

Justice blinked again, the reflection changing. There were little green dots reflected all across his goggles. "Plenty. We're close to a hive."

"How close?"

Justice shrugged. "It shouldn't bother us unless someone opens a gate. It's two floors down and it's big. I can't tell how many monsters."

Gadise Samir grunted. "That means a lot."

Justice tilted his head. "There are human life signs. They're approaching the hive from below. That's a bad idea."

Gadise Samir tapped at her tablet. "There shouldn't be any other squads nearby. Are they from the other fleet?"

Justice's lip curled. "How should I know, Cousin? Either way, if they disturb that hive, we won't have to worry about them. There's something big at the centre. I can't get an accurate reading, but I'm seeing *a lot* of little signs surrounding one *big* sign." He blinked again and pulled his goggles back up onto his forehead, pinning his floppy hair in place. His eyes were back to normal.

"What's a hive?" Iro asked.

Gadise Samir strode over to the cubicles and started pulling the doors open one by one, checking them all. "Some monsters are solitary, like hydrids. Others, like rustlings form swarms. Some monsters even gather in massive hives. We don't know why. They're not places any Hopper squad should go alone."

"Except the Silver Blade did," Toshiko said. "She went into a Vhar hive and killed the warlord." She pressed a button on her cannon and the barrel shifted, splitting into four feet. The Mage placed the cannon on the floor and hopped up onto it, perching on it like a stool.

"That's not the full story," Gadise Samir said as she pushed open another cubicle door. "Eclipse Eyildr. Or the Silver Blade, if you insist on calling her by that ridiculous name, did not enter the hive alone. She had a squad of fourteen Hoppers with her. They went there to destroy the Hive. She did, however, fight the warlord alone after it slaughtered the rest of her squad."

"Oooh." Toshiko swung her smile to Iro. "She's from the Eclipse, too? What's she like?"

"I don't know. I've never met her. I know her daughter, though. She's…" Iro grinned as he thought of her. "She's Eir." He hadn't trained with her for a while and he missed their late night sparring.

"Uh huh," Toshiko said, her grin deepening.

Gadise Samir finished checking the cubicles and closed the door at the far end of the chamber, then strode back to the rest of the squad. "We'll be staying here for a few hours. Try to get some sleep. We'll keep watch in shifts. Myself and Justice will take the first shift. I'll wake Eclipse and Courage for their turn. Then I'll stand with Thousands Suns for her shift as well."

Iro almost raised his hand, but thought better of it. "Um, Squad leader. Aren't we on the fifth level? The Black Cloaks warned us not to Hop this far down. Won't staying here break the accords?"

Gadise Samir leaned against the wall of the closest cubicle and removed her shield from her arm, placing it against the wall next to her. "Only if they find us. Get some sleep, all of you."

CHAPTER 7

TOSHIKO WOKE to something tapping her leg. She groaned, flailed at the offending something, then squeezed her eyes shut. The tapping grew more insistent. She cracked open an eye, squinting against the light, to see the squad leader standing over her, looking every bit as steely and stoic and traditionally boring as before.

The older woman jutted her chin. "It's our watch." She turned and strode away, back straight and proper just as a Hopper should be. It was infuriating.

Toshiko let out a groan, considered closing her eyes again. She noticed Courage Emil watching her. He leaned against the far wall, arms crossed. She wouldn't let him see her as lazy. She clambered to her feet, yawned, hefted Steel Lotus up and rested the strap across her shoulders. She rubbed the sleep from her eyes and turned to Courage Emil with a smile. He closed his eyes.

She wanted to talk to him. Toshiko had wanted to talk to him ever since she'd heard he opened his First Gate. No one else on the Thousand Suns seemed to care much about a trainee opening their gate except that it meant they weren't stalled. Toshiko had seen it differently. Not that Courage Emil had proven that the rest of the fleet wasn't stalled, but that he had shown them how to open their First Gates. He had proven to them all that things needed to be done differently. A Paladin who had learned to enhance himself instead of others. She wanted to ask him how he'd known to do it. He'd broken the mold so effortlessly.

Toshiko picked her way between Flame Horizon Justice and Eclipse Iro, and walked down the line of cubicles. She yawned again, wiped at her eyes. So groggy. Mornings were the worst time of the day. Not that she was sure what time it was. But whenever you woke up, that was a morning. And mornings sucked.

The squad leader leaned against the wall at the far end of the chamber, close to the second doorway. She had something small in her hands, was staring down at it. Toshiko wiped at her eyes again and sauntered closer.

"Is that a book?" Toshiko asked.

Vermillion Gadise glanced up at her. "Keep your voice down, Thousand Suns." It seemed every word out of her mouth was a reproach, though that was something Toshiko was well used to.

"Is that a book?" Toshiko whispered. "An actual book. With paper."

The Vanguard sighed and gently turned the page. "Yes."

"Can I see it?"

"No." She shut the book and tucked up underneath her breastplate.

"I've never seen an actual book. Only heard about them in... well... books. You know..." She tapped a finger against her wrist mounted tablet. "The electronic kind. No pages, just screens and screens of..."

Vermillion Gadise grunted and stared at her with cold, dark eyes. "Yes, I understand how books work, Thousand Suns."

Toshiko decided one day she'd figure out how to make a good first impression, but not today. She started pacing between the cubicles. "So... what do we do on watch?"

"We watch over the others. Stay awake. In case of attack, we either deal with it, or wake everyone."

"So it's just standing around not doing much?"

"Yes."

"Hence the book?"

"Yes."

Vermillion Gadise was not the chatty type. But that was fine, Toshiko knew how to deal with people like her. No one on the Thousand Suns was chatty either, except for her mother and granny Hinata. The trick was to wear people down with questions until they started talking without even realising it.

"How many Hops have you been on?" Toshiko asked.

"Seventy three."

"That's a lot!"

The squad leader gave a non-committal grunt.

"Do you have any exciting stories?"

The Vanguard shook her head. "Nope."

"Have you Hopped with many Mages before?"

"Many."

Toshiko smiled to herself. Vermillion Gadise was a tough one. She was going to take a lot of wearing down.

Hours later, Toshiko had admitted defeat. Despite a barrage of questions, each more demanding than the last, Vermillion Gadise had answered each one with only a few words. Never had Toshiko met anyone so adept at shutting down conversation. After the first hour, Toshiko had gotten so bored, she'd pulled one of the cubicle screens off the wall and dismantled it. She pocketed a couple of parts she was certain she could use to upgrade Steel Lotus's display.

The Vanguard woke the others by stalking among them,

kicking legs. They chewed on some dried bhurbeast meat from their packs, sipped from water bottles, and were ready to go in only a handful of minutes. Toshiko envied people who shook away the edges of sleep so readily.

"We're heading back," Vermillion Gadise declared when they were all awake and ready.

"The way we came?" Eclipse Iro asked.

"Yes."

The Corsair looked around the others as if searching for help. "But you said this was an exploratory Hop, we haven't found anything yet. We just came down to the fifth level, then we're turning around?"

"Correct."

The little automaton buzzed and took off into the air. "Command Query:..."

"Not now," Eclipse Iro said. "Why take us down this far just to turn around and head back?"

Justice chuckled. "Because that was the whole point, wasn't it, Cousin? We didn't come here to explore. We came here to poke the Vhar."

"What?" Courage Emil asked.

The Surveyor sighed. "Obviously not literally. Do try to keep up. This entire Hop was about the Black Cloaks. They warned us not to Hop any deeper than the fourth level. You two were even there when they delivered that warning. So the fleet decided to send you down deeper, stay here for a while, and see if the Black Cloaks turn up to spank your asses again. Tell me I'm wrong, Cousin."

Vermillion Gadise shook her head. "You're correct."

"You brought us down here to be attacked?" Eclipse Iro said.

Toshiko backed away from the raised voices, trying to melt into the background. She hoped no one dragged her into the argument. Conflict made her uncomfortable.

The Vanguard pinned Eclipse Iro with a dark stare. "I brought you down here on fleet orders to determine whether the Black Cloaks could follow through on their threat. I also volunteered to lead the Hop so I could protect you if they showed up. Now, our mission is complete. We're heading back. None of you should be down this deep yet anyway."

"Why me, Cousin?" Justice asked. "I understand why these two are along, but why did you pick me? Why the Mage?"

Vermillion Gadise glanced at her and Toshiko raised a hand to her chest and gave a stupid little wave. Then she dragged her hand down and cursed herself for being so foolish. She should just stay quietly at the back, meek and forgotten, until all the anger and shoutiness was over.

"Because you are expendable, Justice."

The Surveyor drew in a deep breath and stared up at his cousin, his jaw writhing. Then he snatched his pack from the ground, stalked over to the doorway, and stormed out into the corridor. It was all very dramatic.

"What about me?" Toshiko asked in a small voice. "Am I expendable?"

Vermillion Gadise glanced at her again. Toshiko thought she saw the woman's face soften, just for a moment, then it was hard as titansteel. "I asked for a Mage. The Thousands Suns sent you."

Toshiko wilted back into the edges of the argument then. She thought she had been requested. The first trainee from the Thousand Suns to open her First Gate since arriving on titan 02. She had thought she was finally standing out. But they did not request her at all. She was the only member of the squad who wasn't there by request. She was simply someone her ship wanted to be rid of.

"HELP!" the squeal of panic came from the corridor outside.

The squad leader launched herself to the doorway and barrelled through it. Iro and Emil were only a few steps behind, forgetting their packs. They bumped into each other as they reached the door and the Paladin pushed the Corsair out of the way and hurried through first. Toshiko struggled after them, but was far slower, especially carrying the bulky weight of Steel Lotus.

The corridor was almost pitch black save for the sweeping beams of light from the other's flashlights. Toshiko fumbled at her vambrace to turn her own light on. It was a wide corridor with plenty of space. Probably intended for cargo transport, judging by the twin rails running along the floor and mimicked on the ceiling above.

"Justice? JUSTICE?" the squad leader shouted. Up ahead, the beams of light swept about frantically.

Toshiko heard a sound behind her and spun about, pointing her flashlight down along the corridor. Something moved, darting away from the light. When she tried to follow it with her flashlight, there was nothing there. But she was certain she had seen... something.

The light in the room with the cubicles winked out. It didn't come back on.

Toshiko backed up a step. "Hey, squad leader? Emil? What's going on?"

"Stay with the Mage," Vermillion Gadise's voice again. She sounded like she was quite a way up the corridor now. "Justice? Where are you?"

Toshiko shone her light down at Steel Lotus so she could see the display. She tapped the right button and the barrel started shifting, the internal motors shifting the configuration until it was double-barrelled. More noise ahead, claws skittering across the floor. She shone her flashlight down the corridor, saw six little lights shining back for a moment, then gone. Eyes! That was her light reflected in something's eyes.

Toshiko backed up another step and activated her crest. Fuzzy pink light shone around her, lit the nearby walls in a crimson light. She started chanting her litany, collecting energy from her current and pouring it into Steel Lotus.

"The Vermillion is the flagship of the fleet. With a length of eight hundred and twelve feet and a population of just under six thousand, it's one of the most spacious ships."

Something touched her shoulder and Toshiko spun about, pointing both of Steel Lotus' barrels even though the cannon wasn't ready to fire.

"Woah," Eclipse Iro said, holding up his hands. He had his broken sword drawn.

"Scrap it," Toshiko said. She turned around again. "It's home to the Legacy families Samir, Outouda, Geiss, and Ntega."

"Huh?"

"Sorry. Just ignore me." She lowered her voice and kept whispering. Clearly, he didn't understand that she had to keep the litany going.

"Just stick behind me." He slipped past her, standing against the darkness of the corridor. He swept his flashlight back and forth, revealed nothing.

Toshiko hated not being able to hear the squad leader. She wished comms were up, but that was part of what they were doing down here. They needed the signal amplifiers to get their comms network up and running.

Footsteps pounded on the floor behind her a way and Toshiko spun around, keeping up her litany, pouring energy into the cannon.

"Cousin? Cousin, is that you?" Justice's voice, high and panicked.

"Get over here, Justice. What's happening?" Vermillion Gadise asked.

"Gaunts!" the Surveyor said, out of breath. "They're in the walls."

"Scrap!" The squad leader was so far down the corridor Toshiko couldn't see anything of her but a vague sweeping blur of light. "We're facing gaunts. Do not let them take you. Stay in sight of another squad member at all times."

Eclipse Iro glanced over his shoulder at her. "Hey, Toshiko. Do you know what a gaunt is?"

The automaton sitting on Eclipse Iro's shoulder buzzed. "Gaunt: Grade three humanoid variant type monster. Typically eyeless and noseless, they hunt by auditory sense. Gaunts develop scaly protrusions all along the skin. They usually hunt in large packs. Gaunts can turn other humans into gaunts."

"Don't let them take you," Toshiko repeated the squad leader's warning. She glanced down at Steel Lotus' display; the screen read the capacitor at 20%.

"Don't worry," Eclipse Iro said. "I'll protect..."

A scaly creature erupted out of the dark, crashed into the Corsair, bearing him down to the ground. His sword was pinned between his body and the monster, its clawed hands gripping the edge. The gaunt lurched down and bit, sinking sharp fangs into Iro's shoulder, finding a gap in his armour. He screamed.

Toshiko staggered back. "The Vermillion is one of the few ships in the fleet to house external weapons systems." She kept channeling power into her cannon, but she charged so slowly, and her blasts weren't suited to delicately shooting enemies off comrades. But she had to do something.

She ran forward, raised Steel Lotus in her hands and bashed the butt of the cannon down on the gaunt's head. It growled, tilted its eyeless head towards her, unharmed. Iro's crest flared azure beneath him, lighting the corridor an icy hue. His broken sword became whole, the top half formed of his current. The gaunt howled as the searing light of Iro's blade cut through its claws. With a cry of effort, the Corsair heaved the monster off of him and stood, already swinging. He cut the gaunt in half with a single blow.

"That hurt," Eclipse Iro shouted at the dead monster. He rolled his bitten shoulder.

"More!" Toshiko pointed her flashlight to reveal three more scaly shapes crawling along the corridor towards them.

Eclipse Iro vanished, reappeared in front of the lead gaunt, stabbed his blade into it, pinning it to the wall. The next monster leapt at him and he ducked, rolled away from it, leaving his sword behind. He staggered back a few steps next to Toshiko.

"Scrap! My sword."

Another monster leapt out of the darkness towards them. Toshiko rose Steel Lotus to block, the gaunt smashed into the cannon and knocked her down. Blue light flared again as Eclipse Iro formed an entire sword out of his current and swung at the gaunt. The monster squealed and leapt away. Toshiko saw smoke sizzling from where Iro gripped his sword and the Corsair was wincing. His own current was hurting him.

"I need my sword." He swung his light blade, vanished again, reappeared next to the sword he'd left pinning a dead gaunt to the wall. He swept his light blade around his head, forcing the monsters back, then dropped it. The light winked out. Iro grabbed the hilt of his physical sword, wrenched it from the wall, spun and slashed a gaunt in the chest. The blade bit deep, slammed the monster against the corridor wall.

Toshiko realised she'd stopped chanting. She started up her litany again, this time reciting facts about her own ship, pouring current into Steel Lotus. Behind them, she saw Justice pinned against a wall. He had hold of the gaunt's hands, keeping it from clawing at him, and his autodage produced a drill, bore into the monster's skull even as it tried to sink its fangs into him.

Behind Justice, Toshiko could just about make out Emil fighting a gaunt of his own. He grabbed its head in one huge metal fist, slammed it against the wall over and over until it stopped moving. And beyond Emil, the corridor was lit silver with Vermillion Gadise's crest.

The gaunts swarmed at the Vanguard, filling the corridor with scaly bodies. The squad leader was a blur of movement, slamming her shield into monsters, breaking limbs, shattering skulls, knocking them away. But for every gaunt she killed, two more clambered from the walls, the floor, the ceiling.

Steel Lotus' barrels started glowing red. Toshiko looked down at the display. It read 45%. Far from fully charged, but she could make it work. "Ready to fire!" Toshiko yelled.

Gadise threw a gaunt into the swarming mass and glanced back, meeting Toshiko's gaze. She nodded. Then she threw her head back and shouted so loudly Toshiko winced and almost covered her ears. There were no words to the Vanguard's shout, only a cry of challenge. For just a moment, everything seemed to stop. The gaunts paused their assault and all heads turned towards Gadise. Even Emil and Justice stopped to stare at her. Toshiko couldn't tear her eyes away. Then all the monsters lurched back into motion, crawling over each other to get to the Vanguard. The monsters raced past Iro and Toshiko, ignoring them in favour of the only prey they wanted.

The Vanguard raised her shield and a sphere of yellow light surrounded her just moments before the swarm reached her. She disappeared underneath a rising tide of scaly flesh. More of the monsters swarmed past the squad, ignoring them. Justice staggered back behind Toshiko, his goggles cracked, his hand over his mouth. Emil stood in front of them, fists raised and ready, but none of the gaunts cared for him. The corridor beyond was filled with writhing, scaly bodies. Toshiko couldn't see how the squad leader was still under them all.

"Do it, Mage!" Toshiko heard the bellow even over the noise of the swarm.

"Get back," she said. Emil backed up behind her. Toshiko levelled Steel Lotus, and pulled the trigger. There was a percussive boom as the top barrel fired a wave of sound that cracked the walls and staggered the swarming gaunts. They fell about themselves, clawing at their ears, screaming.

The squad leader squirmed her way out of the disorientated swarm, crawling over writhing bodies. She was almost free when a scaly claw wrapped around her ankle. Her eyes went wide and she stared at them all, a snarl on her face. "Fire!" She was dragged back into the swarm, vanished into the scaly mass.

Toshiko grit her teeth and pulled the trigger again. The second of Steel Lotus' barrels roared and a beam of searing white energy tore through the corridor. Walls smoked, scorched, cracked. The floor melted. The ceiling buckled. And the swarm of gaunts disintegrated, burned away to dust and ashes.

Steel Lotus' barrel fell silent as the last of Toshiko's current burned away. The corridor was a twisted ruin of slag and smoking metal and the occasional charred body. The walls glowed with a molten light. Toshiko stared wide eyed. She'd never fired off a Giga Beam like that in an enclosed space before. It was only the third time she'd ever fired off a Giga Beam at all, and she was still learning to control it.

"Remind me never to get in your way," Eclipse Iro said in a quiet voice.

Toshiko paled. "Squad leader?"

The corridor was filling with steam. It was hissing out of one of the cracked walls.

"Cousin?" Justice stepped forward and holding up a hand against the heat.

A scorched shape shifted from the floor, rising amidst a pile of charred corpses. "Scrap that's hot," Vermillion Gadise said. She staggered upright and hurried forward towards the rest of the squad.

Toshiko breathed a sigh of relief. She'd had a terrible feeling for a moment that she had killed her own squad leader. She supposed it would make her stand out once and for all, but not in a good way.

The Vanguard's shield was burning bright and her silver armour was scorched black in places.

"You're tougher than titansteel," Eclipse Iro said, grinning.

"You'd be surprised what a Vanguard can survive."

The corridor was still filling with steam. Along with the glowing walls, it was making the atmosphere uncomfortably hot.

The squad leader stared back down the corridor. "We'll have to find another way back up. Best we get out of here…"

Something in the corridor cracked, burst. Water gushed out of one of the broken walls, filling the corridor, racing towards in a consuming wave.

Toshiko groaned. "Not again."

"Run!" the squad leader shouted.

Toshiko turned, started forwards, but it was too late. The water slammed into her from behind and everything went black and cold.

CHAPTER 8

IRO WOKE half submerged in a tepid puddle. He groaned, coughed out some metallic-tasting water, and sat up slowly. Last thing he remembered was liquid gushing into the corridor so fast he didn't even have time to run. It scooped up, spun about, and slammed into a wall. It was a miracle he hadn't died. And another miracle he had kept hold of his sword and not somehow skewered himself on it.

My sword is my life. And was nearly the end of it, too.

The chamber was dark, with a persistent roaring noise all around. It was cold, too. He shivered. He was standing on a large metal disc about three meters across, and then another meter of grating. In the centre of the disc, a pylon stretched upwards. A red light blinked at the top of the pylon and beyond was nothing but darkness. Water dripped down from somewhere high above, splashing his face. Iro wiped his eyes and turned his flashlight on. It provided scant illumination but convinced him this new chamber was massive.

The disc trembled and water splashed up over the side, washing his boots. Iro approached the edge of the disc and shone his light over the side. He saw nothing but frothing, crashing, black water. He activated his crest, raised his sword, and used Light Blade to make it shine ten times brighter than his flashlight. Still, all around him was nothing but turbulent water, roiling and angry. He made a full circuit of the disc, but it surrounded him on all sides. It was more than he had ever even imagined existed and made him feel small and fragile. The disc shook again as another wave crashed into it. Iro took a step back from the edge. He had no idea where he was, and even less of an idea how to get out of it. He remembered stories Burning Ember Franka told him of drowning. She had not made it sound pleasant.

"Hello?" he screamed against the roar of the thrashing waves. No reply. He tried again, shouting out the names of his squad. No reply. He hoped they hadn't dropped into the water below. For now, he needed to figure out how to escape this chamber, then he could worry whether his squad had survived, and go about finding them.

Iro made another circuit of the disc, holding his shining sword out to provide light. It drained his current, but he could keep the Light Blade active for a while. The disc was suspended about six meters above the churning water. He got down on his belly and slithered forward, peering underneath the disc to discover it sat on another pylon that vanished beneath the waves. None of which helped him figure out how to escape.

He held his Light Blade above him and joined his flashlight to the glow, shining it upwards. There was nothing but darkness above and water dripping down in steady streams.

Iro made another circuit of the disc, talking to himself as he went. "Franka said something about swimming. She seemed to think it was possible to move through water. But I don't know how, and I don't think I want to try that. She also said it was far easier to drown than swim." He completed the circuit and started around again.

"I could Blink Strike upwards and try to reach the ceiling. I guess I must have fallen into this chamber, so maybe I could get out again that way?" He looked upwards, tripped over his own feet. His heart thundered in his chest, but he caught himself before careening over the edge into the water. "But if the drop is too high, I might not reach the ceiling, and then hurt myself on the fall back down. The chance of me escaping with a broken leg seems low."

Panic closed in on Iro, constricting his chest as he thought about how to escape, and discarded each option. He completed another circuit of the disc. "Maybe there are some talents that would help me." He tapped on his tablet screen, flicked through a couple of pages, reading as he paced.

"Phantom Blade. The ability to create a sword out of pure current that can be moved by command. Perfect. I could stand on it and fly out of this chamber. Shame there's no one around to teach me." He closed down his tablet screen and paced some more.

It occurred to him that North could fly. He didn't think the automaton was strong enough to lift him, but he could send it to find help. "North?" he shouted into the roaring room. No answer. He really was alone.

Iro released the Light Blade to let his current recharge and turned off his flashlight to conserve energy. He paced just as well in the dim, blinking glow of red haze above him. He made another circuit, and stopped. There was another light in the distance. Another dim glow, fuzzy in the darkness. It might mean another pylon. He hoped that's what it meant.

"This chamber is on a titan, there has to be an end to it. Four walls, a ceiling. A floor." He glanced over the edge of the disc again and discounted the floor as any sort of option. "If this pylon has a disc attached, it's reasonable to assume that the other red light also has a pylon and therefore a disc. Right? Perfectly reasonable." He was aware he was trying to convince himself. "So how do I reach it?"

The answer seemed obvious when it came. Blink Strikes. Though it looked like a long way away. And if he failed? He'd plunge into the churning black waters below. He'd seen things dropped in water before. They sank.

Iro shook himself. "What else am I going to do? Wait here and hope for rescue?" If the rest of his squad were dead, that rescue would never come. And even if they weren't, how would they find him? The titans were beyond massive, and the very existence of this water-filled chamber proved that. Still, he hoped they weren't dead.

Iro drew his broken sword and activated his crest. It blazed behind him in cold, blue light, fuzzing where the water dripped through the lines from above. He focused on the red light in the distance, so far away it was only a soft glow. He'd never tested just how far a Blink Strike could take him.

"Here we go."

Iro slashed his sword and used a Blink Strike. The world gave that now familiar lurch around him as he was tugged along at an alarming speed, almost as though gravity shifted direction for him. He did not make it to the other pylon. His strike ended short, he slashed at mid air, and fell.

Iro's stomach lurched, he screamed in panic, swung his sword and used another Blink Strike. The force gripped hold of him again just as his foot touched the water. It dragged him upwards at a bizarre angle. He completed his strike, still in mid air, started falling again, the black water rushing up to meet him. He cried out, used another Blink Strike to drag himself upwards again. The red light was gone! He glanced about in a panic. Gravity started dragging him back down.

Iro used another Blink Strike to drag himself up away from the water again. He was getting the hang of it now. At the summit of his slash, he spun about until he locked gaze on the red light, then stabbed out with his sword. The Blink Strike carried him half the distance and he fell again. Iro used an upward slash and his talent dragged him through the air once more. He finished his attack on nothing and landed on the new disc, rolling to a stop.

"I did it!" Iro shouted, jumping to his feet. He let out a whoop of joy. It was almost like flying. He made a quick circuit of the disc, not paying attention. His heart thumped fast as thruster fire and he kept laughing with joy.

"Scrap it. Calm down. You have to figure out where you are now. And stop talking to yourself. It makes you sound crazy."

Iro made a slower circuit around the new disc, shining his flashlight. Everything looked the same as the last disc. Metal plating, grating, pylon, and blinking red light, and the water drizzling down from above. Even down to the single red light in the distance. He had to consider the possibility he'd got turned around and was back on the original disc. Which meant he had to fly all over again.

"Found you!" Master Rollo shouted, sounding oddly elated. "Found you! North has found you!" The little automaton flew out of the darkness and buzzed around Iro's head three times, repeating that it had found him. Then it landed on his shoulder, scuttled across to his other shoulder and back again. "North has found you."

Iro laughed. "You did. But how?"

North buzzed. "Command Iro is Command. North will always find Command."

Iro found himself buoyed by the company. He knew the automaton was just that, a bundle of wires and metal and programming he'd never understand, but it was also company. He was glad to not feel alone. And he was happy the little construct was… alive wasn't the right word. Intact.

"North, I need you to fly around this chamber and scout it.

Find me a way out."

The automaton buzzed into the air and started zipping away, but it stopped. "Do not leave, Command Iro. North will be back. Do not leave." Then flew away into the darkness and falling water.

Iro waited long enough that he was getting worried and was contemplating Blink Striking over to the next pylon. Then North came flying out of the darkness and buzzed around Iro's head again.

"North has found an exit. Command Iro, follow this trajectory." A light beamed out from the little chassis, impossibly bright given the automaton's small size. It shone towards the pylon in the distance.

Iro breathed a sigh of relief. "So if I follow the pylon, I'll find a way out."

"Affirmative."

"Alright then." Iro approached the edge of the disc. "Time to fly."

North landed on Iro's shoulder. He activated his crest and slashed with his sword. The Blink Strike carried him about a third of the distance to the next pylon. Gravity tugged Iro down. He stabbed out and used another Blink Strike to close the distance again.

"Look, North, I'm flying!" Iro shouted as he dropped.

"Command Correction: You are falling consecutively."

Iro slashed with his sword and used a final Blink Strike to reach the pylon. This time he didn't fall onto it, but stepped easily onto the disc. He laughed and punched at the air. He felt strong. His current was a little drained, but he could perform a few more Blink Strikes at least.

"Trajectory?" Iro asked.

North beamed out its light. Iro ran towards the edge of the disc, leapt into the air with a jubilant cry, and slashed his sword.

He reached the next pylon in three quick Blink Strikes, never letting gravity grab hold of him. He landed on the disc without slowing, crossed it in five bounding strides, leapt into the air again. Regardless of North's correction, Iro flew.

He was drained but ecstatic by the time he reached the edge of the chamber. North directed him onto a small ledge with a single large door set into the wall. Iro hit the ledge and slowed, taking a moment to lean against the wall and pant. His current was low, his crest dimmed to a sullen glow, but he had made it. He turned to stare back into the chamber for a few moments. A massive space filled with churning black water, strange pylons thrusting up from the waves. There had to be a purpose for it. Why was the chamber filled with water? What was underneath, pushing it to such violence?

"You're a guide. What purpose does this chamber serve?"

North buzzed and floated off his shoulder. "Unknown. There is no entry in North's databanks."

"Can you make a guess?"

North was silent a moment. "Negative. Guessing is not currently part of North's available functions."

"I should have seen that coming. Can you extrapolate a hypothesis based upon existing data?"

North landed on his shoulder, scurried across the other one, then back again. "Hypothesis: Chamber is used for research. Proximity to the laboratories, and aquatic aeration system would suggest higher than average probability the chamber's intended use was for marine research."

Iro grinned as he pressed the button to open the door. "See, I knew you could guess."

North buzzed but said nothing.

Iro squared his shoulders and strode through the doorway. It was time to find the rest of his squad. Assuming any of them were still alive.

CHAPTER 9

EMIL DUCKED a clawed swipe and rose into an uppercut. He activated his crest and used Strength at the last moment so the punch had extra power to it. The blow took the hairy gaunt under what he decided might be a chin and snapped its head back. He followed up with a thunderous haymaker that sent the monster staggering, and quickly closed the distance between them, grabbing the gaunt by the neck in one huge gauntlet, lifting it off the floor and slamming it down half on the nearby counter. The metal dented and the monster's back snapped. It slid to the floor, dead, trailing purple blood.

Dusting off his gauntlets, Emil took a moment to glance around at the room. It was well lit with circular lights set into the ceiling, probably too deep for the eyeless gaunts to claw out. A long chamber filled with metal counters jutting out from the walls. Cupboards sat beneath the counters. Set into the walls were odd cabinets with metal and glass doors, windows peering into metallic chambers. Each of the strange cabinets had dials and buttons around the door. Some cabinets were smallish, barely large enough for a child. Others were much larger and could have fit an adult or two in them comfortably. Emil wondered if that were the purpose, some sort of sleeping chambers. But then he couldn't figure out what the counters were for. He supposed it didn't matter. The room had been home to three gaunts when he found it, and they had been feasting on the body of a rustling. All three were dead now.

Emil pulled off his left gauntlet and tapped at his tablet screen. Since he was here, and alone, he might as well try to find some parts Roret needed. One bit of tape he'd used to strap the tablet to his vambrace had torn away and the tablet was hanging loose. Emil glanced around for something to tie it back into place and his gaze fell on the hairy gaunt. He shrugged. It was no different to using bhurbeast leather, he supposed. He grabbed a handful of the monster's hair, tore it from its body, and used it to tie his tablet down on his vambrace. That done, he brought up the list of parts Roret needed, and set to searching the room.

The cupboards were full of bowls and plates, some metal, some plastic. Nothing helpful. He approached a cabinet set into the wall and peered in through the glass window. It was one of the larger doors and Emil could see two shelves set into grooves on the cabinet walls. At the back was a large fan. He pressed the button outside the cabinet and nothing happened. He turned the dial as far as it would go. Still nothing. He pulled open the door and hot air wafted out, blasting him in the face. He guessed it was some kind of heater as it was heating up quickly.

Emil heard claws skittering across the floor. He activated his crest and Steeled himself just as a hefty weight smacked into him from behind, slamming him against the cabinet door. Claws scraped across his armor, fangs clanged against his neck, stopped by his enhancement. The heat coming from the cabinet flared to an oppressive level. Emil struggled with the gaunt clinging to his back, slammed into a nearby counter, punched at the monster's head. A claw scraped across his head, tearing out some of his hair, but his skin was too hard to penetrate as long as he held his Steel.

Emil dropped to his knees, wrenched on the gaunt's head, dragging it over his shoulder and slammed it into the open door of the cabinet. It hissed and spat and flailed at him. Emil rose to his feet and shoved the monster deeper into the cabinet, then slammed the door closed and threw his enhanced weight against it. The gaunt screamed and howled, slammed against the door a few times. Then the struggling stopped. Emil pulled away from the door. Through the glass window, he could see the monster cooking inside. He turned away, feeling a little sick and was glad his stomach was already empty.

Emil checked his list of parts again. He was certain he would not find anything in this room, not without pulling apart the electronics behind the cabinets. And if he did that, he'd destroy anything he actually needed.

He plucked his discarded gauntlet from the floor and slipped his hand into the padded interior. What he needed was someone who knew about electronics and parts and tech stuff. It was time to find the rest of his squad, wherever they had ended up.

Emil heard shouts. He knew the voice; Iro. It sounded like the Corsair had got himself into trouble again. Emil launched himself out of the room and put the mystery of why it was filled with dusty old rusting beds out of his mind. He charged along the corridor, feet pounding on metal grating, and wished he had learned the Speed talent. He rounded a corridor and barrelled through an open doorway into a strange chamber with large closed tubes spaced out evenly along all the wall. There didn't appear to be a ceiling, the chamber disappearing into darkness above.

In the centre of the new chamber, lit by powerful yellow strip running in a circle around the wall, was Iro. Four Hoppers all wearing featureless gray armor surrounded him. No black cloaks, though. They were from the other fleet. Iro had his sword drawn, held ready, and was warning the others to stay back. Like monsters circling prey for a kill, the other Hoppers had him penned in.

"Hey!" Emil shouted to get their attention. They all turned to stare at him.

Iro stabbed with his sword, flickered. The large Hopper with a scarred lip reached out quick as spark, grabbed Iro even as he tried to Blink Strike away. Iro cried out. His sword ripped free from his hands by the momentum of his talent and skidded across the floor towards Emil. The Hopper slammed Iro down on the ground, then placed a metal boot on his chest.

"Another little rat," the scarred Hopper said. He had no weapons that Emil could see, but there was something about the way he carried himself. He was confident, either by personal power or by their superior numbers.

Emil stooped and picked up Iro's sword. "Let him go."

"Or what, rat?" the scarred man said. He leaned a little heavier on Iro's chest. "You'll go get more rats to scurry about and infest the place. Take more of what's not yours."

"Huh? Did you take something, Iro?"

"No," Iro grunted. It sounded like he was struggling to breathe with the scarred man's foot pressing down on him.

"This," the scarred man said, raising his arms. "All of this. This titan is ours. We were here first. You." He sneered. "You come here. Start stealing things. You stir up the Black Cloaks." He looked angry now. "Even the monsters are more active. You upset the balance, and we're all paying for it. And now with the Blight, there ain't enough titan for all of us."

"We should use them to send a message, Kettle," said another of the Hoppers, a rangy woman with hollow cheeks. "Kill one, send the other back to his fleet and tell them to scrap off."

The scarred man, Kettle, looked like he was considering it. He rubbed a gauntleted hand across his chin.

Iro's crest flared in front of him, icy lines bright. He formed a glowing dagger in his right hand and stabbed it into Kettle's leg. The scarred man growled and staggered back, though the dagger hadn't penetrated his armor. Iro flicked his dagger towards Emil and vanished, reappearing sliding across the floor in front of Emil. He flipped back onto his feet and snatched his sword from Emil's grip.

"Looks like I saved you again," Emil said.

"What? I clearly saved myself this time. You were just an audience." Iro's voice trembled.

"Do you think we can take them?"

"I don't think they'll give us a choice."

The odds weren't good. There were four of them, and for all Emil knew they could be Fourth Gaters. Even if they were only Second Gaters, they outclassed both Emil and Iro together. They'd barely survived against the mad Corsair Alfvin by unleashing an army of monsters on him.

Iro's automaton drifted down from above, landing on his shoulder. It buzzed. "Threat level: 43."

"Scrap!" Iro said. "That's Second Gate at least."

Emil growled. That put both fighting and running out of the question. If even one of the other Hoppers had opened their Second Gates, they were both faster and stronger than them. And he had a feeling negotiating wouldn't go well.

The other Hoppers clustered together in the centre of the chamber. "They're scared of using too much current," Emil said quietly. "We're close to that nest Justice mentioned. If we can show them we're not weak, maybe they'll back off." And the best way to show someone you weren't weak, was to attack.

"Emil wait..."

Emil rushed forwards. He picked Kettle as his target. If he

could knock the leader down, maybe they could all agree to go their separate ways.

Kettle laughed as he stepped away from Emil's first swing, then swayed from his follow-up jab. "At least they have some spirit. You'll need that when you're back out in the void." He stepped into Emil's third punch.

At the last moment, Emil activated his crest and used Strength on himself. His muscles bulged and his punch crashed into Kettle's chest with a clang as titansteel met titansteel. Kettle grunted, but didn't even budge from the force of the attack. He reached up casually and wrapped a hand around Emil's wrist, holding him in place.

"Wave," Kettle said over his shoulder. "That other one is a Corsair. You deal with him."

The gangly woman who had been waiting at the back of the group stepped forward hesitantly. "What? You... you want me to k-kill him?"

Kettle turned his head to look over his shoulder, still holding onto Emil's wrist as if it was nothing. Emil tugged, trying to pull away, using Strength, but couldn't free himself. "Well, I certainly don't want you to k-k-k-k-kiss him, you simpleton." He chuckled and the other Hoppers joined in.

Emil sent a haymaker slamming into the side of Kettle's head, titansteel slamming into flesh. Kettle turned back to him slowly, one eyebrow raised. "Ow." He tugged on Emil's wrist, pulled him close, drove a knee into Emil's gut. Emil collapsed, spitting blood, the air driven from his lungs. But Kettle still had hold of his wrist and hauled him back up again.

"This is our warning," Kettle snarled into Emil's face. "Take your junker fleet and scrap off. Find your own titan and stop churning up trouble on ours."

Emil was still struggling to catch his breath, caught in Kettle's grip. The scarred Hopper held up a single finger before Emil. His crest flared behind him, an imposing burgundy series of lines. Emil stared at it for a moment and saw the Hopper had unlocked two gates. Only two, and he'd crushed Emil without even trying.

Kettle's finger started to glow, bright yellow as though he were holding a star. He let go of Emil's wrist, placed his finger against his chest, and flicked.

Emil used Retribution.

In a flash of blinding energy, Emil and Kettle flew away from each other. Both crashed into opposite walls of the chamber. Iro turned to run to Emil, and suddenly Wave was standing in front of him. She was rangy, pale skinned with dark hair and eyes that seemed large and unblinking.

"S-sorry ab-bout this," Wave said. She stabbed a long, straight edged sword at him. Iro leapt backwards and brought his own sword up in a guard position. He didn't use Light Blade yet. His current was still low from flying so much earlier.

"I really l-like your s-sword." She stepped forward and whipped a flurry of strikes his way. Iro retreated, slipping into a flowing defence like in training with Eir so many times. Wave pushed him back across the chamber, not letting up for a moment. Her crest hung behind her, searing white lines. Iro glanced at it and saw three concentric circles, two locks. She had opened her Second Gate. But she didn't seem so strong. She was fast, but he could keep up. He could attack.

Iro parried a stab, ducked, drove up and forwards with his sword.

"No," Wave said. She blocked Iro's strike with no effort. Her sword wavered, blinked out of existence, slipped through his own sword. The flat of her blade slapped Iro across the cheek. He staggered back, crying out in pain, holding a hand to his face. It came away bloody.

North buzzed and took to the air. "Threat level: 39. Command Advice: Retreat."

"Oh," Wave said flatly, staring up at North. "That's… s-something." She stepped forward again, slashed at Iro. He blocked and again her sword flickered, passed through his own, sliced across his chest.

Iro cried out and fell backwards, his chest was on fire. He glanced down to see his armour was intact, but he could feel blood running down his stomach. He stood again, gripping his sword tightly. Whatever talent Wave was using, he'd never heard of it before. Shadow Blade could make a sword appear invisible, but her sword seemed to blink out of existence for a moment.

Out of the corner of his eye, Iro saw Emil stir. The Paladin was down, but not dead. That was good. Over the other side of the chamber, Kettle was up, wiping blood from his mouth, his face twisted into an angry snarl.

"He's w-wounded. I th-think they've learned their l-lessons."

"No," Kettle snarled. "Kill him, Wave."

Wave sighed.

Iro Blink Striked to the side, dodging around Wave, then again to cross the chamber to Emil, all in the space of a second. Wave beat him there. She pushed his sword down to the floor, stepped on it and pinned it against the metal grating. "You're v-very slow."

She lashed out with her blade again and Iro didn't even see the strike. Blazing pain trailed like fire across his chest. He staggered back, losing grip on his sword.

"F-fall down."

"No!" Iro growled. He looked around for something to help. Emil was getting up, one hand beneath him, but his other hung limp. North floated above, but the little automaton was no help. He had to do this alone.

"P-please fall down." Wave stepped in, her sword lashing out at him again. Iro formed a Light Blade in his hands and blocked. The blade sizzled in his grip and his hands smoked like he was gripping a heating element.

Iro shoved Wave's blade away and swung. She vanished. Something hard hit Iro on the back of his head and he collapsed. His blade slipped from his grip and burned away. Wave kicked him in the ribs and flipped him over onto his back. She held her sword above him, a breath away from his neck.

"B-beg. B-beg for your l-life."

Iro grit his teeth and stared fury at her. Could he form another Light Blade, knock her sword aside before she could thrust?

"Don't!" For the first time, her voice wasn't flat. She almost sounded like she was the one begging. "Please b-beg for your life."

Emil groaned. He hauled himself to sitting, leaning against the wall and cradling his left arm against his chest. He was in no position to fight on. And Iro had no way to win. Even after opening his First Gate, he stood no chance against Wave. She had opened her Second Gate, and he realised now that put her so far ahead of him, it was like fighting against a trainee for her. The gap between Gates was huge.

"Please," Iro said, forcing the words out through gritted teeth. "Please don't kill us. I beg you."

"D-done." She pulled her sword away and turned. "Humiliated. They c-can carry the m-message back to their f-fleet."

Kettle stalked forward. He had a smear of blood across his chin. Emil had hit him that hard somehow. "I gave you an order, Wave. Kill the little rat. Take his worthless life."

Wave stopped and glanced down at Iro again. "He's a C-corsair." She stopped and plucked Iro's sword from the ground, hefted it up to lean against her shoulder and started walking away. "There. I've t-taken his life."

Kettle shook his head. "That's not…"

"My d-duel. A Corsair's s-sword is their life. I've t-taken his."

Kettle glared at Wave and snorted. "Cute. But no. Kill him."

North had flown across the chamber and was descending next to another doorway.

"They don't need to d-die. They can s-send a message j-just as easily alive."

"We only need one of them to send a message. I'm in charge here, Wave, not you."

"I won't k-kill someone who has already begged for m-mercy."

North was flying in little circles over the other side of the chamber, next to a large silver button. Iro stared at it, and the automaton spun in the air, slammed into the button, then skirted the room, moving faster than Iro had seen it before. The entire chamber started rumbling.

"Who did that?" Kettle asked.

The other Hoppers shrugged and stared about. Wave turned and watched Iro, her head cocked a little to one side. The floor started moving.

Iro realised they were on an elevator. Judging by the size, it was some sort of cargo lift. He twisted, grabbed Emil by the arm, ignoring his pained protest, and pulled the Paladin towards the doorway.

"Stop them!" Kettle shouted. He started forward and Wave stepped to the side in front of him. She was still staring at Iro. She could have Blink Striked over to them in a moment, but she didn't.

The chamber floor was moving upwards, the door disappearing below it. Emil slithered out, dropping the few feet to the corridor below with a grunt of pain. Iro glanced back once, then launched himself through the disappearing gap, his armor grinding against the hole, then he was through. He fell on top of Emil and they both rolled away from each other. North zipped through the gap before it disappeared, the elevator rising out of sight.

"North saved you," the little automaton declared.

Iro nodded and leaned against the wall opposite Emil. He slammed his head against it in frustration. It was like the Black Cloaks all over again. They had proven how much stronger they were, and they had taken Mia. Now these Hoppers from the other fleet had proven they were stronger, and had taken his sword. Was this how it always was? No matter how much power he mustered, there would always be those stronger than him, and they would always take whatever they wanted.

Wave didn't seem like she wanted to fight. But that hadn't stopped her. It hadn't stopped her beating down on someone weaker than her. Iro balled his hands into fists. He wanted to scream, to curse, to run after them and take his sword back. But he couldn't. Not yet.

Before, when the Black Cloaks had taken Mia, he'd made a promise both to Cali and to himself. He promised to rescue her. Now he made another promise. "I will get my sword my back."

Emil grunted behind him. "I'll help. And I'll grind that scrapper Kettle into dust to do it. Are you alright, Iro?"

"I'm fine," Iro snarled, barely recognising his own voice. He surged back to his feet, then staggered as his vision swam. He had to put a hand against the wall to steady himself. His cheek was bleeding from where Wave's sword had slapped him, and his chest was sticky too, but all the cuts seemed shallow. She hadn't been trying to kill him. "You?"

Emil grunted, pushing against the wall to struggle back to his feet. "Can't move my left arm."

"How did you hit Kettle that hard?"

The Paladin chuckled bitterly. "I didn't. He hit himself that hard." He activated his crest in front of him. The lines fizzed a sullen, fiery red. His current ran weak. Emil pointed at one symbol. "Retribution. I bet the scrapper didn't think I could do that."

Iro nodded. It was a poor consolation. Retribution was a Paladin talent that threw back an equal amount of force onto the attacker. But to use it, Emil still had to get hit. It allowed him to punch above his gate, but any hit that beat his opponent would kill him as well. Still, Iro needed something like that, too. A way to fight people stronger than him, not just those weaker.

"We need to go," Emil said. "The fight might draw monsters and we're in no condition to meet them."

North drifted down from above and settled on Iro's shoulder. "Multiple injuries detected. Command Advice: Seek medical treatment."

CHAPTER 10

IRO LET EMIL lead the way. Not that he thought the Paladin had a better idea of where they were going, but that he doubted Emil would let him go first. There was a well of pride as deep as a titan running through him. Besides, Iro was struggling to concentrate. His thoughts kept drifting back to the encounter with the Hoppers from the other fleet. They had left their own wing and flown all the way across the titan to come here. Why would they have done that unless they wanted to meet Hoppers from the Home Fleet?

North buzzed around Iro, scanning him with a beam of light. "Command update: Injuries downgraded to minor. Medical treatment still advised."

"If only we had a Surveyor with us," Emil growled from up ahead. He was in worse shape than Iro. Every step was a limp, he was cradling his left arm against his chest, and occasionally he'd stop and lean against the corridor wall and spend a few moments breathing.

"Thank you, Emil," Iro said. "You didn't have to throw yourself into that situation."

"Yes, I did." The Paladin pushed away from the wall and started limping again. "You're part of my squad, Iro."

They kept going until the corridor ended, then cut through into a large room that looked broken. The walls grew thick with some sort of slimy brown growth. A hole in the floor big enough to throw a bhurbeast down dominated the space, and the entire chamber stank like algae gone to rot. They crossed through it quickly into a new corridor, this one with white walls as pristine as the Eclipse, and blaring strip lighting running all the way along the ceiling. It was strange, the difference as stark as if they had walked from a low ship to an upper ship. The walls and floor were solid bulkhead, not grated, and there wasn't a spot of rust to be seen. There were letters stamped onto some of the bulkhead walls, but written in a language Iro didn't know.

Emil kept trudging on as though he didn't even notice the change to the state of the titan. Iro poked his head in a door, peered around. Waist-high pedestals stood at regular intervals each with a chunk of something on top. Iro stepped into the room and approached the nearest pedestal. The thing on top was about the size of his head, angular and irregular, dark brown. He reached out a finger, almost poked it, then drew back, wary of setting off a trap.

"North, do you know what this is?"

"Scanning databanks." North buzzed. "It is a rock."

"What's that?"

"Geological Definition: a natural substance composed of solid crystals of various minerals fused together."

"A rock?" Iro said.

North buzzed. "It is a rock."

"They're all these… rocks?"

North buzzed around each of the pedestals and flew back to Iro. "Rocks of various compositions are categorised into…"

"Hey!" Emil hissed from the doorway. "Do you hear that?"

"Would Command Iro like a catalogue of the various sounds that are detectible within standard human range?"

Iro shushed the automaton and joined Emil at the doorway. He heard a soft noise, barely audible. It sounded like crying. He met Emil's gaze for a moment, then they were both hurrying down the corridor. Neither of them were in any condition to fight, but if someone was crying, they might be hurt.

They followed the noise into a room filled with lockers. Some hung open, the contents long since taken or rotted away, while others remained closed. Benches lined the middle of the room, and Iro took one side, while Emil crept along the other. The sound was definitely crying. As they came to the end of the lockers, Iro saw half a dozen cubicles, each with an open door and a shower head above. One door was closed and the noise issued from within.

Another sob, followed by a sniff. Iro glanced at Emil. The Paladin had a grim set to his mouth and he edged forwards. Iro reached the shower first and reached out. Emil clenched his right fist in its gauntlet. Iro didn't have his sword anymore, but he could form a Light Blade if he needed. He took a steadying breath and pulled open the door as another sob echoed from within.

Toshiko huddled in the cubicle's corner, curled into as small a ball as she could manage and hugging her oversized cannon against her chest. She squeaked in surprise, stared up at them. Her cheeks glistened damp from tears and she trembled.

"Are you alright, Toshiko?" Iro asked.

The Mage blinked twice, then spun away, pulled her beret from her head and wiped at her face. When she turned back to them, her cheeks were dry, but her eyes were still puffy and red. She struggled to her feet, still trembling.

"I'm fine," Toshiko said, her voice high and tight.

"You were crying," Emil said.

"No I wasn't. I thought… I thought I'd killed you all."

Iro shook his head and smiled at the Mage. "Still alive, just about."

"You're hurt. Steel Lotus is hurt, too." Toshiko hefted her cannon from the floor.

Emil grunted and turned away, stalking back towards the lockers.

"We're not too bad," Iro said, though he thought it might be half a lie. "Nothing to do with your blast. We ran into some trouble with the other fleet."

Toshiko nodded and crept out of the shower. "The others?"

"We haven't found them yet."

"Oh."

"But I'm sure they're fine. Gadise Samir is too tough to die, and I'd bet Justice will outlive us all."

Toshiko let out a small clipped snort and walked past Iro, her hand resting on her cannon. Iro noticed the barrel looked bent out of shape, and now and then a spark of electricity leapt from the main housing.

"There's still gaunts around somewhere." Toshiko coughed and started sounding a little less timid. "Some of them chased me. I lost them and hid in here, but I could hear them searching, clawing, scraping, hissing." She shivered.

Emil grunted as pulled open lockers and checked inside each. "I killed a few a while back."

"Justice mentioned a nest," Iro said. "How close are we?"

Emil shrugged.

North buzzed and landed on Iro's shoulder. "Close."

"Nothing but scrap in any of these," Emil said. "We should move." He limped towards the door.

"Are you ready to go?" Iro asked Toshiko.

The Mage stared at him wide eyed for a moment, then shrugged and walked past him. "Of course I am. You're the one that looks like hammered junk."

They crept along, wary of traps, and checked every room they came across. This section of the titan appeared to be designed with humans in mind. Perhaps a living quarters. But that made no sense to Iro. Again he was confronted with the fact that the titan appeared to be designed for humans, and yet humans could not live on the titan without being attacked by monsters. And if the titan was designed for humans, then by who? Who built it? They were the same questions Torben had wanted answered, before Master Alfvin had killed him.

"Is this what I think it is?" Emil asked. He was ranging ahead, his limp not even slowing him down. Iro and Toshiko hurried to catch up with him as Emil slipped into a large room with a low ceiling. Dust covered every surface with desks set up at various intervals. Some had workstations on them, others had screens and keyboards. A few had glass boxes with circular holes large enough to reach through cut into the sides. A heavy door waited at the far end of the room, locked with a steel bolt across it.

Toshiko hurried into the room behind him. "It's a laboratory. Those are specimen containers."

One of the light strips above flickered, casting much of the lab in shadow. North buzzed about, flying from one desk to another, scanning everything.

"I don't care about any of that," Emil said. He pointed to a device with his one good arm. "Is this a printer?"

Iro hurried over and bent to stare at the device. It was a large printer, capable of working on multiple designs at once. A glass case, six arms, a static bed. He nodded. "I think so." Despite its size, it was still small compared to the printers in the manufactory.

"Alright. Help me take it apart." Emil winced as he shifted his left arm and tapped on his tablet, bringing up Roret's list of parts again. "You know how to find and remove these parts?"

Iro looked at the list and shrugged. "I can try."

"Aren't you a tech?"

"I was," Iro said indignantly. "But I mostly worked on doors and filters. The Courage didn't have a working printer, so I never even saw the broken thing."

Toshiko sighed. "Send me the list, and don't get in the way. Unless I need an extra pair of hands. And find me a bag or something."

"What?" Emil asked. "You're a tech, too?"

Toshiko gave him a withering look. "No. But I built Steel Lotus from scratch all by myself. You wouldn't believe some of the things I had to take apart to scrounge the parts. I hope the Thousand Suns never needs its tertiary grav belt because." She shook her head. "That's not important." She placed her cannon on the floor, cracked her knuckles, and went about removing the main housing of the printer.

Iro stepped back and let Toshiko work. She seemed to know what she was doing and far better than he could have managed. "You built your cannon from scratch?"

"Yup." Toshiko handed Iro a light metal plate as long as his arm. He had no idea if she'd want it back, so placed it on a nearby desk.

"That explains why it looks so different to other Mage cannons."

Toshiko paused and grinned at him. "Isn't she beautiful? I've been building Steel Lotus for years. Wasn't like I had much else to do while floating through the void. But they wouldn't let me take her on a Hop. The Thousands Suns is very… traditional."

Emil leaned against a nearby specimen container and prodded at his left shoulder. "Most Mages use small handheld cannons, right?"

She glanced at Emil, her eyes wide. "Yes. All very standard. A single design for small, controlled talents. A bolt of fiery plasma or a pinpoint energy blast. It was never… me. I always felt like I needed a bigger cannon, something that could channel more current. So I built it. But it wasn't until you opened your First Gate that they let me take her on a Hop."

Emil shifted. "What have I got to do with Mages?"

Toshiko shrugged and went back to fiddling around inside the printer. She pulled out a small circuit board. "We'll need this so keep it safe.

"You have nothing to do with Mages, but you were the first trainee to open your First Gate."

"Actually, that was me," Iro said proudly. Emil short him a dark glare. "What? I beat you by at least thirty seconds."

"You don't count," Toshiko said. "You manifested your first talent here on titan 02. That made you a unique case from the start. But Emil was supposed to be stalled like the rest of us."

Emil slammed a fist into his wounded shoulder and bit back a cry of pain. "I didn't think the Stalling was common knowledge."

"What are you doing?" Iro asked.

"Trying to put my shoulder back in its socket. I think that's what's wrong. My old man knocked his shoulder out once. He fell in the sceptic tank, smacked his arm. I had to half carry him to the doc. She said he'd dislocated it. Then she sort of lifted and pulled, and my dad screamed. But it didn't hurt so much after."

Toshiko pulled her hands out of the printer, holding another board. She placed it with the first. "Help me remove the glass case." Iro hurried to help before Emil could jump in. "The Stalling wasn't common knowledge," Toshiko continued as they hefted the glass case aside to get at the arms. "But the Thousands Suns, despite being so stiflingly traditional, is quite open about communicating with its people. Different ships have different ways of operating, I guess.

"The moment they heard a Paladin had somehow opened the First Gate by learning to enhance themself instead of others, even the stuffy old Hoppers on my ship decided maybe they would allow us all to do things a little differently."

"I'm not sure that's how it happened," Emil said. "I opened the First Gate because Iro... Well, I didn't want to let him fight alone. Not sure it had anything to do with my enhancing myself."

"No?" Toshiko said. She and Iro finished removing the case and shuffled it over to an empty desk. Then she pulled a small screwdriver out from a pouch on her belt and advanced upon the printer's arms. "Well, it worked for me. I took the first opportunity to take Steel Lotus down on a Hop and encountered the gate within ten minutes of boarding the titan. Not a monster or trap in sight. Master Kinsoko was busy telling us all the plan and then suddenly everything went gray and a vast portal appeared in front of me."

"What gate was it? How did you open it?" Iro asked.

Toshiko glanced at him, frowning. "Those seem like very personal questions. I don't know why."

"Because they're your gates, not his," Emil said. "Whatever they represent, and however you open them is no one's business but your own."

Iro stared at the Paladin for a few moments. Emil had never told Iro how he had opened his own gate. They'd been questioned apart and together afterwards, but Iro only now realised that Emil had refused to talk about his own gate.

"So you see," Toshiko said, straining as she pulled on one of the printer arms. "It's all because of you, Courage Emil. I opened my First Gate two days after you did and all because you showed me the way." With one final wrenching pull, the entire arm came away from assembly. Toshiko turned to Emil and smiled at him. "Thank you."

The Paladin blushed and turned away. Iro had never seen Emil embarrassed before, he didn't even think it was possible.

"North has found a data point." The little automaton flew

across the lab, skimming desks, and circled Iro twice. "North has found a data point. Command Request please: North requests orders to access the data point."

Iro shrugged. "Uh, sure. Access the data point, North."

The automaton buzzed, spun in the air and zipped back across the lab towards a wall. There was a small indentation in the wall large enough a child could have crawled inside. The bulkhead around the wall crowded thick with cables and pipes and all of them led to the indentation.

"North," Iro said, he dodged around a desk. "What exactly is a data point?"

Too late. Without hesitation, the automaton flew into the hole. The wall shifted. The bulkhead came alive, closed in around North. All of North's chassis opened up, revealing a host of different parts and ports. Wires snaked out, plugged into the automaton. The wall lit up an electric blue, then a solid metal plate slid down across the indentation, obscuring Iro's view.

"North?" He rounded another desk and closed in on the bulkhead. There was a lot of noise beyond. It sounded like sparking wires, welding torches, saws. "North, are you alright in there?"

No answer.

Emil stepped up beside Iro. "Want me to rip the plate away and free him?"

Toshiko peered around Iro from the other side. "What's it doing in there?"

Iro glanced at her, then back to the wall. Pulses of blue light raced from above and below, funnelling into the wall right where North had flown into the indentation.

"We'll wait," Iro said. "North didn't sound like it was dangerous. So we wait until… whatever is happening is finished."

While they waited for North to finish, Toshiko went back to the printer and finished stripping the parts Roret needed. If they fixed the Courage's printer, they could start producing new filters for air, water, algae. Even such a simple thing would improve the quality of life for everyone aboard a massive amount. It might not be his ship anymore, but the Courage was still home as far as Iro was concerned, and he'd do whatever was needed to help.

Iro searched the laboratory for anything else that might be useful. There were plenty of screens, but most were large things that were too bulky to carry out with them. Though the Courage was also missing things like wiring, and Iro considered ripping out a few bundles for Emil to take back.

The heavy door set into the far wall drew Iro like a gravity well. It had a triple bar securing it to the wall and looked sturdy enough a rampaging bhurbeast would have trouble knocking it down. A small glass window frosted creeping at the edges looked through into a dim chamber. Iro peered in. There were banks of lights. Most were white and blinking, but some were flat and red. They went far back, the chamber disappearing into the depths. Iro rubbed his palm against the glass, trying to clear it a little. There was a console just to the right of the door, but he couldn't make out what was on the screen. Beyond that, the first of the blinking white lights. He pressed his face against the glass.

"It's a pod," Iro said, his breath misting the window.

"What?" Emil limped over and shouldered Iro out of the way to peer through the glass himself. "You're right. Help me get this door open." He winced as he moved his left arm, but the Paladin grabbed hold of one bar securing it to the wall. His crest flared fiery orange and one symbol lit brighter than the rest. His arms seemed to bulge as he heaved on the bar. "I said help, Iro."

"Why?"

Emil strained against the door. "Because there are pods. You mid shippers might have plenty to spare, but the Courage barely has enough pods for its Hoppers." He stopped heaving and straightened up, panting. "And I'm the Courage's only Hopper."

"And what do you expect to do? Haul a pod half way across the titan? We don't know where we are or how to get back to our docking point. We don't even know if the pods fly."

Emil glared at him. "Only one way to find out. I helped you. Now it's time to repay the favour. Help me get this door open."

It was a stupid idea. There was no way they were carting any of the pods back themselves. But he owed Emil. And what harm could opening the door do? He nodded and they both grabbed hold of one bar and started wrenching.

Toshiko cleared her throat. She perched on the edge of a nearby desk, shaking her head. "That won't work. Have you actually looked at the door? Five of you couldn't open it."

"You underestimate my power," Emil said.

Toshiko sighed and threw her head back to stare at the ceiling.

"Fine," the Paladin said, stepping back and gesturing to the door with his good arm. "Blast it open."

Toshiko snorted. She patted her cannon. "Even assuming poor Steel Lotus wasn't hurt, I wouldn't do that. What if the other side is vacuum? I'm pretty sure blowing a hole in the wall would kill us all. And even if it didn't, any blast I levelled at the wall would destroy everything on the other side too."

"Pretty full of yourself," Emil said in a low voice. Toshiko glared at him.

"Hey!" Iro said, determined to stop them before they killed each other. "It's a door. Doors are there to be opened. So there must be a way to open it. We just need to figure out how."

Toshiko let out a pained groan. "Surveyor work."

"Well, we don't currently have a Surveyor," Emil said. "And Justice would probably wet himself and refuse anyway."

The wall where North was secreted away started clanging.

Then the panel covering the indentation moved, sliding aside. North flew out of the hole, spinning in the air, buzzing.

"North. Has. Weapons." The automaton buzzed. Two little ports either side of its chassis opened up and small spikes deployed. North flew over to them. It seemed to be a little larger than before, and vibrating with energy.

"Those are weapons?" Emil asked. "They don't look like much."

North spun about to face Emil. "Charging to full power." Lightning sparked around the spikes. The automaton hovered down level with Emil's chest. "Firing."

"Wait!" Iro said, but it was too late.

Two zaps of lightning arced out from North and struck Emil in the chest. His faded pink breastplate smoked a little from the impact.

The Paladin shook his head. "Wonderful." He turned back to the door.

North buzzed. "North is not a combat model." The twin spikes retracted into its chassis and the ports closed.

"I was worried, North," Iro said. "What happened in there?"

The automaton landed on Iro's shoulder. It was bigger than before and heavier, too. "Data points provide upgrades to hardware and supplemental information packets."

"So you know more? About the titan?"

North buzzed. "North can learn."

"Do you know where are we?" Toshiko said.

North flew into the air and spun in a quick circle. "Archive 16-C: Tropical Fauna and Bioengineering Theory."

"And what's behind this door?" Emil thumped the door for emphasis.

North flew over to the Paladin and scanned the door with a beam of light. "The archive."

Emil grunted. "Can you open it?"

North buzzed and turned to face Iro. "Command: Authorisation required."

"Uh, sure. You have my authority to open the door."

"Activating wireless communications."

The bars on the door shifted, retracting into the wall. A seal popped with a hiss and the door swung open. Cold air blasted out into the laboratory. Iro shivered, and his breath misted before him.

"Huh," Toshiko said, still perched on the desk and peering around Iro. "I was expecting something more dramatic."

Emil grunted, pulled the door all the way open and stepped through. Iro rushed after him. It was freezing inside the archive and every breath puffed out in front of them. A cavernous darkness stretched out before them. The console on the right had a small screen attached with soft green light blaring out. Each of the pods had either a blinking white light or flat red, but they provided very little illumination despite the number of them. There had to be hundreds of pods.

Toshiko followed Iro in. "Oh scrap! It's colder than the void in here." She hugged herself and shivered.

Emil limped over to the first pod. It was three times the size of the pods they used to cross from ship to titan. Two metal steps led up to a frosted glass window. Emil mounted the steps and still had to go onto his toes to stare in. "What the scrap?"

"Command Query: Would you like North to turn on the archive lights?"

"Sure."

North buzzed over to the console and scanned it. A few seconds later, lights started flickering on all along the archive walls, floor, and ceiling. Iro had underestimated the size of the place. Even well lit, it stretched on forever. At first he had thought there were hundreds of pods. Now he had to admit there were thousands, maybe tens of thousands. They weren't just secured to the floor, but to the walls as well, stretching out the entire length of the cavernous archive.

"What is this place?" Iro said, staring around in wonder.

"Archive 16-C: Tropical…"

"Right. But what do they archive?"

Emil stepped down from the pod and gestured for Iro to look. "Monsters."

CHAPTER 11

Emil left the archive behind. There was nothing there of any use. Those things in there weren't pods at all, they were... He wasn't even sure. Pens for monsters? It didn't matter. None of that would help him keep the Courage afloat. So what if whoever had built the titans were weird junkholes who liked to collect monsters? It changed nothing. It didn't matter. At least Toshiko had dug out as many of the parts Roret requested as she could. Emil rummaged through cupboards until he found a bag he could shove them all in.

Iro and his little automaton spent a while in the archive, speculating about why there were pods filled with monsters. But it didn't matter. Still, the few Emil had looked at were creatures he'd never seen before. A long serpent with an immense head, wrapped into a tight coil. A four legged furry creature that was bigger than a person and had brutal looking fangs. A hulking beast that looked almost human except brutishly large with elongated arms.

"Time to go," Emil said, poking his head back into the archive. Even from the doorway, the cold air made the hairs stand up on his bare arms.

Iro was standing at a pod, wrenching on the door, trying to open it. The pod was in a cluster with eight others, but it was the only one with lights on. It had LV426 stamped in black lettering on the gray metal above the door.

"But all of this..." Iro said. A hiss of vapour blasted out from the pod, stirring his hair, but the door didn't open.

"Doesn't matter. We need to find the rest of the squad and get off the titan."

The Corsair stared at him a moment longer, then nodded. "I suppose so. I wonder if the fleet will want to send a team to investigate?"

Emil shrugged.

"More likely, they'll send a team to scrap it all for parts," Toshiko said. "I'm sure I could rip a few upgrades for Steel Lotus from this place." She had spent the time wrestling with her cannon's barrel, trying to straighten the dented plating. Unfortunately, the Mage was all but useless until she fixed her cannon, and a liability even with the thing working. A powerful liability though.

Iro climbed through the archive doorway. His automaton buzzed and the door swung shut behind him, the bolts slid home to lock it back up but ground to a halt. The door stayed open. Emil shook his head in frustration. It was just like the Courage, everything was falling apart.

"Hey, North, do you know how many archives there are?" Iro said.

The automaton was silent for a moment. "Aboard Leviathan there are fifty-two archives split into four subsections; A, B, C, and D."

"Leviathan?" Toshiko asked.

"Affirmative. This titan's designation is Leviathan."

"What does that mean?" Iro asked.

"North does not know. Additional data points will provide

supplemental information packets." The automaton settled on his shoulder.

"What's the purpose of the archives?"

North buzzed. "Access Restricted." It flew into the air, spun in a quick circle. "North will try again." It buzzed. "Access Restricted. Access Restricted. Access Restricted. ERROR. ERROR. ERROR." The automaton fell from the air and hit the ground with a solid thunk. It didn't move. The lights in the laboratory went out.

They all activated their flashlights. Emil had to smack his to get it working again. Beams of white light cut through the darkness, bouncing off floating dust. Iro knelt before the automaton and poked it. "North? North, are you alright?" There was no answer. Iro looked up at them in panic.

"Time to go," Emil said. He had a bad feeling about this. It seemed far too coincidental that the lights went out right after the automaton died.

"What about North?"

"Carry it." Emil threw him a spare satchel he'd found. He stalked towards the exit, ignoring the twinges in his arm and leg. It was only pain. He could work through pain.

He stepped out into the corridor. It was dark, too, lit only by pulsing red lights that raced along the length of the ceiling. He stared first one way, then turned and looked down the way they had first come. The pulsing red lights lit movement just for a moment, bodies crawling along the floor and walls. Lots of them. Gaunts.

"Does anyone have any idea where we're going?" Toshiko asked as she strolled into the corridor to join him.

Emil snapped around to her, shoved a hand over her mouth. But it was too late. In the pulsing red light, Emil saw the gaunts look up. The lead monster hissed, and they all started crawling over each other, swarming down the corridor.

"Go!" Emil shouted. He pushed Toshiko on to get her moving, then limped after her as quickly as he could. He sent a single glance over his shoulder, saw Iro race out of the laboratory behind them, feet pounding on the metal floor. Behind him, the swarm of gaunts filled the corridor, their bodies gleaming in the dim red light, then swallowed by darkness.

Toshiko led, charging along the corridor, cannon bouncing at her hip. Emil ran behind, ignoring the stabbing pain shooting down his leg. The lights pulsed and raced, one moment bathing them in an ominous glow, the next casting them in suffocating darkness. The gaunts hissed and screeched behind them, claws skittering over metal. They sounded so close Emil expected to be dragged down any moment. But there were too many of them to fight. Toshiko's cannon was busted, Iro had lost his sword, and Emil hurt badly enough he wasn't even sure he could swing his left arm. It grated on him, but they couldn't fight. They had to run.

The corridor split in two and Toshiko veered left. Emil couldn't turn in time, slammed into the wall, lurched back into motion. He didn't have time to check on Iro. His leg was slowing him down, each step like knives driving up through his foot all the way to his knee. Toshiko took another turn, sprinting down a new corridor. Emil struggled to keep up. There was a smell on the air, something stale and sharp. No time to puzzle it out.

Toshiko was a dozen steps ahead now. She turned again, ran down a new corridor. Emil grit his teeth, turned, hit the wall again, kept on running. Toshiko was gone. In the pulsing red light racing down this new corridor, he saw nothing but emptiness ahead of him. He surged on, limping. A hand shot out of a doorway, grabbed his arm, pulled him inside.

"Wha…"

Toshiko shoved her hand over his mouth. She was so close their armour ground against each other. She put a single finger up against her own mouth and sank down until she was squatting on her haunches, pulling Emil with her.

Iro barrelled into the room a moment later, glanced at the two of them. He nodded and stepped to the other side of the door, pressed himself against the wall.

Outside the room, claws scraped against metal as the swarm surged on. A gaunt howled, a horrible noise that sounded like a knife trying to cut through metal.

A claw wrapped around the doorframe, clutching at it. In the pulsing red light, the monster stepped through into the room. It stood for a moment, right between where Emil hid with Toshiko and Iro on the other side. It raised its head, cocked it to the side. Its teeth chattered together and it prowled further into the room. Another gaunt followed it in, head tilting this way and that as it searched. This one was bigger, wearing armour just like a Hopper. Emil remembered the squad leader's warning. *Don't let them take you.* This monster had once been a Hopper. It had been human. Not anymore. Its face was a scarred ruin, as though its eyes had been clawed out. Its lips pulled back from sharpened teeth. The armor it wore was fused to it with scaly protrusions erupting from the skin. It stalked into the room after the other monster, still tilting its head as it searched.

Iro shifted his foot. Emil shook his head at him, but the Corsair edged forward, sliding his foot. He peered around the doorframe into the corridor beyond, then stepped back. His boot tapped against the metal floor. The two gaunts in the room hissed and turned, searching for the noise. A third gaunt, twice as big as the others, squeezed its way through the door. Its scaly skin caught against the doorframe, scraped against it, and it growled in annoyance. It had to duck to get through and when it stood up to its full height, Emil shifted away from it. It had to stand at least nine feet tall. This new, huge gaunt, barked something. The others chittered away, teeth clapping together.

Again, Iro edged forward and peered into the corridor, first one way, then the other. He turned back and gave a single nod, then stepped out. Emil and Toshiko rose together. His leg screamed in pain, but Emil bit it back, refusing to utter even a grunt of pain. In the pulsing red light, he saw Toshiko staring at him, frowning, biting her lip. She lifted his arm, slipped underneath it, and helped him from the room, all in silence.

They crept down the corridor as quietly as they could. The swarm of gaunts was everywhere. They stalked in and out of rooms, searching for their missing prey, heads tilting at every tiny sound. One monster passed so close Emil and Toshiko had to flatten against the wall. The creature had a sickly, dusty stench that almost made him gag. Toshiko clapped a hand over her mouth and squeezed her eyes shut until it had passed. By then, Iro was at the end of the corridor. In the pulsing red light, Emil could see him waving for them. Toshiko tightened her grip around Emil's waist, and they struggled on.

The corridor was a dead end but for a single closed door Iro stood in front of. His hand hovered over the button to open it. They had no idea how much noise it might make. It could summon the entire swarm to them in moments. They clustered by the door and stared back down into the corridor. Gaunts prowled in and out of rooms, dozens of the monsters.

Toshiko tapped at the tablet on her vambrace and held it up between the three of them. It read *We can't go back.*

Iro tapped at his own tablet. *Through the door?*

Toshiko shrugged. Emil nodded, not bothering with own tablet. The screen was so cracked it was a pain to type on.

Iro reached for the button to open the door again. His satchel lifted into the air as if drawn upwards by gravity. It buzzed. "Command Query: Why is North in a bag?"

Emil glanced back down the corridor just as gaunts came

howling, swarming out of the rooms, racing down the corridor towards them. "Go!"

Iro slammed the button. The door opened a crack, a hiss of air wafting through carrying a foul smell. He gripped the edge of the door, threw it opened and launched himself through. Toshiko dragged Emil through next. Iro pressed the button on the other side and the door slid shut. He pushed it closed as Emil and Toshiko limped into the towering chamber.

"Scrap!" Toshiko breathed the word.

Emil could only nod in reply. The chamber was massive and spherical, stretching up hundreds of feet. All along the walls, the floor, along every surface were fleshy, scaly growths. Gaunts crawled in and out of ducts, clung to the walls, clawed furrows in the shining growths. And in the centre of the chamber were three twisted cones, each one crackling with black lightning. Clinging to those three spires was a giant gaunt that would have made a bhurbeast look like a bug.

Iro slammed the door closed and turned to join Emil and Toshiko. "What the…"

Emil sighed. "We've found the nest."

CHAPTER 12

THE DOOR BANGED BEHIND THEM. Gaunts on the other side, throwing themselves against the metal. Inside the massive chamber, hundreds of eyeless heads turned their way. From the walls, from ducts, from bridging scaly growths that spanned the chamber, monsters prowled into view.

Iro's satchel floated up beside him. Iro pulled it open and North surged into the air, spinning about. The little automaton buzzed. "Threat Detected."

"That would be an understatement," Iro said. The door behind him thumped again, squealed like talons were raking down it.

"There," Toshiko pointed all the way across the chamber. "Another door."

"What if it leads to more monsters?"

The Mage shot him an incredulous glare. "More than this?"

A gaunt dropped from the wall above, landed in front of Emil and Toshiko. Before it could recover from the drop, Emil stalked forwards, shrugging off Toshiko's help. His crest flared to fiery light behind him and he slammed a gauntleted fist down on the monster's head, crushing it down to the ground with a crack like a whipped cable. The gaunt twitched on the scaly ground, but didn't get back up.

Iro stared around. The gaunts were swarming their way from all over the chamber. The monstrously big one in the centre, still clinging to the three twisted cones, was the only beast not moving. Every time black lightning raced up and between those cones, the massive gaunt shivered. It was absorbing the energy somehow.

"North, fly up there," Iro pointed above. "Cause a distraction."

"Command Clarification: How should North distract..."

"Make noise. Lots of noise." Iro turned and ran after Emil and Toshiko as they led the way.

"Commencing distraction," North said from behind and buzzed away.

Another gaunt leapt out in front of Emil, slashed at him with taloned claws. Emil got his face in the way and the claws skittered off his skin like they would metal. Still, the Paladin fell to one knee. Iro rushed past, activated his crest and formed a small Light Blade in his hand. Searing pain lit his palm on fire and his gloves smoked. It felt like he was gripping a live wire. He thrust the glowing blue blade into the gaunt's neck and kicked the body away. He let go of his Light Blade and winced at the pain in his hand. His current had charred the fabric on his gloves black and it was flaking away.

Toshiko ran past banging on her cannon's barrel, trying to wrench it back into shape, chanting her litany. "The Burning Ember is a Thorn class ship with a population of..."

A loud series of discordant notes started blaring out into the chamber as North launched its distraction with obnoxious gusto. The gaunts crawling across the walls and scaly bridges turned towards the automaton, started swarming after it. North buzzed about, flying around out of reach, playing the shrill music.

Emil thumped another gaunt out of the way and kept on limping. Toshiko was just behind him, whispering her litany. A clawed hand shot out of the floor in front of her, reaching for her foot, but she squeaked and danced away from it, kept running. Iro followed behind, ready to form another Light Blade if he needed. It was working. They were halfway across the chamber, closing in on the way out fast.

The music stopped. "Command Request please: HELP!"

Iro slid to a stop, tripping over a scaly growth on the floor. They had caught North. A gaunt was clinging to the wall of the chamber with one hand, and had the automaton clutched in the other. North buzzed this way and that, but the gaunt held on, claws scratching into North's chassis.

"Leave it, Iro," Emil said from up ahead. "We're almost out."

Emil was probably right. North wasn't a person, wasn't human. It was just an automaton. A construct given a semblance of personality. Its sacrifice would help them all escape. Wires and circuits in exchange for flesh and blood life. And yet... *Command Request please: HELP!*

Iro's crest burst to icy light behind him and he forged a Light Blade in his hands even as he swung it. He crossed the chamber in two lightning quick Blink Strikes and slammed into the gaunt, driving his glowing blade deep into the monster's chest, pinning it to the wall. He flipped around, hand still on the Light Blade's hilt, and stood on the flat of the blade half way up the chamber wall.

North shook free of the dead gaunt's hand and flew circles around Iro's head. "North is free. North is free."

Across the chamber, Iro saw Toshiko and Emil reach the doorway. Gaunts were closing in on them, crawling down the walls, swarming across the chamber floor. Above, they were closing in on him, too, popping out of ducts and charging across scaly bridges. The giant gaunt in the middle of the chamber was still clinging to the twisted cones, absorbing the black lightning every time it sparked between them.

"On me, North," Iro said. The little automaton plopped down on his shoulder. His chassis was a little dented and scratched, but four little legs forced their way out and clung to his pauldron.

Iro let go of the Light Blade still embedded in the gaunt and the wall and formed a new one in his hands. He swung it and used a Blink Strike even as the blade he was standing on faded away.

The world lurched around him as the strange force of his Blink Strike dragged him through the chamber. Something hard and scaly smashed into him and sent him crashing down to the ground. Iro hit the metal flooring hard, rolled to a stop amidst a mass of fleshy growths. He felt like a bhurbeast had trampled him. He'd dropped his Light Blade and it had faded away, but he could forge another, though his current was feeling low. But what had hit him?

In the middle of the chamber, the giant gaunt shifted. It lumbered out from between the cones, still clinging to one of them with a taloned hand. Eyes opened up all along its skin. Thousands of eyes embedded in its arms, its legs, its chest. Iro had a sickening feeling he knew why all the smaller gaunts were eyeless. This giant monster took them all.

North buzzed from Iro's shoulder. "Threat level: 88."

Iro glanced at the automaton and found he agreed. He couldn't fight this monster. It was so massive he couldn't even begin to guess how, and he knew he didn't yet have the power.

Black lightning surged up the cones again and the giant gaunt shivered, every single one of its eyes rolling back in their scaly sockets. Iro seized on the distraction. He forged a new Light Blade and stabbed it forwards even as a smaller gaunt leapt for him. The world blurred as the Blink Strike dragged him, and he slammed to a halt as the giant gaunt reached out with dizzying speed and snatched him from the air.

Toshiko stared in wide-eyed horror as the giant monster clutched at Iro. The Corsair screamed in pain.

Emil flung a gaunt aside only for another of the monsters to leap on him, savaging his one working arm. He wrestled with it for a moment, then slammed it into the ground, knelt on it, crushed its skull in his oversized gauntlet.

"… but the ship has three separate bridges allowing redundancy across command activities…" She kept up her litany, quoting the fleet compendium, channeling current into Steel Lotus even as she wrenched the barrel pieces into position. Her poor cannon sparked and squealed as she manhandled it.

The giant gaunt pulled Iro close to its head, all its thousands of eyes focused on him. He was screaming, dying, being crushed. The black lightning surged along the cones again, and the monster howled victoriously.

"Hurry… up…" Emil said. He was wrestling with one gaunt, while another clawed at his bad leg. Claws tore away pieces of armour, squealed down skin as hard as steel.

Steel Lotus gave a metallic groan as Toshiko forced the last barrel section into place. The cannon began to glow, filled with her current and ready to fire. Toshiko hefted it onto her shoulder, levelled the barrel at the huge gaunt and hoped it would work. "Capacitor charge at Forty-eight percent. Ready to fire."

"Do it!"

She pulled the trigger.

A blast of discordant noise ripped from Steel Lotus in a

rippling wave that knocked the smaller gaunts aside. The barrel exploded outwards, torn asunder by the force. The wave of noise slammed into the giant gaunt and it screamed, staggered back, clutched hands to its head. And it dropped Iro.

A blade of azure light formed in the Corsair's hands even as he tumbled to the ground. He slashed out wildly, vanished, reappeared and slammed into a cone. His blade tore through whatever material formed the cones and Iro bounced off, fell and hit the floor hard. Black lightning burst from the damaged structure, striking everywhere around it, lashing out like a mad serpent.

Toshiko staggered as her drained current refilled, swelled. She felt strong, fast, brimming with surging energy.

The lights in the chamber went out, then dull red lights took their places, flashing and pulsing just like before. An impossibly loud klaxon blared into the chamber, soft then screeching, soft then screeching. The gaunts went mad, staggering around, slashing out at everything, attacking each other. The giant gaunt howled, thrust out a massive hand, smashed through another of the twisted cones.

"CONTAINMENT BREACH." A neutral male voice said over the cacophony. **"EMERGENCY ISOLATION PROTOCOL IN EFFECT."**

Emil shoved a gaunt away and it flailed and span about. It fell on the floor and started clawing at the bulkhead like the metal was its enemy.

Emil threw a punch at another monster, sent it careening away. His current was overflowing, like liquid power running through his veins. He felt mighty, like he could take on the entire titan. His wounds were such inconsequential things in the wake of so much power.

"CONTAINMENT BREACH. EMERGENCY ISOLATION PROTOCOL IN EFFECT."

Across the chamber, at the door they had entered through, a heavy blast door slammed down, sealing it off. Up above, similar blast doors slid into place over the ducts. Emil glanced at Toshiko, she stared back, her mouth moving, but drowned out by the blaring klaxon and that stupid voice repeating about the containment breach over and over.

The noise dulled for just a moment and Toshiko shouted at him. "Blast door!"

Emil limped over to their escape route and raised his hand just as the blast door slammed down. He used Strength, but the force of the door trying to close still knocked him to his knees. He knelt, hand raised above him, holding the door up as it tried to crush him. His crest flared bright as a sun behind him and his current was a geyser that would never run dry, but Emil could only channel so much power into his talent and it wasn't enough. His arms trembled, his knees screamed in pain, his back was about to break. He held on, screaming past the noise and the agony. He had to hold on until they were all out.

"CONTAINMENT BREACH. EMERGENCY ISOLATION PROTOCOL IN EFFECT."

Iro felt a living sun. It was just like when he had opened his First Gate. He was invincible. His current was no longer a shallow thing to be used up. It was endless. And he would use it to lay waste to his enemies.

He rose from the ground slowly. All around him, gaunts were flailing, driven mad by the relentless noise. The giant monster stumbled about, a behemoth unaware of those it crushed beneath its staggering weight. Iro activated his crest and it flared behind him, so bright it turned the red light around him a menacing purple. He formed a Light Blade in each hand and leapt into the fight.

The gaunts clawed at him madly, blindly. He swayed away from attacks, stabbed, slashed, a gushing torrent of glowing swords and violence. He swept the legs from a monster with one sword, slammed his other down on its midsection, cutting it in two. Another gaunt staggered at him and he thrust a blade through its chest, then decapitated it. They kept coming and he met them gladly. His hands burned, but the pain seemed a distant thing. Only the stench of burning flesh annoyed him.

The giant lumbered across his path, crushing smaller gaunts beneath its feet. Iro swept his swords, Blink Striking upwards, then slashed then back down with another Blink Strike. His twin Light Blades carved a huge chunk of eye-ridden flesh from the gaunt's arm. Iro hit the ground and slashed out, slicing another couple of smaller gaunts in two. The giant stumbled away, howling, flailing.

"CONTAINMENT BREACH. EMERGENCY STERILISATION PROTOCOL ACTIVATED." Iro recognised the words had changed, but it didn't matter. His current was endless and he was invincible. And he was going to kill the gaunt no matter how big it was. Finally, he was going to win a fight.

The monster had turned its massive back on him. Iro slashed upwards, Blink Striking onto its scaly flesh. He stabbed both blades down into its skin, slashed, cut, carved. He became a dizzying whirlwind of strikes. Foul blood oozed down the monster's back. It reached for him. He Blink Striked away, turned in midair, used another Blink Strike right back and slashed both Light Blades across the monster's face. It flailed, slammed a claw into him. Iro spun, fell, hit the ground amidst a mad swarm of smaller gaunts. He rose in a flurry, slicing and cutting them down, then screamed at the giant.

"IRO!" a woman shouted. He ignored the quiet voice, flew into the air with a Blink Strike, drove both Light Blades into the giant's chest, carving flesh and popping eyes. Then he leapt backwards, twisted, crashed down to the ground with another Blink Strike and sliced a howling gaunt in two.

"Command Iro." Iro ignored the voice and stabbed another smaller gaunt through the chest.

"Command: Apology." Lightning zapped into Iro's cheek and he stumbled from the shocking pain. The sound rushed in a moment later and he winced from the deafening noise of it all.

"**CONTAINMENT BREACH. EMERGENCY STERILISATION PROTOCOL ACTIVATED.**"

"What?" Iro shouted, trying to hear himself over the noise. What had come over him? He'd been ready to fight the entire nest on his own. There were dead gaunts all around him. His hands were burning. He dropped his Light Blades and stared down at his trembling palms. His gloves were all burned away, his skin was red and weeping.

"Command Request please: Run!" North buzzed in his ear.

Iro glanced at the automaton, then looked about. The gaunts were ignoring everything, flailing at the floor, at the walls, at thin air. The giant was slamming huge hands against the wall over and over as though trying to pound its way out of the chamber. Fierce red light pulsed everywhere and the neutral voice kept repeating about a containment breach. Iro winced and looked about for the others.

They were over by the exit. Toshiko was waving frantically at Iro. Emil stood in the doorway, one hand raised, stopping a blast door from closing. His crest flared bright as a star behind him, but he looked about to buckle from the strain. Toshiko waved at Iro again, then ducked underneath the straining blast door.

Iro forged a Light Blade in his hands again. The pain was a searing fire like trying to hold a furnace. He swept it through the air, Blink Striking over to where Emil held the door up. Iro let go of the blade, rolled underneath the door, then grabbed Emil by his breastplate and hauled the Paladin through after him. The blast door slammed shut, casting them all in darkness and silence.

CHAPTER 13

IRO LEANED against the blast door, staring down at his wounded, trembling hands. Emil was propped up against the wall, eyes closed, his mouth twisted into a grimace of pain. Toshiko had her head in her hands. She looked like she might be crying, but she was doing it silently.

They had done it. They had survived the nest. If the emergency sterilisation protocol was what Iro suspected, they might even have killed the giant gaunt along with all the little ones.

Iro laughed. He couldn't help it. It bubbled up from somewhere deep inside and escaped in a burst. Toshiko wipe her face with her beret, stared at up Iro incredulously. Then her face crumpled and she started giggling. Even Emil started chuckling, his eyes still closed, head thrown back against the wall.

"Does this…" Toshiko paused, clapped a hand over her mouth, giggled even harder. "Does this sort of thing always happen to you two?"

Iro glanced at Emil. The Paladin stared back at him a moment, then they both burst out laughing again.

"Command Query: What is funny?"

Iro laughed again. The others join in until all three of them were cackling helplessly. North buzzed about, scanning each of them. "North does not understand."

"It's a..." Iro stopped and laughed again. "A human thing, I guess."

The blast door against his back was getting hot, and Iro stepped away from it. The laughter died down and they all sagged. He realised the surge of power he'd felt, that swollen, endless depth to his current, had vanished. Cut off as soon as the door had closed behind them. He started wondering what a containment breach meant? What was being contained and how had its release made him so strong? His current had been bursting out of him, swelled to a depth he couldn't hope to contain. Iro shook his head. Too many questions and no answers, and he was far too tired to go searching for them.

"What happened in there, Iro?" Emil asked, serious now. "You went crazy."

Iro shrugged and met Emil's gaze. "I don't know. Do you remember when we opened our gates?"

Emil nodded.

"It was like that. Only more. A lot more. I... I lost control."

Emil nodded like he understood. "Don't do it again." He struggled to stand, cried out in pain and slumped back against the wall. Iro held out a blistered hand. Emil stared at it, and his face went hard. For a moment, Iro thought Emil would knock his hand away and tell him to scrap off. He sighed and grabbed Iro's wrist. Wincing at his own pain, Iro pulled Emil to his feet and both of them staggered, but kept each other upright.

"Time to go?" Toshiko asked. "Finally! I need to get off this titan and see to Steel Lotus."

"How is it?"

Toshiko glared at him.

"Sorry. How is she?" Iro corrected.

"She's hurt. Badly." She shook her head. "If we run into

anything else... well, she won't fire again." The barrel was split and twisted, clearly broken, and some of the internal electronics kept sparking and sizzling.

Iro started forwards, helping Emil along. The big Paladin limped and winced with every step. "And I guess you're useless without it," Emil said. "Maybe you need a smaller back-up cannon just in case?"

Toshiko gasped and hurried along to walk in front of them. "I would never cheat on Steel Lotus like that."

They limped through dark corridors, using their flashlights to navigate. Iro hoped they wouldn't encounter any more gaunts. Or any monsters. He wasn't in any state to fight them. His palms were burned and oozing and stung like he'd run them down a grater. The thought of forging another Light Blade made him queasy. The wounds Wave had given him seemed to have stopped bleeding though, so he was grateful for that. Though she had stolen his sword and he would never forget or forgive.

Toshiko pointed out an elevator and they gathered around it, debated for a minute whether they should take it. Emil staggered inside and sank down against the far wall. It decided for them. They bundled inside.

The elevator carried them up two floors. It was a slow moving thing and it gave them time to rest. Emil was asleep by the time the doors parted. Fingers thrust through the widening gap and forced them open. Standing on the other side was Gadise Samir and Justice. The Vanguard was looking a little battered. She had a few fresh cuts on her face, and her some of her hair had pulled free and was sticking out at odd angles. Justice was soggy, but otherwise looked fine.

Iro laughed and gave Emil a shove. The Paladin grumbled and cracked open an eye. "About time." He closed his eye again and dropped back to sleep in moments.

Toshiko sniffed, lurched forward and wrapped her arms

around Gadise Samir's waist, hugging her despite their armour. The Vanguard suffered it for a few moments, then coughed. "Thousand Suns," she said reproachfully.

"Sorry. Sorry." Toshiko pulled away from her squad leader, then turned to Justice and leapt on him, too, squeezing him in an embrace. Justice squeaked in alarm and went rigid. "I'm so glad I didn't kill anyone."

Justice extracted an arm and patted Toshiko on the head. "Quite surprising, isn't it. I thought for sure you were all dead."

"How did you find us?" Iro asked.

Gadise Samir crossed her arms and stared down at them critically. "Justice has been tracking you since I pulled him out of a croctar's mouth. You went through the nest. Report."

Iro told her everything, from escaping the water-filled chamber to meeting Wave and Kettle and the Hoppers from the other fleet. He told her about the archive and the nest. Toshiko interjected here and there with enthusiasm, but Emil was silent throughout, sleeping.

When he was done, Gadise Samir shook her head at them. "Alright, time to go. Justice thinks he can get us back on track and to our pods in a few hours. Up you get, Courage."

Emil grunted and used the elevator wall to haul himself back to his feet. He limped forward, clutching his hurt arm to his chest. Gadise Samir watched him go, then glanced down at Iro's injured hands. "Any monsters, let me deal with them," she said and stalked ahead.

"No worries there, squad leader," Toshiko said with a smile, but Gadise Samir gave no sign she had even heard. The Mage sighed and fell in beside Emil. Iro hurried to catch up and walked on the other side of the Paladin.

"I don't need your help." Emil stumbled on his bad leg, hissed in pain, almost fell.

"You sure about that?" Iro asked.

Emil's jaw writhed. "No."

Iro slipped underneath Emil's good arm and helped support him. Toshiko took his satchel, filled with parts, and carried it next to Steel Lotus.

"We made a good team," the Mage said happily.

"We almost died," Emil countered. "More than once."

"But we're still alive," Iro said.

Emil grunted. "I can barely walk. You're a Corsair who lost his sword and couldn't hold it even if you hadn't. And the Mage broke her cannon."

"You're so negative," Toshiko said. "We survived being tragically split apart. We valiantly fought off an entire nest of monsters. And by the power of teamwork, we located our missing squad members."

North buzzed from Iro's shoulder. "North found a Datapoint."

"And saved us all with your distraction. So well done, little bot."

The automaton adjusted its footing on Iro's shoulder, and he could swear the little bot was vibrating from Toshiko's praise.

They lapsed into silence, trudging along after their Surveyor and squad leader. Iro thought back to the nest, to the giant gaunt, to the influx of current that had convinced him he could fight all the monsters alone. Like opening a gate. He'd gone wild, swinging his twin Light Blades with so little finesse Master Rollo would have kicked him across the chamber. He'd never fought with twin blades before, and decided he needed to learn how.

"We have a game on the Thousand Suns," Toshiko said as they walked. "One person says a word, then the next person says a word that begins with the same letter the last worded ended on. And no repeating. I'll go first. Star."

"Rustling," Iro said.

"Groan," Emil said pointedly.

Toshiko was ready to drop by the time they made it back to the pods. She was hungry enough to eat a bhurbeast by herself, and was certain she could sleep for a week. Not that she'd have chance. Miho would want a report and nobody aboard the Thousand Suns ever kept the Lead Hopper waiting. She was pure rage condensed into a woman even shorter than Toshiko. She was terrifying. And after that report, which was sure to go poorly, Steel Lotus needed fixing. It was more than a day's work, but Toshiko would get started as soon as she could. She hated the idea of her poor cannon being so injured.

"Get back to your ships," the squad leader said. "Have your injuries seen to. I'll contact you all when we're heading out next."

"So we'll be going out together again?" Iro asked. "I thought this was going to be a single mission? You know, because we're expendable."

Justice glowered but said nothing.

The squad leader shook her head. "Most of you will be joining me again. The council ordered this mission, but I know potential when I see it. Get back to your ships. Rest. Heal."

Toshiko's spirits sank. She knew who the squad leader was talking about.

Justice was the first to go. He climbed into his pod without so much as a wave goodbye. The door shut and he was gone. Emil limped over to his own pod, and Iro opened the door for him.

"I'm fine," Emil growled. "I can do it myself."

"And I can help," Iro said. "It doesn't make you weak, just makes me useful."

Emil snorted, but he smiled and thumped Iro on the arm. "We really brought down a nest, huh?"

Iro grinned. "Mostly me, but you were there, I guess."

Toshiko hurried forward and pulled Emil's satchel over her

head. He collapsed into the pod chair with a hiss of pain and she put the satchel on his lap. "Don't go fiddling around with the contents," she said. "Give them straight to someone who knows what they're doing."

"Roret then?" Iro asked.

Emil nodded. "Roret. He's pretty smart. For a tech."

Iro stared down at his burnt hands. "Say hi to him for me. Tell him I'll find time to come over to the Courage soon."

Emil nodded and pressed the button for the pod door to close. A few seconds later, his pod roared off through the atmospheric guard and into the void. Iro was next to go, pressing the buttons with the back of his hand where he could. Toshiko watched his pod rocket off, then turned to the squad leader.

Vermillion Gadise Samir was waiting by her own pod, eyes fixed on Toshiko. Toshiko placed Steel Lotus down in her pod and crept forwards. She was desperately trying to think of the right words to say. Nothing convincing came to mind, so she settled on the truth. A plea.

"Please don't kick me off the squad," Toshiko said and bowed from the waist. When she straightened up, she found the squad leader had crossed her arms and a hard light shone in her eyes.

"What makes you think it's you?"

Toshiko chewed over the answer for a few seconds. "Because it was all my fault. I blew up the generator and forced you to protect us. My blast ruptured the wall and hit... a water pipe, I guess. I got us all split up. I'm sorry. But please don't kick me off the squad."

"Why are you so determined to stay?"

"Because I like it here. I mean I like the squad. They accept me."

"Courage and Eclipse?"

Toshiko nodded. "I know I'm not exactly a normal Mage. But they're not normal either, so they accept that. Me. They accept me.

I... I feel like I finally fit in somewhere." She knew it was strange. She both wanted to stand out and fit in, and it always seemed like she somehow managed neither all at the same time.

The squad leader sighed. "You have one of the deepest currents I've ever seen in a First Gater," she said. "I know Hoppers well on their way to their Third Gate who would kill for half the amount of power you can summon. But you can't control it. That oversized cannon of yours is a crutch. It allows you to use your current without learning to moderate it."

Toshiko looked up, met the squad leader's hard gaze. "I won't get rid of Steel Lotus."

Vermillion Gadise Samir loosened the straps on her shield and placed it inside her pod. "Even if I tell you the cannon is the problem? Lose the oversized cannon or lose your spot on the squad."

Toshiko clenched her hands into fists. "She's the reason I opened my First Gate. I won't get rid of her. But I'll learn to use her properly. I'll control my current."

The squad leader regarded her for a few more seconds. Toshiko met her cold gaze and refused to look away. "Go home, Thousand Suns. I'll contact you when next we Hop."

"Really?" Toshiko beamed a grin at the Vanguard.

"One more chance."

Toshiko bounced on the spot. "It's all I need!"

CHAPTER 14

Iro was bored. Cooped up in the infirmary, ordered to stay in bed, with nothing to do. He couldn't even use his tablet because his hands were so swathed in bandages he couldn't move a finger. And the worst bit was the itch on the back of his left hand and no way to scratch it.

He had micro-stitches in his cheek and chest, and doc Knud had warned him they were likely to leave scars. The doc had also covered Iro's hands in some sort of stinging gel and wrapped them tight. He claimed Iro could use them again in a few days. A few days of bed rest and nothing to do but stare at the white walls of the infirmary. And suck algae through a straw whenever he needed to eat. It was maddening.

So when the door opened and Eir skipped into the room, Iro sat up with blessed relief.

"Oh, so you are alive," Eir said with a mischievous grin. "I assumed by the lack of reply to any of my messages that you must be dead. It's the only reasonable explanation for such a shunning, so I eagerly await your unreasonable one."

"Hey," Iro said, grinning.

"Hey."

"Sub Command Eir," North said as it launched itself into the air.

"North!" Eir threw her arms wide to hug the automaton. "Have you grown? Is that possible? You look bigger. Did you hit puberty? Is there hair?"

North spun around in midair. "North has been upgraded."

"Well, you look... dented." Eir turned a reproachful glare on Iro. "Did you let poor little North get hurt?" She sat down on the end of Iro's bed and winked at him.

Bjorn squeezed through the door, he had to turn sideways to fit his shoulders through. "You got your own room." He whistled. "Nice. Last time I was here, the doc patched me up outside and kicked my arse out the door. Literally. I had a footprint to prove it. Catch!" He threw a shiny red apple to Iro who winced and let it him in the chest.

"Thanks." Iro waved bandaged hands at Bjorn.

"Don't expect me to feed it to you. Ask Eir."

Iro chuckled. "With her bedside manner? I'd be choking on apple before the first bite."

Eir snorted. "Bite? If I'm feeding it to you, you're eating it whole."

Arne slunk in next, followed by Ylfa and even Ingrid. They all squeezed into Iro's little room. Ylfa flopped down into the chair with a sigh, a disgusted sneer on her beautiful face as though just being in the infirmary was distasteful. Arne wrestled with Bjorn for a spot at the foot of the bed, lost, and sulkily edged to stand behind Ylfa. Ingrid sank down onto her ass on the floor and crossed her legs. Only Eir sat on Iro's bed. Ashvild marched in last, but she stopped in the doorway, leaning against the frame. She said nothing but gave Iro a nod that he hoped was respect.

"So this is what happens when you try to Hop without us to

protect you," Bjorn said once they were all squeezed inside the little room.

"I knew he wasn't scrapping ready," said Ylfa. She caught his stare and shrugged. "No offense."

"Was it a rustling, Iro?" Arne asked, his voice whistling a little around his S's. "Did a little rustling do all this to you? Want us to go beat it up for you?"

Iro chuckled. "No. The cuts..." He waved a bandaged hand at his face. "Were from Wave. Uh, a Corsair from the other fleet. She..." He sighed and shook his head. "The hands I kind of did to myself while fighting a nest of gaunts."

"Gaunts?" Ingrid looked up from the floor, shocked.

"A nest?" Ashvild said from the doorway.

Eir narrowed her eyes and was giving Iro a quizzical look. "Where were the rest of your squad?"

So Iro told them. Not everything. But he told them enough that they'd realise how dangerous real Hops were. Beyond the Black Cloaks and crazy Masters trying to kill them, Iro realised now that every Hop was life and death. Every time he set foot on the titan, he might not make it back. Despite that, he wanted to Hop again. He was eager to get back there. How else was he going to get stronger? And he needed to get stronger. To find Wave and take his sword back. To rescue Mia from the Black Cloaks.

"Sounds scary," Ingrid said.

Bjorn laughed. "Sounds fun. I can't wait to get over there with a real squad and..."

"A real squad?" Ashvild asked.

Bjorn edged around to face her. "Well, sure. I mean..."

Iro didn't hear the rest. He noticed Eir staring at him, all her usual smiles faded away. She looked concerned, opened her mouth as if to say something, then sighed and closed it again. She fidgeted on the bed.

"What the scrap are you all doing in my infirmary?" Doc Knud shouted from the main sick bay.

Ylfa shot to her feet. "Oh quiet down, granda'. We're visiting our scrapping friend." She shoved Bjorn out of the way and squeezed past Ashvild out the door.

"I don't give a void-touched spark who you're visiting, you degenerate excuse for a granddaughter. I've told you before not to come here unless you're hurt."

"Believe me, granda', of all the places on this scrapping ship, this is the last junk site I want to visit."

"Junk site? You little wretch."

They continued shouting at each other. Ashvild cajoled the others out of the room, guiding them away. Ever the squad leader. Eir didn't move from the foot of Iro's bed and Ashvild gave her a brief glance, then followed the others.

Eir rubbed a hand over her bristly scalp, looked down, then to the side. She frowned. Eventually she looked up at North. "Look after him, North."

North buzzed. "Sub Command Eir: Order confirmed."

Eir sighed and then grinned, her eyes lighting up. She stared at Iro. "Don't go getting hurt again. Or any more. Can't have you falling apart before I catch you up."

Iro chuckled. "But you're so slooooow. I thought you'd have overtaken me by now. At this rate, I'll have opened my Second Gate before you even see your First."

Doc Knud appeared in the doorway, his wrinkled face the very picture of displeasure.

Eir pulled an *ooops* face and leapt from Iro's bed, spinning around gracefully and dipping into a bow. "Soon, Iro. Soon. I'm taking my time. Have to learn to walk before I can Hop." She stopped by the door.

"Out," Doc Knud growled.

Eir gave Iro a final wink, and slipped past the doc. She stopped on the other side of him, said something Iro couldn't hear. The doc nodded, then Eir was gone.

Two days later, the doc let Iro out of the infirmary. He gave his patient the once over, removing a few stitches and checking his hands, then declared him fit enough that he could '*Stop taking up my scrapping space*'. Iro was eager to get away. His hands were still bandaged, though no longer swathed, and they stung like a kharapid bite, but at least he could move them now and hold things and even feed himself. Nothing could temper his joy at being able to leave algae through a straw behind.

He made his way to the showers and washed a few days of infirmary stink off himself, then made his way to the mess hall for a real meal. The garden domes were bringing in regular shipments of fruits and bhurbeast meat, and they'd even started growing crops in two of the domes. Those would need harvesting soon. Iro imagined a near future where algae was a thing of the past for all the members of the fleet, not just Hoppers. He was proud that he was helping to make that future happen.

A couple of older Corsairs joined him at his table in the mess. A grizzled veteran named Ulf and a younger woman with a bright smile named Lilja. They congratulated Iro on his first Hop and told him the stories of their own. It was not uncommon for Hoppers to get a bit hurt on their first times, and it made him feel better.

Of course, none of the other Hoppers could claim the same experience as Iro. Until reaching titan 02, or Leviathan as North named it, they hadn't even realised another fleet of humans existed. No other Hoppers, no matter how veteran, had ever encountered Hoppers from another fleet before. Iro knew fights between Hoppers weren't unheard of. Back on titan 01, there were regular duels fought, sometimes for pride or disagreement, sometimes for practice; two Hoppers in their prime cutting loose against each other. There had even been a tournament held every few years. They took place on the titan where the duelists didn't have to worry about damaging the ships. But those duels, those fights had been different. The Hoppers had never been trying to kill each other.

As soon as Iro finished eating, he said goodbye to Ulf and Lilja, and went in search of Rollo. He needed to ask the Corsair Master something.

Iro paused outside the Hopper lounge and hovered his bandaged hand over the door to knock. He bashed the door with his elbow instead.

An audible sigh sounded from within. "Come in," Rollo's muffled voice said.

Iro pulled the door open and stepped inside. He'd never been in the Hopper lounge before. It was quite spacious. There were a few sofas, some chairs, a metal table stained with mug rings, a deck of cards in a pack in the centre. Off to the side of the lounge, stood a series of cabinets, a sink, a coffee maker. And the lights were dimmed, giving it an intimate feel.

Rollo sprawled on a sofa, feet up on the arm, a cushion flopped over his face. He peeled up one corner of the cushion and stared at Iro out of one eye. "Close the door, kid," Rollo said in a lethargic drawl. "The longer you leave it open, the more likely some other idiot will think they can come in. Then, just like Chorns, they'll breed and breed until we can't move or hear ourselves not think."

Iro closed the door and edged inside. He wasn't sure where he should sit. "What's a Chorn?"

Rollo pulled the cushion from his face and shoved it under his head. "You don't know what a Chorn is? What did they teach you over on the Courage, kid?"

Iro sighed. "Mostly how to clean filters, strip wires, and to stay out of the way of grumpy Hoppers. Is it a type of monster?" Iro had looked through the bestiary multiple times now, but he'd never seen an entry for a Chorn.

"Worse. It's a myth. Leave your door open and a Chorn will wonder in, sit in your favourite seat, demand to be fed, scratch up your clothes. Nasty things that leave hair everywhere. Luckily, they're only a myth. Sit down, Iro." He waved to a chair and Iro hastened to it.

Rollo sat up and stretched his neck to the side until it popped. "You look like scrap, kid. That first Hop is a killer, huh?"

Iro leaned back in the chain and nodded. "Yeah."

"Command Query: North does not understand. No member of the squad was killed."

"It's a…"

"Iro," Rollo said, his voice low and dangerous. "Why does that scrapping thing sound like me?"

"Oh! I, uh, had to pick a voice to stop it sounding like me. You were the first person who came to mind and…" He grinned. "North, Command Order or something. Reset your voice."

"Command Order: Accepted," North said in Iro's voice only tinny. He needed to figure out a way for North to find its own voice.

"What happened to your hands?" Rollo asked.

Iro raised his bandaged hands. "Light Blade. No one told me it burned."

Rollo shook his head and chuckled. "You're not supposed to hold it by the blade end, idiot."

"I wasn't." Iro leaned back in his chair and sank into it. "I lost my sword. Well, a Hopper from the other fleet stole it. And I know, before you say it, *my sword is my life*. I shouldn't have let her take it. But she was stronger than me. A lot stronger. She'd opened her Second Gate, and how the scrap am I supposed to compete with that? Anyway, I had to forge a full Light Blade from my current so..."

"You did what?" Rollo asked. He leaned forward, his eyes intense.

Iro shrugged. "You know, I just forged a Light Blade in my hands."

"Without a base weapon?"

Iro nodded.

Rollo sat back in the sofa, rubbing at his chin, silent for a few moments. "Look, kid... Iro. That old saying *My sword is my life*, it's just words. Some old Corsair came up with them because they sounded sparky. Idiot! No different from the Vanguard motto; *I am the shield of humanity.* Or the Paladin saying... what was it?"

"Always protect your Paladin?"

Rollo laughed. "No. That's what the rest of the fleet says. I think it's something like; *To Protect. To Enforce. To Empower.*" He thew up his hands and sighed. "Just words, Iro. But you now have the chance to learn the one spark of wisdom behind our old Corsair saying. Have you figured it out?"

Iro thought about it. *My sword is my life.* It wasn't literal, of course. But Corsairs channelled their current through their swords, so without one they were all but useless. It came to him in a flash. "Always carry a spare."

Rollo nodded. "Always carry a spare. Do know how many knives I take on a Hop, kid?"

Iro shook his head.

"Neither do I, but it's never enough." Rollo leaned back in the sofa again. "So what's eating at you, Iro?"

"Wave crushed me. She's the Corsair from the other fleet. I thought, after Emil and I stood up to Master Alfvin, I'd at least be able to hold my ground against a Second Gater, but... She wasn't even trying. It was like being a trainee all over again."

Rollo shrugged. "That's the heart of it, Iro. I suspect Alfvin was holding back, still struggling against his conscience, maybe. He wasn't a bad guy at heart. But... Scrap him, I'm not gonna make excuses. The void sucker murdered Torben. But he didn't fight you two at full strength or you would not have made it out of there alive.

"Because that's the truth, cold and hard as the darkness outside, Iro. You can't fight against someone stronger than you. You'll lose."

Iro felt like he'd been crushed. "So that's the life of a Hopper?" he asked bitterly. "You punch down on people weaker than you? Run away from anyone stronger."

"Did I run away?" Rollo sounded angry. "When I fought against the Black Cloaks."

"You didn't know they were stronger than you."

Rollo laughed humourlessly. "Don't be an idiot, Iro. I knew that junkhole was stronger the moment he dodged my first strike. But I didn't run. I couldn't win, but I fought them anyway. Why?"

Iro shook his head.

"Why?" Rollo insisted.

Iro shrugged. "Because it was the right thing to do?"

Rollo nodded. "Because I had people to protect. Look, kid, you're not wrong. You'll win against anyone of a lower gate than you, and you'll lose against everyone whose opened a higher gate. Only person I've ever known who can challenge folk stronger than her is Eyildr."

"Eir's mother?"

Rollo laughed and nodded. "The Silver Blade herself. But no one else can do what she can. The truth of it is, Iro, if you come up against someone of a higher gate than you, you either run or you lose. That's it. Those are your options. My suggestion; don't be an idiot. Run." He shrugged.

Iro still didn't like it. He couldn't punch down on people weaker than him. There had to be a way to challenge those stronger. There had to be a way for him to get his sword back from Wave.

"Hey, kid," Rollo said as he stood. "Come on. You need a new sword."

"Actually. I need two. And I need someone to train me to use both."

Rollo knocked on Frigg's door.

"I'm busy," Frigg shouted from inside.

Rollo pulled the door open and walked through. Frigg was hovering over her desk, tablets arrayed around her. She looked tired.

"You must not have heard me," Frigg said in a weary voice.

"What?" Rollo asked as he sauntered over to the only chair in the office. He pushed a couple of tablets onto the floor.

"Don't just…" Frigg sighed. "What do you want, Rollo?"

Rollo collapsed into the chair. "You don't come around the Hopper lounge anymore, Frigg. It's quite pleasant. You know… peaceful."

Frigg wiped a hand over her face and smiled at him. "You could just say you miss me, Rollo. We both know it's true."

Rollo shook his head. "It would mess up the whole dynamic. Have you spoken to Iro since he got back from his first Hop?"

Frigg shook her head and drooped. "I read his report, I think. Honestly, Rollo, being the lead Hopper is impossible. How did Alfvin keep up with everything?"

"By going crazy and trying to kill a bunch of innocent

trainees." Rollo shrugged. He made light of it, but he hadn't forgotten nor forgiven his old friend. If he had the chance, he'd happily hunt down Alfvin and throw him into the void. But reports suggested Alfvin was dead. Rollo did not trust the reports.

Frigg sighed. "I need to find a more constructive way, I think."

"Delegate some duties to someone else. Not me. You're a Hopper, Frigg, you need to get back on the titan. Again, though, not me."

Frigg nodded and closed her eyes, leaning on the desk. "What about Iro?"

Rollo pushed his hands into his pockets and leaned back in the chair, putting his feet up on Frigg's desk. "Are we sure he's a Corsair?"

"Huh?"

"He forged a Light Blade out of pure current. No base weapon."

Frigg didn't even open her eyes as she shook her head. "That's not possible, Rollo. Corsairs focus their current through a sword."

"Thanks for explaining that," Rollo said. He grinned at her as she opened her eyes. "But he did it."

Frigg shook her head. "Maybe it wasn't a Light Blade. Phantom Assault creates swords out of pure current. You don't swing them with your own hands, but…"

"But you still need a weapon to focus your current through. The phantom blade becomes an exact replica of the sword you're wielding."

"Exactly."

Rollo spread his hands. "Iro didn't have a sword. Another Hopper took it from him. He didn't have a weapon of any kind."

"How could he use his talents?" Frigg's eyes went wide. She looked like she was about to collapse. "You're in my chair, Rollo."

"I am."

"I need to sit down."

Rollo stood up and pushed the chair over to Frigg. She fell into it and he leaned against the nearby wall. They were both silent for a few moments.

"Has he ever shown you his crest?" Rollo asked. "I've never seen the symbol at the centre. No one has. It's new, Frigg."

She nodded and buried her head in her hands. "If he's not a Corsair, then what is he?"

CHAPTER 15

EMIL PUSHED the third training dummy into place, so all three of them formed a triangle. The trainees watched him, whispering to each other. He ignored the kids. He'd hoped to practice alone, but there was no way he could chase them away and they were doing no harm.

His arm was mostly better after the doc had pulled it out of its socket and popped it back in again. That had hurt like taking a dip in vacuum, but Emil had grit his teeth through the pain. His shoulder was still stiff, but it was nothing he couldn't ignore. There was nothing to do for his leg but limp off the ache. Emil was finding his body healed quickly now he had opened his First Gate.

"If you're gonna watch, at least get over here and give me a hand," Emil said as he stepped into the centre of the three dummies.

The trainees rushed forward. "What do you need?" asked the girl with wide eyes surrounded by freckles.

"When I say go, turn all the dummies on to their highest settings." It was time to train his talents and his current. He had no idea when the squad leader would next summon him, but he intended to be ready. The printer parts he'd brought back had helped a lot, but the Courage still needed so many supplies they couldn't print. It was up to him to find them, and he would not fail.

Emil activated his crest for the first time since he'd got back to the Courage. One trainee gasped. He glanced over his shoulder. His crest looked different. It felt different, too. It was brighter, the lines like roaring fires flickering and threatening to burn out of control. His current had been swelled by… whatever happened in the nest. For a short while, he'd had unlimited power at his command, like he could have held an enhancement forever. But as he summoned his current now, it was still swollen, bloated, as though the nest had permanently increased the depth of his current. And looking down at the bottom of his crest, the second lock was visible, empty for now, but written in light fiery lines. He hoped it meant he was close to encountering his Second Gate. He hoped he beat Iro there.

Emil Steeled himself, his skin growing tight, his body heavy. "Go!"

The trainees stepped on the buttons to get the dummies going. All three dummies flailed at Emil, smashing him with their arms, whipping strikes at his head and chest, thumping him in a torrent of blows. He stood in the centre of the flurry. Each blow was only a tap against him. He was steel, and nothing could hurt him.

The trainees watched with wide eyes and slack jaws as though Emil were some legendary hero standing against a horde of monsters. He hated to admit it, but he enjoyed the attention and adoration.

After two minutes of standing in the middle of the pounding, Emil summoned his current. It was still strong. He had barely touched his deep reserves. He'd never improve this way. The dummies were too weak.

Emil let the Steel enhancement drop and found himself

battered this way and that by the storm of blows. He weathered it, standing tall, gritting his teeth, grunting past the pain. He enhanced himself with Retribution. The dummies faltered. They still struck him, but each blow they landed hit them with an equal strike. Emil stood still, but the dummies rocked back and forth from their beatings. His current was draining faster now. Retribution took more current to use than Steel, but he could have kept it up for minutes, and he wasn't even striking back. He was just letting the dummies hit him and hit themselves through his talent. But he'd never known that talents used various amounts of current.

The front dummy hissed, clanked, smoked, and ground to a halt. It drooped, dead. Something had broken inside.

"Well, that's a scrapping thing," Phusone said from the doorway. "I'll have to get a tech to come look at it." He limped into the training room and shooed the trainees out of the way, turning the last two dummies off by pressing his cane into the floor buttons. "I assume you're here for a reason, not just to break things?"

Emil nodded, stepped past the dummies. "I need you to teach me something."

Phusone raised an eyebrow. "Trainees, run a few laps. Give me time to talk to our mighty Hopper."

The trainees grumbled, one even saying it wasn't fair. Then the girl took off, sprinting out the doorway. The two boys followed her, not willing to be left behind.

"So..." Phusone growled. "Whatever happened to you over there gave you a boost. I've never seen someone deepen their current that quickly."

Emil activated his crest again, in front of him this time. It lit up the training hall, fiery light bouncing off the rusted walls. It had grown, and there were new symbols worked into it. He saw one that looked like a claw and wondered if it represented a gaunt.

Another looked almost like clasped hands. He let the crest flicker out.

"I need to know how to use two enhancements at once. Retribution is useful, but only if I can take a hit, too. If I could Steel myself at the same time, I could take a hit that would floor me, and bounce it right back onto my attacker. I might have been able to stand up to that scrapping Hopper."

Phusone narrowed his eyes. "I read your report, Emil. There was no way you and Iro were standing up the other Hoppers. You did well just to get out of there."

"Doing well is standing still. I want… I need to do better. I need to excel. To break my boundaries. Teach me how to use multiple enhancements."

The old Paladin shook his head sadly. "You can't."

"What? Some sort of Second Gate scrap? I'm almost there, Phusone. Tell me how and I'll…"

"You can't because it's not possible, Emil. I'm surprised Tannow didn't teach you this. Paladins can only throw out one enhancement at a time. With enough training, and if your current is deep enough, you can bestow that enhancement on multiple Hoppers."

"Except *I* can't."

Phusone nodded. "Except *you* can't."

Emil had learned to enhance himself, something no other Paladin had ever done, but at a cost. By turning his current and his talents inwards, he cut himself off from enhancing others. Emil seethed. If he couldn't use multiple enhancements, what good was he?

"So that's it? I can Steel myself, but I'm just a poor Vanguard. I can Strength myself, but then I'm just a weak Berserker. Retribution can bounce back any hit but is as likely to kill me as them."

Phusone was nodding. "That's about the right of it." The old

Hopper limped over to his chair and perched on it. "The truth about Paladins, Emil, is we're not a combat class. We're there to protect others, to give them strength or protection or resistance when they need it. To bolster others with our current. What you've done to yourself... it's amazing. But ultimately, yes, it's made you useless."

Emil shouted in frustration, turned, smashed the nearest dummy in the face with his fist. "It's not fair!"

Phusone sighed. "Have you heard of the pairings before? Corsairs and Berserkers work well together. Corsairs favour speed and deadly strikes. Berserkers are powerhouses that get stronger as they get weaker. They can both hit hard, and make up for each others' lacks.

"Mages and Mechanists work in the same way. The Mages are living artillery and Mechanists are great at controlling a battlefield through traps and illusions woven by their constructs.

"Paladins and Vanguards are the third pairing. Vanguards are great shields, but on their own they can't do much damage past just hitting things with slabs of metal. But a Paladin can make them even Stronger, faster. Retribution on a Vanguard can wipe out a horde of monsters even as the Vanguard turtles up and protects themself."

"What about Surveyors?" Emil asked.

Phusone grunted. "They don't have a pairing. Useless in combat. You might need a Surveyor to get past the traps, but the moment a fight breaks out you'll wish they were anywhere else."

That made sense. Emil had only met two Surveyors but they had both been liabilities whenever a fight broke out. He hated the idea of having to protect Justice all the time though.

"Look, Emil, it's not all darkness and void here. With the right talents you'll be able to keep up with a low ranked Vanguard or Berserker."

Emil scoffed. "Great. I'm only useful if you can't get the real thing." He thumped the dummy again and started for the door. "If you can't teach me what I need, I'll just learn it myself."

"Stop!" Phusone shouted. It was an order.

Emil paused by the door, but didn't turn around.

"You want to have a tantrum and storm off, fine. Or you can start acting like an adult. Like a Hopper. Because like it or not, Emil, you are not in charge here. Your actions are not just your own. They reflect on the entire ship. Those kids I'm training look up to you. If they see you storming off in a huff, they will emulate that."

Emil heard footsteps behind him. A hand landed on his shoulder and he let Phusone turn him around. "The Courage is rallying around you, Emil. You might not be as sturdy as a Vanguard to hold a line, or as devastating as a Berserker in a melee, but the truth is that you are all we have." He rubbed a hand down his injured leg. "You are the hope of the Courage, Emil. Just one Hop and you've already fixed our printer. You're not useless, but you cannot function like a Paladin, and you cannot take the place of a Vanguard or a Berserker."

"Where does that leave me?" Emil asked.

Phusone slapped him once on the arm. "I don't know. No one does. We all have to figure out for ourselves where we fit in and how. It's not something anyone else can hammer into you."

Emil hated it, but the old Hopper was right. He was angry. More than angry. He'd achieved so much, but he was always going to be a step behind everyone else. Always going to be the Paladin who couldn't enhance others. But that didn't matter. Because the Courage was counting on him. It didn't matter what he couldn't do, only what he had to do. He had to help the ship.

"Sorry," Emil mumbled.

"What was that?"

"Sorry."

"Huh?"

"SORRY!" Heat flushed to his cheeks, but he refused to look away from the old Hopper, even as Phusone grinned at him.

"No apology needed," Phusone said with a wave of his hand. "Now if you've finished hissing like a burst pipe, I have something I can teach you. Paladins can't use two enhancements at once, but we can learn to swiftly switch between enhancements. It's not as good, sure, but it will save you in a pinch. You ready to learn?"

CHAPTER 16

IRO PAUSED outside Eir's quarters. Though he supposed they weren't really Eir's quarters. She was still a trainee, so she lived with Ashvild and Ylfa and Ingrid. But these were her family's quarters. Her mother's quarters. Someone squeezed past behind him as he hovered before the door. The officer chuckled and shook his head, walking away.

"Command Query: Is this portal dangerous?"

Iro laughed. "No. Ominous, maybe."

North buzzed.

"It doesn't matter, North. I'm hesitating."

The automaton buzzed again. "Command Iro is scared."

"I'm not… Maybe I am."

North took off from his shoulder. "Courage, Command Iro. Do you require North to scan the door for threats?"

"Hey, Iro," Eir said as she skipped down the corridor towards him, a grin on her face. "What ya doing?"

"I… uh…"

"Sub Command Eir, North is here." North zipped over towards Eir.

"North!" Eir held out her fist and North bumped against it. Iro wondered when they'd had the chance to figure out that form of greeting, North never seemed to leave his side.

Eir stopped beside Iro, facing the door to her family quarters. She nudged him with her shoulder. He glanced at her to find her smiling, staring straight ahead.

"Nice door, isn't it," she said.

"Looks quite solid."

"See those smudges?" Eir pointed to the lower half of the door. There were a few faded swipes of color against the white. "I did those. When I was a kid, I painted an entire scene on the door. My mother fighting against a horde of rustlings. It was very dramatic."

Iro smiled as he peered at the smudges. "Oh, I can see it. There's the rolling horde of orange. And that green streak must be your mother?"

"It used to be a silver streak. I think someone tried to clean it off and made it worse. So you know I don't live here, right?"

Iro shrugged. "Quite the ego you have there. I'm not here to see you."

Eir staggered as if punched. "Urgh. I'm wounded, Iro. Wounded. I'm bleeding. Urgh, such a mortal blow. You're here to see the Silver Blade, then?"

"I have something to ask her."

"Very mysterious," Eir said as she recovered from her fake stagger. "I love mysteries. Word of warning, my mom does not." She reached for the door, paused. "You do know where I live, Iro?"

"Of course I do. You live with Ashvild and the others."

Eir shot him a quizzical half smile over her shoulder and pulled open the door. She skipped over the threshold without delay. "Hey mom!" she shouted. "I'm collecting my old sword."

"In the cupboard," a voice roared back. "Behind the bucket."

"Why's it there?"

"Because it's the one place I knew you wouldn't look."

Eir pulled open another door and disappeared inside. Iro stared into the quarters. It reminded him a lot of his own mother's quarters back on the Courage. A single corridor with rooms leading off either side, a small kitchen and dining area, and another short corridor with more rooms.

Iro was still waiting outside the door when Eir skipped back into view, carrying a shining, slender sword. It was longer than the one she usually used, but otherwise very similar.

Eir held the sword up and grinned. "Titansteel."

Iro almost laughed at the idea that the Silver Blade, hero Corsair of the fleet, had been keeping a titansteel sword buried in a cupboard behind some buckets. But he'd carried around his sister's titansteel sword for years in his toolbag before manifesting a talent.

Eir stopped before the doorway and frowned at Iro. "You're not avoiding me, are you, Iro?"

Iro shook his head. "What? No. Of course not."

"Good. Because you've not been coming to the training hall at night lately and… I missed it. Besides, I have something to show you. So next time I message you and tell you to come…"

"I'll drop everything and Hop right over. Even if I'm on the titan and fighting a monster. I'll just tell them they have to wait."

Eir grinned at him. "You do that, Hopper." She held his gaze and drew in a deep breath. "Mom, I'm off. My boyfriend is here to see you." She giggled and skipped past Iro.

"Wait. What?" Iro said, staring after Eir as she waltzed away. She didn't reply.

His ears were burning as he turned back to the door in front of him. Inside the quarters, standing with her arms crossed inside the kitchen area, was an older woman. She was tall, slim, with blonde hair starting to grey, and she looked furious. "Inside.

Now," the woman growled. Iro didn't hesitate. "Now shut the door so no one can hear you scream."

Iro fumbled at the door, slid it shut. He turned back to the Silver Blade to find her unmoved, her face still set in lines of rage.

"I'm not..." Iro started, stopped. "Eir isn't... We're just friends." Weren't they?

Eclipse Eyildr cracked her neck to the side.

"That doesn't mean I don't like her. She's lovely. Your daughter is wonderful. It's just we're not... I mean I'm not..."

The Silver Blade took a menacing step forward. She wasn't brawny, but she seemed to fill the small corridor. Iro backed up and bumped against the door behind him.

"Scanning for threats." Before Iro could stop it, the little automaton launched from his shoulder and swept a beam of light across Eir's mother. "ERROR. Cannot calculate threat level."

The Silver Blade raised an eyebrow at North, then moved her glare back to Iro. Her mouth was twitching at the corners. She snorted. "Oh, I can't keep that up. Still, you should see the look on your face, Iro. Eir is going to keel over laughing when I tell her about this."

"What?" Iro asked, still backed up against the door. "What's happening?"

"My daughter was messing with you. She must like you to tease you like that."

"Really? She likes me?" Iro shut his mouth before he said anything else.

The Silver Blade shook her head and snorted again. "Come inside. Sit down." She strode back into the kitchen area.

Iro inched forwards. North landed on his shoulder and buzzed. "ERROR."

"So you said." Iro poked the little automaton.

"Running diagnostic." North went dead and tumbled from his shoulder. Iro staggered forward and caught the bot in bandaged hands before it hit the ground. North was heavier than he realised. The little construct didn't seem this heavy when it perched on his shoulder.

Iro shuffled into the kitchen and placed North on the table, then slid into one of the vacant chairs. The Silver Blade turned, placed a cup of water in front of Iro, and leaned against the counter and cocked her head in exactly the same way Eir did when she was about to ask a question.

"So, what can I do for you, Eclipse Iro?" She even had the same way of using Iro's full name, like Eir. Iro could see why Eir hated being compared to her mother so much, they were so alike. "I'm assuming this isn't about my daughter?" She smiled.

Iro shook his head and took a sip of water. He'd been over this conversation in his head a hundred times, but he still wasn't sure what to say. "I fought against another Hopper on the titan. She had opened her Second Gate. She beat the scrap out of me. Rollo said that's how things are. You can't fight someone of a higher gate than you." He looked up from his water. "But you did. I found a report from titan 01 that said you challenged a Fourth Gater when you were only at the Third Gate, and you won. I want to know how. How can I fight someone stronger than me?"

The Silver Blade nodded. "And I assume you asked Rollo about this?"

"He said I can't do what you can. No one can. He was very vague."

"He's a lazy idiot, but he's right. You can't do what I can, Iro. It's that simple."

Iro clutched the cup hard in his hands, frustration clawing at his better sense. "It might help if you told me what it is you do? How you challenged someone stronger than you."

Eir's mother hopped up on the counter and dangled her legs. "Have you heard of a talent called Burning Adrenaline?"

The name rang a bell from the talents list he'd been reading, but there was no data in the entry. He shook his head. "Not really."

"That's because I'm the only one who can use it."

"Oh," Iro said, dejected. "It's your unique talent?"

"Oh no," the Silver Blade said. "But I am the only one who can safely use it. Let me explain. Burning Adrenaline is a supportive talent. It supercharges you and any other talents you use. Makes you stronger, faster. Multiplies the potential of your talents."

Iro looked up eagerly. "That sounds amazing. It's exactly what I want."

"Sure. For all the three heartbeats you could use it. It supercharges you, but also drains your current at an unsustainable rate. You've opened your First Gate?"

He nodded.

"You might get two seconds of boosted power from Burning Adrenaline. One if you try to use another talent. Even if you open your Second Gate, you'll manage five seconds. And after that, your current will be completely drained. You'll be weaker than a first year trainee until it recharges."

Iro remembered talking to Eir about her mother, about her unique talent, and it made sense. "But you can use it because your unique talent allows you to store your current in objects and draw the energy out again."

"I'm the only one who can use Burning Adrenaline without being left helpless. And even then, I have to spend weeks storing my current in my armor to use that talent for even a few minutes."

"But it was enough to allow you to beat a Fourth Gater even when you were weaker than them. Could you challenge a Grand now you've opened your Fourth Gate?"

She chuckled. "No chance. The gulf between Fourth and Fifth Gate is wider than between a trainee and the Fourth. The Grands are... something else." She sighed and shook her head. "I'm sorry,

Iro. I know you were hoping this would be the answer, but it's not. It's nothing but another way to lose."

Iro thought back to the nest, to the way his current had surged, swelled. It had felt bottomless and he had been infinite. How much had he been capable of in that moment if he'd been able to use Burning Adrenaline to push himself past his limits? And ever since that time in the nest, his current felt deeper. Deeper than it should be. Maybe deep enough.

"Can you teach me?" Iro asked.

The Silver Blade sighed. "Yes, but I won't. Iro, I mean this, Burning Adrenaline is not the talent for you."

"But it's my choice? I get to choose the talents I learn."

"Yes, but…"

"I choose Burning Adrenaline. Please teach me."

Eyildr sat in silence for a few seconds. Iro matched the void and stared back at her, keeping his will strong. Eventually she rolled her eyes. "It's not a decision to make lightly, Iro. Think on it. Take a day, sleep. Maybe talk to Rollo again. If you still want to learn it, I will teach you the talent. But I'm warning you not to. It's a poor choice."

"I won't change my mind," Iro said, hoping it was true.

"We'll see. Take some time to think about it."

✿✿✿

"Shouldn't you be in bed?" Eir asked as Iro strode into the training hall. "Doctor's orders or something." She lowered her voice into a terrible impression of Doc Knud's growl. "Mighty Hoppers need their rest."

Iro smiled and dropped into the same stretchy pose Eir was holding. She liked to call it the Farting Rustling, which convinced Iro for once and all that she made the names up on the spot. North floated in the air around them, buzzing softly.

"I was in bed," Iro said as he sat and pulled his legs beneath him, then rolled forward until his head touched the fraying yellow floor mat. "But you made it very clear earlier you couldn't live without me."

Eir snorted. "Oh? Because I've been living without you for weeks now, Iro. And yet the moment I say come here, you come running." She rolled forward into the dreaded Exploding Starfish handstand and thrust her legs into the air. "So maybe it's you who can't live without me."

"It's true." Iro matched her, rolling into his own handstand. He didn't fall over. "You're the very *air* I breathe."

Eir giggled, swayed, almost toppled, but kept her composure. "That was a good one," she said, no hint of strain in her voice.

"Thank you." It was taking all his concentration to keep his balance. "Can I admit I've been saving it for the right occasion?"

"Ash would be proud of your preparation. Here, check this out." Eir pulled one of her hands from the floor so she was supporting herself upside down with the one hand. She frowned in concentration, then performed the splits. "Your turn."

Iro tried to lift one hand from the floor, overbalanced and went sprawling.

"Yeah, I can't do that. A human can't do that. I've come to the conclusion you're not human. You must be a monster somehow snuck aboard." He sat up, rubbing his still-injured hands together. He had a feeling doc Knud would kill him if he knew what Iro was doing.

Eir grinned at him, still upside down. Her face was turning red as a rustling. "Keep watching." She grunted and pushed herself up onto her fingertips so she was supporting her entire handstand on five tiny points of contact.

Iro gawked. "You're not human."

"Wait." The grin slipped from her face and she frowned hard. "There's more." Slowly, still upside down, performing the splits, and on her fingertips, she lowered herself into a single one handed press up, then pushed back up until her arm was straight again. She collapsed, falling sideways and sprawling on the mats, panting and sweating.

"That might be the most impressive thing I've ever seen. And I recently saw a Mage blow a hole in the titan."

Eir chuckled, still lying on the floor. "You're Hopping with a Mage?"

Iro shrugged and stood. He sauntered over to the sword rack. "Mostly, I'm just trying to stay out of her blast radius. Did I mention the blowing a hole in the titan?"

"Sounds exciting. I can't wait to meet my new squad."

Iro stared at the training blade he had used in this hall. It was roughly the same shape as his sister's sword. The sword he had both broken, and now lost. A massive blade, far too big for someone Iro's size. Yet he'd learned to use it all the same. Still, now it was gone, maybe it was time to use a different sword. A sword better suited to him. The thought left a bitter taste.

"Wait. What did you say?" Iro said, turning. "New squad?"

"Finally!" Eir jumped to her feet. "I thought I was going to have to repeat myself." She turned to North. "Scan me."

North swept a beam of light over Eir. "Threat Level: 28."

"Yes!" Eir leapt into the air. "Eighteen points higher than last time. You hear that Iro, I'm a threat now."

"You opened your First Gate?" Iro rushed over to Eir. He couldn't keep the grin from his face. "That's scrapping amazing. What was it like? How did it feel? Were there monsters? What did you have to do?"

Eir grinned wider and wider with each question. She was trembling, almost vibrating with excitement. "You can hug me!"

Without thinking, Iro lurched forward and wrapped his arms around her. Eir giggled as he squeezed her.

"I'm so happy for you," Iro said. He breathed in. Eir smelled almost earthy, like the wind in the forest dome.

Iro pulled away, feeling embarrassed.

They sat while Eir described opening her gate in great detail. Well, Iro sat. Eir shifted, wriggled, jumped up, danced about, mimed out the story. The Eclipse trainees had been on an exploratory Hop. Bjorn triggered a trap that had slammed huge bulkhead doors down around them all, separating them. Eir had been stuck with Ylfa, cut off from all the others. Apparently, the other girl did not like enclosed spaces and panicked. Eir unleashed a string of curses that could only have come from Ylfa. Then the world had frozen and her First Gate had appeared. Eir refused to tell Iro how she had opened it. After that, she used her new strength to scale the bulkhead and tear open the ceiling panels, then dragged Ylfa, kicking and screaming to safety.

"What's your new talent?" Iro asked when Eir breathlessly finished her story.

"Ooh, it's really fun." She ran over to the wall of swords and picked her training blade out. Eir's crest fuzzed into light behind her. It glowed a soft, but intense purple, and was much bigger than the last time Iro had seen it. The lock at the top, the proof she had opened her First Gate had a strange symbol in it of a triangle with the point upwards touching the point of an identical, inverted triangle.

"Patience," Iro said, staring at Eir's rest. "You said your gate had Patience written above it."

Eir nodded, flipping her sword from hand to hand. "Scrapping frustrating thing. Anyway, watch."

She raised her sword and held it in a ready pose, as if to strike. One of the other symbols on her crest glowed brighter for a moment. Eir stepped away and left an ethereal purple outline of her sword behind. Iro leapt to his feet and ran over to it. A few paces away, Eir bounced up and down in excitement. The purple sword, a replica of the one in her hands but formed of soft light, hung in mid air.

"It's like a Light Blade but... not attached to anything. What does it do?"

Eir grinned. "It's called Phantom Assault." She thrust her own sword out. The phantom blade made the same movement, poking Iro in the chest.

Iro stepped back. "So you can control it?"

"Kind of," Eir said in a strained voice. She made a wild swipe, followed by another. The phantom blade mimicked the movements. It faded away, leaving no trace. Eir bent over double, panting. "It's tough to control. Master Rollo says I'll eventually be able to form more than one and to control them all independently. Which sounds like a lot of fun."

"Ashvild must be so jealous. Think of the traps she could plant with a talent like that."

"So..." Eir straightened up, stretching backwards into a cartwheel, she flowed into a combat ready stance. "Sparring?" She grinned.

Iro shook out his hands. They still hurt, but not enough he couldn't swing a sword a few times and show Eir she still had a way to go. He grabbed his old training sword from the wall. It felt ludicrously light in his hands these days. "Talents?"

Eir twirled her sword in the air dramatically. "You think you'd stand a chance without them?"

Iro activated his crest and opened with a Blink Strike. He closed the gap between them in a heartbeat and swung for her leg. Eir blocked, her own crest lighting up behind her. She slid away along the momentum of his strike, her Parry talent making her weightless for a few seconds.

"Huh." Eir she strode around Iro. "I used to think you were fast." She stuck her tongue out at him.

Iro rushed in again with a cross slashing combo. Eir ducked

the first strike, parried the second, then stabbed out with her sword. Iro spun away from her lazy attack into a sweeping upper-cut. She jumped, used Parry again, so Iro's strike carried her up and over his shoulders. She landed on the other side of him and again strolled away a few paces.

Iro was about to Blink Strike behind her when Eir turned to him. "It's over, Iro," she said in mock seriousness. "I have you flanked." She giggled.

"Huh?" Iro straightened up.

Eir gave her sword a little thrust in mid air and something poked Iro in the shoulder. He turned to find another of her Phantom Assault blades hovering above him. The sword gave a little flourish to mock him, and faded.

Iro glared at the empty air. He'd lost again. In a few simple moves, Eir had beaten him. She'd only opened her First Gate the day before and already she was stronger than him. Rollo was right. Iro was useless for everything except punching down on those weaker than him.

"Hey. Are you alright, Iro? I didn't hit you too hard?" Eir asked tentatively.

Iro took a deep breath and pushed his anger down. Eir didn't need it. She didn't deserve it. He wasn't angry at her for beating him. He was angry at himself for losing. Again. He plastered a smile on his face and turned to her.

"You're going to be a terror with that talent."

Eir stared at him a moment, then cracked into a grin. "If I can learn to use it properly. It's exhausting."

"You already beat me with it."

She snorted. "You weren't trying." She flipped her sword into her other hand and sauntered closed, pressing the flat of the blade against his ribs and leaning into it. "Next time, Eclipse Iro, I demand you give it your all."

Iro remembered the Silver Blade saying his name the same

way, and the way she had gone along with Eir's joke. He laughed and shook his head. "You and your mother really are alike."

Eir's smiled dropped. She leaned back from him, pulling her sword away. She spun around and marched over to the sword rack, slotted her blade into position, then turned again and strode for the door. Iro watched, certain he had done something horribly wrong, but unsure what.

Eir paused at the door and glanced over her shoulder at him. She looked distressed. "Why would you say that?" She didn't wait for an answer, but paced through the door and was gone.

North floated down from above and landed on Iro's shoulder. "Command Query..."

"I messed up," Iro said, cutting the little automaton off. "First, I lost the fight. Then I messed up. I'm just not sure how."

North buzzed. "Command Iro can learn."

Iro glanced at the automaton resting on his shoulder. He nodded. "You're right. Command Iro can learn. I can learn not to lose anymore. And Eir's mother can teach me." He'd made up his mind. Regardless of her objections, Iro was going to learn Burning Adrenaline. And he was going to stop losing.

CHAPTER 17

MUSTER WAS a daily chore for Toshiko. No other ship in the fleet kept the stupid old tradition, but the Thousand Suns never met a stuffy practice it wouldn't happily sentence half its Hoppers to death to protect. Muster was one of the absolute worst.

Every day, at 0600 Ship Central Time - which was a time zone that no other ship in the fleet kept - the Thousand Suns blared out its alarms to call the entire ship gather in their designated areas to be judged by officers and captains and lead Hoppers, and whoever else thought they were in charge. It didn't matter if you were sick or injured, or twenty hours into the longest shift of your life, or if you had just returned from a death defying Hop. Everyone on the Thousand Suns was called to muster. And they always found Toshiko wanting.

She rushed to the pod bay as though she were preparing to Hop across to the titan, which she would have preferred given the choice. Of course, she was late. It wasn't her fault, but Steel Lotus weighed a lot more than any of the other Mage's cannons, and that slowed her down. The alarm had stopped by the time she reached the bay and she barrelled in to find the others already lined up and standing still and silent. Except for the smirks. A lot of smirks pointed her way.

Kichiro, the assistant lead Hopper in charge of the inspection, ignored her as Toshiko hurried past and slipped into line. He ignored her, but he also radiated displeasure in a way that somehow filled the expansive pod bay and made Toshiko feel like trying to breathe in vacuum.

Toshiko stood to attention and waited for her turn to be berated. Across the bay, she watched the others. Pod bays on the Thousand Suns were large rooms with banks of eight pods on either side. It was unfortunate because it meant that every single muster Toshiko had to put up with eight other Hoppers staring at her, watching her dressing down. They all wore the same armor, carried the same pair of hand cannons. Most of them even wore their hair the same way. Tradition.

Kichiro stepped in front of Toshiko and stared down at her. She tried not to flinch even as he shook his head in disappointment. "How many times must I tell you to stop wearing this?" he snarled as he pulled Toshiko's beret off her head and threw it to the floor. He stamped on it, grinding his heel in. He found fault in her hair, because she had dyed it blue and that wasn't a traditionally approved colour and it was both too short for a woman's cut and too long for a man's style. Her armor was still too lightweight, the wrong shade of red, and scuffed from her last Hop. She also wasn't standing straight enough, and he snarled at her to tuck her bum in more and more and more. Then he came to Steel Lotus. Muster was every day, and every day Kichiro took great pleasure in insulting Toshiko's poor injured cannon.

"This abomination will get you killed, Toshiko," Kichiro said. She'd heard the same speech from him almost twenty times now, but he never seemed to grow bored with it. "Worse, it will get your squad killed. Do you even care how that will reflect upon the Thousand Suns?" He snorted. "Such selfishness.

"We have refined our cannons into art, Toshiko. Function and performance fine-tuned. Generations of research and craft and experimentation. And yet, you think you can do better? You think this oversized bucket is better?"

Toshiko didn't answer. She'd tried that the first time, but it had led to a half-hour lecture on the intricacies and benefits of the standard Thousand Suns cannon model, oh so lovingly named TCX-556. Besides, she had to admit that Kichiro was right. The TCX-556 was the perfect cannon for any Mage. Except her.

"Get rid of it," Kichiro finished. He turned to advance down the line.

"Is that an order, sir?" Toshiko asked. "From the council?"

Kichiro stopped, ground his teeth, stared furious anger at her. Toshiko stared ahead, refusing to meet his gaze. He turned again and continued down the line. Her one minor victory was that he couldn't order her to get rid of Steel Lotus.

When muster finished, Kichiro dismissed them all. Before Toshiko could pick up her beret, the Hopper next to her walked over it, then the next and the next. She had to wait while six other Hoppers trampled over it. Then she snatched it from the ground and tried her best to dust it off.

Toshiko trudged into the armory. No matter how she fluffed it up or pulled it about, she couldn't seem to get her beret to sit right on her head anymore. Her mother had made her the hat when she was still a girl, and now Toshiko had a horrible feeling it was ruined. And with her malady, her mother wouldn't be able to knit her another.

"I know those feet," Hinata said from her desk. The ancient Hopper didn't even look up. She was perched on her stool, hunched over the desk, fiddling with some old parts, or fixing a

TCX-556. "It's the way you step, Toshiko. That cannon of yours is a weight and you favour your right leg because of it."

Toshiko carried Steel Lotus into the armory, found a mostly empty table, and hefted the cannon atop it. Then she turned and gave Hinata a respectful bow even though the old woman was too blind to see it. "Hello, granny."

Hinata chuckled and spun around on her stool. She was wrinkled as an old dishcloth, with milky pale eyes, and a host of burn scars around them. Blind as a dead screen, but still deft with her fingers despite her extreme age. That was why she was in charge of the armory, because even despite her blindness there was no one better at the job. And she knew more about the TCX-556 than anyone else alive because she had designed it.

"Not even my own grand kids call me granny," Hinata said as she hopped from her stool and waddled forward.

Toshiko shrugged. "Steel Lotus does." She patted her injured cannon.

Hinata grumbled and reached out, running a gnarled hand over the cannon's frame. "I wouldn't know about that, girl. She only talks to you."

"Only because she's shy. But she remembers you. You helped build her."

"Bah!" Hinata waved a hand at Toshiko. "Don't go spreading that around. The fools will all start venerating her like she's the next model, and then she won't be unique anymore."

"At least she'd be easier to fix if there were parts designed for her," Toshiko said. She wandered over to the supply cabinet and pulled it open. Inside sat row upon row of perfect, shining, never before used TCX-556s. So dull and lifeless. A perfect tool for the Thousand Suns Mages, but utterly uniform and soulless. Toshiko hated them. "I'm taking one of these, granny."

Hinata grunted, but didn't turn from running her hands over Steel Lotus. "I can't let you do that. There's already more than a few of my 556s in this little girl's design. Any more go missing and I'll be explaining it to the captain."

"I'm not going to dismantle this one, I promise. I'm taking it as a backup in case Steel Lotus gets hurt again. I'll sign it out." Toshiko slotted the 556 into the holster on her left hip. It felt wrong. Too light, too flimsy, too weak. Worse, it felt like she was cheating on Steel Lotus by carrying the 556 around.

Hinata grumbled. "She's banged up good, Toshiko. There are a few superficial scratches on the chassis. The display screen is cracked and needs replacing. Some of the wires are burned out. How much current are you channelling through her?"

Toshiko sighed and leaned her elbows on the table opposite Hinata. She peered at her wounded cannon. "More than the capacitors can handle. I maxed it at seventy percent of my potential, but it fried half her insides. We have nothing on the ship that can handle it."

Hinata laughed. "That can handle you, you mean."

Toshiko nodded. "I designed and built Steel Lotus specifically for me. We were supposed to work together. Instead I broke her."

Hinata pulled open a draw and started rifling through it. She pulled out a screwdriver and paused. "I'm going to open her up."

Toshiko nodded sullenly. She patted her wounded cannon. "It's alright. This is Granny Hinata, you remember her. She's going to take a peek inside and help get you better."

Even though Hinata couldn't see it, she set to taking apart Steel Lotus' chassis.

"You built this little girl when you were a trainee," Hinata said as she worked.

"I did. You know that, Granny. You looked the other way while I stole parts enough times." Not to mention all the times she gave advice or added an extra pair of hands.

Hinata cackled. "I saw nothing, and no one can prove otherwise. But it stands to reason you built her to channel your old current. You've opened your First Gate now. You're trying to force a flood through a straw and something was bound to burst. Makes sense she's going to need an upgrade to keep up with you."

"But we don't have any capacitors that will work. You designed the 556s to handle small bursts of current. And I... I don't work like that." She thought back to the last Hop. To Vermillion Gadise Samir telling her she needed to learn to control her current better.

Hinata popped open the first panel on Steel Lotus' chassis. The wires beneath were burned out and needed replacing. The old armorer sucked at her teeth as she ran her hand over them.

"Not here on the ship, no," the old woman said. "But you'll find plenty on the titan. We need to make sure you can salvage them and repurpose them into this little girl."

Toshiko perked up. "Upgrade her mid Hop?"

Hinata looked up, her blind eyes shining. She grinned. "I have some thoughts on her design, if you'd like to hear them."

"Yes. Yes! Please." Toshiko bounced. She'd never even dreamed Hinata would actively help her improve Steel Lotus.

"Well, alright then." Hinata swept her hands over to Steel Lotus' bent barrel platings. "You've got a variable design here that's nothing short of genius."

Toshiko grinned at Hinata over the barrel. "It allows for three different configurations. A focused shot for range and power, a wide angled blast with very little control, or twin barrels for channelling separate spells at once."

Hinata shook her head. "*Channeling separate spells at once*, she says as if she hasn't just revolutionised the whole Mage class. Most Hoppers carry two separate cannons and can't channel individual spells, girl. Now, what if we designed a standard housing array to make the entire design modular?"

Toshiko gawked at the idea. "It would allow me to make

repairs and upgrades at a moment's notice as long as I was carrying the correct docks."

"It won't fix the capacitor problem, but it will allow you to fix it if you find the right parts. A substantial rebuild of the cannon is required. You got time?"

Toshiko grinned and snatched the screwdriver. "Let's do it!"

CHAPTER 18

Iʀᴏ sᴛʀᴏᴅᴇ into the Power Acceleration Chamber with his new sword in hand. He'd had Freya print it to the exact specifications of his old sword before he'd broken the blade. Neya's sword. He knew it was still too big for him, but it was a connection to his sister he wouldn't give up. He'd had Freya print him a second sword as well, much smaller. The type of sword Rollo had suggested he use. But it was only a backup in case someone disarmed him again.

Eyildr waited for him in the chamber. She was rangy, her face starting to collect a host of wrinkles to go along with the scars. The Silver Blade wasn't young, but she wasn't too old to keep Hopping. Yet Iro hadn't heard of her crossing over to Leviathan even once. Nor did she take on trainees these days. He wondered if something had happened to her and thought maybe he should ask Eir. If he ever spoke to Eir again. She hadn't sent him a message since their sparring in the training hall a few days ago. He had a sour curdling in his gut that he'd ruined things between them.

"It's about time, Hopper," Eyildr said, crossing her arms. "I used to make my trainees run laps when they were late."

Iro chuckled. "I'd happily run laps. Alfyn knocked us flat with his stylus when any of us were late."

The Silver Blade gave him a pitying look. "Sorry about Alfyn. I should have trained him better, I suppose."

Iro shook his head. "It's not your fault." He tried to think of a way to change the subject. "How's Eir? Is she still angry? I didn't mean…"

The Silver Blade cocked an eyebrow. "Hopper Iro, I'm in no position to comment on my daughter's feelings. Only she is qualified for that. And sometimes I think even she isn't." She sighed and shook her head. "Don't have children, Iro." She looked up and fixed Iro with an intense glare. "Do not have children."

"Uhhh…" Iro had the urge to turn and run from the chamber.

"Threat detected." North took to the air, buzzing away from Iro. "Unable to calculate threat level. Command suggestion: run."

"So… Burning Adrenaline?" Iro asked.

Eyildr walked over to one of the half spheres embedded in the floor and rested her foot on it. It was spongy and, Iro knew from firsthand experience, oddly sticky to the touch. He had no idea how they worked, but the chamber sort of bounced expended current back at the Hopper, allowing them to reabsorb it. It was the closest condition to being aboard the titans they could manufacture aboard ship, but anyone who spent too long in the chamber suffered from Current Sickness. Iro had experienced the sickness before, and he had no wish to go through it again. It was all trembling and nausea and feeling like he was going to die.

"Last chance to back out, Iro. I've warned you this talent isn't for you. It isn't for anyone. Chances are it'll get you killed."

Iro nodded. "It'll allow me to punch above my gate."

"For brief moments. Then it'll leave you…"

"I've made my decision," Iro interrupted her. He'd been doubting himself too much of late. This was his decision. He'd live with the consequences. *Or die with them. But let's hope it's the former.*

"Alright. I won't ask again." Eyildr turned and walked over to him. "Activate your crest."

Iro flared his crest into azure light in front of him. Again he marvelled at how much bigger it was since his last Hop. The lock on his Second Gate was visible now, a blank circle near the bottom of the concentric rings.

"Interesting," Eyildr said.

"Why does everyone say that when they see my crest?"

Eyildr smiled, one corner of her mouth tugging up. "This is going to hurt." She activated her own crest, silver lines shimmering in the air so bright Iro had to squint to keep himself from being blinded. She shrank her crest down to match his own and stepped forward until they were touching. The light from both their crests fizzed and crackled where it mingled, sending shards of washed out blue sparking in every direction. For a moment, Iro thought he perceived the Silver Blade's full power. She was an ocean, churning with enough power to drown a titan. Beside her, he was a puddle not yet deep enough to do anything but splash a few boots.

The Silver Blade reached out. "Press your hand against mine."

Iro did as she said. Pain lanced through him so sharply he was certain she had impaled him, a sword thrusting through his chest, skewering his heart. He gasped, dropped to his knees. He couldn't breathe past the pain, his limbs were heavy as steel, his mind a blank blur.

Eyildr pulled her hand away and stepped back. Her crest faded away to nothing and the chamber seemed a much darker place without it. Iro knelt on the floor, gasping. He clutched at his chest. The pain was gone, but the memory of it still hurt.

"It's not that bad. Get up, Hopper," Eyildr said.

Iro struggled back to his feet. Apart from the pain, he felt no different. But his crest had changed. It had a new symbol written in its icy lines. A blue flame with a circle in the centre.

"Congratulations, Iro. You now have a talent that will probably get you killed. And you can't learn another until you open your Second Gate."

Iro stared at the new symbol, the representation of his latest talent. His way to be stronger, to fight those stronger than him. He traced a finger around it, the lines tingling to the touch. "How do I use it?"

Eyildr sighed. "Pick up your sword. With your other talents you draw upon your current, focus it through your blade, push it into the form you need. With Blink Strike, you visualize the attack you want to make, and push the current into it. Burning Adrenaline is different.

"Draw on your current, focus it into your sword."

Iro did as he was instructed. His current felt deep, so much deeper since the last Hop. He felt like he could use a hundred Blink Strikes before he depleted his battery.

"Now, instead of trying to form an attack with the current. Take it back from your sword. First, push it into your blade, then pull it back into your battery."

Iro wasn't sure how. Drawing on his current had become as natural as breathing. It fizzed inside his chest like a spark of electricity. Pushing it into a sword was as simple as making a connection, a circuit so the current flowed from him into the blade. He visualised a new circuit, one leading from the sword, back into his battery.

Lightning raced through Iro and he staggered from the force of it. His current raged through him, around him. Blue light erupted from his skin. He was stronger. So much stronger. The world was sharper around him, like he was seeing everything in sharper resolution. He smelled old sweat, blood spilled on the floor, a hint of apples from the Silver Blade. He heard North's anti-grav rings buzzing, the hum of the extractor fan in the ceiling, boots ringing across the metal floor in the corridor outside.

"Disorientating, isn't it," Eyildr said. "Try moving. Slowly."

Iro tried to walk forwards. Instead he ran. In just a moment, he crossed the distance between himself and Eyildr, careened past her, bounced off a sphere imbedded in the floor.

"That'll happen," Eyildr said.

Iro's current ran out. The strength and the power left him in a rush and he collapsed, unable to even hold himself upright. He went from strong enough to break the titan in half, to weak as a limp wire. He sprawled against the spongy sphere and blinked away groggy confusion, trying to think.

Eyildr squatted down in front of him on her haunches. "Do you see what I mean yet?"

"I felt so powerful," Iro said, still trying to comprehend it. "I moved so fast. Like Blink Striking, only I just walked."

The Silver Blade nodded. "How long do you think it lasted?"

Iro shook his head. How long had he kept Burning Adrenaline active? "A few minutes?"

"Eight seconds, Iro. You managed eight seconds of Burning Adrenaline and all you did was stand there for half of it, then run a few steps and fall over. And how do you feel now?"

"Drained." But that was a lie. He wasn't just drained. His current was empty. He felt raw and used up, so weak he couldn't stand, so tired his eyes kept drooping closed.

Eyildr stood, seeming to tower over him. "You emptied yourself, Iro. Give yourself fifteen minutes and your current will recharge. Might take a while until it's full again. Until then, you're as weak as a trainee. Worse, even. And you didn't even use a talent with it. Burning Adrenaline super charges you, but you use up your current..." She snapped her fingers. "You want to learn to use it in a way that won't leave you this vulnerable. Brief bursts, that's the only thing you can do." She reached out a hand to him.

Iro took her hand and Eyildr pulled him upright. His sword fell from his fingers and clattered on the floor. He looked down at it, tried to summon the strength to bend down and pick it up, but his body wouldn't respond.

"Practice, Iro. Every moment you can get in this chamber, practice. Because if you die from a talent I taught you, my daughter will never speak to me again."

CHAPTER 19

IT WAS the lightest landing his pod had ever performed. Emil was impressed. Not only had the techs used the printer to replace enough parts they had got a full eight pods working, but they had improved the scrapping things so that not every landing was a crash. He made a note to thank Roret once they were all out.

Emil pressed the button to open his pod door. The door gave a quiet hiss, and nothing. He sighed, all goodwill towards the techs evaporating in an instant. He growled out a sigh.

"Fix one scrapping thing, break another. Of course." He thumped on the door three times until it creaked open a jar. Then he wrenched it open the rest of the way.

Cool air fresher than any he'd smelled in a long time assaulted him. A breeze wafted his way, tickling his skin. Trees stretched up before him and the emerald leaves whispered in the wind. Back in the dome again, but things were much different this time. Everything was different and not just because he'd opened his First Gate.

Emil stepped out of the pod onto spongy earth baked black by thruster fire. Hoppers milled around everywhere. Dozens of them, hundreds even. Some were from upper ships or midships, but many more were from the lower ships. This was a joint Hop the likes of which the fleet hadn't seen since they first arrived at titan 02. A couple of Hoppers called greetings to Emil as if they knew him. He nodded back and turned to deal with his charges.

The other seven pods from the Courage were landing one by one just behind his own. They'd been set to follow-the-leader, and Emil guessed that made him the leader. It was a good job he had taught himself to fly the things.

He reached the first pod as the door clunked. It didn't open. Emil sighed. No matter what else they fixed, it seemed every scrapping door on the Courage refused to work. Emil wrenched the door open to find Roret with his head dangling down beneath the floor of the pod. The little tech looked up, a spanner in one hand.

"I was going to fix the door," Roret said.

Emil reached into the pod, grabbed the tech by his collar, hauled him out onto the earth. "You're not here to do that. Fix it later."

The other pods were opening up now, six other terrified heads poking out to stare in wonder at trees for the first time. "Come on, over here. Stick together where I can see you all."

Three drudges, two techs, two officers, all young enough to have still been children when titan 01 exploded. They crept out of their pods.

"What are they?" One drudge asked. He was a young man with a hairy top lip.

"Trees," Emil replied.

"Are they dangerous?" this from the other tech, a gangly woman with eyes as dark as the void.

"Not unless you fall out of them."

"What's wrong with the floor?" said the oldest of the bunch, an officer who should know better.

"It's not metal. Enough with the questions. Just stick together, don't go wandering off to lick anything."

"Why would we lick anything?" Roret asked.

"What do the trees taste of?" asked the drudge.

Emil shook his head. He was never this stupid. Sure, he'd been shocked by the trees, too, but not like this.

"Courage!" Emil recognised the voice as belonging to the Squad Leader. He turned and straightened up to see her striding across the earth, her shield already strapped to her arm. "Why aren't you responding to comms?"

A trio of pods rocketed overhead and Emil had to wait until they had passed before answering. "I didn't realise..." He looked down at his tablet. Sure enough, there was an audio communication request.

The squad leader stopped in front of him, eyed the talentless from the Courage, then dismissed them. "Put your earpiece in, Courage."

Emil ground his teeth, looked away. "I can't."

"Why not?"

"Because I don't have one."

"Why not?"

He looked up, met the squad leader's gaze. "Because we don't have a single working earpiece on the entire ship."

Her glare softened. Again she looked at the talentless from the Courage. "Here," she said. "Take one of my spares." She pulled an earpiece from underneath her tablet and tossed it to him. Emil gripped the earpiece for a moment, considered crushing it in his fist. So easily, they just gave things away. A single earpiece meant nothing to someone from the upper ships, yet it was more than the entire Courage could scrounge together. And they didn't even realise the disparity. He hated her a little for that, even as he realised it wasn't her fault.

"Roret?" Iro shouted as he ran over. "Hey, Roret! What are you doing here?"

Emil held the squad leader's confused stare a few more moments, then relented and slotted the earpiece into his ear. He tapped his tablet a few times to link himself into the squad comms.

Iro reached them, enfolded his little tech friend in a hug that looked like it crushed the smaller man.

"We've got more pods than Hoppers," Roret said in a small voice once Iro had put him down. "Everyone has to help with the harvest and the chief volunteered me."

"You should have volunteered yourself first," the squad leader said.

Roret gawked up at her. "Yes sir."

The squad leader crossed her arms. "Everyone in the fleet has to do their part."

"Yes sir."

Emil couldn't help but notice there were more talentless from the lower ships than upper or mid.

"Courage, Eclipse, with me." The squad leader turned and started away.

Iro grabbed Roret into another hug. "We'll talk later!" He ran after the squad leader.

Emil waited behind. It took about ten seconds before the squad leader realised he wasn't following. Her voice came through the comms in Emil's ear.

"Fall in, Courage."

Emil shook his head. "No, boss. I've got seven talentless people from my ship here. None of them have any idea where they are or what they're doing. It's dangerous here. I will not leave them alone."

Another set of pods roared overhead.

"They're not alone, Courage," the squad leader replied in his ear. "They're surrounded by the largest collection of Hoppers we've assembled since we arrived. They're here to help with the harvest. Someone will be along to organise them soon enough, but that's not our job. We're on patrol. Now fall in."

Emil clenched his fists and fought against his better judgement. In the end, he had to accept she was right. The talentless were here for a reason. They weren't alone. There were plenty of other talentless from other ships. All low ships. All ships who couldn't field enough Hoppers.

"Stay close to each other, and stay here by the pods until someone comes to collect you," Emil said. "Roret, you're in charge. Keep them steady." He chose the tech because he was the only one Emil knew by name, but it seemed to embolden the man.

With that done, Emil turned and hurried after the squad leader.

"Urgh! Where are you guys?" Toshiko's voice came over the comms a little tinny. "Justice is so boring."

"I can hear you," Justice said in an crackly voice.

"I should hope so. You're standing close enough I can smell you."

"When this squad eventually dies," Justice said. "And it will with me attached. I hope you go first, Toshiko."

"Well, at least I'll be freed from the smell."

Iro pressed the button on his own earpiece to transmit. "You won't die first, Toshiko. I'll be there protecting you."

Toshiko gasped dramatically over the comms. "My hero."

"It doesn't matter which order you die in," Justice said. "I'll be last. I'll survive. I always do."

Emil pressed the button on his earpiece. "Because you're a coward who hides at the back of the fight."

A damning silence settled over the comms. Iro turned to stare at Emil and threw up his hands in exasperation.

"What?" Emil asked without transmitting.

Iro pressed his earpiece again. "Don't mind Emil. He was born in vacuum."

Toshiko snorted over the comms. "That explains his ability to suck the joy out of a room."

They continued on for a couple more minutes, trading jokes and insults. Emil didn't join in again. He stared around at the gathering Hoppers. A mighty expedition with hundreds of Hoppers from all ships in the fleet. Just as many talentless, too, all of them drawn from the lower ships. The crops they had planted when they first arrived on titan 02 had grown and it was time to take everything they could back to the fleet. Back on titan 01, it was a job that had only been carried out by Hoppers, but they didn't have the numbers anymore.

The squad leader greeted other Hoppers as they went. She seemed to know everyone by name and by ship. She led them along a well trodden dirt path around the forest edge until Toshiko and Justice came into view. The Mage and Surveyor were sitting side by side on a crashed pod that had clearly been there a while considering the moss growing over it. Toshiko waved the moment she spotted them. Her hair had changed, now blue instead of blond. It suited her though Emil would be damned before he'd say anything about it.

"Our mission today is simple," the squad leader said once everyone was together. "We're patrolling while the harvest is under way. This many people gathered in one spot will draw monsters. It's our job to make sure they don't reach the harvest or the lines transporting the crops back to the pods. It's a long way to the fields, and a lot of ground to cover, but we won't be the only patrolling squad. Hopefully there won't be anything more dangerous than a bhurbeast to fight, but you never know when this many people gather."

Already there were people marching along the path, carrying tools and pushing carts with crates loaded on top.

"Command Query..." North said from Iro's shoulder.

"Go ahead," the squad leader said. They all stared at her a moment and she coughed into her hand, looked a little embarrassed. "Your automaton can ask its question."

North buzzed. "Why include those who are unable to absorb current?"

"The talentless?" Iro said.

"Affirmative."

"And why are they only from the lower ships?" Emil asked, glaring at the squad leader.

Gadise Samir nodded. "Because the lower ships can't field enough Hoppers, but the work still needs doing."

Emil snorted. "And because people from the lower ships are expendable?"

The squad leader fixed him with a stare. "No one is expendable."

The silence held for a few seconds. Then Toshiko coughed. "Except Justice."

The squad leader tightened the straps of her shield around her forearm. "Except Justice," she said.

"Hey!" Justice leapt off the downed pod, but the squad leader was already striding away.

CHAPTER 20

IRO DECIDED that of all the places he'd visited so far, the garden domes were his favourite. Maybe it was because for the last two weeks he'd spent every moment possible inside the Power Acceleration Chamber training his new talent, but there was something about the air in the garden dome. He liked the smell of the forest, fresh and earthy and fragrant. The noises, hooting and calling of little animals, the wind shushing through the leaves, the crunch and snap of sticks under foot. He loved the openness. It was so different to living aboard a ship. Though he supposed he was still aboard a ship. The size of the titan still played havoc with his perspective.

He wondered what it would be like to live every day with this much space around him, to not have to squeeze past people in corridors all the time. To see things growing everywhere he looked. Then again, as much as he enjoyed the whisper of the wind rustling through trees, he found he almost missed the mechanical buzz of air passing through filters. The smell here was so fresh that he longed for the dull tang of shipboard air reprocessed a million times.

"Did you get Steel Lotus fixed?" Iro asked Toshiko as they

patrolled. They were walking through the forest, trees on every side. Now and then, they spotted another Hopper group, but there had been no monsters yet. They hadn't even heard a battle.

"You remembered her name," Toshiko said with a smile. "And yes. She's all fixed and upgraded." She slapped the little cannon. "Good as new. Better, even."

"Ready to blow us all to scrap again?"

"Only if you keep getting in the way."

Justice was upfront with Gadise Samir, and the two seemed to be deep in conversation. Iro wondered if they were talking family matters. He wasn't sure how the Legacy families worked, but Justice was related to Gadise Samir somehow even though they came from different ships. Emil paced along behind them, hands already bunched in his gauntlets like he was spoiling for a fight. Iro understood that well enough. He was itching to use his new talent, even knowing it would floor him for a while afterwards. Despite training it for weeks, he still couldn't use Burning Adrenaline for over eight seconds, and less if he used it to boost one of his other talents. The Silver Blade's suggestion of using it in short bursts was not as easy as she had made it sound.

"I also have this, in case she gets hurt again," Toshiko said. She leaned down and whispered to the cannon, "Don't get jealous." She pulled out a much smaller Mage cannon that fit in one hand. It was like the designs Iro had seen other Mages wield.

"A backup?" Iro asked.

"A backup. I feel like I'm cheating on Steel Lotus just carrying it around. Is that weird?"

Iro turned around and patted his own second sword strapped to his thigh. "A backup."

Toshiko mock gasped. "We both learned our lessons. Good for us."

Emil groaned from behind. "At least neither of you will be useless now."

They both ignored him. Toshiko spun her little cannon around on her finger a few times, then tossed it to Iro. "Ever fired one before?"

Iro shook his head. "I'm not a Mage."

"You don't need to be a Mage to fire a cannon. You just need to channel current."

"Really?" Emil said as he surged forward and slotted himself between them. Of all the things Iro had thought the Paladin would get excited about, this would have been low on the list.

Toshiko danced to the side to step around a bundle of knotty roots erupting from the earth. "It's easier being a Mage. We can do it more efficiently, and we have talents to help shape the current and guide it and all sorts, but anyone can use a cannon. Well, anyone who can channel current." She glanced around and lowered her voice to a whisper. "Just don't tell anyone I told you that. I'm probably breaking some sort of secret Mage code or something."

Iro stared at the little cannon in his hands. He turned it over a few times, inspecting it. It had a textured grip that was snug in his hand and a single barrel that bowed out at the end like a bell. There was a trigger for his finger, and on top of the cannon was a tiny display screen that was blank.

"So I channel my current into it?"

"Sure do." Toshiko skipped around another root. "Push as much as you can in, then pull the trigger and POW!" She wiggled her fingers dramatically.

Iro activated his crest and channelled into the little cannon in the same way he did with his sword. He let his current flow and directed it through his hands, into the weapon. The display screen on top came to life with a blinking 1 written in dull green. He felt his current draining away. The cannon seemed to have a voracious appetite compared to his sword.

"See, charged already," Toshiko said, barely suppressing a smile. "Now aim and pull the trigger."

Iro pointed the cannon into the forest and winced as he pulled the trigger, expecting a massive blast of energy. A spark of current fizzed out from the barrel and scored a small line of ash across a nearby tree. It was the most anti-climatic thing he could have imagined.

Toshiko giggled.

"Is that it?" Emil asked. "That's all you've got? What's it go up to?"

Toshiko had a hand over her mouth and spoke around her fingers. "The display is a charge percentage. You channeled it to one percent of capacity, Iro."

Iro stared down at the cannon and frowned. "It must be broken. North, scan the cannon."

North buzzed down from above and swept a beam of light over the cannon. "Device functioning within normal parameters."

Iro shook the cannon. "Maybe there's still some of my current stuck in there." He pulled the trigger a few more times, but nothing happened. The display screen read 0.

"Give me a go." Emil snatched the cannon away. His crest flared to fiery light behind him and he frowned as he channelled current into the cannon. The light of his crest dimmed. He pointed the cannon at the earth and pulled the trigger. A thud of energy hit the ground and dust puffed around it. They all stared down at the one inch shallow crater Emil had created.

"You were right," Emil said sulkily. "It's broken."

Toshiko giggled and plucked the cannon from Emil's hands. "Just because you *can* use it," she said in a haughty voice. "Doesn't mean that you should. Mages will always have an efficiency and potency you lesser classes simply can't match." She grinned and her pink crest flared to life behind her. The display screen blinked to life with a flurry of ascending numbers until it hit 150. She pointed the little cannon at the same tree Iro had scorched, and pulled the trigger.

A blast of white light roared out of the cannon and struck the tree with a crack. The trunk splintered apart, shards of wood flying everywhere. Then the tree gave a loud groan and leaned over and over and fell with a crash that sent little creatures scurrying into the undergrowth for safety.

Toshiko bit her lip and winced. "Scrap!"

"Thousand Suns," Gadise Samir said over the comms. "Up front with me. Now."

"Have you learned to control your current yet?"

"Yes," Toshiko lied. "Sort of. Mostly yes, but also sort of no. Alright, no. No, I haven't."

The squad leader remained damningly silent. Toshiko felt the need to fill the void.

"But I fixed Steel Lotus, so I can fire her again. And, look, I brought a 556. Uh, a standard cannon, so I can use that instead if I need to." She stroked a hand across Steel Lotus' chassis. "Don't worry, I'm not replacing you."

The squad leader frowned.

"Steel Lotus gets jealous."

The squad leader tightened the straps on her shield. Toshiko noticed she often did that when she was about to say something. Maybe it was her way of psyching herself up to it. Maybe she wasn't all cold titansteel, but had to force herself to be. Toshiko liked the idea of that. That the legendary Vermillion Gadise Samir was human after all.

"Justice, go scout ahead," the squad leader said.

"And miss out on this juicy confrontation? No thanks, Cousin. I'll just…"

"Now, Justice."

Justice sighed and threw his hands up in the air. His autodage threw its own little hand up in mimicry. The Surveyor strode ahead.

"I agreed you could stay with the squad as long as you learned to control your current, Thousand Suns," the squad leader said once Justice was far enough ahead he wouldn't hear.

"I know," Toshiko said, taking her beret in her hands and twisting it. She had to save the situation somehow. "I meant to. But it's not easy and I had to fix Steel Lotus. She was pretty banged up after the last Hop and fixing her took more time than I thought. Actually, we didn't just fix her. We did a full redesign of her internals so she can be—"

"I need to trust you, Thousand Suns. That oversized cannon is a danger to everyone around you every time you fire it."

Toshiko already knew what was coming. "But we're a team, Steel Lotus and me."

"You are not to fire that cannon without my express permission, Thousand Suns."

Toshiko shook her head as if she could will the decision away.

"Unless I give you the order, you will use your standard 556 cannon. Are we clear?"

"No," Toshiko whispered. The squad leader turned her head to glare at her. "I mean, yes. I understand. But… this little thing isn't me."

"Are. We. Clear?"

Toshiko slumped and nodded. "Yes. Clear, Squad Leader."

She twisted her beret in her hands some more and felt wretched. If she wasn't allowed to fire Steel Lotus, then what was the point of bringing her? And if she couldn't bring Steel Lotus, then did she really want to be part of the squad? Without Steel Lotus, Toshiko wouldn't stand out. But with her, she didn't fit in the squad. It was impossible.

Toshiko trudged along in misery. The squad leader marching beside her in silence. Eventually she spoke, and her voice had softened some. "I like your hair. Blue suits you."

Toshiko nodded. Her hair was another way she had tried to stand out from everyone else. And most people didn't even notice. Somehow, it seemed worse that only the squad leader had. Because what Toshiko wanted was to stand out for her ability as a Mage, for doing things differently. Not because she'd changed her stupid hair color.

CHAPTER 21

IRO TRIPPED on a root and stumbled into Emil. The Paladin shoved him back.

"What are you doing?" Emil asked.

"Nothing," Iro said. "Looking at my screen."

"Well, stop it. We're supposed to be patrolling for monsters." He took a couple of steps away and kept marching forwards.

Toshiko was with Gadise Samir up ahead and Justice ranged even further ahead. That left Iro and Emil to bring up the rear. But the forest was peaceful apart from the occasional rustle of leaves or a hooting call of a little beasty. Iro went back to staring at his vambrace-mounted screen. The message prompt blinked at him, waiting, accusing.

"Detecting elevated heart rate," North said from Iro's shoulder.

"I'm nervous."

"Command Query: Why is Command Iro nervous?"

"Because I don't know what to put in the message."

One of the first things the Hoppers had done upon landing in the dome was set up the last few signal amplifiers. Communications were up, fleet wide. That meant Iro could message anyone.

He had Eir's contact blinking at him, waiting for him to type a message. He hadn't spoken to her in over a week, not since she'd opened her First Gate and they'd sparred, and he'd said something wrong. He still wasn't even sure what he'd said wrong. Now he didn't know what to say.

A rustle in the bush to his right drew his attention. Iro stopped and peered into the undergrowth. A set of red eyes stared back at him. They shifted and the creature scampered forwards into the open. It stood no higher than his knee, had four little legs, a bushy white tail, and two teeth that stuck out of its mouth and looked like they could shear through metal. It opened its mouth and screamed so shrilly Iro pressed a hand over one of his ears. The little beast turned and scaled the nearest tree in a blur of motion.

"Eclipse?" Gadise Samir's voice over the squad comms.

Iro pressed the button on his own earpiece to communicate. "Just a little beast with a set of lungs, Squad Leader."

"Don't fall behind."

Iro hurried to catch up with Emil and went back to staring at his screen.

"Stop being a coward," Emil said.

"What?"

He nodded at Iro's screen. "It's the bald one, right?"

Iro glanced at his blinking screen again. He thought about denying it, but he didn't want to be a coward. "Eir."

"Just type something. Doesn't matter what. Tell her you have three feet and hate windows. Who cares?"

Iro shook his head, lost for words. "You're awful at this."

Emil shrugged.

"Not to mention you take playful insults way too far. Is this how you act with your friends on the Courage?"

"I don't have any friends," Emil said bluntly.

"What? I always thought you were popular. Mia and Cali used to hang on your every word."

Emil kicked at a root sticking out of the dirt. "Yeah, well, they're gone now. And…" He frowned, staring straight ahead. "I used to have friends, I think. When I was young. My mom used to take me to class. She taught in the school, lessons on biology and something else. All the other kids were older than me, but they used to talk to me. Then mom died."

"Sorry," Iro said. "How? Was she a Hopper?"

Emil shook his head, crossed his arms, then uncrossed them again and cracked his knuckles. "She never set foot on the titan. She died of Myers syndrome. Organs shutting down and stuff. Easy to scrapping fix with a few pills, but only the manufactory could make them."

"So after titan 01 exploded?"

Emil sent a dark glance at Iro. "Nope. Before."

"But we had access to a manufactory on 01."

"Sure. The fleet did. And mom was on a waiting list. She never made it to the front of the queue. They kept pushing her back because this upper ship needed some new bedding, or some Legacy scrapper needed a new pair of shoes. Mom died because the Courage wasn't allowed anywhere near the manufactory."

"Sorry." Iro couldn't think of anything else to say. There wasn't anything else to say.

Emil shrugged. "After she died, my old man looked after me. I didn't get to go to class anymore. I had to follow him around his jobs. He's a Drudge. Used to make me crawl down pipes to clean them. Said he was too big, but I was the perfect size. I knew it was scrap. He was making me do his work, but… He was my dad. Mom was gone, and I wanted him to feel useful. Worth keeping around, I guess.

"When I manifested Steel and dad pushed me into training. Said I had no time for friends. I had to be the strongest Hopper on the Courage to pull our family out of the Drudges and put us up where we belonged.

"So I never had time for friends."

"Until now," Iro said, smiling.

Emil glanced at him, snorted and looked away. But he didn't tell Iro to scrap off, so he considered that progress.

"So..." Emil pointed at Iro's screen. "What are you gonna say?"

North scuttled from one shoulder to the other. "Observation: Humans often open lines of communication with banal greetings."

Emil chuckled. "Takes the bot to tell you to just say hi."

"And a better suggestion than *I've got three feet*."

"Shut up!"

Iro paced along beside Emil and hovered his hand over the screen. A message flashed up from Eir.

Hey.

Iro panicked, his heart racing. It was always so much easier in person.

Hey.

He typed back and wished he had something better to say. He waited for a response, unable to tear his eyes away from the screen.

You know I've had a blank message request open from you for about 30 minutes?

Iro felt sweat on his forehead.

I figured you were desperately trying to think of something to say, but my digital beauty stunned you into silence.

Either that or I opened the message request by accident and had no idea it was there.

He waited a few agonising seconds for a response.

Nah. I like my thing better.

Iro smiled at the screen, realised he probably looked stupid. He glanced up, but none of the squad were paying him any attention.

Are you on the titan?

Yup. I don't like the garden domes much. Too open. I miss recycled air. That's weird, right?

Iro looked up to see another group of Hoppers walking towards them. Justice was with them.

What's weird for most is normal for you. I think I prefer the weird.

"Eclipse, Courage, over here," the squad leader said.

Iro hurried to where Toshiko was waiting. The Mage looked crestfallen. "Did you get in trouble?" he asked.

Toshiko nodded. She seemed unhappy. "No more than I'm used to."

The squad leader tapped at her screen a few times, then looked up at them. A gust of wind stirred her hair and she tucked a couple of braids behind her ear. "Wait here, all of you. Keep your eyes open. There's something..." She trailed off as the other squad approached with Justice in their midst.

The other squad stopped a dozen feet away, and Gadise Samir went to join them. They were older, veteran Hoppers by the looks of them, but Iro didn't recognise any of the symbols on their armor.

"Upper shippers," Emil said with distaste. "All of them."

"They do have that sort of look about them," Toshiko agreed. "Kinda haughty."

Emil grunted. "Clean and well-fed."

North launched from Iro's shoulder. "Command Query: Should North scan for threats?"

"No!" Iro said and reached out, pulling North back before the automaton could fly off and get him into trouble. His screen pinged with a new message.

North buzzed. "Communication received from Sub Command Eir. Would Command like North to read it?"

"No!" Iro said. The last thing he wanted was the rest of the squad hearing his messages.

"Who's Eir?" Toshiko asked.

"No one."

Emil crossed his arms and leaned against a tree trunk. "Some bald girl Iro likes."

Toshiko grinned. "That's exciting."

Iro shook his head. "It's not." He pointed at North. "Shut up." Then he pointed at Emil. "Shut up." He wanted to look at the message, but forced himself to ignore it.

There was a burst of laughter from the other Hopper group and Gadise Samir pointed back towards them. Justice threw up his hands and stropped away. A few moments later, he stopped beside Emil and glared back towards the other group.

"Kicked out?" Emil asked.

Justice sulked. "They're discussing command decisions I'm not privy to."

"Who are they?"

Justice sighed. "The colossal idiot with the beard who can't stop grinning is Verdant Grave Ulysses Blanc. He's a Berserker who thinks he's the funniest thing the universe has ever produced."

"I assume he's not?" Toshiko said.

"Rotting algae is funnier. Smells better, too."

"You don't like him?"

Justice fidgeted a little. "He always punches me on the arm. Berserkers hit hard.

"The smaller woman next to him is Leaf on the Wind Mei Ling." She was small, but stout, with black spiky hair. Little flying constructs surrounded her like flies. "She's a Mechanist. Tipped to join the Council of Grands pretty soon."

"Are they all Legacy family?" Emil asked.

Justice glared at the Paladin. "Not all. See the smug junk hole with the three autodages on his arm? That's Flame Horizon Mercy." The Surveyor said it with such venom Iro almost took a step back. "My older brother and the best thing to ever happen to my family. *Have you heard what magical scrapping feat Mercy did now? Why can't you be more like Mercy? Mercy wouldn't have lost an entire squad.* And, of course, while my parents are saying all that, he's standing there pretending to be embarrassed saying *It's not Justice's fault.* And *He's trying his best.*"

"He doesn't sound too bad," Toshiko said.

"He's a condescending void sucker."

"Sorry," Toshiko said. "Want me to glare at him for you?"

Justice crossed his arms and hunched in on himself. "Yes."

Toshiko set to glaring at the other group of Hoppers.

"What about the rest of them?" Emil asked.

Iro glanced down at his screen. He still had a message waiting from Eir. The others were busy listening to Justice, so he tapped on the message.

> See now that's the sort of thing a girl wants to hear. Well done.

Iro couldn't decide if she was being genuine. It was hard to tell with text only. He hoped she was.

> The rest of my squad are SO dull. How's yours?
> Fought any monsters yet?

Iro glanced up at the others. Justice was still busy insulting the other squad.

> My squad is anything but boring. No monsters yet, but if I find any, I'll be sure to let you know so you can be suitably jealous.

"I think we need a squad name," Toshiko said.

Justice sighed. "We have one. Vermillion Gadise Samir's squad."

"Urgh! Something better. Something more dramatic like..." Toshiko frowned. "Killsquad Alpha. No, that's awful. Something though. What do you think, Emil?"

Emil was staring hard at the other Hopper squad and startled as if he hadn't been paying attention. "I dunno. Courage Squad?"

Toshiko stared at him in dumb shock. "You really have no imagination."

"What?" Emil said. He glanced at Iro.

"She's right," Iro said. "It's terrible."

"Fine. You come up with something."

Iro's screen pinged and he looked at it. The message from Eir read.

Too late. I have to go fight a knoblar. Now who's
jealous?

Iro fought the urge to open up the bestiary to look up a
knoblar.

"Uh, Team… Super… Win?"

Toshiko stared at Iro for a few seconds, her mouth open. "How
are you even worse than Emil?"

Emil nodded sagely. "Much worse."

"How about squad Four Home?" Justice said. They all turned
to look at him. "I mean, because we're part of the Home Fleet and
there's four of us."

"But there's five of us," Iro said, waving a hand toward Gadise
Samir still talking to the other squad.

"I guess," Justice said. "Five Home?"

Toshiko shook her head. "I like Four Home. That's why we
Hop, right? For home."

Iro grinned and nodded. "Four Home."

Emil pushed away from the tree. "I still like Courage
Squad."

Gadise Samir had finished talking with the other squad and
was striding back towards them all.

The other squad started moving again, walking past the
members of Four Home.

The Surveyor, Justice's brother waved a hand in the air. "Be
good, little bro," he shouted. "Don't get lost. And try not to lose
another squad." They all laughed.

Justice balled his fists and stared hard at the ground. His little
autodage balled its hand into a fist and shook it at the other
Hoppers.

Gadise Samir was frowning as she rejoined them all. She
looked distracted. There was something the other squad had said
that was weighing on her, but she clearly wasn't about to share it.

Iro remembered Rollo saying she was Legacy and therefore not to be trusted.

"We're heading to the western fields," Gadise Samir said. "Our updated mission is to take over watching the harvesters there. For now." She sighed out a deep breath. "Justice, lead the way. Move out."

They all started marching through the forest again, but Iro couldn't help but feel something was off. He checked his screen again. No new messages from Eir. He hoped she was alright.

They reached the edge of the forest and looked down on gently rolling hills filled with tilled earth and green plants. Toshiko was amazed by the way the trees just ended rather than thinned out, as if adhering to some line in the dirt they weren't allowed to cross. It hinted at organisation rather than chance.

There were harvesters working the fields, a group of twenty untalented from the Home Fleet digging up things from the earth and chucking them into a massive cart that followed them about on great, grinding wheels. They seemed hard at it and Toshiko had to admit that it looked like tiresome labor. But then the people of the fleet, Hoppers, drudges, techs, officers, all were used to hard work and long hours. If they weren't, the fleet would have crumbled generations ago.

"We'll stop here, watch over the harvesters until the next squad arrives to relieve us," said the squad leader. Despite the hours of walking, she stood with her back straight as a doorframe. Toshiko stood next to her and made an effort to stand a little straighter herself. The Vanguard intimidated her a little, but it just made Toshiko want to appear stronger and more capable in the woman's eyes.

"Or we could help." Emil crossed his arms and leaned against one of the last trees before the fields. It had a knobbly trunk, gnarled and deep brown, and huge branches higher up that stretched out and almost interlocked with those from other trees. Higher up, the trees exploded into a vast riot of green leaves.

"No," the squad leader said. "We're here to watch, guard, remain vigilant. Easier to do that with a good vantage point." She looked up and then sprang onto one of the lowest branches above. It was a good twenty feet, but she made the jump look easy and landed so gracefully.

"Show off," Justice grumbled.

Emil thrust his hands into his huge gauntlets and leapt at the tree next to him. He only cleared about ten feet, then slammed his hands into the tree, metal fingers digging into the bark. He climbed the rest of the way until he reached a large branch, just a few feet above the squad leader.

Iro whipped his new sword from over his shoulder and stabbed upwards. He vanished and reappeared a heartbeat later, standing on his own branch. They all made it look so easy.

Toshiko gave an experimental jump on the spot. She might clear five feet, if she was being generous. Better than a trainee, but not enough to reach a branch, and there was no way she was scrambling up a trunk like Emil.

"Feeling left out?" Justice asked as he paced around her.

"A little bit," Toshiko admitted. "Except you're here, too."

"The difference is I don't want to be up there. I'm more than happy down here on the ground, thank you. Much safer."

"I thought you Surveyors were supposed to be all about mobility and traversing a battlefield?"

Justice laughed, but it had a mocking edge to it. "No! Well, some maybe. I took Scan as a talent for a reason. Now I can survey from a nice safe distance and stay out of trouble."

"Good luck staying out of trouble in this squad," Toshiko said.

She considered how else she might scale the tree. If she

charged Steel Lotus and fired her straight down, would it give her a boost up, lift her off the floor? It was a terrible idea. With her luck, she'd blow a hole straight through the garden dome into whatever was underneath. Besides, even if she lifted off, she'd have no control. Nope. There was nothing for it, she needed to take a mobility talent as soon as possible.

There were several mobility talents for Mages to choose from. Most mages seemed to think Casting was the best option, as it was teleportation in the truest sense. Unlike Iro's Blink Strike, which appeared to temporarily alter gravitational pulls, Casting just moved the Mage from one point to another instantly. But it had its drawbacks. It was a cannon talent, or shot as the Mages like to call them, so needed to be channeled through a weapon. The Mage had to fire a blast to where they wanted to teleport to. That made it too predictable for Toshiko. While the teleportation itself was instant, the planning and execution of it took time. She'd need to ready the shot, channel the current, fire the blast. And it was so telegraphed. A wily enemy would see where she was Casting to.

Boost was another mobility talent and far more to her liking. It fell under the spell category of Mage talents as it didn't need a cannon to use. It allowed the Mage to fire off a short, unfocused blast of energy from any part of their body. Like a ship firing thrusters, it allowed for quick manoeuvrability, and if used with sufficient current, Toshiko was certain she could give herself enough thrust to make gigantic leaps. The downside was that Boost consumed a massive amount of current to use. Every talent was like that. Pros and cons. Cost and effect.

"Need a lift?" Iro called from above.

Toshiko squinted up at him. Part of her would have liked to say no, but then she'd much rather be with the rest of the squad than stuck below with Justice. She nodded and Iro stepped off the branch and fell the earth, landing so easily as if he hadn't just dropped twenty feet.

"Hold on tight," he said as he stepped close and wrapped an arm around Toshiko's waist.

She clutched at him with one hand and held Steel Lotus close with the other. Iro stabbed upwards with his sword, and the world lurched. Then they were standing on the branch high above. Toshiko's stomach caught up with her and she staggered away along the nobbly wood, fell to her knees, and fought the need to throw up.

"Horrible, isn't it?" Emil said.

"You get used to it," said Iro.

Toshiko squeezed her eyes shut. "I'd rather not." It took her a few more seconds before she opened her eyes and another minute before her stomach settled. Eventually, she stood and crossed to the same branch the squad leader was standing on. She had a commanding view from there.

From her new vantage point, Toshiko could see the crop fields, the hills beyond, and even further still to the fuzzy haze of the dome wall rising until it connected with the glass panes that formed the ceiling. Outside those panes was nothing but the darkness of the void. Toshiko wondered where the light came from. It was so bright in the garden dome. Night never fell here. She thought maybe there were strip lights above, between the glass panes of the dome roof.

"How much longer will the harvesters be working?" Iro asked.

"As long as it takes," the squad leader said. "We planted a lot of crops the moment we arrived on 02 and secured this dome. They have an accelerated growth cycle, but it's imperative we harvest them before they rot. This yield will feed the fleet for months. Along with regular culling of bhurbeasts and other edible monsters, we can get back to a point where no one in the fleet needs to go hungry."

"No more algae?" Emil asked.

The squad leader shook her head, her braids twisting. "We'll still need the algae vats. But they'll be supplemental to more substantial foods."

"Right. Lower shippers still gotta eat algae. But I bet you upper shippers won't touch the stuff any more?"

The squad leader glanced at Emil, but she didn't argue with him.

Toshiko squinted as she stared into the distance. There was a cloud of dust drifting across the hills from the dome walls.

"Where did the carts come from?" Iro asked.

"We found them here on the titan," the squad leader said. "We think the domes were set up to be used as gardens to grow crops just like this. Not all the machinery works though. The carts are simple enough they haven't broken down."

"How many harvesters are here working?" Toshiko asked.

The squad leader tapped at her tablet screen. "This group is twenty-two strong, but we have harvesters all over the dome working all the fields, and others carting the crops back to the pods. As well as the Hoppers guarding it all. This is the largest operation we've run since arriving on 02. Maybe two thousand people."

"Won't that attract monsters?"

The squad leader remained silent for a moment. "Yes."

Toshiko pointed at the dust cloud racing across the hills. It was heading straight towards the harvesters. "Like that?"

They all peered in the direction of the dust cloud. Toshiko raised her TCX556 and peered through the sight. She saw a thicket of tusks. "It's a bhurbeast!" A true adult that must have stood thirty feet high at the shoulder, and it was bearing down on the talentless workers.

"Let's do this, Iro," Emil said.

"Hold!" the squad leader snapped in a tone that brooked no argument. "We wait."

"What?" Emil said. "There's a monster closing in on our people."

The squad leader turned to him, crossed over to Emil's branch and stood over the Paladin. "I said to hold here. We wait."

"Wait for what? Those people down there don't have talents. They can't fight. That bhurbeast will kill them."

"Maybe not," the squad leader said.

The bhurbeast sped towards the workers. It crested a hill, moving so fast. The harvesters saw it, started pointing, their work stopped as they milled about.

"Scrap this," Emil snarled. He made to jump down from the tree, but the squad leader grabbed his shoulder, pushed him back against the trunk and held him there. "What are you doing?"

"Following orders," the squad leader growled. "As will you, Courage."

Emil struggled, but he couldn't dislodge himself from the squad leader's grip. He leaned to the side, glanced past her. "Iro!"

Iro drew his sword. "Right."

"Hold, Eclipse!" the squad leader roared. Iro froze, caught between wanting to help and the need to follow orders.

"Toshiko," Emil said. "Shoot it!"

"I can't." She patted Steel Lotus. "She isn't charged and at this range I'd be as likely to hit the people." Maybe she could add a sharp shooter mode to Steel Lotus in the future, but that wouldn't help matters now.

"Do nothing, Thousand Suns," the squad leader said.

Toshiko shrank down. She hated conflict, and she hated being part of the conflict even more. The harvesters were panicking now the monster was bearing down on them. They left the cart, started running for the forest, but they weren't going to make it. The bhurbeast was closing too quickly.

"Get off me," Emil shouted. "Let me go help."

"These are my orders, Courage," the squad leader shouted back. "And yours. Stand down."

"What orders?" Iro asked. "To do nothing and watch as monsters slaughter our people?"

The squad leader looked over her shoulder, stared at Iro. She winced as if in pain, looked down at the fleeing harvesters. The bhurbeast was almost on them. It ploughed into the abandoned cart, knocking it over and sending the gathered crops flying.

Emil made to shove away from her, and the squad leader pushed him back against the tree without even looking.

"We have to help them," Emil said. "Iro, go!"

"We follow our orders," the squad leader hissed between her teeth.

"Cousin," Justice shouted from below. The squad leader looked down. He shook his head at her. "Don't do this."

The squad leader stared back to the fields and the fleeing harvesters. The bhurbeast was massive and they had only seconds before it caught them. Gadise Samir let out a ragged sigh. "Eclipse. Help them!"

Iro's crest flared to light and the tree he was standing on exploded. He was gone.

CHAPTER 22

Iro hit the bhurbeast like a falling star. He cleaved it in two and stumbled out through the other side. Behind him, the bhurbeast fell in two pieces, gore seeping out into the earth.

His crest flickered out of existence. He'd used Light Blade and Blink Strike and super charged himself with Burning Adrenaline. In less than a second, he'd burned through his entire battery of current. He sank to his knees, exhausted. He had to lean on his sword just to stop from keeling over.

The harvesters turned and cheered. Iro saw overalls and uniforms, not a single scrap of armor or a weapon more dangerous than a spade between them all. They would never have stood a chance against the bhurbeast, or any monster. They surrounded him. Some cheered, others clapped him on the back. One of them even worked up the courage to approach the leaking monster corpse and spit on it. Now Iro looked a little more closely, there was something off about the corpse, but he didn't have time to think about it.

Emil and the squad leader were bounding down the hill away from the trees, closing on them all, but they were still a few seconds away. Iro couldn't quite believe how much distance he'd crossed with a single Blink Strike. His new talent boosted his abilities so much. He struggled back to his feet, waving the harvesters away, and stepped closer to the corpse.

The bhurbeast was a great, shaggy mound of hair, flesh, blood, and horn. Its guts spilled out on the earth, glistening and ropey. And moving. Coils of worms writhed within the stinking mass. They crawled around, linking to each other, digging into the corpse. It was disgusting.

The squad leader was the first to arrive and started organising the harvesters, ordering them to retrieve the cart. It was lying on its side, wheels spinning. The muddy tubers the harvesters had been collecting were scattered around.

Emil ran up to Iro and slapped him so hard on the back Iro staggered to his knees. His current was only starting to refill. Faster than in the Power Acceleration Chamber, but still so slow. "You did it!" the Paladin said.

Iro struggled back to his feet and pointed at the corpse. "Are you seeing this?"

More and more of the worms inside the bhurbeast wriggled, coiling around each other. It must have been full of them. As Iro watched, the front half of the monster shifted as the worms constricted, pulling the two halves back together.

"What the scrap?" Emil said.

One worm whipped free of the corpse, flailed about, slapping against the ground. Some of the blood wiped away and Iro realised it was metallic. They all were. Metal worms infesting the bhurbeast, reassembling it.

The two halves of the bhurbeast squelched together. The skin bulged, worms wriggling about beneath the flesh. Then the monster shifted, legs flailing, and rolled back to its feet. It turned a gleaming red gaze on Iro and Emil.

The squad leader bounded between them, swung her shield and smashed it into the bhurbeast's side. It toppled and flew away from her, rolling in the dirt, shaking the earth. But it didn't fall apart again.

"What is that thing?" Iro asked.

The squad leader shook her head. "I don't know."

"It put itself back together," Emil said. "It… came back to life."

The earth shook.

"Cousin!" Justice shouted over the squad comms. "Get the harvesters back."

The squad leader raised her hand to her earpiece, but Toshiko's panicked voice shouted over them. "There are more monsters coming. A lot more!"

The bhurbeast spasmed back to its feet again.

"Courage, go get the workers," the squad leader said. "Tell them to run back to the pods. We'll hold the monsters here until they're gone."

She ran at the bhurbeast and her crest shone giant and silver behind her. She leapt, slammed, her shield against the monster's chest, then kicked away from it, flipped and landed in a crouch. A shining silver copy of her crest glowed on the reanimated bhurbeast's chest. It pulsed fiercely for a few more seconds, then detonated. The monster exploded into so many pieces there was no way the worms were going to put it back together.

Emil herded the workers, shoving them on, leaving the cart behind. They were so slow, but at least they were moving.

"You alright there, Eclipse?" the squad leader asked.

Iro's current had recharged enough he thought he could manage a Blink Strike if he needed to. He nodded. "Just taking a breather."

"No time for that, Hopper." She stepped up beside him. Emil stopped on Iro's other side as the last of the harvesters ran past them. "We hold the line here until the workers are gone."

Justice and Toshiko sprinted down from the tree line. Iro stood with Emil and Gadise Samir. A deep green kharapid crested the hillside and charged straight for them. It was the first of many.

The bodies piled up around Emil. He rolled away from a kharapid's slashing limbs, darted back in, used Strength, crushed the monster's carapace with a thunderous punch. It reared back, screamed, bit at him. Emil used Steel on himself in a flash and the kharapid's mandibles shattered on his exposed arm. He grabbed one of its flailing arms, tore it from the socket, then thrust the bladed end into the kharapid's eyes. The monster fell away, twitching to join the rest of the pile.

They had been fighting for what felt like hours. There was no end to the monsters. Every time he killed one, another leapt the corpse to attack him. And some of them kept getting back up. Those strange snaking cables infested one monster in every ten, pulled the creatures back together no matter how many parts they separated them into.

Iro was struggling. He fought to Emil's left, holding the line against the monsters. Now and then, his blade lit up like azure frost, but the Corsair only managed a chop or two before the light flickered out again.

A beam of white light roared over Emil's shoulder, reducing a marsh mite to a smoking wreckage of flesh. He glanced over his shoulder to see Toshiko's hand cannon smoking, the little barrel glowing.

"What's a marsh mite doing here?" Toshiko shouted. "They live in water, never go on land."

Emil didn't have time to answer. A giant adult bhurbeast barrelled through a mountain of corpses, bearing down on the squad leader. Toshiko aimed, pulled the trigger, and another blast of searing white light roared and cut a hole right through the beasts. It dropped, missing its head.

The squad leader fought on, racking up kills far faster than the rest of them. In her hands, even a shield was a deadly weapon. A kharapid leapt at her. She slapped the attack away with her shield, then ripped its head from its body in one easy motion, tossed both head and body aside.

"Why don't they stop coming?" Iro shouted as he shoved his sword down the mouth of a blue serpentine creature that had erupted out of the earth below him.

Gadise Samir's crest flared to silver light and a sphere of crackling yellow lightning surrounded her. A kharapid scuttled forward, electrocuted itself on the sphere, followed by another and another.

"All the fields are under attack," the squad leader's voice came across the comms. "Some of our Hoppers have opened new gates. It's drawing even more monsters in."

A rising scream of noise reached Emil's ears. It sounded like many voices all overlapping each other. He shoved aside a kharapid and it stumbled into Iro's sword arc. Emil jumped up onto a dead bhurbeast's shoulder, stared across the fields. There was a sea of rusted red rolling towards them, screaming. Rustlings, a true horde of them, thousands strong.

"Squad leader!" Emil shouted, pointing at the swarm as it gibbered and flowed their way.

"Scrap!" Gadise Samir swore. "Thousand Suns. You have my full permission."

Toshiko shook her head wildly. "I need time to charge Steel Lotus."

Gadise Samir backed up, waved for the rest of them to get behind her. "We hold here."

"For how long?" Justice asked, his voice high. "The workers have gone. We need to flee."

"We hold until my orders say otherwise, Justice."

More orders. Emil grimaced. "Who gave those orders? Same people who told you to leave a bunch of talentless workers to die?"

"Now is not the time, Courage. Everyone stay behind me. Eclipse, Courage, protect the others."

She slammed a fist against her shield, releasing a ringing gong of sound. The swarm of rustlings rolled over the corpses, a seething mass of angry red balls, each one waving jagged metal knives on the end of stumpy limbs. Gadise Samir's crest flared again and her shield burst into yellow light, the lines extending outwards until it looked like she was holding a shield five times her size. The swarm hit her, bouncing off her giant shield, scrabbling to find a way around or over. The rustlings flowed forwards, surrounded them.

Gadise Samir held the front, her feet sliding in the earth as he held back the brunt of the swarm. A bloody red light oozed from her skin into a murderous aura.

Emil used Steel, switched to Strength, back to Steel. He punched out, swung his gauntlets, crunched bones, pulverised flesh. Wicked daggers flicked at him, bounced off his armour, squealed against his Steeled skin. The world receded to a fine point. Punch, block, punch again. Rustlings piled up around him. His arms grew tired, his current ached from exhaustion. He fought on, crushing their little bodies. They kept coming. An endless horde slashing at him.

Justice screamed. Emil shoved a rustling away, turned, pulled another of the little monsters off the Surveyor. It pivoted in his grip, bit down on his gauntlet, teeth scraping against metal. Another of the monsters leapt on him, daggers flailing at his neck, striking his Steeled skin. Emil tried to move, but another of the rustlings jumped on him, knocked him down. He fell beneath a gibbering horde as they piled on top of him, stabbing, biting. All he could see was rustlings writhing atop him, stabbing, biting, clawing at him. Only his Steeled skin kept him alive, but he couldn't move, could barely breathe past the press of stinking red bodies.

A blast of white light roared overhead, piercing a rustling, blowing it away. Another, then another freed Emil's hands. He switched to Strength and roared to his feet, throwing fists this way and that, screaming at the monsters.

Toshiko stood in the centre of their group, her big cannon hanging at her hip, her little cannon in her hand. She fired blast after blast into the horde, chanting her litany, something about the fuel capacity of a standard ship engine. Even as she fired off blasts with her little hand cannon, she tapped at the display on Steel Lotus and the cannon's barrels twisted and rotated into one giant barrel, the metal glowing brighter and brighter every moment until they shone blindingly.

"Charged to forty-nine percent of capacity. Ready to fire," Toshiko shouted. She holstered her little hand cannon and hefted up Steel Lotus.

"Everyone down!" Gadise Samir's shout came over the comms.

They all threw themselves to the ground just as Toshiko pulled the trigger. Her cannon roared and Emil felt like fire passed over head it was so hot. The Mage swept around them all in a great arc, burning away the gibbering horde of rustlings, cutting down hundreds in one overpowered blast.

When it was done and the white light faded away, Toshiko staggered back. Justice caught her before she fell. "Whoo," Toshiko said, blinking. "Tired now." Dark smoke trailed up from the cannon in her hands.

Emil rose to his feet to survey the carnage. Smoking bodies lay everywhere. He gawked. He could have fought for hours and not managed the damage Toshiko had wrought in a single blast. It shouldn't have surprised him. Mages were heavy hitters, built to deal damage.

"There's more of them," Iro said. He was up again, leaning on his sword.

Toshiko's blast had bought them a few seconds, knocked back the swarm, but it had barely put a dent in their numbers. The rustlings were still coming, so many of them the fields ran red.

"Where are the other squads?" Emil asked.

Justice tapped at his tablet, pressed the button on his earpiece. "Fleet comms say there's fighting in the forest."

Iro's tablet pinged, and he looked down at it. "It's from Eir. Her squad is fighting Hoppers from the other fleet."

The chittering of the horde rose to painful levels as they swarmed forwards again, tumbling over the bodies of their slain brethren.

"Cousin," Justice snapped. "The harvesters are all gone. We need to run before we can't join them."

Gadise Samire slapped aside the first rustling to reach her, her backhand flinging it far away. "All of you go," she roared. "I'll hold them here."

"We're not leaving you," Toshiko said. "We're not leaving her, right?"

Emil glanced at Iro. The Corsair stared right back and for just a moment he thought they understood each other without words. Neither of them trusted the squad leader, but nobody was getting left behind.

"No," Iro said. "We're not leaving." His crest flared to light behind him, icy lines flickering but not going out.

"That's an order!" Gadise Samire roared. "I'm made to hold the line. My unique talent..." The swarm of rustlings crested the smoking remains blocking them and rolled forwards, a tide of red death swamping the squad leader.

Something boomed behind them all in the forest. It was so loud a shockwave pushed out, felling trees, rushing forwards and smashing into the squad and rustling horde alike. Emil steadied himself by digging a fist into the earth. The rustlings gibbered, squeaked, fell over each other in confusion. Another percussive boom and a beam of energy shot upwards out of the forest, tearing towards the dome above. The clouds spiralled away from it. At the head of the beam of energy, something solid smashed into the glass dome, punched straight through it into the void beyond.

They all stood in shocked silence for a few moments. "Alright, it wasn't me this time," Toshiko said. In that quiet, Emil realised the rustling horde was silent.

Clouds were sucked up through the hole in the dome, pulled from the air like liquid down a tube, thrown out into the cold black, crystallising instantly. Enormous cracks snaked along the already fractured glass panel. Then the whole panel shattered and was sucked out into nothing. It looked small, but it was anything but. That one panel was as large as the Courage. Wind rushed past Emil now, tugging at the grass, at the trees, the leaves, his hair. A funnel of air being sucked in space. Cracks snaked along another of the glass panels above, and another, and another. The whole dome was breaking.

The rustling horde squealed, chittered, turned, fell over each other as they all tried to run. Air roared above, like some colossal beast.

"Justice," Gadise Samir shouted. "Where's the nearest exit?"

The Surveyor's sickly green crest lit behind him and he knelt, slammed his palm against the earth. When he stood, he looked pale. Justice pointed a single finger after the fleeing horde of rustlings. "The closest exit. The only close exit in range, is right through them."

"What about the pods?" Toshiko asked.

"No time," Gadise Samir said. "The dome is coming down. Now move!"

They ran straight into and through the milling horde of rustlings. Each of the monsters was no taller than a person's waist, but they were thick as oil and crashing against each other. Gadise Samir led the way, shoving them aside with her shield, throwing them from their path. Iro followed, his sword a blur as he slashed left and right, cutting a swathe through the monsters. Toshiko and Justice followed in their wake. The Mage had slung her huge cannon and was using the little hand cannon to fire blasts at any rustlings who took an interest. Emil took the rear, following at a jog, ready to jump in if any of the others got into trouble.

They were moving too slowly. The rustlings all but ignored them in their blind panic to flee, but the wall in the distance was still hazy. So far away.

A crash from above and the roaring wind grew louder, stronger, tugging at them all. Emil risked a glance over his shoulder. It looked like two more glass panels had cracked and were gone. A funnel of water, twisted, winding as it was sucked up and out into the void. Trees ripped from the earth, sent spinning upwards. Smaller shapes that looked like bodies. He hoped none of them were from the Home Fleet. He hoped his seven harvesters from the Courage had got back to their pods.

A rustling screamed and leapt at Emil, knives flashing. He blocked with one gauntlet, punched it away. The roaring wind caught it, pulled it up and up and it was gone.

"Keep moving," Gadise Samir shouted over the comms. "Almost there."

They didn't look like they were almost there. Justice stumbled over a dead rustling, fell. Emil hauled him up, not breaking stride, pushed him on. Another panel shattered overhead and the wind grew stronger still. Rustlings either side of Emil screamed as they lifted from the ground, pulled away in twisting currents to be ejected out into the void. Emil glanced over his shoulder again. Panels everywhere were gone. There were dozes of spinning streams of earth and water, trees and monsters, people. All being sucked up and out into space.

The squad leader broke through the ranks of the rustlings even as the monsters squealed and struggled against the tearing wind. The wall was only a hundred feet away, the door large, a red light blinking above it.

"Move!" Gadise Samir shouted into the wind. She struggled on, fighting against the howling gale threatening to pull her off the ground. They all followed her, no longer running, but slogging forwards. The dirt rose around them in whipping, stinging clouds.

Fifty feet from the door. Twenty. Gadise Samir streaked ahead, the power of a Fourth Gate behind her. She reached the door, pressed the button to open it. Nothing happened. Emil watched her wedge the edge of her shield into the crack. She shouted, but the sound didn't reach him, as she wrenched the door open.

Toshiko screamed as the wind took her. She was smaller, lighter. Her beret whipped from her head, vanishing into the air. And then her feet were off the ground and she was pulled away. Emil reached for her, his fingers snagged around Steel Lotus' strap. Toshiko wailed, her face a picture of terror as the wind tried to take her. She held on to her cannon and so did Emil. Then the strap snapped and the wind snatched Toshiko.

Iro streaked past Emil in a blur, flying. He slammed into the Mage, grabbed her around the waist and they were both spinning upwards. He slashed with his sword and they both flickered, his talent dragging them against the roaring current of the wind, but the two forces pulling on them were as strong as each other. Iro slashed again and again, each of his Blink Strikes only carrying them forward a few flickering feet at a time.

Justice screamed. Emil turned just in time to see the Surveyor ripped from his feet by the wind. He reached out, grabbed the smaller man by his trailing leg, pulled him close. Emil felt the wind lifting him as. well. He activated his crest, Steeled himself to increase his weight. His boots sank into the rising dirt all around. Justice clutched at him and Emil slogged on, one foot after another, squinting against the stinging dirt. Another crash from above and the wind only got stronger. Emil leaned into it, powered forward, Justice slung over his shoulder, Steel Lotus under his arm.

The squad leader had the door open, just a jar, enough to throw her own body between the two slabs of metal and push. Even with the strength of a Fourth Gate, she was struggling to hold it open.

Iro and Toshiko flickered past Emil. The Corsair was grimacing, shouting, stabbing forwards again and again. His crest was dimming, his current almost gone. Emil's own current was draining fast and knew if he lost his Steel enhancement, both he and Justice would be torn from the ground in a second.

Iro stabbed forward, flickered one final time, reached the door. He shoved Toshiko ahead of him, through the gap the squad leader was holding open. Then the Corsair dived through after her.

Emil waded on, fell to his hands and knees, crawled forward. Justice clung to him, screaming in his ear. The squad leader was shouting, but the roar of the wind stripped her voice away.

Another deafening crash from above, then another and another. The whole dome was breaking.

Emil reached the door, grabbed hold of the metal. He switched to Strength, and the wind tugged his legs into the air, but he shoved Justice through the gap. Then he pulled himself through, screaming against the pain as his crest dimmed and guttered, his current ran out. He hit the ground on the other side of the door, rolled over and stared through the gap to see the entire dome shattering, everything in it being sucked out into the void.

The squad leader leapt through the door as it slammed shut behind her. Everything went silent. All five of them sat about, panting, exhausted, trembling. They had survived. But the dome had shattered, and Emil already knew not everyone had been as lucky as they had.

CHAPTER 23

THE SOFT GREEN striplights in the corridor stuttered, casting them all in darkness for a couple of seconds. When they came back on, Iro saw a small sphere about twenty paces away. He squinted. It was a single rustling, standing in the centre of the corridor. Its legs were short and stumpy, its arms drooped by its side. Its toothy maw drooped at the sides. It stared at him with eyes black as space. Then it shouted in alarm, turned and ran, thin arms waving in the air. There was a *whunk* and a flash of something shiny. The rustling stumbled a step, and burst into five pieces, showering the corridor with blood.

"Trap," Iro said, pointing. He was still sitting on the floor, propped up against the wall, and couldn't spare any energy to say anything else.

"Really?" Justice asked. "What gave it away?"

Iro didn't bother responding. As long as the Surveyor did his job, he could be as grumpy as he liked. They had all nearly died. They all deserved to be a bit grumpy.

Emil was leaning against one wall, his head drooping, eyes closed. Gadise Samir leaned against the opposite wall, panting. Toshiko knelt on the floor, hugging Steel Lotus to her chest, eyes squeezed shut. He wasn't surprised. So many consecutive Blink Strikes had turned his own stomach, and he was used to being dragged around like that. Her hair was a mess, blown about by the wind and sticking up at crazy angles. And it appeared to have turned blue.

"Now what?" Toshiko asked in a quiet voice. "How do we get home?"

They all looked at the squad leader. She squeezed her eyes shut for a moment, then tightened the straps on her shield. "We rest here for a few minutes. Justice will find us a way back around the dome."

"To what end, Cousin?" Justice asked. "Our pods were in the dome. We have no way back."

"What if we find a dock somewhere?" Iro asked. "Contact the fleet and request a pickup."

Gadise Samir tapped at her tablet. "Comms are down. That means we're too far from any of the signal boosters. We're on squad comms only. Very limited range."

Emil thumped a gauntlet against the wall. "So, how do we get home? Because they probably think we're dead."

Iro felt sick to his stomach. How many others had lost their lives? How many techs, drudges, Hoppers? What about Roret? What about Eir? Everyone who didn't get back to the pods, or didn't reach an exit, couldn't have survived the dome shattering. He lurched to his feet, anxiety lending him new strength. "We have to get back. Get in range of a signal booster or something. Justice, you have the map of the titan. Can you lead us to a booster?"

The Surveyor shrugged. "We should already be in range of one. I don't know why we're not. But I can try to lead us to another."

"What just happened, though?" Toshiko asked. "First there were monsters. Then they started reassembling themselves even after they were dead. Then there were *more* monsters. And the dome... broke." Her voice rose until she was squeaking in alarm.

"It was a coordinated assault," Gadise Samir said with steel certainty. "All our fields came under attack at once. The monsters were being driven towards us. Some of our Hoppers opened gates, which only drew in more monsters. A sort of feedback loop. I don't know about the dome, but it sounded like there were Hoppers from the other fleet in the forest, fighting with our people. I guess one of them shattered the dome, but... that shouldn't be possible."

Emil shoved away from the wall. "We're forgetting something. The part where you ordered us to leave a bunch of talentless workers to be slaughtered by monsters."

The squad leader shot him a guilty glance. "I was following orders, Courage."

"Whose orders?" Emil took a step forward, squaring up to the squad leader. She met him, towering over him.

"The council's orders."

"Why the scrap would the council order a bunch of talentless workers to their death's?"

"To put them in danger," Iro said, realising the truth. "They were hoping to get more of us to spontaneously manifest talents. Like I did." But he'd been a mistake. He was never supposed to set foot on the titan. The council were sending defenceless, talentless people into danger on purpose. And they were willing to sacrifice them in the slim hope of discovering a few new Hoppers.

Emil shook his head. "That's why all the workers were from lower ships. The Courage, the Curse Hammer, the Braided Fold, the Burning Ember. All lower ships. Because this was a scrapping risk, so you sent in the expendable people from the ships you don't care about."

Gadise Samir didn't argue with him. She stood, tall and straight backed. "Those were the orders," she said.

"Orders you followed," Emil snarled. For a moment, Iro thought he was going to punch the squad leader, but the Paladin turned away and started down the corridor.

Iro leapt to his feet. "Stop! Emil, stop." He ran in front of the Paladin. Emil tried to walk through him, but Iro pushed him back.

Emil glared. "Get out of my way, Iro."

"The trap," Iro said, pointing down the corridor towards the dismembered rustling. "You can't go anywhere until Justice has disarmed the trap. And besides, we're on the titan, Emil. You can't run off in a huff all alone."

Emil glared at him.

"You're part of a squad now, Emil," Iro said. "Our squad. We need you. We rely on you. All of us."

"Four Home?" Toshiko said.

Emil sighed out a deep breath and relented. "Four Home," he said bitterly. He stalked back to the others, refusing to meet the squad leader's gaze.

"Justice, can you deal with the trap?" Iro asked.

The Surveyor nodded and pulled his goggles down over his eyes. He took two steps, then turned back, staring at the squad leader. "I thought you were better than that, Cousin." Then he inched forward, his little autodage waving in the air in front of him.

Gadise Samir looked pained, as though Justice had stabbed her. "It's my job to get you all out of here. That's what I'm going to do. You don't have to like me. But I will get you all back to the fleet. We've lost enough Hoppers today."

North detached from Iro's shoulder and took to the air, buzzing. "Elevated heart rates detected. Command Query: should North scan for threats?"

Iro shook his head. "Not now, North. This isn't a fight situation, it's an argument situation. Right now, we need to figure out a way to get home."

The automaton buzzed. "Suggestion: Spire detected."

Gadise Samir looked up sharply. "That's a terrible suggestion. None of you are ready for a Spire."

The automaton twisted in the air, floated closer to the squad leader. "Spires act as transmitters. At their full extension signal is boosted to allow communication between titans." North buzzed. "Suggestion: Use the Spire's communication array to contact Home Fleet."

"I thought you didn't know what the purpose of the Spires was, North?" Iro said.

North buzzed. "North has received significant information packets from the Datapoint. Data banks currently sit at 5.7% of capacity. North is learning."

"Is that possible?" Toshiko asked. "Using the Spire to boost the signal?"

The squad leader shook her head. "I... don't know. But even if I was stupid enough to let you four into a Spire, we'd have no way in. Spires only open sporadically and for a brief period."

North buzzed again. "Correction: Spires open when full extension is reached to allow for ease of transmit. Detected Spire is approximately three hundred and twenty-six minutes from full extension."

"Aha!" Justice crowed from upfront. "I have it." There was a loud *whunk* and something shiny flashed out. Justice fell away with a cry, but he seemed unharmed. "Almost. I almost have it."

"So if we find this Spire and climb it," Iro said. "We can use its comm devices to contact the Home Fleet and tell them we're alive? We can ask them to send pods to pick us up?"

North buzzed. "Theoretically."

The squad leader sighed. "You're missing the part where Spires are filled with the worst monsters and traps we've ever seen. And all of you are still First Gaters."

"Correction:" North said, turning to the squad leader again.

"Security in Spires is correlational to the designated transmit location."

"What the scrap did any of that mean?" Emil asked.

"I think," Iro said. "It means that traps and monsters are specifically placed in the Spires. By who?"

North spun to face him, tilted. "By the intelligence responsible for contact initiation. In this case, by Leviathan."

"The titan? You're saying titan 02 has initiated contact with another titan? And that 02, um Leviathan, will have placed traps and monsters in the Spire as a security measure?"

North buzzed. "Affirmative."

Toshiko stood, shouldering her cannon. "And you're saying titan 02 is an intelligence? Has intelligence?"

North vibrated. "ERROR. Pathway not found. ERROR."

Iro had seen North do this before. Whenever it encountered an error, it shut down for a while and they couldn't afford that right now. He jumped up, grabbed the automaton in both hands. "North, uh… Command Override: forget previous information request."

The automaton stopped vibrating and fell silent. Iro let go and it floated up into the air. "We best stay clear of that question for now."

North buzzed. "Command Request please: Restate query."

"Sorry," Toshiko said. "I didn't mean to break him."

"I've got it!" Justice announced. "I've definitely got it this time. See…" He tapped the corridor wall, then gingerly took a step forward, bunching up as if ready to leap for safety. Nothing happened. He turned pushed his goggles up onto his head. "One disarmed trap."

"Hey, Iro," Emil said. "Can your toy direct us to the emerging Spire?"

Iro shrugged. "North?"

North buzzed. "Negative. North does not contain a map of this section. A Datapoint is needed for information transfer."

"I have a map," Justice said as he rejoined the rest of the squad. "Or at least I can see a map. Scan the surrounding area. It's a Surveyor talent." He placed a hand against the wall and his sickly green crest sizzled into light behind him. Iro could swear he saw a schematic imprinted on the Surveyor's eyes. "I have a map here. I don't see a Spire though."

North spun in mid-air and rushed over to Justice. It landed the opposite shoulder to his autodage and its chassis opened up, revealing one of its little weapons. It sent an arc of electricity into Justice's neck.

The Surveyor stumbled. "Argh! What the scrap? Wait. Oh, I see it now."

Justice's autodage crouched down and pounced at North. North buzzed and launched back into the air. "Approximate location of emerging Spire located. Map downloaded from biological Datapoint."

Justice took his hand away from the wall and rubbed at his neck. "What did you call me?" His autodage contorted itself into a shape that seemed to be a rude gesture directed at North.

North buzzed around Iro's head twice. "North has learned."

Iro stared at the little automaton in wonder. It had interacted with Justice's talent, showing the Surveyor where to find the Spire, and taking the map from him. It was something that needed investigating further. But they had far more important things to worry about.

"So you really want us to climb a Spire then?" Justice asked. "I was starting to think you wouldn't all die, but sure. If you want to throw yourselves to the fire."

CHAPTER 24

IRO CHECKED his tablet for the fifth time in the last minute. He had the chat thread with Eir up on the screen. The last message was from her, warning him about the Hoppers from the other fleet.

Hey!

He waited for a response. None came.

The squad walked in sullen silence. Justice led the way with goggles down, his autodage waving an array of small sensors in the air. North floated along above the Surveyor's shoulder. The automaton didn't have the same sensors as the autodage, but North seemed eager to help. Justice's autodage, on the other hand, seemed eager to take swipes at North.

Gadise Samir followed close behind the Surveyor. Occasionally she pressed the button on her earpiece, said a few words. If she got any reply, she didn't mention it.

Iro and Toshiko followed at a short distance with Emil brooding behind. Iro couldn't blame him considering what they had learned, but he also couldn't take the silence. He was far too worried about Roret and Eir.

He glanced down at his screen again. Still no answer from Eir.

You there?

"Thanks for saving me back there," Toshiko said.

Iro dragged his attention from the screen. "You saved all of us, so thank you."

"Yay! We all saved each other."

"Except Justice," Emil muttered from behind.

"He disarmed the trap," Iro said.

The Paladin grumbled something under his breath.

"Hey," Toshiko said. "Why do you think North keeps shutting down when it encounters an error like that?"

"I think there are intentional blocks placed within North's memory. When it first found me, it knew almost nothing. Since we found that first Datapoint, North has a greater understanding of… everything. But when we prompt it for information it doesn't have access to yet, it breaks. It's like a puzzle, but with pieces missing. A lot of pieces."

"So if we find more Datapoints, it will fill in the puzzle. But you said you think the blocks are intentional. Who placed them?"

This was the part where Iro thought he was crazy. He lowered his voice to a whisper. "The titan."

Emil snorted. "This thing can't think?" He slammed a fist against the nearby wall. "It's a ship, Iro. Nothing but a big ship. Like the Courage or the Eclipse or the Thousand Suns, but much scrapping bigger."

Iro wasn't so sure. He remembered Torben telling him how much of the Home Fleet's history was corrupted, so they didn't know where they had come from. They had almost no history from before titan 01. And the systems aboard the titans were eerily similar to those aboard the ships of the fleet.

Justice pulled them all to a halt. The corridor ahead was

gloomy, the lights buzzing with an ancient hum that reminded Iro of the Courage. But a strange shimmer hung in the air. The Surveyor stroked his chin and paced back and forth a few times. His autodage twisted about, waving its array in the air all the time. Justice stopped, glanced at it, then shifted his goggles up on his forehead.

Iro checked his screen again. Still no answer from Eir.

> Please answer me.

> Be alive!

"We need to backtrack a short way," Justice announced.

"Some sort of trap, cousin?"

Justice snorted. "Yes. Far too complex for me to disarm. Watch." He knelt down and his autodage scuttled forward onto his arm. A tiny welding torch sparked to life and the autodage removed a small section of metal from the grated flooring. Then Justice stood and tossed the little strip of metal down the corridor. It hit the shimmer and stopped dead. It didn't drop, but hung motionless.

"Oooh, that's fascinating," Toshiko said, hurrying forward.

"Don't get too close." Justice held out a hand to stop her. "I can't explain it, but time is broken here."

"Broken how?" Iro asked.

"It doesn't work."

"That's not much of an explanation."

Justice threw up his hands. "Well, tell you what. You go fetch a more experienced Surveyor and tell them to take a look. Maybe they can figure out what the scrap is going on. Perhaps, time-space theory and meta-dimensional physics are light reading for them. But I am just terrible at my job. So feel free to walk into some frozen time. Or, we can back track a bit and cut through a couple of chambers. It's not as direct a route, but at least you won't die. Probably."

The chamber they cut through turned out to be filled with some sort of processing equipment. There were conveyor belts, empty vats with stirring devices inside. One wall contained several storage tanks, but three of the seven had cracked open, glass shards scattered on the floor. A thick layer of dust covered everything, which was a little unusual as the titan was rarely dusty unless monsters like rustlings lived nearby. But there were no footprints in the dust, which suggested the area was abandoned.

The next chamber was almost identical except that the doors leading out from it were huge, large enough to fit eight people walking abreast. Old carts lined up near one doorway. They were empty, but judging by the detritus at the bottom of a few, they hadn't always been.

The squad passed through the large doors into a chamber that was wide enough to accommodate them all walking side by side with plenty of room to spare. Two sets of twin rails ran along the floor, spaced evenly apart. The corridor stretched on for a long way, turning so it eventually disappeared around a bend.

Justice consulted with North, then started them walking again.

"People used to live on the titans, didn't they?" Iro asked as he sped up to walk alongside Gadise Samir.

The squad leader was silent for a few seconds. "We believe so."

"Those were processing chambers." Iro thumbing over his shoulder. "Designed to take the harvest from the garden dome and... do something with it."

Gadise Samir nodded. "It makes sense."

"And most of the titan is designed with people in mind, not monsters."

"Yep."

"So, where did the monsters come from? Why do they hunt people?"

The squad leader glanced down at him. "I don't know."

"That doesn't make sense," Toshiko said, rushing forward to join them. "If people... if we lived on the titans once. Why did we move onto the ships?"

"Because of monsters. Obviously," Emil said.

"But again, where did the monsters come from?" Iro asked.

Emil shrugged. "Doesn't matter. They're here. They're in our way."

"Where did the ships of the fleet come from?" Toshiko asked. "If we lived on the titans before the monsters, we wouldn't need ships."

Gadise Samir tightened the strap on her shield as she stepped over one the rails along the floor. "And now we know there are more titans. And yet there are monsters on all of them. Not just that, but the same monsters. We've encountered rustlings, bhurbeasts, Vhar, countless others on both titans. How did so many types of monster invade all the titans at once? If we did once live on the titans, how were we all kicked off at the same time?"

"You really don't know?" Iro asked.

"I really do not."

Up ahead, Justice stopped, knelt down with one hand on a railing. "Something is coming."

Iro knelt and placed his own hand on the railing. It vibrated. A rhythmic pulse shivering through the metal, getting stronger with each pulse.

"Hide!" Gadise Samir snapped. "Into the alcoves."

They each picked an alcove and wedged themselves inside. They were only big enough for one person, but at least the alcoves were shadowed, hiding them from view.

Iro shifted uncomfortably. His armor had caught on something sharp that wedged its way in between two of the plates on his back, poking him in the skin. Every time he breathed in, it stabbed him a little deeper. He was about to force his way out of the alcove and pick another when he heard a rumbling noise echoing down the long service corridor. He held his breath, and shoved himself back into the shadows.

The rumbling grew louder, metal grating on metal. He had such a small field of view, only a tiny portion of the corridor, the two sets of twin railings on the floor, lit by the frosty yellow glow from above.

"Everybody quiet," Gadise Samir whispered over the comms. "Keep hidden."

Iro waited. The rumbling grew louder still, and a cart trundled into view. It was attached to one set of the tracks. A man in flat grey armor stood at the front, his hands on some sort of controls. The cart rumbled on and Iro saw crates piled on the cart, each one stamped with a ship logo. There were five crates on that first cart stamped with the flightless bird logo of the Courage. He hid in the darkness, seething as a second cart passed into view. Hoppers in grey armor walked alongside this cart, many of them. Some were silent and watchful, peering about as if searching for danger, others walked in pairs or threes, laughing with each other.

Six carts trundled past as Iro hid in the darkness. He counted at least thirty Hoppers escorting them, a sizeable force. He wanted to leap out and attack. These were the Hoppers from the other fleet who had attacked the dome. Each cart was piled with crates from the Home Fleet. They had stolen the harvest before destroying the dome. First, they took valuable supplies the Home Fleet needed to survive, then they killed dozens of Hoppers, of talentless workers. Perhaps even Roret. Maybe even Eir.

Iro reached up for his sword, couldn't quite draw it in the confined space. He wriggled, tried to squeeze himself out of the alcove, but whatever had snagged him had worked its way under one of his armor plates.

The last cart rumbled out of view. Two more figures walked behind it. One was a giant of a man in grey armor. He had a crooked nose, a bald head, and a thick black beard. Beside him walked a smaller, much younger man wearing the same armor. The smaller man had a cruel, pinched face with a scarred lip.

"I know it made sense, Wheel," the smaller man said. "But destroying the dome was dangerous."

The big one, Wheel, snorted. "Best way to get rid of the Blighted monsters we drove in. And we crippled the enemy's forces. It was tactically sound."

"But we destroyed a dome. If we want to take this wing from them, an un-Blighted wing, we should have found another way."

Wheel stopped, spun around and grabbed the smaller man by his collar. "Are you questioning the Emperor's orders, Ink?"

They were in front of Iro now. He let go of the hilt of his sword and tried to wedge himself a little further back. There was something about these two, like a charge in the atmosphere, he could almost feel the current flowing around them. They were more monstrous than any actual monster he'd ever faced.

"Take your hand off me or lose it," the pinched-faced man, Ink, said, his voice cold as the void.

The giant held on a few seconds longer, then let go. Ink stretched his neck to the side and slapped one hand against his chest. "Of course I don't question *his* orders. The Emperor is the fleet. The Emperor is eternal. I just wish we could have done it without unleashing Blighted monsters on this wing. They already have half the titan."

Wheel laughed. "Hyperbole. Trust in the Emperor. He has a plan." He sniffed the air twice. "Let's go. This place smells of junker."

Both men walked on out of view and Iro sighed out, relaxing a little. With them gone, he could breathe again. He waited there for a long time, until the rumbling of the carts faded into the far distance. Until his leg cramped from being wedged into the alcove.

Emil appeared at the opening to his alcove. "You alright in there, Iro?"

Iro tried to move. Something still snagged him, digging under his armor, and was sharp against his skin. He grunted and tried to force his way out again, but was wedged tight. He sagged, feeling tired.

North launched from his shoulder and flew around Emil's head. "Command is stuck."

Emil leaned against the wall and raised an eyebrow. "Need a hand?"

"No." Iro wriggled again, couldn't move. He closed his eyes for a moment. It was a struggle to open them again.

"Hey, everyone. Iro's stuck," Emil said. "Come see."

Iro sighed and held out a hand. "Fine. I need a hand."

Emil grinned and grabbed his hand, tugged. Iro still didn't move. If anything, the sharp pain sticking into his back only got sharper. Emil wedged a foot against the wall, grabbed Iro's hand in both of his own and pulled. Nothing.

Toshiko poked her head around the corner of the alcove and peered in at him. "How are you stuck? Emil managed fine, and he's much fatter than you are."

"Hey!"

Toshiko grinned at him. "Sorry. I'm sure it's all muscle."

Iro sagged again. He was so tired. "I'm snagged on something. There's something poking into my back."

"Alright, let's see it." Emil pointed his left hand at Iro and slapped his flashlight a few times to get it working. A bright beam of light burst to life and Iro heard a loud hiss.

"What the scrap?" Emil staggered back.

Iro tried to twist around to see what they were looking at. What had hold of him? He didn't know if it was a trap or a monster or if the titan itself was trying to take him.

"Shoot it!" Emil said, still pointing his flashlight.

Another hiss from behind and above. North scanned his beam of light over whatever it was. "Threat level: 35."

Toshiko drew her little cannon and chanted a few words. Her crest lit up behind her and she fired a short blast of white light above Iro. The thing that had him let out a warbling cry and tugged Iro even further back into the alcove. His armor grated against the walls.

Emil lurched forward and grabbed Iro's hand. "Shoot it more!"

"Water capacity is twenty-five thousand litres..." Toshiko started chanting again. She fired off three more quick blasts from her little cannon. The thing above Iro snarled, tugged at him. The stabbing pain in his back grew sharper.

Emil's crest flared behind him and his arms seemed to swell. He growled and heaved on Iro's hand. The pain intensified so Iro was gasping, certain his spine was being ripped out his back. Toshiko fired another blast and the thing behind Iro screeched and released him. He tumbled forwards, hitting Emil so they both sprawled on the corridor floor, rolling up against a rail. Toshiko fired off a few more blasts, but the monster darted in and out of the shadows, a slick sinuous serpent that wound between her shots. It battered its way through a grate, shunting the metal aside, and was gone.

"What's happening?" Gadise Samir said as she jogged up the corridor towards them, Justice close behind her.

North buzzed around as though unable to sit still. "Command was in danger."

"A monster had Iro," Toshiko said, still pointing her little cannon at the grate the monster had slithered into.

Gadise Samir reached them. "Are you alright, Eclipse?"

Iro struggled to sit. "I'm tired. Like I'm..." He tried to activate his crest. It flickered into weak blue light twice, then fizzled out. "It was draining my current."

"There are monsters that can do that?" Emil asked.

Gadise Samir didn't answer him. "Justice, see to Eclipse's wounds."

Justice set about looking at Iro's back. The monster had cracked one of his armor plates and had pierced his flesh in two places. Luckily, neither of the wounds were too close to his spine. Justice sealed them both with a Surveyor talent and the squad decided it was time to move on.

Iro glanced behind as they set off. He didn't like the idea of a monster out there somewhere with his stolen current. He didn't like the idea there were monsters that could suck a Hopper's current out of them. And the Hoppers from the other fleet. They had mentioned Blighted monsters. Wave had said something similar before she had stolen Iro's sword, something about the Blight. Iro had a feeling it was connected to the strange cables that had slithered within the bhurbeast corpse and stitched it back together. One more mystery of Leviathan they had to solve.

CHAPTER 25

THEY CUT AWAY from the service corridor at the first opportunity. None of them wanted to be trudging along behind the raiding party from the other fleet. Emil would have liked to catch them up, pound their heads into the wall, and take back the harvest they had stolen. He'd liked revenge for all the workers and Hoppers they had killed. But even he wasn't hardheaded enough to think that would go well. He'd felt something from the final two raiders, a charged air as they walked past. It was a level of power not even the squad leader possessed, and she had already opened her Fourth Gate. No, he had to admit that the raiders from the other fleet were beyond them for now.

Justice led them deeper into the titan. There were chambers full of dormant machinery, great cart-looking things with enormous wheels and some bladed grinder on the front. The squad leader called it an automated harvester. Apparently, they were still close enough to the garden dome that most of the chambers revolved around it. Not that it was there anymore. The dome shattered. Everything that had been inside was gone, ejected into the void. Now it would be nothing but a cold, dead expanse.

Emil noticed Iro kept twitching, looking behind him. The

Corsair's hand was wrapped tight around the hilt of his sword.

"Nervous?" Emil asked.

Iro frowned and eased his hand away from the hilt, flexing it a few times. "I can feel it following me."

"What?"

"That thing that had me in the corridor. It sucked out some of my current. It's following me. I think it wants to finish the job."

Emil grunted and shoved Iro's shoulder. "Let it try. We'll tear it apart." He thumped a fist into an open palm.

Iro nodded fretfully. "Hey, do you think most of the others made it out of the dome?"

Emil grunted. "Roret is quick. In the head, I mean. He'd have figured out what was happening. And he knows the pods like no one else. He'll have made it back to the Courage. Probably already fixing a door or something."

Iro shot him a frown. "You know Roret does more than just fix things, right? He's not an automaton."

"Of course I do!" Emil stalked ahead a few paces. But he couldn't help but consider it. He didn't really know anything about Roret, or any of the techs. Or any of the people aboard the Courage, now he thought about it. He'd never really considered they each lived their own lives. They'd supported him, dug deep and provided him with armor when he had none, and he knew nothing about any of them. That needed to change. Just as soon as he made it back.

Justice pulled them to a halt outside a small door with a rusted wheel lock standing out proudly. The Surveyor pulled his goggles down over his eyes and placed his hand against the door. His sickly green crest oozed into light behind him.

"We're here," the Surveyor announced. "No monsters. No humans. The chamber is empty, but the Spire is still closed."

North buzzed and spun in a circle. "Affirmative. Spire is still twenty-one minutes from full extension."

The squad leader shook her head and tapped at her tablet, then pressed the button on her earpiece. "Home Fleet, this is Vermillion Gadise Samir, do you read me?" She didn't receive an answer. She paced back and forth. "This is a bad idea. None of you are ready for a Spire."

"So says you," Emil growled. He was sick of her telling them all what to do. Her orders had been to leave a group of helpless workers to slaughter. He shoved Justice aside, put his hand on the wheel lock and spun it. The door clunked a few times, then rattled.

"Stand down, Courage."

Emil didn't give her the chance to stop him. He pushed the door inwards and it swung open on silent hinges.

The noise was the first thing to hit Emil. There was a constant squealing of metal grinding against metal. It filled the air and left no room for anything else. He winced but strode into the chamber regardless. The chamber might have been massive once, except for the Spire that was busy thrusting its way up through the floor and roof like a screw being driven through the titan's hull. Around the floor, jagged metal strips were bending upwards from the force of the Spire's journey. That was where the noise was coming from. Emil had expected the Spires to grow out of the titan somehow, but it appeared they were forced up through it like a blade through skin.

The squad leader shouldered Emil aside. She had her shield up and crept further into the room as if expecting an attack despite their Surveyor declaring it safe.

There wasn't much in the chamber except for row upon row of empty shelving stretching from floor to ceiling. Though many of those shelves had been knocked aside or rent in two by the growing Spire. It bisected the chamber and probably a few more besides. Emil tried to reason it, but he knew he was seeing only a small section of the Spire. It twisted, grinding the floor and driving upwards. Just ahead of them was a small control panel with a dead screen and several buttons. To either side, at the far ends of the chamber, was a large closed blast door, the type that closed vertically. Stacked in one corner of the chamber were dozens of metal crates. He thought maybe there had once been more crates stacked on the shelves, but they were now scattered haphazardly across the floor, no doubt displaced by the violence of the emerging Spire.

Emil skirted the panel and stepped up beside the squad leader. He stared at the Spire, winced at the grinding metal as another floor plate popped free of its welding, bent, scratched, tore into jagged edges.

"Where's the door?" he asked. No one heard him over the screeching metal. He pressed his earpiece to transmit. "Where's the Spire door?"

Iro's automaton answered over the comms. "Spire is still nineteen minutes from full extension."

He stared at the bot as it hovered in the air. "And the door will emerge here?"

"Affirmative."

Toshiko's voice crackled over the comms. "How did you know about the Spire, North? Or where its door will be at full extension?"

The bot started spinning. "ERROR. ERROR."

Iro ran towards it, pressing his own earpiece. "North. Command Override: Forget previous query."

The automaton stopped spinning.

"We need to find you a new Dataport or something," Iro said over the comms.

The automaton flew towards Iro and orbited his head a few times. "A Dataport will provide significant upgrades to North's processing and capabilities."

The squad leader was standing just a dozen paces from where

the Spire was grinding its way out of the floor. Justice stood next to her. Emil joined them. He still didn't trust the squad leader, but he couldn't ignore that she was the strongest of them.

"I still think this is a bad idea."

"Do you have a better one?" Justice shouted over the cacophony of squealing metal. "Because I do not want to go in there."

The squad leader said nothing.

Iro's toy was bang on in its prediction. The Spire thrust and twisted its way up through the titan for nineteen more minutes until a door appeared on its surface. Then it ground to a halt, the door just a few feet above the floor. Red strip lights rimmed the door and they flicked over to green and the door split in the middle and started sliding open.

The squad leader turned to them all before they could rush through. She stood between them and the opening door and wore a severe frown. "You all need to know what you're getting your-selves into before we step foot in there.

"When we pass through the door, it will close behind us. It will not open again until the Spire has completed its function."

Iro's automaton spun around in mid air. "Spires serve as communications arrays for contacting other titans."

"Right," the squad leader said. "Once that has happened, and only then, we will be able to open the door and escape. We'll need to fight our way to the summit to access the communications array to contact the fleet." She shook her head. "I don't know what we'll encounter in there. Spires on 01 were full of the worst traps and most powerful monsters. But no one from the Home Fleet has entered a Spire here on 02 yet."

"But there'll be loot, too?" Toshiko asked. "That's what all the stories say. That Spires are full of monsters and loot."

Behind the squad leader, the door finished sliding open. "Spires often contain items that can enhance a Hopper's abilities.

But our objective here is to reach the array. We need to notify the Home Fleet we're alive so they can send pods to retrieve us."

Emil leaned to the side and stared past the squad leader. Beyond the doors, he could see a pool of standing water shimmering in strobing yellow light. And there were steps beyond that, leading both up and down.

"When we are in there, you will follow my orders," the squad leader said. Emil noticed she was staring at him when she said it. "And listen to Justice."

"Me? Cousin, I've never been in a Spire before."

"You're our Surveyor," the squad leader said. "You'll be surveying."

Justice seemed to deflate. "Wonderful. Please don't blame me when you all die."

"How many floors is it?" Iro asked. "I mean up to the communications array?"

"5," the automaton said in a voice that sounded far too happy.

Iro nodded and let out a sigh. "That doesn't sound... too bad?"

"Five floors full of the worst traps and deadliest monsters the titan can throw at us," Justice said. "Doesn't sound too bad? Are you insane?"

The squad leader took two steps towards the open door and paused. She shook her head. "This is a bad idea." She took another step, paused again, and didn't move.

Emil realised she had gone gray. The Spire had gone gray, too. All color had drained from the chamber. He grinned, pumped his fist in the air. Everything had gone gray and frozen and that could mean only one thing. His Second Gate! He had encountered his Second Gate. Now all he had to do was figure out how to open it.

"What the scrap?" Iro said.

Emil spun about on his heel. The chamber was still gray, but Iro was not.

CHAPTER 26

IRO POINTED AT EMIL. "What are you doing here?"

"Me?" The Paladin stalked towards him. "It's my Second Gate. You're supposed to be frozen and colorless. So… freeze already."

Iro squared up to the bigger man. "Unless it's my gate, and you're getting in my way."

Emil looked like he was about to throw a punch, but he stopped and shook his head. "We don't have time for this. Look, the color is already draining back into the chamber."

Iro stared up to the ceiling where the Spire had ruptured through in a riot of twisted metal. The reddish hue of the Spire was visible at the top, crawling slowly downwards.

"Have you ever heard of two people being unfrozen when a gate appears?" Iro asked.

"No," Emil said, staring about the chamber. "But nobody told me anything about the gates other than good luck." He stalked over to the squad leader, glared at her a moment, then thumped her on the arm.

"What are you doing?"

"Nothing." The Paladin's face went a little red. "Doubt I'll get another chance. Where's my gate?"

"Or mine," Iro said. It was a little worrying that neither of their gates had appeared. He wondered if they had triggered some sort of trap and were now frozen in time like Justice had warned them about?

Emil crept towards to the Spire door and poked his head through. "Nothing in there."

Iro hurried further back into the chamber, towards the little control panel. He looked left to see the door at the far side was closed, then right. The door to the right was open. He squinted into the grey gloom and saw the chamber beyond was long and thin and with cupboards on either side, and standing right in the centre of it were two gates.

"Emil!" Iro shouted, his voice echoing in the frozen space. "They're over here. Come on." He started into a jog towards the doorway, heard Emil sprinting to catch up.

There was about a hundred paces between the control panel and the doorway and Iro was only halfway there when a black shadow faded into view next to the door. It was vaguely person shaped though with no features. The shade slapped a hand against a button on the left side of the doorway and the door slammed down fast as a heartbeat. The shadow faded away as if it had never been.

"No!" Emil shouted. "What did you do, Iro?"

Iro reached the closed door, hammered on the same button the shade had used to close it. It didn't open. He crossed to the other side of the door where there was an identical button. He pressed it but nothing happened. Emil hit the door hard, not even slowing down from his sprint. He tried to wedge his fingers in the seam as if he could pull the door open.

"That's not going to work, Emil." Iro paced back and forth. "It's a blast door."

"Shut up!" Emil growled, still trying to get a grip on the door where it met the floor. "If I can get my fingers in, I can use Strength to..." He trailed off.

"We don't have our talents." Here in the grayspace of the gates they didn't have access to talents or current. They were as weak as day one trainees again.

"Scrap it!" Emil stood and punched the door. "How do we open it?" He stared up at the ceiling.

Iro followed his gaze. The white panelling of the walls crept downwards. Iro guessed they had already used an eighth of their allotted time before the color filled the chamber again. If they hadn't passed through their gates by then, the world would unfreeze and they would both be stalled, forever stuck at their First Gates and unable to get any stronger.

"Maybe if we press both buttons at the same time?" Iro said. He waved at Emil to move to the right, while he took the left one. They both hovered their hands over the buttons and Iro counted down. They pressed the buttons at the same time. Nothing happened.

"Maybe you counted wrong?" Emil counted down quickly and they both slammed the buttons. Nothing happened.

"SCRAP!" Emil shouted. "Any more bright ideas?" He punched the door again.

"Maybe. Or maybe you'd like to hit things some more?"

Emil shot him a dangerous glare. "Puzzles aren't my thing." He threw up his hands and turned away, then stopped. "There's a light on the control panel over there."

Both of them launched into a sprint back towards the control panel. Most of it was still dead and gray, but a single small square button was lit with a purple light. Emil pressed it without waiting. Behind them, the door shot upwards, opening again. Iro could see both gates still waiting beyond.

"Yes!" Emil shouted. Both sprinted for the doorway. Again,

they were less than half way when a shade of fuzzing shadow faded into existence. It drifted two paces towards the button on the left of the door and pressed it. The door slammed shut. The shade faded away.

Emil slid to a stop and shouted. He slammed a fist against the floor, turned, sprinted back to the control panel. Iro ran the other way towards the door.

Emil pressed the button again and the door slammed open in a second. Iro slid to a halt just as the shade appeared. It lurched towards the button on the side of the door, and Iro drew his sword and cut the dark shadow in half. It faded away.

"Come on!" he shouted, waving for Emil. The Paladin sprinted.

Another shadow faded into view on the other side of the door. Iro launched towards it, but he was already too late. The shade hit the button before Iro could slay it and the door slammed shut. The shade vanished.

Emil slowed to a stop, panting. "Scrap! What does it want from us?"

Iro glanced up at the color draining back into the room. They had used half their time already. "What if only one of us can pass through?" he said.

Emil glared at him. Then glanced back at the control panel. The Paladin crossed his arms. "Well, I'm not running back to the control panel again."

Iro screwed his eyes shut for a moment. The color was draining back into the room and they didn't have time. "Fine." He started running for the control panel. "The shades appear one at a time on either side of the door. You have to sprint between them, hold them off until I reach you."

"I'm not an idiot," Emil said.

Iro reached the control panel, slammed a hand down on the

purple button, turned, launched into a sprint back towards the now open door.

The door slammed open behind Emil and the first shade appeared out of thin air, already reaching for the button to close the door again. He turned and thumped it in what passed for a face. His fist passed through it like it wasn't there, but the shade evaporated into nothing. Emil turned, sprinted towards the other side of the door. He reached it just as another shade formed. This one he back-handed away, already turning again and running for the other side.

The next shade almost got its fingers to the button before Emil reached it, shoved it away. He grit his teeth and sprinted back towards the other side.

"Hurry up, Iro!"

The shades were appearing fast, more energetically reaching for the button to close the door. Emil reached the next one, punched it. It vanished. He turned, slipped, already knowing he'd not reach the other side in time.

"Now!" Iro shouted as he sprinted through the open door.

Emil leapt for the opening. The door slammed shut and he smacked against the solid metal. Iro was through. He was not.

Emil screamed. He punched the door again and again and again. His fist stung inside his gauntlet, but he didn't care. It wasn't fair. "No. No. No. No. No!"

The color was still seeping back into the chamber. Time slipping away. He had to get through the door. To open his gate. He would not be stalled. His father was stalled. Being stalled was no different from death.

Emil turned and sprinted back to the control panel. He didn't have long, the color was almost down to the top of the door now.

He mashed the purple button and launched himself back towards the door.

The door slammed open and Iro leapt through, sword already drawn. He skewered the first shade and was already running for the next.

"You waited?" Emil panted out as he ran.

"Shut up and run!" Iro shouted back. He slashed another shade out of existence and leapt towards the next, hitting it with a strike that would have decapitated it.

Emil put his head down and ran. His legs burned, his breath heaved, but he ran. Iro leapt from one side of the door to the next, slashing through shades. But they kept coming quicker and quicker. The color was head high now and still draining back into the chamber.

Iro stabbed another ghost, turned, threw his sword across the doorway to vanquish another. Two shades appeared, one either side of the door, both reaching for the button. Emil tackled Iro and carried them both careening through the open door just a moment before it slammed shut behind them.

They both scrambled to their feet and ran for the gates. The color was halfway down this new chamber and Emil could swear it was speeding up.

"Which is yours and which is mine?" Iro asked.

"Does is matter?"

Both gates had the same word written at the top of them. *Co-Operation*. One had a rectangular frame with colored wires running all around it. The closed doorway was solid metal. The other gate was a fluid arch that appeared to be made of water and had multi-colored lights pulsing within the water. Its doorway was a bizarre film like a sheet of algae.

"What if we go through the wrong gates?" Iro asked. "Will you end up with Corsair talents?"

"Scrap that. I'm not learning to use a sword."

They stared at the two gates for a few seconds as the color reached them and kept draining into the chamber. "There!" Emil said. He pointed at the rectangular gate. There was blue crest outlined on the metal door. He looked over to the watery gate and saw a faint red crest burning on the greenish mat of algae door. Emil didn't know why the gates appeared as they did, but it seemed odd that his would be so fluid, while Iro's was more like a circuit board.

"Alright then," Iro said. The Corsair strode forward and pushed against the door with the blue crest. It didn't budge. He slammed his shoulder against it, strained. Still nothing.

Emil rushed forward and placed his hands against the algae door. It was spongy beneath his touch and he pushed, but it held firm and sprang back into place.

The color had drained down to their hips now. Emil pushed again against the spongy door. It held firm. "What do we do?"

"Together?" Iro asked. He counted down quickly, and they both pushed on their doors at the same time. Still, both doors held.

Emil growled in frustration. There had to be a way. Something they were missing. He looked up at the door, his gaze catching on the word written at the top of both. *Co-Operation.* "Switch gates."

"But…"

He tugged Iro out of the way and shoved the Corsair in front of the algae gate, then stepped in front of the circuit board gate. "Now push."

They both pushed and the doors swung open. A gale hit them both, a stream of force blasting from the gates, pushing them back. Emil tried to fight against it, leaning into it, scrabbling at the floor with his gauntlets. The force blasting out of the gates was invisible but too strong, he couldn't fight against it.

"Switch again," Iro shouted as if screaming into a tempest despite the gates making no noise.

Emil threw himself to the side, rolling underneath Iro as the Corsair leapt over him. The color had almost hit the bottom of the chamber now.

As soon as they were each in front of their own gates, the force pushing them back stopped. Emil shared a single glance with Iro, then they both launched themselves through the gates.

CHAPTER 27

IRO WHOOPED FOR JOY. He felt strong. Really strong. Just like after opening his First Gate and back in the nest when the reactor had been breached, he felt invincible, like he could take on the entire titan. A soft blue light surrounded him like icy fire burning along his skin. He activated his crest and it was so bright he had to squint against it. His current was deeper than ever before and it was churning inside of him like it wanted to be used.

Beside him, Emil was surrounded by his own light, a fiery red like flames from a furnace. He looked up, caught Iro's gaze, then grinned. Iro grinned back. Both of them shouted for joy and launched into a hug. Their auras crackled and turned purple where they touched.

"We did it!" Iro shouted.

Emil thumped him on the back. "Too scrapping right, we did! Two nobodies from a lower ship."

They separated, both still grinning, and Emil clapped his hands together then gave Iro a push on the chest. Iro flew backwards, slammed into the wall.

"Scrap!" Emil said, his grin dropping. "Sorry. I didn't mean to…" He looked down at his hands. "It's gonna take a while to get used to this."

Iro shook his head to clear away the sparkling lights and lurched back to his feet. A manic laugh burst from his lips. Emil had thrown him against a bulkhead, and he barely felt it. He needed to test out what he was capable of.

Iro crouched down, then leapt straight upwards. He smashed into the chamber roof a good fifteen feet above, smacked his head on a hanging light, then plummeted back to the ground. He landed on his feet and bent his knees, absorbing the impact.

Emil gawked at him. "I have to try that!" The Paladin leapt upward and hit the ceiling. He grabbed hold of the swinging light and hung there for a few moments, then swung his feet up and pushed off the ceiling, spun in midair and hit the floor so hard the bulkhead dented beneath him. "This is scrapping brilliant."

"What does your crest look like?" Iro asked.

Emil activated his crest. It roared to fiery light, so bright and huge. All the lines looked like molten flames coursing down a mold. His second lock was open, the symbol in it looking like a pair of clasped hands. It matched the symbol in Iro's second lock. But Emil's crest was larger than his by far, and on the left side Iro saw a faint circle that almost looked like another lock. Did that mean Emil was almost at his Third Gate already? Iro searched his own crest, but couldn't see any sign of a similar circle. His joy curdled a little in his gut. He knew he should be happy for Emil, did feel happy for him. But he also didn't like the idea of being left behind. He needed to work harder.

"Courage, Eclipse, where are you?" Gadise Samir said over the squad comms.

"We opened our Second Gates," Iro said into the comms as he and Emil jogged for the door back in the Spire chamber.

"What? Both of you?"

"Yup," Emil said. "What? You surprised?"

There was a couple of seconds silence, then Gadise Samir spoke again, her voice urgent. "Get back here now."

"Why what's…" Emil trailed off and stared at Iro.

"Monsters are drawn to Hoppers opening gates," Iro said. Behind them, down the far end of the long, thin chamber, another door opened. A brutish monster with six arms thick with muscle stood silhouetted in the doorway.

"Is that a Vhar?" Emil asked.

Iro slapped a button on the wall and the door slid open. He saw Gadise Samir hurrying their way. She barged in between them and raised her shield at the same time the Vhar howled, a pulse of sound ricocheting down the long chamber. Gadise Samir activated her crest and a barrier of interlocking amber energy formed outward from her shield, filling the chamber. The Vhar vanished, reappeared as the wave of sound hit them. It slammed into the Vanguard's shield, clawed hands scrabbling at the energy barrier. Up close, it was a hulking thing, eight feet tall and each arm so thick with muscle it was as big as Iro's leg. Its face was a distended thing like a human had grown a muzzle.

"Go!" Gadise Samir shouted. She braced her feet and put her shoulder behind her shield, holding back the Vhar. "Get to the Spire." With her free hand, she pressed a series of symbols floating before her in the energy barrier. Then she stepped back and away. The barrier held, even as the Vhar clawed against it, sparks flying as it gouged wounds in the energy field.

The Vanguard turned, shoved Iro forward. "Go! That won't hold long."

Iro started running. Emil had already gone ahead. "Shouldn't we fight it?"

Gadise Samir jogged alongside him. "Look around, Eclipse. Vhar never hunt alone."

The door at the far side of the chamber slid open and a hulking Vhar even larger than the caster lumbered into the chamber. It looked about and roared. A large section of grating clattered to the floor from above and Iro didn't dare look up.

The brute hit the ground in front of them, the floor denting from the impact. It must have been ten feet tall and had four arms, each one wielding a sword or axe. Its snoutish face was a haphazard mess of pointed teeth.

"Keep running," Gadise Samir said. She sped a little, aimed herself at the Vhar brute.

A beam of white light seared out from the Spire as Toshiko fired her cannon. The blast hit the brute in the back, severing one of its arms, staggering it. But it didn't fall, didn't die. Gadise Samir leapt even as the brute recovered, slammed her shield across its face, launching the brute away and into a shelving unit. The Vanguard hit the ground, rolled back onto her feet still running. Iro followed in her wake.

"My sword!" Iro slid to a halt, spun around. He'd thrown his sword at a shade. It was still lying by the doorway, had clattered to a halt by the wall. Forty paces away, the Spire maybe fifty paces behind him. He couldn't lose another sword. Not again. Besides… He grinned. Now he'd opened his Second Gate, he was sure he could make it.

Iro drew his smaller sword and activated his crest. He used a Blink Strike to cross the distance. It was faster than before. Like the force pulling him around was stronger. The power of his Second Gate had made his current swell. He scooped up his sword into his offhand and turned. The downed Vhar brute had recovered, was back on its feet. The huge one was lumbering towards him. Above, another grate clattered down from above and gleaming red eyes peered out.

"Eclipse, what are you doing?" Gadise Samir roared over the comms. "Get back here."

Iro pressed the button on his earpiece. "On my way, squad lea…"

There was a mighty crash as the Vhar caster trapped in the next chamber shattered Gadise Samir's barrier and barrelled through the open doorway. It screamed and the noise staggered Iro like a haymaker to the head. Then the caster vanished and reappeared in front of him, two fists thundering into his gut so hard his printed armor cracked and it threw him away to smash against the bulkhead wall.

Iro found himself on his knees. He tried to get back to his feet, but his legs didn't seem to work right. He coughed, sputtered, spat blood onto the metal floor. One punch. The Vhar had hit him with a single punch and he could barely move. He growled past the pain in his chest. It wasn't right. He'd opened his Second Gate and still he could only punch down on those weaker than him.

He still had hold of his swords, used the larger one as a crutch to help push him back to his feet. The caster stalked towards him. Its six arms spread wide, taloned fists clenching and unclenching with every step. It was talking. Gibbering something.

"Get out of there, Eclipse!"

Iro swiped with his shorter blade, Blink Striking to the side to get around the Vhar. The monster screamed and beat him to his destination. A fist smacked into the side of his head and he tumbled away, crashed against the control panel.

"I'm on my way," Gadise Samir said over comms.

Iro blinked away his fuzzy vision and saw the Vanguard running towards him. Another Vhar dropped from above, landed in front of her.

Iro pressed the button on his ear piece. "Get back to the Spire. I've got this."

The caster was stalking towards him again, and Iro stood unsteadily to meet it. It was stronger than him. Faster than him. Even with his Second Gate open, he stood no chance against even the weakest Vhar. But that was why he'd gone to the Silver Blade. That was why he demanded she teach him Burning Adrenaline.

Iro pushed his current flooding into his swords, then pulled it back into his body, honing his speed and strength to a razor edge. He surged back to his feet, both swords light as air in his hands.

The caster screamed, a wall of noise roaring at him. The monster vanished, reappeared in front of him, clutched at him with clawed hands. Supercharged with Burning Adrenaline, Iro saw the attack coming. He ducked, slipped under the reaching hands, spun away and sliced out with his smaller sword.

Blood spurted out from the Vhar's cut leg and it roared, stumbled. Iro's current was deeper than before now he'd opened his Second Gate, but draining away so fast with Burning Adrenaline active. And he hadn't even used another talent with it yet.

Iro drew his swords together as the Vhar lurched for him again. He slashed them apart and poured his current into them, Blink Striking. For a moment, there was two of him, one being dragged to the left, and the other to the right. The Vhar snatched out, grabbed the image of Iro being dragged left. It was the wrong one. That image of Iro vanished and he slid to a halt behind the caster. He dropped his smaller sword, grabbed his larger blade in both hands and swung, putting the full force of his Second Gate Burning Adrenaline boosted strength into the blow. The blade bit into the caster's side and cleaved the monster in two. Its scream died on its distended lips and the monster fell away dead.

"Behind you, Iro!" Emil shouted over the comms.

Iro flung himself forwards, snatching up his fallen sword and rolling. The huge Vhar brute slammed four arms down on the metal flooring right where he had been a moment earlier. Iro rolled back to his feet, stumbled. His current was almost gone, his crest flickering. The brute towered over him, shards of metal armor sewn into its skin all over its flesh. He already knew he didn't have enough left to fight it.

The brute lurched forward, one arm swinging a giant rusty knife at him. Iro swipe his smaller sword to the side and channeled the last of his current into a Blink Strike. It dragged him away from the attack, flew him through the chamber. His crest flickered out and he hit the ground ten paces from the Spire, rolling to a painful stop. He had nothing left. His arms and legs trembled. He couldn't even stand.

Gadise Samir reached him, knelt, picked him up and flung him over her shoulder. She turned and sprinted through the Spire door. Behind them, Iro saw ten Vhar charging forwards. Brutes, warriors, casters. A whole war band there for them.

"Close it," Gadise Samir shouted.

Justice pressed the button and the door started to slide shut. It was so slow. Toshiko stepped in front of the door, her cannon levelled. She pulled the trigger and a white blast shot out between the closing doors. It hit the lead Vhar square in the chest, knocked the brute down but didn't kill it. Another of the monsters leapt over its staggered comrade, charged on. Toshiko fired again, the second barrel roaring. The Vhar was ready, lurched to the side to avoid the blast, kept running.

"I'm out," Toshiko squeaked and backed away from the door. Both Steel Lotus' barrels were smoking.

"My turn," Emil stepped in front of the Mage. His fiery orange crest lit up behind him, blazing like a forge.

The lead Vhar reached the closing door, one hand either side, started squeezing through. Emil moved to meet it, swung a gauntleted fist. At the last moment, his arms swelled as though with new muscle. His fist crunched against the Vhar's snarling face with a spray of blood and smashed teeth. The monster flew away.

The doors were almost closed as Gadise Samir laid Iro down against a small bench. Another of the monsters leapt half way through the door, one hand reaching forwards, closed around Emil's arm. It tried to drag him back, but the Paladin switched his talent and Steel strengthened his skin, made him weigh twice as much. The Vhar tugged on him again once, then the door closed on it, crushing its arm at the elbow.

The door boomed to a close. Emil stepped back, staring at the monstrous hand still wrapped around his wrist. He shook it violently until it fell away.

"All good?" Gadise Samir asked, her voice echoing in the silence of that first chamber.

Justice leaned against the wall, next to the door. "Not even remotely, Cousin."

Emil cracked his knuckled within his gauntlets. "Better than ever."

Toshiko had placed Steel Lotus down barrel up and was blowing on them as though trying to cool them down. "Uh, sure? Really need to find some upgrades in here."

The squad leader glanced down at Iro. He tried to speak, couldn't remember how to form words. His current battery was empty and he was beyond exhausted. He heroically raised a single trembling hand and gave her a thumbs up.

"Good," Gadise Samir said as she sat down on the bench Iro was propped against. "Because that was the easy part. Now is where the real test begins. We have a Spire to climb."

CHAPTER 28

TOSHIKO WOULD HAVE LIKED to say she wasn't jealous, but she already knew that would be a lie. Both Iro and Emil had opened their gates. Together. It had given Iro enough power to kill a Vhar! Although he now looked like a limp wire, unable to even stand. Still, the strength to kill a Vhar had to be enormous. She'd hit one with a blast that would have fried a bhurbeast inside out, and the Vhar shrugged it off like a stubbed toe. Of course, part of the problem was Steel Lotus. Toshiko couldn't put her full current into a proper Giga Beam for fear of burning her poor cannon out again. First she needed to find a capacitor upgrade, then she needed to open her Second Gate… somehow. Preferably before Justice did. Toshiko did *not* want to get left behind.

While the others collected themselves and waited for Iro to suck up enough current to stand again, Toshiko did a lap of the chamber. Considering the massive size of the Spire, this room was small. She could walk all around it in a couple of minutes. At the far end, opposite the door, was a staircase leading both up and down. She started there and peered upwards. The staircase doubled back on itself after a short way and kept leading up. It was brightly lit with white wall strips, but the walls were metal, silver and rusting in places as though the Spire had been here a long time rather than grown out of the titan in the last few hours. That seemed strange. And some panels didn't look like they lined up. She saw a faded red stain splashed along a panel that just ended. The next panel was spotless. It was as though they were pulled from two different areas. Like the titan had constructed the Spire from many parts of itself, old and new. There was noise echoing down from far above, too, clanging and whirring. It sounded almost like the engineering deck aboard the Thousands Suns.

Toshiko chewed on her lip and dreamed. What she wouldn't give for a few hours alone in a manufactory. She could rebuild Steel Lotus with titan steel parts that wouldn't just withstand her current, but would resonate with her and amplify it. She was halfway up the first staircase before Gadise Samir's voice sounded in her comms.

"We're waiting here, Thousand Suns, until Eclipse is recovered."

Toshiko turned, flashed the squad leader a smile and skipped back down the stairs. She could wait, though it ground against her nerves.

She checked out the staircase leading down. After the first step, it was filled with a smoky, inky darkness like a pool of oil. She peered into it, squinted, shone her flashlight. No light penetrated the darkness, but it wasn't solid. She poked a toe down, and the tip of her boot disappeared. She pulled it back out and her boot was fine. The darkness wasn't smoke or liquid. It was just darkness. Toshiko backed away from that. She'd never liked darkness. Even safely aboard the Thousand Suns, snug in her own room, she slept with a light on.

The small pool in the centre of the chamber was shallow enough she'd have had trouble bathing. It was clear as plexiglass and Toshiko could see small holes in the bottom, each one as large as a finger. Justice was sitting on the edge of the pool, one hand hovering above the still surface. His little automaton scuttled down his arm and extended its sensor array, dipping it into the water. Justice cocked his head as though listening to something far away.

"It's clean," he said, sounding surprised. "Pure. We can drink it."

"You first," Toshiko said, narrowing her eyes.

Justice stared at her a moment, then pulled his hand away from the water and crossed his arms. "I'm not thirsty right now."

"Convenient, neither am I," Toshiko lied. She was parched enough to plunge her head into the pool and drink until she burst.

"That's surprising. It's been hours since any of us drank anything. Surely you're scratchy? Like you have a dry spot you can't seen to moisten no matter how many times you swallow." The Surveyor smiled.

Toshiko tried to swallow but her mouth had gone dry as dust. She held Justice's gaze and refused to break.

Emil surged between them, leaned down the edge of the pool and dunked his head into the water, gulping down huge mouthfuls. After seconds that seemed like forever, he pulled back and gasped. "Oh, that felt good." He sank down to lean against the edge of the pool. The disturbed water lapped against the side, sploshing out and running down his neck, but he didn't seem to mind.

Justice stared at Emil for a moment, then looked to Toshiko. "Uhh, how do you feel, Paladin?"

Emil frowned. "Don't call me that. The name is Courage Emil. Pick one. And I'm fine. Why shouldn't I be?"

Justice shrugged. "No burning sensation in the stomach? Limbs aren't seizing up?"

Emil shifted. "No. Why? You said it was safe to drink, right?"

Justice shared another look with Toshiko. She shrugged back at him. Then they both leapt towards the pool. Justice started scooping up handfuls while Toshiko shoved her face in and started slurping.

Toshiko sat back with a grateful sigh, contented, her thirst quenched. She grinned at Emil, though the Paladin was looking a little cross eyed. She gave him a light shove with her boot and he started shaking, choking. He collapsed sideways and hit the ground, eyes unfocused.

"Oh scrap. Oh scrap. Oh scrap," Toshiko said. "What do we do?"

"Uh…" Justice looked around, stared down at the pool. "Oh no!"

Emil's choking turned to laughter and he rolled over onto his back, staring up at them both, grinning.

Toshiko kicked him in the chest, not softly this time. "Not funny!"

Emil's chuckle faded to a smile, then to his usual deadly serious expression.

"Made me laugh," Iro said from where Gadise Samir had propped him up on the bench.

The squad leader strode forward and dipped her own hands in the pool, cupping some water and slurping it down. When she straightened up, her back gave a crack and she stretched it out. "Check the cupboards," she said, pointing to the wall behind Toshiko. "The Spires often have supplies on the lowest level." She cracked her neck from one side to the other. "It's like the titans want us to climb them."

Toshiko sauntered over to the cupboards and found North hovering above her shoulder, also eager to have a look. They were set in the bulkhead walls, each with a thin door sporting a handle and nothing else. Toshiko pulled open the first and peered inside.

It was stacked high with foil-wrapped bars. She picked one up and turned it over in her hands, then peeled the plain foil away to reveal a brown stick of something grainy.

North scanned it with a beam of light. "Analysis: Nutrient rich proto bar. Designed for feeding workers. Shelf life: two-hundred-and-fifteen-years ERROR standard."

Toshiko glanced up at the floating automaton. "So it's edible?"

North spun around and announced in a cheery voice, "A proto bar will provide an adult human with all the energy they need for a productive day of work." It floated down to scan the rest of the cupboard. "Hypothesis: An automated processing unit must still be running in this quadrant."

"Automated processing unit?" Toshiko asked. "Is that like a manufactory?"

North spun around to face her and went still for a few seconds. "No." The bot turned and flew away back towards Iro.

Toshiko shrugged and nibbled on a corner of the brown bar. It tasted of dry, which until then Toshiko would not have identified as a flavor. She scooped up an armful of the bars and carried them back to the squad while nibbling on more.

The rest of the cupboards provided little else. Many were filled with more of the bars, some had ratty old clothing that was half disintegrated. One contained a small plasma welding torch, which Justice jumped on, claiming it would make a fine addition to his autodage. That was something at least. They hadn't even started climbing the Spire and already had their first piece of loot; a standard techy welding torch. Not quite worthy of retirement.

It took Iro almost an hour before he'd recovered enough to walk again, and even then he was slow and uncoordinated.

Gadise Samir led the way to the staircase. She stopped on the first step, the rest of them crowding behind her. "Be careful. Follow orders. No more heroics."

Emil snorted and started up the stairs, walking past the squad leader. Gadise Samir ground her teeth, looked like she wanted to break the Paladin in two, then hurried up the stairs after him. Iro followed, taking each step carefully as though it were a monumental climb. North hovered above him, zipping from shoulder to shoulder.

"What's down there?" Toshiko asked Justice, pointing towards the stairs leading down into the darkness.

Justice stared at it for a second. "I don't know. No one does. Every Spire has stairs leading down, but they're also shrouded in darkness that no light can penetrate." He shrugged. "Or so I've heard. First time in a Spire for me. Probably last, too. Have I mentioned we're going to die in here?"

Toshiko hefted Steel Lotus and started up the stairs. "Even you?"

Justice spent a few more seconds staring into the dark, then hurried up to walk beside her. "Not me. I always seem to survive. Part of my curse."

"Seems like a lucky curse. You always survive even though everyone else dies."

Iro wished he had earplugs by the time they reached the first chamber of the Spire, although he was also hard pressed to call it a chamber. It was a small stretch of corridor that normally he could have run across in twenty seconds, except for the giant metal rods thrusting out from the walls at regular intervals.

Every ten paces, there were circular holes in the walls. Huge metal tubes thrust out of the holes, slammed together, interlocking, then rotated at dizzying speeds that charged the air to static. Then they stopped, separated, and pulled back into the walls. A few seconds later, the rods thrust out again and repeated the interlocking and rotating. It happened all down the corridor twenty times. At the far end of the corridor, there were steps leading up.

"Trap," Iro said during a brief lull.

Justice turned to him with a glare, but the Surveyor's retort was drowned out when the front couple of rods slammed together and started spinning.

"Justice, can you shut these things down?" Gadise Samir said.

She was standing close enough to the rods that the spinning stirred her hair. The rods stopped, pulled apart, then retracted back into the walls. The squad leader leaned forwards a little, peering into the holes. She jerked backwards as the rods thrust out again with a metallic clash as they collided. They interlocked and started rotating once more, charging the air.

Justice had his hand pressed against the wall. The bulkhead there was bent like it had been pushed outwards. The metal was dark and pitted, pock marked with burn scars. It looked so different to the next panels along, like the titan had cobbled together the entire chamber with spare parts. It almost reminded Iro of the Courage, and a pang of homesickness ran through him.

A puff of smoke belched out from the damaged section of wall and hit Justice in the face. The Surveyor waved a hand in front of his face and coughed. "Acrid. Smells like burning oil. I ca…"

The front most rods slammed together again and started spinning at ear-splitting volume. Justice sighed, then pressed the button on his earpiece. "I can't stop it. These things serve some sort of function in the chamber above and the controls are routed up there."

"So how do we get past?" Emil asked. He was standing next to the squad leader as if daring himself to get close to the rotating rods.

"With great care," Justice said. "Unless you want to be paste."

"Do they remind you of anything?" Toshiko said.

Iro nodded. Several systems on board their ships used a similar design only written in miniature. Even some of their hand-held tools when they dismantled. "Gears."

"Makes you wonder what they're driving up above, huh?" The Mage hugged her cannon to her chest.

"Want me to Blink Strike you across?" Iro asked. He was far from certain his current had recharged enough, but it had to be easier than running through the forest of shifting, spinning rods.

"Um, no, thank you. I'd much rather be in full control of my potential demise than subject to your gravity shifting zoomies. What if you time it wrong? Or can't stop in time? Or you run out of current half way through a strike and then BAM!" Toshiko clapped her hands together. "Hopper pancake."

"What's a pancake?"

"You don't have those?" Toshiko shook her head at him. "You take algae paste, fry it into a flat cake, then roll it around something with some flavour."

"That sounds horrible."

She shrugged. "Yeah, tastes like algae."

"We move one at a time," Gadise Samir said over the comms so she could be heard over the clashing, spinning rods. "You'll have a few seconds to cross each danger zone, and a couple of feet of safety between each one. Do not rush. Only move when you are ready, but when you are, move quickly. Do not hesitate once you've decided to move."

Justice groaned.

"What, Cousin?"

"Oh, nothing," the Surveyor said. "I'm just not looking forward to seeing you all crushed."

Gadise Samir shook her head at him. "Your armor won't protect you. Do NOT stop in the danger zones no matter what."

The squad leader took a few deep breaths and waited while

the first of the gears launched from the walls, slammed together in front of her, then span up. The moment they separated, she leapt forwards. The gears slammed back together and span again. It took a few seconds before Iro and the others saw Gadise Samir safe and sound in the couple of feet of safe space. She waited for the next set of gears to retract, and ran forwards again.

Emil was next up. He waited a few rotations after the squad leader was out of sight. Twice he looked like he was about to make the first run, but he didn't, pulling back a step.

"Want me to go first? Paladin?" Justice said. "Show you how it's done."

"Scrap you!" Emil said in a tight voice. As soon as the rods retracted, he launched himself across, only pulling in his trailing hand in before the rods slammed together behind him.

Justice stepped forward to go next. He waited and waited and waited again. "It's all about timing," he mumbled to himself. His autodage clicked in response. "Every tenth rotation, I see." The next time the rods retracted, he walked calmly across.

"You next," Iro said. "I'll hold up the rear."

Toshiko laughed nervously. She clutched her cannon and stopped before the first gear as it span up, then stopped, and pulled back. She screamed high and tight as she barrelled across. The rods slammed back together and Iro had to wait until they separated again.

Toshiko stood on the other side, grinning back at him. "I made it!" She gave him a wave. The gears smashed together again and started spinning. The next time they separated, Toshiko was gone. He hoped she had made it across the next set of gears.

It was his turn. "Hold tight, North." The automaton huddled close on his shoulder, its little legs clinging to his pauldron.

The next time the gears pulled apart, Iro dashed across. The rods slammed back together behind him. They started spinning and his skin tingled beneath his armor. Ahead of him, the next set of gears pulled apart. He saw a glimpse of Toshiko. He waited for another couple of rotations, then leapt across the next pair of rods. He made this one with a second to spare and huddled close in the safe zone with gears spinning both before and behind him. The charged air made his hair stand on end.

"I'm across," Gadise Samir said over the comms. "Keep moving. Take your time with each crossing. You'll be fine."

Iro knew she was speaking to the entire squad, a general encouragement, but it felt like she meant the words for him alone and in that moment it bolstered him. He ran across the next gear as soon as it separated and made the next safe zone.

Confidence surged through his veins and he leapt into the next crossing as soon as the rods pulled back. His feet hit the safe zone as the gear in front separated and retracted. Iro crossed the safe zone in two quick strides and leapt forward. A flash of silver in the corner of his eye warned him of his mistake, but he had no time to stop. The gears slammed together in a booming crash. They caught his armor, scraped his backplate, sent him careening to the ground in the safe zone a breath away from the next spinning gear.

Iro rolled away from the rods and lay on his back in the safe zone, trying to calm his rapid breathing. North scuttled onto his chest and swept a beam of light over him.

"Detecting elevated heart rate. Minor injuries. Command Query: Would Command like North to scan for threats?"

Iro chuckled despite himself. "We're surrounded by threats, North."

The gears beside him slammed back together, started spinning again. Iro turned his head to the side. He could see Toshiko's feet underneath the gear, watched her dance on the spot a few times then rush forwards. The gear she was passing slammed together and she was gone. A thought occurred to him.

"If any of us die here, would the others even know?"

North buzzed. "Yes. Biological organisms are quite messy when dead."

Iro got back to his feet and waited for the next crossing, only taking it when he was ready. He passed the next two at a steady pace, no longer overconfident and giving the trap the respect it deserved.

Iro guessed he was over half way. No one else had said anything over the comms, but he was sure Emil must have made it by now. He wouldn't even consider the alternative. He waited for the next gear to complete its spin and launched forwards. The rods slammed back together and he pulled up short. They were misaligned, the cogs grinding against each other as they tried to slot into place. The gear didn't spin, but pulled apart, slammed together, pulled apart, slammed together. Both rods retracted into the wall and were gone.

Iro waited for what seemed like minutes. The rods did not reappear. There was nothing but darkness in the two holes in the walls.

"I guess I'll cross."

"Command Suggestion: Crossing is not advised until pattern can be discerned."

"What if there is no pattern?"

North buzzed, sounding agitated. It crossed over to his other shoulder and back again. "Everything is patterns."

Iro took a deep breath and readied himself to make the crossing to the next safe zone. The gears beyond were still working, slamming into each other and spinning. But this one that had stopped. He glanced down at the floor, ready to make the run, and stopped. There was something embedded in the floor, a black box about a foot across in each way. It had golden lettering around the edges that looked a lot like the arcane symbols he saw on crests. A silver ring sat in the middle of the box, attached to a bracket so it could be lifted. The box clearly didn't belong there, surrounded by silver bulkheads. The entire chamber looked like it had been cobbled together from different parts, so maybe the box was there by mistake. And yet, Iro couldn't stop staring at the golden lettering.

He grinned wide. "Loot," he breathed. It had to be. Everyone said the Spires had powerful items that could enhance a Hopper's abilities, but they were always dangerous to attain. Well, this piece of loot was right in the middle of a trap, and it didn't get much more dangerous than that.

Iro stared into the dark recesses again, saw no sign of the rods. He launched forward and slid to a stop above the box. He reached down, grabbed the ring, and hauled. It didn't budge. He planted his feet and heaved, heard groaning metal. Still, it didn't move or open.

"If only I had Emil's Strength talent."

North buzzed. "Command Suggestion: Move."

Iro activated his crest and pushed his current into his sword strapped to his back, then completed the circuit and let it flow back into him. Burning Adrenaline ignited in his veins and his current surged around him, surrounding him like blue fire. He hauled on the ring again with both hands, strained, heard the clasps snap. The lid popped open.

Iro saw a flash of silver. He leapt to the side with current enhanced speed as the rods slammed together, crushing the box lid between them.

Iro released Burning Adrenaline. His current was drained but not empty. He could still move. He waited, panting for breath, until the rods separated again, then dashed into the vacated space and thrust his hand down into the box, not waiting to see what was inside. His hand closed around a small object, smooth to the touch, about the size of his outstretched palm. He grabbed it and rolled to the side as the gear slammed together again.

Iro laughed as he sat on the metal floor of the safe zone and stared at the object. It was almost circular except for a small indentation at the top and bottom. Metallic and flat, and had a bulbous glass display in the middle that was dark and blank. He shook the item and faint yellow lines like circuitry lit up along the flat silver metal. When he stopped shaking, the lines faded away.

"Any idea what this is?" Iro said.

North scanned the item. "Device is functioning within normal parameters."

"But what is it?"

North buzzed. "North has no entry in its databanks for the device."

"Eclipse, where are you?" Gadise Samir said over the comms.

Iro pressed the button on his earpiece. "On my way."

The rest of the crossing felt almost easy. Iro had the timing on the rods down and was energised enough that he leapt through them. He was glad to find that all the others had made it unscathed and they were waiting for him at the bottom of the steps. Gadise Samir gave him a curt nod, then turned and mounted the first step.

"Wait," Iro said, holding up his loot. "I found something."

Toshiko gasped. "Is that loot? What does it do? What does it do?"

"I don't know."

Emil crossed his arms and leaned back against the wall, but Gadise Samir turned and strode back. She took the item from Iro and twisted it about in her hands, then gave a rare smile. "It's a Strikebreaker."

Justice crowded forwards and pulled down his goggles over his eyes. He plucked the device from the squad leader's hands and peered at it. His autodage waddled closer and waved its sensor bank. Gadise Samir tapped at her tablet, and Iro's tablet pinged. She'd sent him a file.

"Do you want me to attach it?" Justice asked.

Iro glanced between the Surveyor and Gadise Samir. "What does it do?"

"Strikebreakers create a momentary shield around the Hopper. Only a second or two, and only enough charge to block a single strike, but if timed right it can stop even a deadly blow."

"A shield?" Iro said, crestfallen. "So a Vanguard item. Do you want it?" His first piece of loot and he couldn't even use the scrapping thing.

Gadise Samir shook her head. "It's useless for me. Strikebreakers charge by passive kinetic force. The more the Hopper moves, the faster they charge. It takes a lot of movement to charge one. My passive talent is Bulwark. The longer I spend in one place, the tougher and stronger I become, but the moment I move my feet, it fades in seconds. I'm built to hold, not to move. Whereas you, Eclipse, never stop moving."

Iro grinned. "So it is my loot?"

"You can give it away," the squad leader said.

"No!" Iro grabbed the Strikebreaker from Justice. He shook it again and the faint yellow lines lit up along the metal planes of the device. The display was alive now and read 0.01%.

"Do you want me to attach it?" Justice asked again. "It'll only work if attached to your armor, so choose a piece you're not likely to replace soon."

Iro nodded and chose his right vambrace, the same one his tablet was attached to. He could reach it with his left hand to activate the Strikebreaker once charged. Justice set to work, his little autodage welding the Strikebreaker to Iro's armor. Once it was firmly attached, little wiry filaments wormed out of the device and connected to Iro's tablet. A new option appeared on the screen and when he selected it, it showed the status of the Strikebreaker, both its charge percent and approximate time to full charge based on his current movement. The reading estimated forty-four hours to charge. Iro felt like going for a run to see how fast he could fill it.

They mounted the steps away from the slamming gears and Iro had to stop himself from jogging up them. He was eager to test out his new loot.

CHAPTER 29

THE STAIRCASE LED UP into a chaos of movement and noise and machinery. Toshiko couldn't help the grin spreading across her face. A manufactory! Then the scale of it hit her. A manufactory of proportions she had never dreamed of. It seemed to go on forever, as far as she could see, and all was in constant motion. Huge mechanical arms swung about, some empty, some carrying half-made things, others sporting a thicket of tools. Sparks flew from one as a giant welding torch seared two blocks of metal together. A plume of steam erupted from somewhere further in as molten metal poured into a giant mould. A machine behind them stretched out bundles of cable and wrapped them in conducting filament. The entire manufactory was in operation building... something.

A construct buzzed overhead, floating on the same anti-gravity rings that kept North aloft, only much bigger. The construct was twice the size of a pod, each of the rings as big as Toshiko. It carried what looked a lot like an arm; metal plates interlocking over pistons and cables, a docking port for a claw at the end.

"Is this place building itself?" Toshiko asked.

Gadise Samir coughed, tightened the straps on her shield. "It appears so." She moved to the edge of the platform and peered over the edge.

The stairs had deposited them on a solid metal platform just about large enough for them all to stretch out on. There didn't appear to be any easy way down into the manufactory, and also no clear passage through. The titan hadn't built this manufactory with humans in mind. It was all automated.

"We need to find a way through," Gadise Samir said over the comms. The noise of the place was so loud her voice was lost otherwise. "There should be a way up to the next level somewhere. North, you said it has five levels?"

North buzzed and landed on Iro's shoulder. "No."

The squad leader frowned and advanced on Iro. "What? You said there were five levels."

North scuttled across to Iro's other shoulder. "Outdated information based upon approximate..."

"What?"

North buzzed. "Clarification: The layout of this Spire is not fixed."

Another construct buzzed overhead carrying a rounded metal clump with dozens of cables dangling from the sphere.

"North," Iro said. "Can you scout ahead? Find us a way up."

"No."

Iro sighed. "North. Command order: Scout..."

North buzzed. "North is scared."

Justice turned at that. He'd been standing close to the edge of the platform. "You can't be scared. You're an automaton."

North seemed to shrink as it lowered itself down Iro's back, clinging to his armor. "North is scared."

Iro tried to look over his shoulder at the automaton. "Why are you scared, North?"

The bot buzzed against his back and didn't answer. Iro shrugged. "It's never refused to answer before."

"We're wasting time," Emil said. "We have a Surveyor. Get down there and survey us a way through."

"Uh." Toshiko coughed. "This is a manufactory. Can't we manufacture some things while we're here?" She patted Steel Lotus.

"A new sword," Iro said.

"Some better armor," Emil said.

Gadise Samir shook her head as another construct buzzed overhead. "I don't see any control panels. This place looks automated. Building itself. Or the Spire. I don't know. Building something." She shook her head. "And no monsters. Best we climb as quickly as possible and find the communications array. Justice, find us a way through."

The floor sparked with electricity like an open conduit, so Justice led them a different way. They had to jump up onto a behemothic arm mounting and cling to the base while the arm swung about above them, soldering, cutting, fusing, showering them with sparks. From there it was up and onto a giant printer housing. The case was translucent and Toshiko peered down inside where four separate printing armatures were busy forming a series of designs that looked like pneumatic parts. Constructs buzzed around inside the case, removing the parts whenever they were complete and ferrying them off through a small tunnel set in the case's side.

Emil tapped Toshiko on the shoulder and got her moving again. The rest of the squad had already clambered down onto a bundle of cables each one as big as her waist. All around them the manufactory was fusing, building, printing, forging, moving, constructing. But there were no finished products. The flying constructs that hovered overhead carted all the pieces elsewhere. Something nagged at Toshiko, and she couldn't quite grasp it. The manufactory was building many things, not one thing. The parts were too uniform, constructed en mass.

"Where are the materials coming from?" Iro asked over the comms as he balanced his way along the cables. "In the other manufactory, huge conduits on the floor above transported materials and energy."

"Energy!" Toshiko shouted as it all made sense. A construct buzzed by overhead and she stared after it, then pressed the button on her earpiece. "Energy supplies."

"What are you talking about, Thousand Suns?" Gadise Samir asked.

"This manufactory is building constructs. All these are constituent parts being assembled elsewhere. But any construct needs an internal energy supply. A battery. Just like North."

The little automaton buzzed over the comms. "North has a Radiant Series energy supply unit capable of outputting 50…"

Toshiko spoke over the automaton. "If this place is building constructs, then somewhere it has to be building batteries. That means it also has to be constructing capacitors."

The squad leader stopped up ahead and turned around on the cable. "What does all that mean?"

"It means we need to find where the manufactory is constructing them."

"Why?"

Another construct buzzed by overhead and Toshiko considered leaping for the lower limbs. Maybe if she grabbed hold, it would carry her to where she needed to go. "Um, because energy supply units are invaluable to the fleet?"

Gadise Samir stared at her a moment later, then turned away and leapt up, following Justice onto a narrow walkway that teetered over a titansteel forge. "We're not here to gather supplies for the fleet. We're here to find a way home."

Emil stepped up close behind Toshiko. "What do you need?" he asked, not using the comms.

Toshiko half turned to him, nearly slipped on a cable. He reached out and steadied her with a hand on her arm. "A power supply unit would be nice. I might be able to create some sort of current storage within Steel Lotus' housing that would allow me to charge her, or at least partially charge her, independently of the main battery." She started walking again, picking her way along the cables. "I'd be able... Hopefully, I'd be able to fire her a lot faster, drawing from that separate power supply.

"Titansteel housing would make her sturdier and lighter. You won't believe the cramps I get in my shoulders. And if I could forge the variable barrel parts from titansteel, it would significantly reduce the risk of stress fractures and deformation warping. Printed metal just doesn't have the strength to stand up to repeated current transference. Not to mention the conductivity means that approximately 4.7% of all current transfer is lost into the metal. In comparison, titansteel only loses 2.1% of the current channeled into it."

Emil's mouth hung open.

Toshiko came to the walkway and looked up at a six foot jump to reach it. She glared for a moment and Emil edged around her. He cupped his hands and nodded for her to step up. She did, and he heaved her up without so much as a grunt of effort. She landed on the walkway, clutching at Steel Lotus and stumbled forwards as Emil leapt up nimbly behind her.

"All that sounds nice," the Paladin said. "But what do you need? Right now."

"A capacitor. One that can handle my current so I don't blow out her internals every time I fire her at even half her full potential."

Emil nodded. "I have no idea what that looks like, but we'll find you one. I don't care what the squad leader says. You helped me find parts for the Courage's printer. I'll help you find whatever you need for the cannon."

"Steel Lotus," Toshiko said.

Emil waved her on. "Steel Lotus."

Iro knew they had reached the centre of the manufactory when all the floating constructs converged and flew upwards into a hole in the roof about fifty feet above. There were hundreds of them, flying in from every part of the manufactory, each carrying different parts that the Spire had built. Others flew back down into the manufactory, newly unburdened, where they zipped off to collect more parts.

The squad gathered on a large metal disc that was flat enough they didn't need to balance, but hummed beneath their feet and was warm to the touch. It sat almost directly below the orifice in the ceiling, and they all stood, staring up at it.

"I know it's my job to secure the path forward," Justice said dourly. "Or in this case, upward... But I have no scrapping clue how."

"I know how," Emil said.

Gadise Samir ignored him. "We'll scout around closer to the walls, find an elevator or ladder."

"I could fly up there," Iro said. "Drag one of you with me?" He wasn't sure about that, it was a long way up. He tapped at his tablet. His Strikebreaker only read 4% charge despite their hike through the manufactory.

Emil snorted and shifted over to the edge of the disc shaped platform. He waited a few seconds, then leapt upwards and grabbed hold of a passing construct as it floated overhead. It dipped, shuddered, then righted itself and struggled against the increased weight. Despite its additional burden, it started rising.

"Courage," Gadise Samir snapped over the comms. "Get down here."

Emil clung to the top of the construct as it rose. He stared down at them, pressed the button on his earpiece. "What's that *squad leader*? You're breaking up."

Gadise Samir growled in frustration and leapt up, catching hold of another construct as it started rising. "Eclipse, help the others up," she said over the comms. She stood straight and stared upwards as the construct followed Emil's ride.

Iro moved towards Justice and grabbed him by the back of his lime green armor. Such a lightweight suit, with only a few plates over the vital areas, barely protection at all. "You ready?"

"No!" Justice said. "No, I'm not. And just how are you planning on getting me up there?"

Iro shrugged and grinned at the Surveyor. "I'm going to toss you."

"What?"

"It's easy. Just grab hold when you hit the construct."

"I'm not…"

"And don't let go."

Justice tried to turn, but Iro kept hold of his back plate. A floating construct carrying a long, thin strip of metal drifted into view. "Now." Iro hefted Justice by his armor and threw the man up and into the construct. It was surprisingly easy and he decided then he liked the raw strength his Second Gate gave him.

Justice landed on the back of the construct, slipped and tumbled over the side. He caught hold of the strip of metal the construct was carrying and dangled there.

"Help! Help!"

"Remember," Iro shouted up at him. "Don't let go."

"Will he be alright?" Toshiko asked as she stepped up beside Iro. The little Mage was a lot smaller than Justice, so he wagered she'd be easier to toss. She was also a lot braver than him.

"If his curse is real, he'll be fine. More likely to accidentally kill all of us, I think."

"That's not particularly comforting."

"He'll be fine. He's not as useless as he wants us to believe." Iro grinned at her. "You ready?"

"I don't like being thrown," the Mage said, hugging her cannon. "Can you carry me up there instead?"

Iro's current had recharged enough to allow for a few Blink Strikes. More than that, if he was being honest. It amazed him how quickly his current battery recharged.

"Hold on." Toshiko lurched into him and wrapped her arms around his waist. Iro drew his smaller sword and sliced upwards. The Blink Strike dragged them both upwards far more quickly than he expected. They scrambled onto the top of the construct and it dipped, struggling with both of them as an extra load.

"I'll be right behind you," Iro said. He leapt from the construct down onto the next in line. It wobbled beneath him, but righted itself and started rising.

He rode the construct up and stared down at the manufactory busy forging parts for whatever the Spire was building. If only they could turn the place to their own ends. With a manufactory of this size, they'd arm every Hopper in hours, fix every ship in the fleet within weeks. They could build themselves a new ship. But if Gadise Samir was right, once the Spire had completed its purpose, it would retract back into the titan. But that meant this manufactory would have to go somewhere? Iro wondered if they could find it again afterwards.

The construct rose into the hole in the roof, cutting off the manufactory from view. Iro realised it wasn't sheer metal either side of him. The walls here seemed to be formed of hundreds of bound cables. Thousands of them; tangled, overlapping, wrapping around each other, and glowing with a fierce inner yellow light. Power cables, he realised, carrying so much energy they glowed and generated an intense heat that turned the air to a shimmer.

It felt private with the cables so close, the noise and heat so encompassing. "What are you scared of, North?" He realised they'd only asked the automaton how it was scared, not what terrified it.

North crawled up onto his shoulder and launched into the air, orbiting around his head, rising at the same pace as the construct beneath Iro's feet.

"North does not want to be re-formatted."

"Re-formatted?"

The automaton tilted to one side and buzzed again. "Spire manufactory designated 0F1XGG592 has been assigned re-formatting purposes in preparation for invasion."

"Wait! I still don't understand re-formatting. And what invasion?"

"Re-format. To format again or into an alternate designation. North is currently designated as Command Iro's guide and chronicler. North does not want to be re-formatted."

The construct he was standing on cleared the hole and started floating up into the next chamber. It was a vast cavernous space, filled with hundreds of mechanical arms hanging down from above, the ceiling crawling with looping cables and mechanical housings. Most of the arms were in motion, retrieving parts from massive stacks near the walls, connecting parts together, welding them, assembling. All along the floor there were rows of circular depressions each with a frame in the centre. And on those frames, the mechanical arms were building monsters.

Iro leapt down from the flying construct as it started carting its load towards the stacks at the walls. He joined the rest of the squad on the floor as they stared at the massive assembly operation in awe. Directly before them, not thirty paces away in one of the circular depressions, four mechanical arms busied about building a lithe, four-legged monster. It almost looked like a bhurbeast but much smaller, only as tall as Iro himself. Its head was big and brutish, though the lower jaw had yet to be attached. The mouth was full of hooked teeth on a belt that looked like a chainsaw some of the zero g techs used to tear through damaged hull sections. Iro watched as an armature slotted a titansteel plate in, covering the mouth, then welded in place.

"Four legs will make that thing fast," Justice said in a quiet voice. "That mouth will shred armor. And the claws on its legs, too. It's a hunter. I mean, it's built... designed to hunt."

"Not us, though," Gadise Samir said. "Look."

The mechanical arms finished welding on titansteel plates. Not a complete suit of armor, but Iro suspected it covered the most vital or vulnerable parts. He could still see the pistons of the legs, cables wrapped around them. The main body underneath the armor plating was a flexible construct designed to move with the monster.

"There!" Toshiko said, pointing. One of the mechanical arms had retrieved a cylinder that had an effervescent blue glowing from within. "The power supply."

North buzzed. "A Starlight series energy supply unit."

"That's different from your Radiant series?" Iro asked.

"Affirmative. The Radiant series energy supply unit is designed to be upgradeable to meet the scaling power requirements of many variable constructs."

"Designed by who?" Justice asked.

"ERROR ERROR..."

"Command override," Iro said without thinking. "Forget previous request." North settled down on his shoulder.

The mechanical arm with the power supply slotted the glowing cylinder down through the hunter's back, then retracted. The opening closed, sealing the power supply inside. A new, heavier mechanical arm swung into view and reached down. It clasped the frame at four points, then lifted the frame with the construct still attached. It doubled back on itself, sliding across the roof past cables and other arms. Iro lost track of it amidst all the hustle. A new frame thrust up in the centre of the shallow depression and mechanical arms started retrieving parts to build another hunter. And it was happening all around them. Dozens, maybe hundreds of monsters being assembled at once. But why?

"No one else is going to say it?" Emil asked. "So, is this where the monsters come from? They're built?"

A mechanical arm carried half a hunter's torso overhead. "No," Gadise Samir said. "The monsters we've been fighting weren't machines."

"Except that bhurbeast we killed back at the dome. The one that knitted itself back together like... I don't know. What does that?"

The squad leader shook her head, frowning. "We hunt bhurbeast, eat them. They aren't all mechanical or infested with self-repairing cables."

"We've never seen constructs like this before," Justice said. The Surveyor pulled his goggles down over his eyes, knelt, pressed his hand against the metal floor. His sickly green crest fizzed into light behind him. "The finished constructs are being taken that way, to the far end of this chamber. There's a freight elevator over there, carting hundreds of them at a time up to the next level."

"What's on the next level?" Iro asked.

Justice shook his head. "I don't know. It's mostly empty, I think." He stood, pulled his goggles up. "My Scan talents gives me rough layouts and can track things like heat sources, but I use it to track life signs. Apart from us, there's nothing living in the Spire."

Toshiko took a few steps towards the depression where armatures were fixing the first of the hunter's legs into place. "Let's grab one before it's finished. Take it apart. There has to be some juicy parts I can salvage from one of these hunters."

"No." Gadise Samir grabbed the Mage by her back plate and pulled her away. "No one is going near these things. We don't know what will happen if we impede construction. Justice, lead us to the freight elevator. We'll ride up to the chamber with the next load of constructs. None of you touch anything."

Emil glared at the squad leader, but didn't disobey her. He was getting more and more rebellious though, and Iro wasn't sure how to stop him, or even if he should. He didn't disagree with Emil, and couldn't forget what Gadise Samir had done, ordering them not to save the workers. Rollo had told him not to trust her. She was a Legacy family, an upper shipper. But she was also in charge, the strongest of them all, the most experienced. Iro shook his head and followed Toshiko as she weaved in between the depressions staring as the armatures assembled the constructs before their eyes.

Not all the constructs were of the same design. The hunters looked savage and dangerous, every bit of them a deadly weapon. But there were others, too, some much larger, standing on squat legs, heavily armored. Iro didn't see any weapons on them, but by their sheer size and bulk they would be dangerous. Some of the constructs looked almost human. Like metal skeletons with all the skin removed. He liked those least of all. There was something creepy about titansteel muscle and bone, and the dull red eyes fixed in leering silver skulls.

The freight elevator was crowded with dormant constructs, each one still attached to a metal frame and stacked in rows, on top of each other, packed together. The elevator rumbled, then started inching into the air. The whole squad burst into a run to reach it in time. They all clambered on and balanced on the edge where there was a little space not filled with construct.

Iro peered at the nearest hunter. Its shoulder was about level with his neck, and it was longer than he was tall.

"North, can you scan this thing?"

The automaton swept a beam of light over the hunter. "Threat level: 36."

Emil stepped up beside Iro. "That doesn't sound too bad. We're Second Gaters now. We can handle thirty-six with ease, right?"

North buzzed and floated in front of Emil. "Threat level diagnostic is a scaling algorithm based upon the relative strength of Command Iro."

"Huh?"

"The threat levels have already been adjusted to my opening of my Second Gate?" Iro asked.

"Affirmative."

Emil shook his head. "Mind telling me what the scrap that means?"

Iro shrugged. "It's relative to my strength. Thirty-six will always be dangerous whether I'm First Gate or Fifth Gate. Toshiko, do you remember what North first calculated your threat as?"

Toshiko shrugged. "Thirty... something, I think. I don't know. Higher than Emil." She grinned.

"North, scan Toshiko."

"Threat level: 18."

"What?" Toshiko pouted. "That's not fair. What about Justice?"

"Please don't scan me," Justice whined.

"Threat level: 5."

The Surveyor sighed. "We'll see what you say when you're caught in a trap and begging to be let out."

Iro gave Justice a good natured nudge. "Surely if we're caught in a trap, you've already failed at your job?"

Justice blinked at him twice and sagged. "I hate you."

The elevator rumbled on, the assembly floor disappearing into darkness below. The roof was a madness of shifting mechanical arms and trembling cables. It was a wonder that they didn't all tangle up in each other. Then they were rising through the roof and up into the next chamber.

The elevator bumped to a halt sitting flush with the metal floor and all of them stepped off. This chamber was cavernous and far more dormant than the previous two had been. Occasional spot lights lit the chamber in infrequent intervals, giving it an expansive, chilly air. And as far as Iro could see, lined up in banks and rows, reaching from the floor to the ceiling, thousands of constructs rested dormant in their frames.

CHAPTER 30

THE SQUAD LEADER set off down the line of constructs with a casual, "Nobody touch anything."

Emil watched her go. That was all she ever seemed to say. *Nobody touch anything. Nobody do anything. Nobody save anyone.* Emil had had enough of being told what to do by upper shippers who didn't care a damn about people like him.

He turned to Toshiko as the Mage bit her lip and leaned in close to one of the dangling hunters. "You think this thing has what you need inside of it?"

Toshiko glanced at him and shrugged. "I think so. It has a power source capable of generating—"

"Where?" Emil asked before she could get going. Whenever she and Iro started talking techy, he found himself lost and didn't like having no idea what they were talking about. Reminded him of being a child and his father speaking over him.

Toshiko scratched at her head. "Near the power source, I would imagine. Hard to say without a proper look inside."

"Justice, can you do your scanny thing and look inside this hunter? Like you do when you scout out the titan, but inside a construct?"

"Uhhh…" Justice closed his mouth, frowned. "I have no idea. I don't think anyone has ever tried. If it has a power source, it should generate heat, so theoretically it might be possible."

Toshiko grinned and advanced on the Surveyor. "Want to try?"

Justice shook his head. "Cousin told us not to touch anything." He tucked his hands under his armpits. His autodage scuttled around his arm and dangled from his elbow. He glanced at it. "Quiet."

"You can talk to it?" Emil asked.

"No!" Justice said too quickly.

"I met another Surveyor once. Burning Ember Franka. She could talk to her autodage."

Justice sighed. "Fine. Yes, I can. I choose not to, because the more I engage with him, the more incessant he becomes. It's the first thing Surveyors are taught right after how to construct an autodage. First how to talk to them, and then how to get them to shut up!" he said the last pointedly, poking at his autodage. The bot dangled floppily from his arm.

"Alright," Emil said. "So you might be able to scan this thing?" He waved at the hunter. "Do it."

"Cousin told us…"

"Your scrapping cousin told us to leave a bunch of workers to die," Emil interrupted him. "But you didn't." Emil stalked closer to the hunter, placed a hand against it and gave it a solid shove. It rocked a little in its frame. "Touched. See, nothing happened."

Justice crept closer to the hunter, winced, placed a single finger against it. When nothing happened again, he sighed. His apprehension annoyed Emil, but he swallowed it down. The Surveyor pulled his goggles down and placed his full hand against the hunter. His autodage scuttled down his arm and placed its own appendage against the metal. Justice's sickly green crest lit up behind him.

All the lights in the chamber shut off with a sound like a slamming door. Two seconds later red strip lights flickered to life on the walls and ceiling.

"I knew it," Justice said, backing away from the hunter. "I knew it. I knew it. I knew it. This is how it happens. This is how you all die. And they'll blame me again."

Iro was the first to get back to them, his sword drawn. A few seconds later, the squad leader came thundering down the aisle of hanging constructs. "What happened?" she shouted.

Justice hung his head. "I was..."

Emil stepped in front of him. "I touched a hunter." He might not like Justice, but he wasn't about to let the man get in trouble for something he'd goaded him into.

"After I specifically told you *not* to?" the squad leader roared as she stared down at him.

Emil looked up and met her furious gaze. "That's right."

The squad leader's nostrils flared, her fists clenched. Emil braced for the punch. He couldn't fight a Fourth Gater, but he'd use Retribution and hit her back for one punch. But she didn't hit him. She let out a growl of frustration and turned away. "We need to find a way up. Now. Justice, we need an exit."

Justice knelt and placed a hand on the floor, his crest lighting up again.

Iro edged to the side and peered down the ranks of hanging constructs. "Uh oh! Squad leader, I think we woke them up."

A hunter shook free of its frame and took its first steps, claws scraping metal as it paced along, winding its way through its hanging brethren. Hunting them.

Justice stood, pointed. "That way, I think. It's, um... It's something."

"A way up?" the squad leader asked.

The Surveyor looked unsure. "Yes?"

"Good enough. Go! Courage, take the rear." The squad leader

lurched into a run, sprinting down an aisle of hanging constructs. Justice followed, struggling to keep up as best he could, then Iro, then Toshiko. Emil hung back a few seconds, watched the hunter prowling towards him, then sprinted after them. He wanted to attack, to tear it apart and take the component Toshiko needed, but the others were running and he couldn't hang around.

Up ahead, another hunter crashed into the squad leader. She got her shield up and the construct clawed at the metal, knocking her aside. "Keep running!" She braced, hefted the monster up and over her head and slammed it down on the bulkhead floor. Justice and Toshiko ran past her. The squad leader thumped her fist into the thrashing hunter once, twice, a third time. The construct shrugged off the blows and rolled back to its feet, wheeling around on claws that scored the metal.

Iro stabbed out with his oversized sword, vanished, slammed into the hunter, driving his blade between armor plates and deep into its machinery. It bucked and thrashed, bouncing Iro around as he held onto his blade. Then the hunter turned and darted off, carting Iro away down a row of dormant constructs.

Next to the squad leader, a hunter dropped free of its frame and leapt at her. She went down under its weight, scrabbling to get her shield between herself and its shredding claws. "Get the others out of here," she shouted at Emil, catching his eye for a moment. The hunter's mouth closed around her arm and it bounded away, dragging her along. Emil thundered on, increasing his pace to catch up with Justice and Toshiko. Someone needed to protect the two vulnerable members of the squad.

Emil heard claws skittering on metal behind him, turned and used Steel as a hunter leapt at him. The construct hit and Emil slid backwards, his increased weight bringing them both to a lurching stop. Claws scratched at him, shredding the printing armor on his legs. He held the hunter by its snout, stopping the sawing teeth from closing on him.

His heart thundered in his ears, but he wasn't scared. He was happy. He wanted this. A real fight. He wanted to test himself like he hadn't been able to since opening his Second Gate.

Emil growled and switched talents to Strengthen himself. He twisted and pulled the hunter around, tripped it up, slammed it down onto the metal floor. He switched back to Steel to increase his weight and fell upon the hunter even as it slipped his grip and its teeth closed around his wrist. Grinding pressure clamped down on his arm as its teeth started sawing. If he wasn't Steeled, it would have chewed through his arm in moments, but the teeth only sparked against his hardened skin. It still hurt like his skin and bones were being crushed though. He wrenched his hand out of its mouth in a spray of sparks, punched the monster in its gleaming red eye. Nothing happened. He wasn't strong enough. Emil scrambled over the hunter, away from its scrabbling claws, but kept his weight on it. He switched back to Strength and punched its eye again. The glassy light shattered beneath his strength and his titansteel gauntlet.

The hunter scrambled and flipped back to its feet. It shook its head, electricity sparking from its broken eye. Emil stood to face the monster and stepped left, keeping himself on the broken eye side. If he could keep attacking from its blind spot, it shouldn't be able to get him. Now to see how much damage it took to break one of these things.

The hunter lurched forward, snapped at him. Emil stepped left, punched at the head and sent the construct reeling. The armor plating was a problem. He couldn't penetrate titansteel. The hunter leapt at him again. Another step left, a combo of punches aimed at the damaged eye. The hunter sparked, half collapsed. It was twitching now, the right side of its head half caved in. Claws raked at the ground, and the construct leapt right, then flung itself left, trying to body check Emil. He leapt over the clumsy strike, grabbed its head in his gauntlets and wrenched.

The armor plating came away from its damaged eye with a shower of sparks and a squeal of tested metal. Emil threw the plating away, reached back and punched. His gauntlet burst through the hunter's head in a spray of oil and sparks and machinery. The hunter staggered a couple of steps, its legs twitching and bucking. The construct collapsed, dead.

"Ha!" Emil shouted and thumped his fists together. "Scrap you, junk pile."

To his right, another hunter dropped free from its frame. And then another one.

CHAPTER 31

"ALL SHIPS in the fleet are separated into three core designs," Toshiko quoted from the Fleet Compendium, using the chant to channel current into Steel Lotus. She and Justice were alone, the others either carried off by hunters, or stopped to hold them back.

"Here," Justice said as they reached the sheer wall of the side of the Spire. "I think. This is where the way up to the next level should be."

There was nothing. Only a flat wall, bowing in just slight as it rose high above them. There was an indentation, a square groove cut into the wall, like there should have been an elevator. No way up. No way out.

Toshiko spun around to face the hanging racks of constructs. The red light gave a bloody gleam to the silver titansteel. It was tough to see anything past the ranks of metallic monsters, but Toshiko held Steel Lotus ready and waited. The others were coming. They had to be coming.

A hunter prowled into view, stepping around some of its dormant brethren still hanging in their frames. Its eyes shone a malevolent red and it turned its head, focused on them. Its mouth opened in something like a snarl, and the bladed teeth started to saw on their chain belt.

"The Indictor model is the largest of the three designs," Toshiko chanted, channelling more current into Steel Lotus. The hunter turned towards them, metal claws scraping at the floor. The monster lowered itself, ready to pounce.

Steel Lotus' top barrel started glowing. Toshiko grinned. "Charged to 35%. Ready to fire." The hunter leapt into a loping sprint towards her and she levelled the cannon and pulled the trigger. A blast of white energy seared forth and smashed into the hunter, sending the bot careening backwards. It knocked into another hanging construct, spun about, came to a steaming stop on the floor. Its legs twitched. Then the hunter shifted and righted itself.

"You didn't kill it!" Justice said unhelpfully.

"I noticed that." Toshiko used the words as a chant, already channelling current into Steel Lotus' second barrel, but far too slowly. Unless the hunter decided to sit and wait for a couple of minutes, she'd never get a chance to fire again.

"Why didn't you hit it harder?"

"Because I can't. If I fire Steel Lotus at anything above 50% power, I'll blow out her circuits. That's why I need a better capacitor, so she can handle my current." Toshiko pulled out her little cannon and aimed, already knowing it was useless. If she couldn't channel enough current through Steel Lotus to kill a hunter, there was no chance with the smaller 556.

"Where are the others?" Justice said in a pleading voice.

"They're coming."

"What if they're not? I've killed them. It's my curse all over again. They're dead. You're going to die, too. I'll survive by some stupid fluke because…"

"Shut up, Justice!" Toshiko kicked him in the shin.

The hunter had reached its feet. One back leg was trailing and its mouth hung open at a broken angle. She might not have killed the construct, but she'd done some damage.

"I am not dying here." She used the words as a chant and fired a blast from her little cannon right into the hunter's body.

"I'm too young." Another blast.

"Too stubborn." Another blast.

"And I'm not done upgrading Steel Lotus. So I am not dying here." That last smashed through the hunter's lower jaw and took it clean off. The construct staggered, then righted itself, fixed its bloody gaze on them and limped their way.

Emil launched out from the ranks of hanging constructs and hit the hunter in the body. It staggered, its back leg collapsing. Emil ducked into a roll, reached his feet and sprinted towards Toshiko and Justice. A moment later, another hunter slid into view, clawed feet scrabbling at the metal. It collided with the damaged hunter and they both crashed down. A third hunter leapt over the tangle and snapped at Emil, sawing teeth barely missing his ankle.

"A little help, Toshiko," Emil shouted as he ran.

"Any time you want to find us a way up, Justice," Toshiko said, channelling desperately.

The hunter leapt, took a swipe at Emil. The claw caught his back, hammered him to the ground. Steel Lotus wasn't charged, but she didn't have time. Toshiko aimed and pulled the trigger. It wasn't so much a blast as a flash of energy, but it smacked into the hunter and staggered it just long enough for Emil to get his feet under the torso and kick the monster away. He scrambled upright and crossed the rest of the distance to stand before Toshiko and Justice.

"Way out?" Emil asked. He was bleeding from a cut on his head and a gash on his left arm, but held up his gauntlets ready to defend them all the same.

"Justice is working on it, aren't you?" Toshiko said.

"I... uh... I don't know," Justice said. "This is it. I mean, it should be the way up."

"Useful as always," Emil growled.

The three hunters were back on their feet now. Two were undamaged, prowling towards them. The last was a jerking, sparking wreck. But even a wreck was deadly enough to kill them if it got too close.

"Stay behind me," Emil said. His fiery crest flared to burning light behind him. The hunters spread out to surround them. Toshiko whispered her chant, channeling current into Steel Lotus even though both barrels were still smoking from the last blasts she fired. Any more and she risked damaging the poor cannon.

An icy blue light zipped through the ranks of hanging constructs high above. Iro, his crest a freezing blue mist behind him, North clinging to his shoulder. Iro hung in the air above them for a moment, then sliced downwards with his sword and vanished. He hit the lead hunter like a lightning strike, smashing it to the ground. There was an almighty clang as his blade hit titansteel armor and rebounded. Iro staggered backwards, thrown off balance.

The hunter behind Iro crouched, pounced at him. Emil rushed forwards, barged Iro aside, met the hunter mid leap. Both went down in a shower of sparks as the hunter clawed at Emil's armor and tried to bite through his arm.

The damaged hunter limped past the struggle, back leg trailing sparks. It leapt at Toshiko and she cringed. Justice threw himself in front of her and the hunter smashed into him. It bucked, thrashed, ragged the Surveyor about, claws raking at his armor, slicing the skin beneath. His autodage ran down his arm, leapt onto the construct, wriggled its way down past an armor plate and burrowed into the machine's guts.

Toshiko pulled out her little cannon, aimed. The hunter thrashed about and she couldn't get a shot, too scared of hitting

Justice. The hunter spun them both around and the trailing leg smacked against Toshiko. She stumbled backwards, careening into the square gap in the wall.

Something grabbed her. A force like Iro's Blink Strike. Toshiko couldn't move, couldn't get away. She squeaked in alarm as gravity shifted and flung her upwards at a speed that left her stomach behind.

Emil wrestled with the hunter as it ragged him about. He thumped it with gauntleted fists, tried to get a grip on its armor, all the while keeping his Steel active; the only thing stopping it from tearing him to shreds.

Toshiko screamed. Emil saw her sucked upwards, faster and faster until she vanished through the roof.

"Iro," Emil shouted. "Go after her!"

Iro had his big sword thrust through the body of his own hunter. He pulled out his smaller sword, stabbed it into the constructs mouth. His crest flared and both blades shone with a blazing azure light. The hunter sizzled, sparked, and collapsed in smoking ruin. Iro pulled both swords free in a shower of sparks, and turned to where Toshiko had disappeared.

"I'm on it," the Corsair shouted as he leapt into the square indentation. The same force that had lifted Toshiko grabbed hold of Iro and he was gone, sucked upwards.

Emil struggled, writhed, shoved his hand deeper into the hunter's mouth and grabbed hold of the rasping chain belt with his gauntlet. He shouted in victory as he ripped the belt and all the teeth out of the hunter in a spray of razor sharp metal. The construct reared, tried to fling him away, but Emil held on. He flipped himself on top of it, using his enhanced weight to flatten it the floor. Then he switched to Strength and heaved, tearing the hunter's head from its body in a gout of spilled oil and shards of metal.

Emil was panting, exhausted. His crest was flickering, his current battery almost empty. Still, he staggered back to his feet and raised his fists, ready to save Justice. Only it was too late.

The hunter was ragging Justice back and forth across the floor in stuttering motions. Sparks flew from its damaged leg, its smoking body, its scorched head. It gave one last lurch, throwing Justice's body across the floor. The construct jerked, shuddered, and collapsed sideways with a solid thunk. Justice's little autodagc ripped its way free from the hunter's carcass. It was carrying something long and cylindrical, holding it above itself in victory as it waddled down the construct's body on three stunty little legs. It hopped down to the floor, and scuttled across to Justice's body.

The Surveyor lurched upright with a gasp followed by a succession of ow's and whines. He was bleeding from his head, his arms, his legs, and his chest. His lightweight armor was shredded in a dozen places, and a thick crack ran through one pane of his goggles. But at least he was alive.

The autodage leapt onto Justice's leg, scuttled up onto his arm, and waved its prize at the Surveyor. Justice nodded wearily. "You got it. Well done." The autodage settled down on his shoulder, clutching its prize tightly like a child with their favourite toy.

Emil held out a hand to Justice. The autodage dropped its prize and slapped Emil's palm. Justice stared at Emil's hand like it was another enemy come to savage him, then sighed and grabbed hold. Emil hauled him to his feet and the man made another whine as if all his cuts and scrapes were about to kill him.

"This is why I don't do combat," Justice said in a pitiful voice. "It really hurts."

Emil grunted and scanned the ranks of hanging constructs. The three dead hunters around them sparked and sizzled, but no others had dropped to attack them yet. Despite that, he could hear the sounds of fighting somewhere.

"Where's the squad leader?" Emil asked.

"I haven't seen cousin Gadise since these brutish things started attacking." Justice aimed a kick at the one that almost killed him.

"I'm surprised you care."

Emil glanced at the Surveyor and away. "I'm not leaving anyone behind." Unlike the squad leader, he didn't care what orders he received. He would bring his entire squad home or die trying, even if they were upper ship junk holes who needed a good kicking.

"There!" Justice said, pointing. He was kneeling, had one hand on the floor, his crest glowing behind him.

The squad leader had her feet planted between two rows of hanging constructs. There were three dead hunters, ripped apart, lying at her feet. Two live constructs had her flanked, were darting in trying to take bites. A dirty red haze darkened the air around her. She twisted, not moving her feet, slammed a fist into one hunter, punched straight through its eye, and ripped her fist free bringing a chunk of machinery with it. The hunter stuttered and sparked, dropped. The second construct leapt on her, claws slashing as it tried to use its weight to bring her down. Its mouth closed around the rim of her shield and the whirring clang of its teeth scraping against metal echoed down the chamber. Despite holding up the weight of the construct, the squad leader didn't move her feet. She reached over, grabbed the top of the hunter's head in her hand, then ripped her shield free in a spray of sparks, oil, and electronics. The hunter's head cleaved in two and the construct fell amidst the other four bodies.

The squad leader turned and started walking towards Emil and Justice. The red haze faded away around her. Her passive talent, she said it was called Bulwark, strengthened her and made

315

her tougher the longer she remained in one spot. Emil nodded grudgingly. He could see that would be a useful talent to have.

The top of the hunter's jaw was still clinging to the squad leader's shield, one tooth having dented the titansteel. The squad leader plucked it free and dropped it behind her.

"Report," she said as she reached them. "Justice, are you alright?"

"No," Justice said. "Well, yes. But no."

The squad leader looked at Emil, gave him a curt nod. "Where are Eclipse and Thousand Suns?"

CHAPTER 32

THE GRAVITY CHUTE spat Iro out into syrupy darkness. He hit the ground in a roll and leapt back to his feet, ready for whatever this new chamber had to throw at him. But there was nothing. Nothing but a void so thick he couldn't see his own nose. And someone crying in wild sobs.

Iro fumbled at his vambrace and flicked his flashlight on. North launched from his shoulder and flew off into the chamber. "Toshiko?" He spun in a slow circle, sweeping his beam of light ahead of him. He heard a crackle like sparking electricity.

The light washed over Toshiko curled up around Steel Lotus, her back against the solid bulkhead wall. She looked pale and ghastly in the washed out light of Iro's flashlight. He hurried over to her.

"Toshiko? Are you hurt?"

When he knelt before her, Toshiko's eyes flicked open. She uncurled and launched herself at him, slammed into him and wrapped her arms around him. Iro tensed, unsure what to do. Toshiko sobbed into his armor, hands scrabbling, trying to find purchase.

Iro patted her on the back. "Hey. It's alright. What happened?"

The sobbing quieted to a few strangled gasps and then Toshiko pulled away and scootched back to her cannon. "Sorry." Her face crumpled. "I don't like being alone. Or the dark. And especially being alone in the dark."

"It's alright." Iro took a slow step forward, laid his hand on her shoulder. "Even if you find yourself alone, we'll come find you. You're part of the squad."

Toshiko stared up at him and looked close to bursting into tears again. Then Justice came warbling up the gravity chute and Toshiko turned away, rubbing at her face.

Iro turned and shone his light at the Surveyor as he hit the ground and crawled away making noises like he was about to puke. Iro sometimes forgot that not everyone was used to being pulled around by bizarre gravitational forces. Justice was bloody, but didn't look too badly hurt. Emil was next up the chute, his arms and legs flailing like a bird learning to fly. He hit the floor feet first, stumbled, fell head over arse and sprawled next to Justice. Gadise Samir was last up. She had her arms crossed and stepped out of the gravity chute as if she hadn't been flung upwards at a stomach curdling speed.

"Eclipse, where's Thousand Suns?" Gadise Samir switched on her flashlight, scanning the chamber.

"I'm here." Toshiko rushed forwards with a bounce in her step and smiled a little too forcefully.

Gadise Samir shone her flashlight in Toshiko's face for a few seconds, frowned, then swept it across the chamber. "Courage, on your feet. Guard that gravity chute in case anything follows us."

Emil pressed the button to turn his flashlight on. Nothing happened. He slammed his gauntlet against it and the light flickered on. Then he stalked further into the room, ignoring the squad leader's orders.

"I've got it," Iro said. He backed up a few paces, shone his flashlight at the top of the gravity chute. He rested his sword across his shoulders and waited. If anything came up behind them, he'd chop it in two before it had a chance to attack. He looked at his tablet to check on his Strikebreaker charge. It read 55.21%. Blink Strikes must charge it faster than normal walking or running.

"Hey, Toshiko," Justice said. He staggered to his feet and approached the shaking Mage. "Here. We got this for you." He reached up and grabbed the cylinder. He had to wrestle a little to get the little autodage to let go, then handed it to Toshiko.

Toshiko gasped. "A capacitor!"

"Yup. Dug right out of a live hunter. I hope it helps because it was a pain to retrieve. I almost died, you know."

Toshiko gave him a brief hug, then retreated to the wall and set about working on Steel Lotus.

"I almost died," Justice repeated.

Iro shifted a little and patted Justice on the shoulder.

"This chamber is riddled with spiralling cones like we saw in the nest," Emil said, his voice echoing in the chamber. "Only smaller."

Iro turned. He remembered the cones well, the black lightning crackling around them, the super gaunt clinging to them like it was feeding off them. He also remembered the feeling of unlimited current when one cone was damaged. The disembodied voice had claimed it was a reactor leak.

Iro grabbed Justice and manoeuvred the Surveyor in front of the gravity chute. "Keep watch."

"What if one of those hunters comes up?"

"Just, uh, tear out its capacitor again." Iro strode into the chamber, his flashlight held up to illuminate the first of the cones. It jutted up from the floor, its spiralling design crackling with black lightning. A corresponding cone hung from the ceiling right above it. Now and then, the dark energy would snap between the two cones, and Iro felt the air charge with it.

"You've encountered this before?" Gadise Samir asked, peering at a cone, sweeping her light across it.

"In the nest with the super gaunt," Iro said. "It was, um, feeding off them, I think? The cones there were much larger though."

"And there were fewer of them," Emil said.

"And when we damaged one…"

"When you damaged one."

Iro sighed. "When I damaged one, it felt like the nest filled with… current. Like I filled with current? I couldn't use it all. It was…"

"Like opening a gate," Emil said. "Only the current didn't run dry."

"Exactly!"

Gadise Samir fiddled with the straps of her shield. "Current generators? I've never heard of such a thing."

"We're not lying," Emil snapped.

"I never said you were. But this… We always thought the current came from the titans somehow, but Hoppers generate it themselves. It runs through all of us." She turned, stared at Iro. "You said the gaunts were feeding from one of these generators?"

Iro nodded as everything made sense. "That's why monsters attack us, isn't it? That's why they hunt humans. It's not us they're after. They're hunting current and we generate it. That's why they're drawn to opening gates, too, because it's a massive excess burst of current." He remembered the shadow back in the freight corridor. It had dug its claws into him, was sucking out his current. Feeding on him like the super gaunt on the cones.

Gadise Samir started pacing. "But why?"

"It makes the monsters stronger, too. Only one gaunt was feeding off the cones in the nest. The big one. The super gaunt. All the others were, uh, minions to it, I guess. That's how the monsters grow, by feeding off the current they syphon from the generators."

"Or from us," Emil said. "That super gaunt got so big from the generators. But maybe it started by killing enough Hoppers to dominate all the other gaunts."

"The council needs to know about this," Gadise Samir said, still pacing between the cones. Emil snorted, but the squad leader ignored him and continued. "All the more reason we need to get to the top of this Spire and contact the fleet. Nobody touch any of the generators. Justice, find us a way up."

Iro saw Emil clench his jaw, crack his neck to the side. "Don't..." He was too late.

Emil reached out and wrapped his gauntlet around the top of the nearest cone. Black lightning surged around him and Emil went rigid, his eyes wide, his mouth open. It crackled over him, around him, through him. His eyes lit crimson like fire burning within.

Low white strip lights slammed on in the chamber. On the wall, close to Toshiko, a bank of twelve screens flickered on. The control panel beneath them whirring to life. A monotone voice scratched out of some speakers somewhere.

"ENERGY TRANSFER INTERRUPTED. BEGINNING TRANSFERENCE COUNTDOWN."

Numbers appeared on one screen: 1800.00. They began counting down.

"Scrap!" Gadise Samir launched herself at Emil. His hand was still wrapped around the cone, black lightning crackling all around him. She hit him with her shield, body checked him away from the cone and slammed him up against the nearest wall, his feet held off the ground. "What did I just say, Courage?"

Emil blinked, coming around. Black energy sparked off him and his eyes were still lit with blazing inner fire. He met the squad leader's furious gaze and snarled back, reached up with one hand and wrapped his gauntlet around her arm pinning him to the wall.

Iro hovered nearby, not sure what to do. He didn't think this collision was a good idea, especially not with the timer to… whatever counting down. But he had no idea how to stop them. Emil was acting like an idiot, disobeying every order he could. But he also wasn't sure all the squad leader's orders were worth following.

Emil growled as he twisted Gadise Samir's hand away from his collar. She looked shocked. A Second Gater matching her strength for strength. Then the black lightning stopped sparking from Emil and his eyes dulled, the fire going out. His unreal strength vanished with it and Gadise Samir snapped her hand back, grabbed the rim of his breastplate, lifted him up against the wall again. Emil struggled again, tried to shift her grip. He failed and hung limp. She let him go and he sagged against the wall.

"I am your squad leader, Courage," Gadise Samir said in a voice harder than titansteel. "You *will* listen to me."

Emil shook his head. "No. I will not listen to someone I can't trust."

"What? What is this about, Courage?"

"The dome! You ordered us to let those workers die. Why should we follow you? Why should we listen to you?" He made to push past her, but Gadise Samir shoved him back against the wall.

"I was following orders. You might understand that one day. Sometimes… Sometimes far too often, you don't like or agree with the orders, but you have no choice but to follow them. Because if you don't, people will die."

"You were ordering us to let people die."

"Because those were *my* orders. Because the Hoppers above me, the council, know better than I do. The same way the admirals knew better when they ordered us to leave the Sunset behind on the trip to 02." The Sunset was the first ship that had broken down on the journey between titans. The fleet had left it there, floating out in the black, full of people.

Emil snorted out a bitter laugh. "The Sunset. The workers you ordered us to watch die. You know what they have in common, *squad leader?* Lower ships. I wonder if you'd be in such a rush to follow your orders if it was upper shippers on the line?"

Gadise Samir dropped Emil and stepped back. She didn't answer him.

"That's what I thought." Emil stepped past the squad leader, stalked further into the chamber, but he didn't touch the cones again.

Iro couldn't help but wonder if Emil was right. Gadise Samir, the council, they were ready to sacrifice lower shippers like pieces on a game board. It wasn't right. But she had been following orders, and in the end she chose to disobey those orders.

"Why us?" Iro asked. "Why did you pick us for your squad? Two lower shippers and a mid shipper. You're Legacy family. You could pick your squad from anywhere, any of the upper ships. Why us? I get it before, we were expendable and you needed to test the Black Cloaks to see if they'd appear. But you kept us as your squad. Why?"

Emil stopped, turned to listen.

Gadise Samir wrenched on her shield straps, tightening them hard. "Because you're the future. Even the most powerful Hoppers have a limited lifespan. The dangers of the titans catch up to us all. It's important those of us who are stronger and wiser, teach the younger generations how to fight. How to survive." She turned and met his gaze then. "And no one else wanted you.

"You were going to be left to rot. A lower ship Corsair pretending at being a mid shipper. A Paladin who broke his own class so he couldn't enhance others. A Mage who can only function with an oversized cannon she can barely carry. You were all considered a poor bet. Bad luck. I don't believe in luck. But I believe in you.

"I've seen it in you. The way you fight. The way you work together, protect each other. You three are change. You're growing stronger at a rate most Hoppers couldn't even dream of.

"That's why you're still on my squad. Because you're not expendable. The three of you are progressing differently, but that does not make you poor bets or bad luck. You're the future of the fleet, and I hope to help you prove it."

Justice had drifted closer as she was speaking. "What about me, Cousin?"

Gadise Samir sighed as she looked at him. "You already know no one else wanted you, Justice. They made up this junkpile of a curse and threw the accusation at you so often you started believing it yourself. I told you I don't believe in luck or curses. And every moment this squad stays alive you're proving me right. We're all still alive. You've helped us all stay alive. You'll continue to help us stay alive.

"Now. I am trying to get you all home. It would be a scrap load easier if you would stop fighting me and start helping." She stepped in front of Iro. "What do you say, Eclipse?"

Iro thought about it and found he believed her. Despite Emil's justified anger. Despite Rollo's mistrust. Gadise Samir had their best interests at heart. The orders she had received were scrap, but she hadn't followed them maliciously. "To the top of the Spire," he said.

She clapped him on the arm and turned to Emil. "What about you, Courage?"

Emil didn't look so convinced. He gave her a curt nod and nothing more.

"I've done it!" Toshiko jumped to her feet and twirled on the spot, swinging Steel Lotus around.

"Done what?" Gadise Samir asked.

"I replaced the old capacitor with the new one Justice pulled from the hunter. Hinata is going to shed rust when she hears the modular design worked." Toshiko glanced around at all their blank faces. "It means I can fire Steel Lotus at full power again. Or close to full power, at least."

"You've been holding back?" Gadise Samir asked.

Toshiko nodded. "Didn't want to blow out her circuits again. Not any more. Full power, ish, and ready to fire! Well, not yet. I have to charge her first."

"I don't mean to alarm anyone," Justice said. "But..." He waved towards the screen counting down. It read **TRANSFERENCE IN** 1487:00. They were measured in seconds. Iro calculated they had just under twenty-fire minutes until TRANSFERENCE, whatever that was.

"Find us a way up to the next level, Justice," Gadise Samir said.

Justice pointed to a dark alcove beside the bank of screens. "Staircase looks good to me, Cousin."

Emil watched the others ascend the steps and waited in the chamber with the cones and the black lightning. When he'd touched one, the energy had rushed into him, swelling his current to unbearable depths. He'd felt like he was spilling over, unable to contain the power, like having eaten so much he was bloated and swollen. And he'd been strong. Strong enough to match the squad leader, a Fourth Gater, even if only for a few seconds. He'd used up that swell of current so quickly.

He stared at a cone and watched the lightning lance around the structure. Was it possible to swell his current again and gorge himself until he artificially encountered his Third Gate? When he activated his crest, the third lock was visible, still empty, barring his way forward. He'd only recently opened his Second Gate, but what if he could jump ahead? Emil flexed his hand, inched towards the cone. Memories of the nest flashed before him, the super gaunt. The monster was hideous and bloated, covered in stolen eyes. When the beast rampaged, it had crushed minions underfoot, not caring for their lives. He'd felt that way when the black lightning surged through him. It had made him strong, yes, but in that moment he hadn't cared about the others. He would have fought the squad leader, killed her. If that was the tradeoff for jumping ahead, he didn't want it.

Emil turned from the cone and strode towards the staircase leading up. Something was wedged into the floor ahead of him, in the centre of the chamber. He knelt down to look. A metal gear about the size of his splayed hand set into a small, shaped depression. Conduits like circuitry zigzagged through the floor, leading to the gear from all over the chamber. Every few seconds, a conduit flashed black with lightning as though funnelling the strange energy into the gear. Feeding it.

He reached out and touched the gear with a single finger. Nothing. No rush of energy, no swelling of current. Emil wrapped his fingers around the spokes, heaved. He wasn't sure why, but the gear felt important. It didn't budge. He set his knees, squared his shoulders, tried again. Still, it didn't come free. But like the trap below, gears were meant to rotate. Emil tried again, this time turning the cog. A grinding noise filled the chamber, echoing from the cones. Then the gear popped free in Emil's hand. The conduits running along the floor all went dark, but nothing else happened. The black electricity kept racing around the cones, leaping from the ones on the floor to those on the ceiling. The screens continued counting down to TRANSFERENCE. He'd removed the mysterious gear, and it felt… anticlimactic.

The squad leader's voice sounded over the comms, "Courage, keep up."

Emil stood and stared at the gear in his hands. He considered putting it back. But he couldn't bring himself to. He wasn't even sure why. He slipped the cog under his breastplate, wriggled a bit until it sat comfortably, then hurried up the stairs to the others.

CHAPTER 33

TOSHIKO WADED THROUGH LOW-HANGING FOG. This mist clung to the floor of the chamber, seeped in through her armor, sapped the warmth from the room and made her shiver. She hefted Steel Lotus a little higher on her shoulder and hugged herself, trying to warm up.

The chambers were getting smaller. They were still large, this one could have fit a few thousand people in with space to spare, but they were shrinking with every level up and at a rate she didn't think was equal to the outer size of the Spire. She had a suspicion the walls were getting thicker almost as though the tip of the spire was reinforced.

Apart from the fog shrouding the floor from the knee down, this chamber was mostly empty. There were screens all over the walls, each one displaying the countdown to TRANSFERENCE. But most notable was the immense sphere of what appeared to be solid metal hovering in the centre of the chamber. It was spinning slowly and the same black lightning from before was lancing up from the floor into the metal mass. A heat shimmer surrounded the sphere, which Toshiko guessed explained the fog. The sphere was generating a massive amount of heat, and the titan was pumping cold air into the room to keep it from burning up.

Emil reached the top of the stairs, paused, staring at the sphere. Toshiko waited for him to gawk for a few moments. She'd been waiting for him, but saw no sense in trying to steal attention away from the sphere. Emil blinked a few times, glanced at her, nodded and stalked on. Toshiko fell in beside him.

Toshiko tried to think of a tactful way into the conversation, came up blank. "Sorry. About, um…" She sighed. "I hope no one you know died in the dome. And I'm sorry if anyone did."

Emil crossed his arms. He looked angry, but he always looked angry. Toshiko remembered when she had first been told she was going to get to meet him, the Paladin who changed everything, who had done things differently, broken his own class to enhance himself. She'd been so excited to meet the Hopper who had made it possible for her to do things differently too. He'd never quite lived up to the image she'd made of him in her head. She'd just never expected him to be so standoffish.

"Does it matter?" Emil said. "If I knew the people who died or not. People still died in the dome. Talentless workers as well as Hoppers because the Council of Grands decided to experiment with their lives. To see if they could force new Hoppers to manifest. Scrapping fools! Callous idiots!"

He was so angry all the time. But Toshiko thought he had every right to rage over this. She should be furious, too. "You're right," she said with a firm nod of her head. "Scrap them, stupid junkers. But I'm still sorry."

Emil's scowl softened a little. "Thanks. So what is this thing?"

"It appears to be a big floaty sphere."

He glanced down at her and shook his head. "Thought you knew about techy stuff?"

"If I could shove it into Steel Lotus to increase her power

output, I would be right next to Justice running tests. But it's a bit big. And I have no idea what it does. Pretty though."

"New capacitor is working out though, yeah?"

Toshiko grinned. "I hope so. Can't wait to fire a few shots. So, you know, feel free to start a fight with something."

Emil opened his mouth to reply.

"Something other than the squad leader."

He shut his mouth again.

"Thanks."

Emil shrugged. "Justice ripped the part out of the hunter. Or at least his autodage did. He might not be as useless as he seems. I've never seen a Surveyor be anything but a burden, but he killed that hunter even as the scrapping thing was tearing him to shreds. Impressive."

"That was a compliment. You complimented an upper shipper."

"Credit where it's due," he said. Toshiko glanced up to find Emil staring at Gadise Samir. "She killed at least five hunters all on her own. Just planted her feet and tore them apart, surrounded by a red haze. Her unique talent."

Toshiko shook her head. "You mean her passive talent. Gadise Samir's unique talent is taking one for the team."

Emil looked down at her, an eyebrow raised.

"Literally. She can take a hit for another Hopper. She takes all the damage, and the other Hopper won't even feel the hit. It's pretty much the most Vanguard talent I've ever heard of."

"How do you know that?"

"I did my research," Toshiko said. "On all of you. The moment I heard who my squad was going to be I read everything about all of you. Gadise Samir is a legend. They tell stories about her on my ship right alongside the Silver Blade. She was at the first landing on 02. I saw a video. She held back that giant fire-breathing monster long enough for everyone else to escape."

Over by the sphere, Justice took a small step closer. He was staring at his vambrace mounted tablet, tapping at the screen. His little autodage clung to his shoulder and was leaning forward waving its little sensor array at the sphere. North floated nearby, drifting closer, then backing up. Justice shuffled back a step and reached into a pocket, pulling out a bit of lint. He held it up, then let go. The lint zipped towards the sphere and burnt up in a flash of fire. Justice tapped at his tablet again, then mumbled something to North.

"North agrees," the automaton said.

"Cousin," Justice said. "We need to leave. Now."

Gadise Samir stalked over from the side of the room where she had been poking at a console. "What is it, Justice?"

"The sphere is speeding up. Quickly." The Surveyor glanced at the closest screen that showed the countdown to TRANSFERENCE. "I believe it has something to do with... whatever that is."

"Explain."

Justice sighed as the squad gathered around. "Oh wonderful, an audience. The sphere is some sort of gravitational funnel. It's spinning. I know it looks like it's spinning slowly, but it's not. That thing is spinning very VERY fast. And getting faster. It's already creating its own gravitational pull and that pull is getting stronger. DO NOT TOUCH IT!" That last he snapped at Emil who started reaching a hand towards the sphere.

Justice stepped in front of Emil and tried to push the Paladin away. He might as well have tried to push a steel wall. Emil stared at him looking unimpressed.

"I don't mean don't touch the sphere because it might give you a jolt like those cones below. I mean don't touch the scrapping sphere because it will snatch you up and separate you into your constituent parts."

"Huh?"

"It will kill you. Violently and instantly. You really don't understand how fast that thing is already spinning."

Toshiko peered at the sphere. It was solid, uniform metal, silvery in color and unblemished. It looked to be spinning lazily on a jaunty axis. A slight wobbly heat haze surrounding it, and the fog at their feet was spinning, twisting, being drawn into the sphere.

"Alright. Nobody touch the sphere," Gadise Samir said.

"That's what I've been saying!" Justice complained.

"What is it, Justice?"

"I don't know. But it's speeding up and in line with the countdown to TRANSFERENCE. By the time the counter reaches zero, this sphere will be spinning so fast that we might as well be standing before a black hole. Everything in this chamber will be sucked into it. Scrap, for all I know the whole Spire might be sucked into the scrapping thing. Its gravity will outstrip the artificial gravity on the titan by a degrading factor of..."

Gadise Samir sighed. "Theories?"

Justice blinked a few times and blew out his lips. "The titan is trying to warp space-time?"

"Why?"

"Because it's a giant scrapping ship and it can? I don't know, Cousin. I'm just running the math and telling you if we stay here, we will all die."

"You said a degrading factor?" Iro asked. "So assuming the current rate of speed increase and that when the countdown reaches zero, it will be terminal velocity. What's our safe distance?"

"Command Correction: You mean maximum rotational velocity." North drifted closer to the sphere and had to fly away again. "Terminal velocity is the constant speed that a freely falling object will reach when the resistance of the medium through which it is falling prevents further acceleration."

Iro frowned at the bot. "Thanks."

North buzzed.

Justice tapped at his tablet. "Based upon standard human gravitational tolerance. We need to be two-hundred-and-thirty-four meters away or we'll all be paste."

"Calculating... North agrees."

"Can we stop it?" Gadise Samir asked.

Toshiko stepped forward, finally with something to add. "I can blast it."

"No! No. No. No. No." Justice waved his hands in the air. "Cousin, do not let her shoot the sphere." He wagged a finger at Toshiko. "No!"

"I'm hearing a lot of yes," she teased.

He glared at her a moment longer then turned to the squad leader. "If she blows the sphere up, I see one of two outcomes. Either her lunatic plan works and she shuts down the whole thing, or it will explode and take us, the Spire, possibly the titan, and maybe the whole universe with it."

Toshiko's eyes widened and she took a step back, found Emil next to her. "That'd be an accolade for sure. Destroy the entire universe."

Toshiko chuckled. "Nobody could ever top it." The very idea that such a thing was possible terrified her. She decided Justice had to be exaggerating. Not that she was going to test that theory.

"What are the odds?" Gadise Samir asked.

"Does it matter?" Justice said exasperated. "Even if it's infinitesimally small, the barest chance that she could destroy the titan should rule it out."

"Alright," the squad leader said. "We keep climbing. Justice, find us another way up. We reach the top, access the comms array, and shut this sphere down before it does whatever it's designed to do. And before it crushes us all."

Justice already had his cracked goggles over his eyes and his hand on the floor. His crest flickered into light behind him. The fog streamed past him on all sides, moving faster now. "Urgh, I think the gravity is interfering with my scan. This way." He stood and set off. "And cousin, the gravity is going to steadily increase unless we turn this thing off."

Toshiko glanced at the nearest screen. The countdown timer read: TRANSFERENCE 512:00. They had less than ten minutes.

CHAPTER 34

AT FIRST IRO thought he was imagining it, but as they climbed the staircase, every step was a little tougher, like each one was bigger than the last. North was buzzing more loudly than normal and halfway up the staircase, the little automaton gave up and landed on Iro's shoulder. It felt like a bhurbeast had perched there. They climbed through it, Gadise Samir leading the way.

The walls were closing in. Some were spotted with rust, others had dents or gouges. Their only light was from their flashlights.

They emerged from the winding staircase into the final chamber, the pinnacle of the Spire. It was large enough Iro could have run laps around it and counted it a good workout. It rose into darkness, but above, the walls leaned in as the Spire rose to its eventual spear. The walls had strange coils embedded into them, running from the floor all the way up. There were also banks of screens around the walls. Most displayed the same countdown: TRANSFERENCE 489:00. But one had TARGET: COLLUSSUS on the display.

In the centre of the chamber was a huge circular metal platform with four pillars arrayed around it. A control panel sat in front of the platform, and in front of the control panel was a massive chunk of metal, tubes, wiring, and pistons standing at least thirty feet high.

Gadise Samir took only a few moments to stare at the grandeur of the final chamber, then turned to the rest of the squad. "Justice, stop the sphere. North, where is this comms array?"

The construct launched awkwardly from Iro's shoulder, its rings buzzing to keep it aloft. "North will interface with the array." The automaton hovered towards the screen bank with TARGET: COLLUSSUS on the display.

"Justice," the squad leader said. "The sphere. Now."

Justice slumped and started trudging towards the metal platform in the centre of the room. "Sure sure. The easy job."

"Bout time you earned your spot, Surveyor," Emil said, but the Paladin was grinning and went with Justice.

"What about us?" Iro asked. But Toshiko had already wandered away, dragging her feet a little with each step against the increasing gravity.

"Be ready for anything, Eclipse."

Iro hurried after Toshiko. She had stopped before the giant chunk of metal and wiring, was staring up at it. A pit of worry formed in his gut.

"Is it just me," he said as he reached Toshiko. "Or does this thing look a bit like a giant hunter?"

Toshiko turned to him, her eyes alight. "Think of the parts I could strip from it."

"Alright," Justice shouted. "There's a menu system on this console for this TRANSFERENCE thing. Assuming the sphere is tied into whatever that is I might be able…"

"Just do it, Justice," Gadise Samir shouted back.

North's tinny voice sounded over the squad comms. "Communications array accessed. Patching it in to squad comms. Any message sent will be a general communication."

"What does that mean?" the squad leader asked.

Iro knew what it meant. "It means the other fleet will hear us, too."

"Scrap!" Gadise Samir said. "Do it, North. Patch me in."

North buzzed over the comms. "You have access."

The giant hunk of metal and wires shifted. Toshiko gasped in awe, but Iro grabbed her by the arm and pulled her away. In a series of clunking, jerky motions, the massive construct started unfolding. Behind it, Emil grabbed Justice and all but carried him away from the console. The construct snapped forward onto six legs, each one big enough to crush any of the Hoppers. Its torso was an armoured mass of overlapping plates topped with a sensor array that shone with red lights like malevolent eyes. Four prehensile arms unfurled from behind it. One arm had a claw, another a blade twice as long as Iro was tall. The final two arms had barrels, one huge like Steel Lotus, and the other a series of smaller barrels arranged in a circle. A spherical grid of yellow lines flashed around the construct.

Iro pulled Toshiko back behind the squad leader. Gadise Samir held her shield up and waited. Emil and Justice reached them at a run just as the construct whirred to life again and took a thundering step forward. Its red eyes flashed and beams of light scanned the chamber.

"INTRUDERS DETECTED. INTITIATING FIRST STRIKE PROTOCAL."

Justice paled. "That doesn't sound…"

The series of smaller barrels started spinning, rotating. A moment later, they unleashed the construct's fire. Gadise Samir screamed in pain, fell to one knee, raised her shield. All around the squad, solid projectiles were ricocheting off the metal floor, sparking. The squad leader's crest flared bright in front of her and the shots impacted against the barrier, metal pellets dropping to the ground once robbed of their force.

Justice hurried forward to the squad leader's side. "You're hit."

Gadise Samir was bleeding from where two of the bullets had ripped through her thigh. Justice and his autodage went to work, searing the wounds closed.

"Just patch me up," Gadise Samir growled. A red haze rose around her. "Listen to me, all of you. My passive talent is Bulwark. I can hold here, but unless that construct comes close there's nothing I can do. Thousand Suns, time to put that new upgrade to the test. Full power!"

"Yes!" Toshiko jumped up and activated her pink crest, already chanting to channel her current.

"Courage, Eclipse, get out there and distract it. Do as much as damage as you can, but do not die! We hold until Thousand Suns can hit it with everything she has."

Iro glanced at Emil. The Paladin looked back, grinned. "Bet I kill it before then."

Iro scoffed. "Not if I kill it first."

"This is teamwork," Gadise Samir said, the red haze thick around her. "Not a competition."

Emil shrugged. "Why can't it be both?"

Iro nodded. "I'm good with both."

"Hey, Iro," Toshiko said. She pointed at the arm with the multiple barrels still raining metal down on them. "That weapon. Steel Lotus wants it. Fetch!"

Emil activated his crest and launched himself out of the cover of the squad leader's barrier. A bullet pinged off his Steeled skin and he stumbled, but ran on. Iro poured his current into his Blink Strikes, slashed left, right, left again, cutting an icy blue zig-zag across the chamber towards the construct. He slid to a stop before its front feet, slashed upwards, activating Light Blade to give his sword a cutting edge as the Blink Strike dragged him towards the arm with the rotating cannon. Yellow lines lit up around the construct, and his sword rebounded from them. Iro fell away and the sword arm of the construct slashed out at him, fast as lightning. He brought his own blade to block and the force of the attack flung him away. The ground hit him far harder than normal, the increased gravity dragging him down. The arm with the single huge barrel swung his way, glowed. Iro Blink Striked to the side just as a beam of white light shot out and scored molten lines across the metal floor, chasing him.

Emil reached the foot of the construct, smashed into the light barrier. His crest flared again and his arms swelled. He unleashed a combo of punches against the barrier, each one rebounding in a shower of fading sparks. The sword arm raising for a downward stab. Iro thrust, Blink Striking next to Emil, grabbed the Paladin and tugged him away just as the construct's sword stabbed down, cutting into the metal floor. Emil recovered, rushed forward, punched the flat of the construct's sword. The blade shuddered and the construct stumbled, its six legs stamping to find new purchase.

Iro slashed out with his Light Blade, the strike rebounding against the barrier again. He swept to the side, using three quick Blink Strikes to get behind the construct, stabbed out into its blind spot. Still, the barrier flared yellow and repelled his attack in a plume of sparks.

Gadise Samir's voice came over the comms. "I know that type of shield. Just like a Vanguard's. Energy barriers have damage thresholds. You either need to hit it hard enough in one strike, or keep up a constant barrage to overload it."

Iro glanced at the countdown timer. It was down to 276:00. That explained the gravity pulling down on him, making him twice as heavy as normal. He considered turbo-boosting himself Burning Adrenaline, but unless he could finish the construct in one strike, it was too dangerous. They needed to bring down the barrier first.

Iro unleashed a flurry of Blink Strikes, each one a sideways slash trailing sparks across the barrier. The claw arm flipped around, grabbed for him, but Iro sliced away from it, striking the barrier again and again. A chime sounded from his tablet and he glanced down. His Strikebreaker was charged and ready for use.

On the other side of the giant construct, Emil thumped the barrier over and over, dodging away as the sword arm stabbed at him. They were too close for the cannons, but the construct kept up a constant barrage on the rest of the squad, riddling Gadise Samir with bullets and energy blasts. The red haze around her was so thick it seemed an impenetrable cloud. The gravity kept increasing its pull dragging Iro down, slowing his every movement.

"Iro," Emil said over comms. "I need a boost."

Iro slashed upwards, sailing over the top of the construct, his sword trailing sparks along its barrier. He fell to the ground the other side, next to Emil. The gravity was so strong he stumbled and crashed down onto one knee.

"Up," Emil growled through gritted teeth. The sword arm stabbed down again and he lurched to the side, punched out and sent it off course.

Iro swung his sword hilt up onto his shoulder, the point trailing on the ground behind him. He'd seen Bjorn and Torben pull off the trick once, and neither of them had opened a gate. Emil stepped onto the sword, and Iro pulled on the handle, pivoting it on his shoulder and flinging Emil upwards. The Paladin leapt at the same time and surged into the air despite the sucking gravity. He landed on top of the energy barrier and it flared to yellow incandescence, sparking with his every step. Emil punched down at it over and over.

The sword arm lifted. Iro leapt at it, sliced his own blade against it, knocking it aside. A huge metal foot flashed out of the barrier and stomped down at him. Iro didn't have time to run or

Blink Strike away. He slapped his hand against his tablet and activated his Strikebreaker. Golden lines of energy wove around him in an instant, forming a circular barrier of light. The construct's foot slammed down on the barrier and rebounded, staggering the bot. The golden barrier shattered around Iro, the single strike deflected.

"Ha!" Iro shouted. "It worked. The Strikebreaker worked." He glanced at his tablet and saw the Strikebreaker's charge was back to 0%.

The squad leader's voice came over the comms. "Stop celebrating and hit it while it's staggered, Eclipse."

Too late. The construct regained its footing and sighted on Iro. The rotating cannon arm swivelled and unleashed a barrage of bullets. Iro spun his sword about, used it as a shield, threw his shoulder against it. Bullets pinged off it, blew chips off his armor, sparked off the floor all around. Pain screamed to life in his ankle. Iro dropped to one knee, hot blood leaking into his boot. But he couldn't move, not while it focused the cannon on him.

The barrier gave one last flash around the construct and vanished. Emil dropped a couple of feet onto its torso. The claw arm swung for him and he met it with Strength enhanced gauntlets, wrestling with it.

A sound like a struck gong sounded from the squad leader and Iro couldn't help but turn his head to stare, his attention stolen by her Taunt. The construct's aim drifted away from him. The bullets tore in Gadise Samir's shield and she shouted something.

Iro didn't know how long he had before the barrier recharged itself. He might only have one try, so he needed to make it count. He flared Burning Adrenaline and blue light surrounded him, bleeding from his skin. He poured boosted current into both his Light Blade and Blink Strike, and slashed upwards. The metal floor burst apart behind him as he launched off and he completed his strike above the construct. He spun his sword about even as gravity took hold, then used another Blink Strike straight down. Iro hit the ground, his knees buckling, the metal flooring denting from the impact. The rotating cannon arm hit the ground a second later, sheared straight through by his Light Blade. Iro turned off Burning Adrenaline and staggered. He'd used so much current in a single second.

The countdown read 150:00. They had less than three minutes.

"Almost ready," Toshiko said over the comms. "I need to know where to hit it."

"Justice," Emil said, his voice strained as he wrestled with the claw arm. "Scan it like you did the hunter."

The sword arm flashed out and Iro blocked with his own sword. The strike knocked him back and he slid across the floor. He could barely stand, the gravity was so strong. But the construct seemed slower than before. Without the barrier up, the crushing gravity was affecting it, too.

Justice broke the cover of Gadise Samir's Bulwark and staggered towards the hulking construct. It swung its main cannon arm towards him, but Emil slipped away from the claw and brought both hands down in a slam against its sensor array. The construct reeled and the cannon blast swung wide, scoring molten lines just a few meters away from Justice.

"Mess—ssaggggee ssss—eentttt," North said, its voice slurring, stuttering, more tinny than ever. Iro saw his automaton try to fly away from the comms array. It crashed down to the ground. Sparks flew from its chassis and at least one of its rings crumpled from the gravity. "Co—ooooooorrrdiiinaaaattteeeesss giiiii—vvvnnnn." With one last spark and fizz, North fell silent and its lights blinked out.

Justice reached the construct, his goggles already over his eyes, his hand outstretched. The construct whirred, its front foot twitching, sparking like it was trying to move. Nothing happened. It thrust its sword arm at the Surveyor. Iro threw himself in the way, met blade with blade, knocked the strike into the floor. Broken lights and scraps of metal fell from above as Emil ripped a section of the construct's sensor array apart. It slammed its claw arm into him and the Paladin fell, hit the ground hard as gravity tugged him down so fast.

"Got it," Justice shouted over the comms. He fell to his knees, couldn't stand back up. "Sending... you the target." He ripped his hand from the floor, tapped at his tablet a few times. "That's... the power... source unit." He collapsed face down on the bulkhead floor, whining and unable to move.

"Out of the way," Gadise Samir said over the comms.

Iro grabbed Justice. Lifting one of his arms felt like he was holding up the titan, but he dragged the Surveyor up and slipped under his arm. Then Emil was there on the other side of Justice. They staggered away from the groaning construct.

"Get back behind me." Even the squad leader sounded strained to breaking.

Iro glanced sideways at the countdown timer. They were down to 88 seconds.

Steel Lotus' barrel was glowing like a star by the time Iro and Emil carrying Justice reached them.

"Charged at 77% of maximum. Ready to fire," Toshiko said, her voice a tight squeak.

"Do it, Thousand Suns!"

Toshiko glanced down at the schematic Justice had sent her, took careful aim, and pulled the trigger. White light spilled from the cannon, then burst out with a roar like thruster fire. The construct rocked backwards, enveloped by the light. Iro fell to his knees, dropped Justice, flailed a hand in front of his eyes to shield himself from the light. Something exploded. The construct screamed the cry of warping metal.

Then it was over. The light faded away. Toshiko collapsed,

slumped forward over Steel Lotus, groaned something about not being able to move.

"Scrap!" Gadise Samir shouted. "What'll it take?"

Iro blinked away the blinding stars in his eyes to see the construct still just about upright. It slumped to one side, two of its legs broken ruins. The sword arm was gone, reduced to molten slag. A hole had been torn through its torso, metal burned away. Through that hole, in the centre of its chassis, was a pulsing blue light. Its power supply unit. Toshiko had torn away its armor, opened up its chassis, but her current had run out before she had felled the bot.

The timer was down to 42 seconds. The construct sparked, stuttered, whirred. It twisted its last cannon arm around and took aim. The barrel glowed white to rival Toshiko's blast.

Iro slid around on his knees, raised his sword and pushed his current into one more Blink Strike. He lurched forwards, the clumsiest strike since his first day training, and swung. The gravity pulled him down and his hands slipped from his sword hilt just as he used the Blink Strike. The sword vanished, reappeared thrusting straight into the construct's power supply. Iro hit the ground and couldn't move. He barely had time to register what he had done. He'd thrown the sword with a Blink Strike.

"Brace yourselves," Gadise Samir shouted. A sphere of sparking yellow lights surrounded them as she threw up a barrier.

The construct exploded. Fire roared past them on all sides, scoring along the Vanguard's barrier. Bits of metal and other debris rained around them. For long seconds everything was noise and flames and the crushing weight of gravity.

The flames burned away, leaving little patches of scorching fire. The bits of construct stopped raining down around them. Iro struggled to breathe. The gravity was too strong, even forcing air into his lungs was almost impossible. Toshiko and Justice were both down, not moving. Emil was on his knees, his hands locked inside his gauntlets and weighted to the floor. Only the squad leader was still upright, but even she was struggling, trembling. The Vanguard barrier shattered around them, yellow lights fizzing out.

"Have to…" Gadise Samir said as she dragged a single foot forward. "Stop… sphere…" She managed one more step and then collapsed to her hands and knees.

The timer was down to 19 seconds and running. The whole chamber was buzzing, the coils embedded into the walls started glowing an angry neon pink.

"Eclipse… stop… timer…" Gadise Samir gasped out her last breath, collapsed entirely.

Iro thrust the last of his current into all his talents at once. He used Light Blade to forge a burning sword in his hands. He used Burning Adrenaline to overcharge his body, to give him the strength to stand. And he used a Blink Strike to cross the distance, through the wreckage of the construct, to the console.

Blue light shone from his eyes, but not from his skin as he held all the current inside. The Light Blade was a burning brand in his hands, but Iro kept hold of it. He needed a sword to keep Burning Adrenaline active, and it was the only thing keeping him upright. He slumped against the console and stared down at the screen, trying to make sense of it. The screen was cracked, the console was sizzling, sparking. The timer was down to 8 seconds. Iro saw a menu selection on the screen for TRANSFERENCE. He pressed it, hoping there was a way to cancel it. Nothing happened. He pressed it again and again. Still nothing. The console was too damaged from the construct's explosion. He'd failed.

Iro stared at the timer as it ran down. 3. 2. 1.

White noise roared into the chamber. The pillars around the metal platform lit up with an impossible black light. The coils in the walls glowed bright as starlight. And the crushing pull of gravity stopped.

All gravity stopped.

Iro felt light as air. His feet lifted from the floor and he floated, spinning. He made a clutch for the console, but it was too late, it slipped away from him. He spun about in the air and saw the rest of the squad lifting off as gravity released its hold on them all. Gadise Samir grabbed hold of a melted section of the bulkhead floor, anchored herself to it and grabbed Justice too. Toshiko gasped and her eyes flicked open, she stared about in panic as she floated towards Iro. Emil floundered about as though he were trying to swim.

Pain lanced through Iro's palms and he realised he was still holding his Light Blade. He still had Burning Adrenaline active, the boosted strength coursing through his limbs. But it shouldn't be possible. His current should have run out by now. His arms trembled, his stomach lurched. He looked inside for his current and it felt like a dark stain was spreading through it. He recognised it right away. Current sickness. Just like the time he'd spent too long in the Power Acceleration Chamber. He let his Light Blade go, turned off Burning Adrenaline. The light shining from his eyes vanished. His limbs went weak and wobbly, even in the zero gravity.

Toshiko laughed as she floated towards him. She reached out and Iro met her with trembling hands. They clutched at each other, spinning in the air.

Then gravity slammed them both back to the ground.

CHAPTER 35

EMIL'S SPINE popped as gravity reasserted itself. Not the crushing gravity of before, but titan-normal gravity. Iro and Toshiko crashed down to the ground with strangled cries. Behind Emil, Justice groaned.

"Heads up," Gadise Samir said. She struggled to get back to her feet and her wounded leg collapsed beneath her.

On the circular metal platform, stood three new figures. A Hopper with dark brown skin and a mop of curly black hair, in battered tan armor, much of it already shredded, the black weave beneath also torn and bloody. The other two newcomers were Vhar, both standing well over a head taller than the Hopper, each with four arms and wielding wicked curved blades.

The two Vhar staggered. The new Hopper stumbled like a drunk, but lifted his head and aimed towards the squad.

"Oh fantastic, I made it," he slurred a little, blinking. "A little help, if you please." He lurched forward into a run and sprinted past Iro and Toshiko even as they helped each other to their feet.

The Vhar recovered next. They snapped a few brutish words to each other. Then they screamed, shimmered and vanished, reappearing at the far sides of the chamber. They screamed again, and both Iro and Toshiko staggered from the impact of the noise. The Vhar shimmered and vanished, reappeared behind Iro and Toshiko, curved blades already swinging. Too late to stop them. If Emil had been a real Paladin, he could have enhanced one of them, but he was broken. He raised a hand impotently and watched his friends die.

The Vhar froze, both leaping in perfect unison, blades mere inches from Iro and Toshiko's backs. The new Hopper froze as well, running from the Vhar towards the rest of the squad. Emil spun around and found Justice and the squad leader frozen, their faces and armor gray. The gate! His Third Gate. It had manifested right when he needed it most.

Emil spun around. There were two gates again. One behind Iro, between him and the Vhar. The other behind Toshiko. A sour curdling bubbled in Emil's gut and he rushed towards them, already dreading what he might see. Color drained into the chamber. So fast. He had maybe thirty seconds to figure out the puzzle.

The gates were identical, a mesmerising swirl of an arch that reminded him of the cones below. There were even carved bolts of lightning running along the swirls. And at the top of each gate, a single word stood proudly in that same language he didn't know yet understood. It read SACRIFICE.

"No." The word fell flat in that frozen space. Emil looked from Iro to Toshiko and back again. Neither of them had any idea what was about to happen. They held to each other, helping each other stand. The Vhar reared up behind them, already attacking. Iro didn't have a sword, had no chance of Blink Striking away. Their armor was printed ship steel, too weak to hold up against a determined attack from a Vhar. Iro's face was frozen in surprise, just registering the Vhar behind Toshiko. Toshiko was caught in a half blink and looked gormless. They were going to die. One of them was going to die.

The color rushed down the chamber walls now, time running

out. Emil glanced around, hoping for something to help. Two gates, but no one else was unfrozen. They were both his gates, both embossed with his crest on the metal door. The squad leader was too far away, her leg injured. She couldn't make it in time. Justice couldn't help even if he was unfrozen. The new Hopper fled without a backwards glance.

Emil pushed at Iro, but the Corsair didn't budge. Just like always, everyone was locked in place. Emil tried to drag Toshiko out of the way just in case. Nothing. The color was most of the way down the wall now.

Emil crossed to the gate behind Iro, placed his hand against the arch. The metal door swung open at his touch. The Vhar snarled through that open arch. He could step through, use Steel, block the Vhar, save Iro. But Toshiko would die. He crossed to the Mage, opened the gate behind her with a touch and saw the other Vhar, blades swinging. The color had reached it now, lighting its distended, snarling face with a savage motley of browny blues. Emil could save Toshiko, trust that Iro would survive somehow. But an unprotected strike to the back like that would kill him.

He ducked underneath his friends' arms, their hands gripping each other. He had to choose who to save. Who to sacrifice. Emil had to choose which of his friends died. Because there was no alternative.

Unless... He had one other choice.

"Scrap you!" Emil snarled, staring at his gates. The color was most of the way down them now. The silver swirls, the black lighting. His gates were trying to make him choose between his friends. Well, he wouldn't. He'd take the only other option open to him.

Emil stood between Iro and Toshiko and took hold of their hands. They couldn't feel it, but he gave them both a squeeze. Color finished draining into the chamber and time snapped back into motion. Emil dragged both his friends back and away from the Vhar's blades and he used Retribution.

The Vhar hit him, blades slicing across his chest and back. Emil didn't feel a thing. He'd saved both his friends, that was what mattered. Both Vhar gurgled, staggered about around him, then fell to the ground in two pieces, cut through. Emil waited for the pain to kick in. He waited to die.

Nothing happened.

"Cousin?" Justice screeched.

Emil spun around. The squad leader knelt, her armour rent in two across her chest and back. Blood sluiced down from her wounds, washing her knees. She had taken the hit for him. Used her unique talent to absorb a strike that should have killed him. Vermillion Gadise Samir had saved his life as surely as he had saved Iro and Toshiko's. She had sacrificed herself for him.

Iro saw Emil drop to his knees. The Paladin stared at his hands like he couldn't understand what he was seeing.

"Toshiko, check on Emil," Iro said. "Justice, help the squad leader."

"I... I... I don't know..."

"Just do it!" Iro snapped at the Surveyor.

He forged a Light Blade in his hands and swung, Blink Striking in front of the new Hopper in the ruined scraps of tan armor. The man was dark-skinned, with scraggly black hair and a sparse beard. He looked like he'd been through a fight or two of his own. He slid to a halt when Iro appeared in front of him and Iro held up his Light Blade to the man's neck. His palms sizzled and burned, his arms trembled, but Iro gritted his teeth past the pain.

"Oooh, very scary," the newcomer said. He raised a single

finger and tapped Iro's Light Blade, pulled it away with a gasp and sucked on it. "I surrender," he slurred around the finger in his mouth.

"Who are you? How did you get here?" Iro asked. He heard Gadise Samir gurgling behind him. "Justice, how is she doing?"

"Not good!" Justice shouted. "Please don't die, Cousin."

The new Hopper leaned to the side, away from Iro's sizzling blade. He stared past him, winced. "That looks bad. I can help. Want me to help?" He met Iro's stare, smiled.

"You're a Surveyor?"

"I'm many things."

Iro winced at the pain in his hand. He smelled burning flesh.

The new Hopper smiled again and pointed past Iro. "If you would just let me. Happy to help. Repay you for saving my life. Very grateful for that, by the way."

"Justice?" Iro shouted, not removing his blade from the Hopper's neck.

"I'm not a medic, Iro. She's cut deep and I don't know what I'm doing."

"You can help her?" Iro asked.

The newcomer shrugged. "I can try."

Iro dropped his Light Blade. "Do it."

The Hopper edged around Iro as if he were a monster likely to bite, then ran to where Justice was trying to save Gadise Samir.

"Who are you?" Justice asked.

The new Hopper knelt beside him. "Mutar, nice to meet you. You're a Surveyor?"

Justice nodded.

"Excellent, place your hands there and do exactly as I tell you. Oh my, that is A LOT of blood." The new Hopper activated a small purple crest in front of his left hand. The crest then moved, wrapped around his hand, the lines and symbols spreading out across his skin like a tattoo. He started prodding at Gadise Samir's wound and the Vanguard groaned and writhed.

Iro turned away. The rest of the squad needed seeing to. "How is he?" Iro asked Toshiko as he paced closer to Emil.

"Fine," Toshiko said. "As far as I can tell. A few scratches, but those Vhar's blades didn't touch him."

The two dead Vhar were close by, four halves bleeding out onto the metal floor. Iro crouched down in front of Emil, shook him by the shoulder. "Are you alright?"

Emil looked up at him, his gaze somehow hollow. "I... I messed up."

"You saved us," Iro said. "Both of us."

Emil shook his head. "But it cost..."

"She'll be fine." Iro glanced at the squad leader. He hoped she'd be fine.

Emil seemed to snap out of it then. He stood and pushed Iro away. "I'm alright." He stalked away, heading towards Gadise Samir.

"Emil," Iro said. The Paladin stopped. "Thank you. For saving us."

"Yes," Toshiko said. She bowed at the waist even though Emil couldn't see it. "Thank you."

The Paladin shrugged. "You're my squad." Then he walked away.

Iro couldn't stop his arms trembling. He lifted his hands before him, saw himself shaking. He clutched his hands together, tried to still them. "North!" He remembered the gravity had crushed the little automaton.

Iro lurched into a run, crossed over to where the automaton was lying on the floor. Its chassis was bent in multiple places, at least three of the rings that kept it aloft were cracked. But worst of all, it wasn't moving. There were no lights on. It was dead.

"North?" Iro poked the little automaton. A bent plate of its chassis fell away. A spark sizzled out of the hole, smoke drifting up. The automaton shook, buzzed, fell still. A single light flicked on.

"Norrrrrth i-i-i-is da-a-a-aaaaamaged. F-f-f-fixxx m-m-m-meeeee."

"How?"

"D-d-d-d-d-d-data p-point-t-t."

Iro stood, clasped his trembling hands and stared around the chamber. He couldn't see anything resembling a Datapoint to slot North into. But he had trained as a tech for years, surely there was some way to help. And Toshiko had tools with her, to fix Steel Lotus.

He scooped up North and as many of the parts spilling out of the construct as possible and walked over to where the rest of the squad gathered around Gadise Samir. The new Hopper and Justice were still working on her, their crests lit up.

"Toshiko, I need your help," Iro said as he laid North down. She set down Steel Lotus and shuffled closer. Iro pointed with trembling hands at the wounds, the rent metal, the sparking innards. "I need to repair North. A patch job until we can find a data point."

"You're shaking, Iro," Toshiko said as she pushed his trembling hands out of the way to peer into North's broken shell.

The new Hopper glanced over. He pulled a bloody hand away from Gadise Samir and waved it at Iro. Small purple crests flared to light around his eyes like goggles. "Huh. Strange, but you're an odd bunch. You're suffering from Current Sickness. Not sure how. But right now it's poisoning your current and that'll only get worse unless you do something about it."

"How do I do something about it?"

"Well, you can either let it dissipate naturally. Or you need a Paladin with the Charge talent to cleanse you."

Iro looked over to Emil. He shrugged. "I've never even heard of a Charge talent."

"Are you a Paladin?" the newcomer asked. He peered at Emil, the crests around his eyes rotating. "Oh, you are. Sort of. Bizarre."

Iro and Toshiko crowded around North. His hands trembled too much to do any of the fine work, so he left it to Toshiko and just advised. They had to cut away another section of the automaton's chassis and found the power supply was cracked, a soft wispy white vapor escaping from it. There was nothing they could do about that but put tape over it and hope it held. Neither of them understood what they were doing. The housing was damaged, too, and some wires were frayed and sparking. They debated about what to do, but in the end tore them out. North wheezed like it was in pain, but the lights didn't go out. With a little soldering, a few wraps of tape, and one cobbled together brace, they stabilised North. The little automaton couldn't fly, desperately still needed a Datapoint, and slurred its speech, but it declared it would survive. It scuttled about on its four little legs, one of them bent and trailing behind.

Gadise Samir took longer to stabilise and by the time the new Hopper declared she would live, he was sweating and exhausted. Justice, too, looked like he was about to drop. They both sat back, Justice with wide eyes. Gadise Samir was unconscious but breathing.

Iro squatted on his haunches in front of the new Hopper. Emil stepped up behind the man. "Thank you," Iro said. "Now it's time for some answers."

CHAPTER 36

"Oooh, this is exciting," the newcomer said. "You can beat til I'm blue, coppa. I ain't tellin' you nothin'."

Iro stared at the man for a moment, not sure if he had just gone insane. "What?"

The Hopper shrugged and grinned. "I've always wanted to say that. You ever seen any of those old... No, I suppose you haven't. Doesn't matter. Shoot away." He dipped into a dramatic bow. "My life is an open book, but please be gentle with the pages."

"Are you insane?" Emil asked.

"Yes. No. Yes. No. Yes. Stop it." He grinned over his shoulder at Emil. "That was a joke. You people do have humor wherever you come from?"

"When it's appropriate," Justice said, still kneeling beside his cousin's body.

"Point taken. I shall attempt to be more serious with my answers. No, I am not insane. I have been accused of being a tad dramatic."

"Who are you?" Iro said.

"Mufar." He spread his hands. "Adventurer extraordinaire.

My friend, I have sailed the seven black seas between stars and visited titans for which you have no name. I have seen a sun in its death throes and I have witnessed the birth of monsters. My name is sung…"

"So Mufar then?"

"Yes. And I would be most grateful if I could have your names? After all, my hands are still sticky with blood and it only seems fair I know the name of the bleeder."

"Her name is Vermillion Gadise Samir. I'm Eclipse Iro."

"Justice. Or Flame Horizon Justice, I suppose."

Toshiko startled. She'd been sitting at the edge of the conversation as usual. "Uh, Thousand Suns Toshiko. Nice to meet you, Mufar."

Mufar dipped into another bow. "And you, lady Toshiko. Such a beauty to outstrip starlight."

Toshiko blushed and looked a little scared. "Huh?"

"And what about you?" Mufar turned to Emil.

Emil crossed his arms and said nothing.

"I see. Very well, I'll just call you Stoic." He slapped Emil on the arm. "I must admit you all have quite lengthy names."

"We're from the Home Fleet," Toshiko said.

"I see. Which one is that?"

"Where did you come from?" Iro asked.

"Colossus. Well, not originally, but most recently. And unless I am very much mistaken, this is Leviathan?"

"Aaaaafffirmaaatiiiivvvvv," North stuttered.

"Oh." Mufar glanced down at the little automaton as it scuttled about on the floor and bumped into Iro's leg, then fell over. "You talk?"

Iro bent down and plucked North up, placed the little bot on his shoulder. The three working legs clung to his pauldron. "You came from another titan?"

"Well, yes." Mufar glanced around at them all, as if expecting something.

"How?"

Mufar sighed. "This might be a little complex. Do you mind if we talk on the road? I'd rather not get locked in a Spire. Terrible things to get out of once they start retracting."

"On the road?" Emil asked.

"Oh, you people are so backward. Yes, talk on the road. While we're walking. I'll spill my guts while we mosey on out of here." He glanced around at them all again. "We need to leave the Spire before it retracts. I'll tell you whatever you want to know while we are leaving."

Emil snorted. "Couldn't have just said that the first time?"

Mufar glared at the Paladin. "I did."

Iro turned to the squad leader. "Justice, can we move her?"

"She can move herself," Gadise Samir said with a groan. Her eyes slipped open and she struggled to sit up, wincing as if in great pain. Justice helped her. "Thank you for saving my life, Mufar."

Mufar turned, grinning. "Why, no thanks is needed at all. To save the life of one so radiant as yourself is all the gratification I could ever need."

"Uh huh. Help me stand, Justice." She groaned as he helped her up, and leaned on him. Justice looked about to collapse. "He's right. We should go now."

Toshiko ran over to the scorched remains of the giant construct. She found the rotating barrel cannon Iro had cut off. It was almost as big as she was. Despite that, she looped a couple of cables around it and started dragging it behind her.

"Leave it, Thousand Suns," Gadise Samir said as Justice helped her along.

"No."

"Need a hand carrying it?" Iro asked.

"No." Toshiko squared her shoulders, leaned into the weight, and dragged it on. With Steel Lotus still hanging from her shoulders as well, she struggled, but didn't stop.

They all shuffled towards the stairs down, wounded and exhausted. But they had reached the pinnacle of the Spire and they had sent out their distress call. Now they just had to hope the Home Fleet had heard it.

"How did you get here?" Iro asked Mufar as they started down the stairs to the chamber with the sphere in it.

"I shall try my best to explain it to you, dear boy."

Iro prickled at being called *boy*, but kept his mouth shut, eager to hear answers.

"You realise that Spires are communications platforms the titans use to talk to one another?" When no one answered him, Mufar turned around on the steps, walking backwards down them unerringly. "You understand that there are many titans all very, VERY far apart across the vastness of space. And that for the titans to communicate with each other, they need to erect massive communications arrays to direct concentrated beams of information from one point to another?"

Until a few hours ago, Iro had no idea what the Spires were. He had been told they were strange protrusions that grew out of the titan's hull. That they were filled with monsters, traps, and loot. And that only the strongest of Hoppers formed teams to enter the Spires, and salvage the powerful artefacts within. He was starting to think the Home Fleet knew even less about the titans than they claimed.

"Oh dear," Mufar said. He turned around on the steps, still not so much as tripping. "Well, now you know. Spires are communications platforms. Occasionally, the titans also need to transfer solid items between each other. This is where the Tucker Sphere comes in."

"That big spinning sphere we encountered?" Toshiko asked, her voice strained from dragging her burden.

Mufar clapped his hands together. "Exactly! A big spinny sphere thing, yes. Though that might be the most rudimentary term for anything that I've ever heard."

They entered the chamber that had contained the Tucker Sphere. Only it was gone. There was nothing in the centre of the chamber now. An inch of water sloshed about their feet, draining away.

Mufar crossed to one bank of screens, now blank, and pulled out a keyboard from a slot Iro hadn't even realised was there. He tapped on it a few times and a series of numbers flashed across the screen.

"What are you doing?" Iro said, hurrying over.

"Nothing," Mufar said. "Just running a quick diagnostic aaaaaaaaaaannd done." He slammed the keyboard away. The screen flashed a single word. *SENDING*. Then it went blank again.

"So, the Tucker Sphere." Mufar sloshed his way back to the centre of the chamber. "Originally theorised by some big brained boffin many many many oooohhhh so many years ago. The titans, back when they were close enough to form a network, before they drifted apart, turned the theory into a working concept. Only they didn't have the power source required to… you know… power it. That's where the current comes in."

"I think you're moving too fast," Iro said.

"If I am, it's because we're running out of time. On we go." He skipped through the draining water to the next set of steps and started down them. Iro hurried to catch up, trusting the others would follow behind.

"The Tucker Sphere, when under sufficient power, spins at a high enough velocity to generate its own localised gravity fields strong enough to quite literally punch a hole in space time."

"I knew it!" Justice shouted from behind. "That's what I said."

"No one likes a show off, kid," Mufar said and barrelled on.

"What is space time?" Iro asked.

Mufar sighed. He was walking faster now, almost jogging down the steps. "Space and time. They're the same thing. Keep up." He increased his pace again and Iro surged after him, leaving the others behind.

"Now because of the frankly insane amount of power required, and almost certainly considering the sheer reality warping stress factors involved of breaking space in two, the Tucker Sphere, when it reaches a sufficient velocity, can only open this breach in space time for a ridiculously short period. It's something like 0.00000... um... 0001 of a second? Very short, you understand. But in that incredibly brief moment, time is broken because a hole has been punched through it. And because space is the same thing and has also been broken, neither distance nor time have any meaning. Understand?"

They reached the chamber with the cones dotted all along the floor and ceiling. They were dormant now, none of the black lightning racing along them. Iro stumbled into the chamber, his mind reeling as he tried to understand. He didn't. Anyway he looked at it, none of it made sense to him. Mufar paced into the centre of the chamber and stared down at the floor.

"Interesting. A little frustrating, too, if I'm being honest," Mufar said and walked away.

The others shuffled into the chamber. Toshiko still dragging her two cannons. Justice helping the squad leader along. Emil at the rear, still looking dazed.

"So when the Tucker Sphere opens a hole in space time," Iro said. "It allows for travel between the titans?"

"Yes. I mean, if you insist on putting it that simply. Instantaneous, or at least so it appears to all known methods of time keeping, transference between two titans. Everything in the contact zone on this titan goes to the other one, and vice versa."

"And vi—ser ver?"

"Vice versa. The same thing but the other way around."

"So you came here from the Colossus titan?"

Mufar clapped again. "I do believe he's cracked it."

"But why weren't we sent to the Colossus?" Iro said.

"Because you weren't in the contact zone."

"The platform in the centre of the pinnacle?"

"Yes." Mufar rolled his eyes. "And everything below it. But really you should be glad you weren't in the contact zone. No one wants to be on Colossus right now." He whistled and strolled towards the gravity chute.

"How do we… get down?" Gadise Samir asked, her words a little slurred. She seemed on the verge of collapse and Iro had to admit it was a miracle she was still alive. "The gravity chute… propels us up."

Mufar turned to them with a helpless look on his face. "Oh, you are so simple. It's cute." The purple crests lit up around his eyes again, and he turned to stare at the wall. Strangely, his crest didn't flare up anywhere else. It was as if he had somehow localised his crest around his eyes. Both eyes. Two crests. There was so much about him they didn't know. And he seemed to know so much about the titans.

"Here we are." Mufar thumped the wall and a panel sprang open. There was a small lever hidden inside the wall. He pulled the lever down. Nothing seemed to change. "Right then. Down we go."

"Wait!" Iro ran forwards. "There are hunters down there."

Mufar looked at him blankly. "There's what?"

"Hunters. Constructs."

"Oh." Mufar laughed. "Right." He stepped into the chute and was sucked down into the chamber below.

Iro turned around, but the others just stared at him. Not even

Emil had anything to say. With a worrying pit of fear in his stomach, Iro leapt into the chute and plunged .

The gravity tugged at him, pulling him down, but never too fast. He touched down on the metal ground and stepped clear, already marvelling at the empty chamber before him. The mechanical arms were all tucked away in the ceiling alcoves. The banks and rows of frames were gone. Every single construct had vanished. Suddenly he understood. They had all been transferred to Colossus. Leviathan had sent an army of constructs to one of the other titans.

Toshiko hit the ground next, her cannons floating down just behind her. She started trudging on again, dragging the construct's rotating cannon behind her, teeth gritted. "I'm going to feel my shoulders for weeks after this."

Gadise Samir hit the floor next and crumpled. Iro rushed to her side and slipped her arm over his shoulders, lifting her up. Justice was next and then Emil, who barely even seemed to register that he had hit the ground.

"Keep up, children," Mufar shouted. He was already strolling across the vast, empty chamber. "And you, too, miss bleeding radiance."

"Hey, Mufar," Iro shouted back. "Why did Leviathan send an army of constructs to Colossus?"

"Aha!" Mufar spun around on the spot, clapped his hands, and danced side to side a few times. "Finally, you're asking some decent questions. The really important ones. Buuuut, I'm afraid you might not like the answers. And that's assuming you even understand them, which I'm far from certain you will." He sped up his pace, skipping towards the freight elevator. Iro struggled to catch up, Gadise Samir was a dragging weight.

"Hurry hurry hurry," Mufar shouted, waving at them all. He slapped a button on the elevator and it rumbled into motion, dropping as slowly as it had risen. Mufar just stood there, smiling as he lowered.

Iro hurried forward and dropped two feet onto the moving elevator, dragging Gadise Samir with him. She groaned as he laid her down. Emil was next, still moving in a daze, he dropped and started pacing on the elevator. Justice was next and wailed as he fell. Toshiko was last, still dragging her burden. She shouted a heads up and threw the rotating cannon down. Iro caught it and placed it on the rumbling elevator floor. Toshiko landed a few seconds later and collapsed. She was sweating and laid out next to the squad leader.

"Stop running ahead of us," Justice said, sitting cross-legged on the floor. "You're our prisoner."

Mufar simpered at him. "Ahhh, that's precious. Would you like to lock me up? Throw away the key." He struck an arrogant pose. "There's not a prison built that can hold me."

"What?"

Mufar sighed. "You don't have books, shows? What do you people do for fun aboard your fleet?"

"Hit things," Emil said in a voice fuzzy with disinterest.

"Fix things mostly," Iro said, thinking of the gears Freya gave him to clean.

"I read," Toshiko said. "I have quite a big library, though I'm not supposed to. The Rangers would confiscate it if they ever found me reading dream books."

"Dream books?" Mufar said. "That's cute. I like it."

The assembly rumbled into view. It was dormant now. All the depressions were empty of frames and constructs. The mechanical arms retreated into the ceiling just like above. All the constructs were gone, even the flying ones that carted around parts.

"The army of constructs," Iro prodded Mufar. "Why?"

"Why indeed?" Mufar paced towards the edge of the elevator and sat down his legs dangling over the side. "Do you think the titans are friends? All chummy and idly chatting with each other over distances that make your mind quake? Well, maybe they are. But do you always agree with your friends? What if Stoic over there decided to push miss Starlight beauty over the edge of this elevator?"

"He wouldn't," Toshiko said. "Would you?"

Emil glanced up, shook his head.

Mufar sighed. "This is what we call a hypothetical. It's a made up situation for…"

Toshiko glared at him. "I know what hypothetical means."

Mufar waved his hands in surrender. "Miss Starlight has teeth. They're very pretty teeth. You must brush regularly. Does your fleet have hygiene? As a rule, I mean?"

Iro realised what the man was doing now. He was distracting them from the real questions, the ones they were asking him. This was all a show, dangling information in front of them then changing the subject to delay further answers.

"The army," Iro said.

Mufar glanced at him and shrugged. "The titans fight, from time to time, as brothers and friends are likely to do. The distances are obviously too great for any conventional weaponry, but the Tucker Sphere provide a novel way to do battle. Titans construct their forces and throw them at each other. Right now, Colossus is a battleground. And if the Leviathan constructs force their way to the Colossus' core…" He clapped his hands together. "Boom."

Gadise Samir groaned as she levered herself to sitting again. "The titans can destroy each other?"

Mufar nodded. "They can. And do. Occasionally. Very occasionally. And it usually requires a concerted effort."

"Is that what happened to 01?"

Mufar shrugged. "01?"

"Our first titan. It blew up just over five years ago."

"That's who you are!" Mufar grinned. "You're the fleet from

Kraken. Oh, no wonder you're so backward. Catch up when you can, nomads." He threw himself off the elevator and dropped the last fifty feet to the assembly floor. He landed and strolled off towards the hole down to the manufactory.

"Scrap!" Iro stared over the edge of the elevator. He was uncertain he could survive the drop unscathed, and the others needed help.

Mufar had dropped to the manufactory level long before the elevator reached the floor. Iro picked up the squad leader again and they all limped their way to the hole leading down. It was a long distance, a deadly drop, and there were no constructs to carry them down this time. In the end, Iro had to carry each of them down in a series of Blink Strikes. Despite his trembling hands and the current sickness eating away at him, making him feel like monsters were clawing at his insides, he retrieved his entire squad, including Toshiko's two cannons. Mufar was nowhere to be seen.

They picked their way through the dormant manufactory. Puffs of steam shot out of cracked pipes and now and then they heard the groan of some metal housing as it cooled and settled back into place. But otherwise the manufactory was quiet. There were no questions about using it for their own purposes.

They found Mufar leaning against the main door of the Spire. He had wet his scraggly dark hair in the pool and it was now slick back against his head. He grinned at them as they filed down the stairs.

"It's about time," he said spreading his arms wide. "I was starting to think you'd been waylaid by nothing. But we're all here now, ready to leave."

"Wait!" Justice said, hurrying forwards. "There are Vhar outside."

"Oh, I wouldn't worry about that." Mufar slammed his hand

against the button and hummed a tune, dancing with a single foot as the door split apart.

"You didn't answer all our questions," Iro said.

"True. But we're out of time, Eclipse Iro of the Home Fleet. I tell you what. We have a few seconds until this door opens. Ask away. One more question."

Iro looked around at the rest of the squad, but none of them seemed forthcoming with a question. And he still had one left unanswered. "Why did Leviathan attack Colossus?"

Mufar wagged a finger in the air even as the door slid open. "Because of the Blight."

The door finished opening with a solid clunk, revealing a dozen dismembered Vhar lying around the chamber beyond. And standing in the midst of the bodies waited two figures dressed in black cloaks.

CHAPTER 37

IRO'S BLOOD froze in his veins. Anger seared cold blue lines into his eyes. He wrestled with it, with his own fury roaring within him, urging him to action he knew was foolish. He lost.

"Ahh, boss," Mufar said as he sauntered out of the Spire. "Am I glad to see you. I..."

Iro activated his crest, forged a Light Blade, gripped it hard.

"Eclipse, don't."

He ignored the squad leader, ignored the trembling in his limbs, ignored the searing pain in his palms and the smell of burning flesh. Iro focused his entire will on the big black cloak and his oversized shield, his golden armor polished to a shine. He could see nothing of the man's face beneath his hood, but he knew him all the same.

"SHOTA!" Iro roared.

The black cloak turned his hood, and Iro felt the weight of his stare. "Do I know you?"

Iro knew it was stupid. He had no chance. But he didn't care. This black cloak and his comrade had beaten Master Rollo, had kidnapped Mia. They had killed Master Tannow. And Iro had learned Burning Adrenaline precisely for this moment. He activated it, felt the power flood through him as his current became unleashed. He swung. His Blink Strike was so fast it left an image of him behind.

Shota was faster.

The black cloak shifted and Iro's strike rebounded against his shield. His Light Blade didn't even scratch the metal.

Iro backed up a step. "Where's Goro?"

Shota's hood tilted. "Back home with the little ones. Why? Who are you?"

Iro swept his blade to the side, Blink Striking away, then back behind the man. He stabbed out into Shota's back. The black cloak didn't even move. Iro's blade seared through his cloak, stopped dead against the man's armor. "Where's Mia?"

Again the hood tilted. "Who?"

It was too much for Iro. Too much to be ignored, to be forgotten. He couldn't penetrate the man's shield or armor, so he only had one choice. To go for the head. He swept his sword back, Blink Striking away, then drew his little sword in his off-hand. He slashed both swords at once, Blink Striking in again, sending an image of himself the other way to distract. Something snapped inside and pain lanced through his chest like shards of ice stabbing into his heart. Just one more thing to ignore. Shota turned towards the false image. Iro sliced his blade upwards, Blink Striking above the black cloak. He spun in midair and chopped down, pouring every bit of current he had into the final Blink Strike.

Shota's crest burst to golden light. It was massive, seemed to fill the chamber, and had three connected circles. Iro rebounded off it, his Light Blade shattering in his hands. He hit the ground hard, rolled to a stop. It made no sense. Shota didn't have one crest, he had three. Three circles linked by arcane lines, each one a different shade of gold. Each one so massive it dwarfed his own. And the man had flung him away simply by activating his crest.

Shota reached up and pulled down his hood, stared at Iro. He had a neck thick with muscle, a jutting chin, skin pale as bone, and his eyes dark as the cloak he wore. His hair was shorn short and grey as static. "Interesting," he drawled. Then he turned away and Iro was ignored again.

"What are you doing here, Mufar?"

"Oh, you know, just out for a walk. Ooops, fell into a Spire and was flung half way across the galaxy."

The growl Shota let loose was audible even a dozen paces away.

"Right," Mufar said and spread his hands. "Blight threshold crossed 61% on Colossus. The other titans have begun their assault. Including Leviathan, obviously."

Iro felt a prick in his neck and turned, scrambling away. He'd forgotten about the second black cloak. The man was painfully thin with grey skin that seemed to cling to his bones. He wore only a few pieces of turquoise armor plates over his vitals and his cloak hung awkwardly from his shoulders. He held a vial in one gnarly hand and tapped a tiny blade at the mouth of it. A single drop of blood splashed into the vial. Iro's blood.

He pressed a trembling hand to his neck, pulled it away to find a smear of red across his fingers. The thin black cloak stoppered the vial, then grinned and walked away without a word.

Toshiko had been ready to charge Steel Lotus the moment Iro attacked. She'd dropped the rotating cannon arm and hurried out through the door with all the others. But the moment she activated her crest, Emil had held up a hand in front of her. The Paladin hadn't moved to help Iro, and he'd made it clear he'd stop anyone else from helping, too. Now Iro sprawled on the ground. The black cloak in gold hadn't even moved, yet Iro looked utterly defeated.

"What about the others?" Shota said.

"What others, boss?" Mufar shook his head and leaned against Shota's giant shield. "I sent Alex to Behemoth and Nunez to Hydra. That's it. Everyone else is dead."

"How?"

Mufar stopped leaning against the shield and shook his head. "Scrap!"

"What do we do?" Toshiko asked in a whisper.

"Nothing," Gadise Samir said, her voice heavy with pain. "We've broken none of their rules. We hope they let us go."

Emil stepped in front of Toshiko, looked back over his shoulder at her and shook his head. He seemed different somehow, as though the fire had gone out of him.

"Where's the gear?" Shota asked.

"Didn't find one, boss."

Shota reached out, grabbed Mufar by his battered breastplate. "You wouldn't lie to me, Mufar?"

Mufar held up his hands. "I know the lay of things, boss."

Shota turned his gaze on the squad, and let Mufar drop. "Then one of these junkers must have it."

"I don't think so," Mufar said. "Boss, they didn't even know the Spire is a comms platform."

Shota turned an incredulous gaze on Mufar.

"Exactly! They're the fleet from Kraken."

Shota grunted. "Are any of them infected?"

"Not a one, Boss. I checked them all thoroughly." Mufar winked at them.

"Shota!" Iro shouted. He staggered upright, shaking as though freezing cold. "What did you do with Mia?"

Shota sighed. "This again. I don't know what you're talking about, child."

"You kidnapped her."

"And you think that narrows it down? Do you know how many children I have taken, boy? Hundreds. Do you care how many junkers like you I have killed? Thousands. And it is a single star in the night sky compared to what I will do." His jaw writhed. "I will protect humanity even if I need to slaughter every one of you to do so."

Iro opened his mouth to shout, and froze. Shota froze, too. They all did. Toshiko stared around at a world turned gray. She grinned. Just when everything was feeling like bad news. She spun around in a circle, searching for the gate. Back in the Spire, through the doorway and in front of the frozen pool.

She hurried through the Spire door. Her gate was shaped like a burning flame, bowing out in the middle and reaching up to a point. The frame looked like circuitry with boards and wires, all gray and lifeless. Color drained down into the chamber and Toshiko guessed she had a minute at most. She loved a good puzzle, but putting a timer on them always added a level of stress she wasn't comfortable with. Especially as she had to solve the puzzle alone. There was something creepy about the frozen space the gates existed in. Everyone was outside and just stopped. As if they were somehow removed from the world, but still there. It made no sense to her. Was the universe frozen? Or did the frozen bubble only extend so far?

She couldn't help but imagine the possibility of something else in the frozen world with her. What if something hunted her through the paused gate time and no matter how much she screamed and begged, her friends couldn't help her. The hunter would catch her and kill her right in front of them and her friends wouldn't even realise and…

Toshiko slapped both hands against her cheeks. She was letting her imagination run away with a scary story, wasting time.

The color wouldn't stop draining into the frozen gate world while she made a fool of herself.

She paced around the gate, studying it. Like before, a plaque sat at the top, a single word written on it. *ALONE*. A sinking, gnawing pit settled in Toshiko's gut. The door was closed, looked like a single printed sheet of metal. Her crest sat embossed upon it. She gave it an experimental push. It didn't give. She rushed around to the other side of the door, pushed again, still no give.

The color had reached the top of the gate already. The word *ALONE* revealed in glaring neon pink, which only seemed to make it more offensive. Toshiko hated being alone. Not just on the titan, but especially on the titan. Her imagination turned every shadow into a gaping maw, every sound into a monster, every breath into a cacophony of noise shouting her presence to anything that might be creeping or crawling around. She could ignore the fear with others around her, but whenever she was alone, the fears crept out through every door and seeped up through the bulkhead floors. Toshiko stared past her gate towards the stairs. The pit of darkness leading down into the guts of the Spire. Was there something waiting for her? Something watching, ready to erupt from the shadow and attack the moment she was alone?

"You're doing it again," she said, her voice loud but flat in the frozen world. As if the sound had nowhere to go and stuck in her throat. Could she choke on her own voice? Asphyxiate here alone. Would the timer runout, the world unfreeze? Would her squad turn to find her dead on the floor?

"Stop it stop it stop it." Toshiko clutched at Steel Lotus, the only company she had. If only her cannon could talk like North, then she'd never be alone.

The button next to the Spire door was lit, a soft red. The color hadn't reached it yet. Toshiko knew what she had to do, how to solve this puzzle. But she hesitated. She'd be alone. She'd be choosing to be alone. To lock herself away from the others.

"Face your fears, Toshiko," she said in a silly voice, pretending it belonged to Steel Lotus. "You can do this. I'll be right by your side."

She patted the cannon. Oddly, pretending Steel Lotus talked helped. "You're a good friend despite being an inanimate object."

"Stop hesitating and get on with it. Time waits for no woman, Toshiko."

Toshiko stepped up to the Spire door and stared out at her frozen squad. The black cloaks were still there as well and she had to hope they didn't mean the squad any harm. Mufar hadn't seemed too dangerous.

"Good luck," she shouted at them. Then more quietly to herself. "Good luck to you, too, Toshiko. Yeah, you can do this, Toshiko. We believe in you. Yay!"

She hesitated. She bit her lip, screwed her eyes shut, and slammed her hand against the button. Nothing happened.

Icy hands crawled across her neck, and Toshiko spun around, squeaking in alarm, eyes flying open. Nothing there.

"That was my imagination, right?"

Nobody answered.

Her gate hung open now. But the Spire door was closed. She was alone. She had locked herself away from her squad. Her choice was made.

Toshiko clutched Steel Lotus close and stepped through her Second Gate.

The world unfroze in a great lurching motion that had Toshiko stumbling. The water sloshed in the pool, the walls spun around her.

Her crest exploded into electric pink lines, so much larger than before, so much brighter. New strength flooded her limbs and she felt like she could run the length of the titan, lift a bhurbeast in one hand.

Toshiko turned, hoping the door was open again, that she could run out and join the rest of her squad. But the door wasn't just closed, it was gone. The walls were moving. Twisting, grinding, spinning down into the floor. The chamber shook, the metallic scream of metal against metal sounding from somewhere above. The floor shook and Toshiko stumbled, barely kept her feet.

"Of course. The Spires retract into the titan when they've been explored. And I just locked myself inside."

"Only one way out now, Toshiko," she said in her Steel Lotus voice.

"Yes, I know. Well aware. And also that I have to stop pretending you can talk before everyone thinks I'm crazy."

The darkness in the staircase leading down was an oily black pool threatening to swallow everything. But it was the only possible way out.

Another shattering squeal from above as the Spire crushed itself back down into the titan. "Time to do this," she said. "All on my own. Into the dark where countless monsters no doubt wait to tear me limb from limb and feast on my poor remains."

Steel Lotus said nothing.

Toshiko reached down and picked up the rotating cannon. She grunted as she slung it up over her shoulder and rested it against her back. The cannon was almost as big her, yet she could carry it now with ease. With one hand holding the cannon in place, and the other resting on Steel Lotus, Toshiko ventured down the steps. The darkness swallowed her.

CHAPTER 38

EMIL LEFT Justice and the squad leader and stalked over to Iro. His friend was trying to summon the current to create another sword out of light. It flickered once, then vanished. He tried again. He was done, spent, yet he couldn't seem to stop. Emil grabbed the rim of his breastplate and dragged Iro around until he couldn't see the black cloaks anymore. He shook him.

"Snap out of it, Iro," Emil said. "Killing yourself here won't help anyone. You can't fight them."

Iro snarled and Emil shook him again. The Corsair blinked a few times, then the anger fled his face and he slumped. Emil caught him.

"Sorry, I…" Iro shook his head. He was trembling. "I don't know what I… I'm sorry."

The automaton clinging to his shoulder scuttled in a circle. "N—n—north is connnnnnncerned."

"Boss," Mufar said. "The Spire door closed."

"Scrap," Shota snarled. "Then we're done here. Time to go." He turned and strode away. The thin black cloak waited a few seconds, a grin flickering across his ugly face. Emil wanted to punch that face. Then the man turned and slunk away. That left only Mufar.

"Current sickness, Iro," Mufar said. The purple crests appeared around his eyes again and he came forward, peered down at Iro still slumped in Emil's arms. "What you did just now was amazing. Honestly, even Shota is impressed. Never seen anyone do anything like it before. But it's going to kill you. You need to stop."

"What did I do?" Iro asked. He stood on his own then, trembling from the effort, stared down at his burned hands.

Mufar smiled and shook his head in wonder. "You closed the circuit. Created a feedback loop within yourself."

"Toshiko?" Justice shouted. "Toshiko, where are you?" The Surveyor spun around in a circle. "She's gone!"

The Spire started moving. Metal squealed as the whole massive structure, rotated and retracted. The door vanished below the floor.

"She went back into the Spire," Mufar said over the racket. He turned his crest circled eyes on the structure. "She's still in there."

"Mufar," Shota shouted.

"Coming, boss." Mufar turned back to Emil and Iro. "You should know the only possible way out at this point is down, so that's where she'll be heading if she's as smart as I think she is."

"She hates being alone," Iro said.

"Don't we all. Part of the human condition, I think." The crests around Mufar's eyes rotated, tiny symbols flaring brighter. "Also, she appears to have opened her Second Gate. Good for her. That means this place will be swarming with new monsters soon though. Best get going before that happens. A few dead Vhar won't scare them off."

"Mufar, now!" Shota shouted.

Mufar waved a lazy hand in the air. "Hold still, Little Guide." He reached out and slapped a hand down on top of North's dented chassis. His crests spun around his eyes again and North buzzed.

"C—cooooordiiinates receeeeeeiivvved."

"Excellent. These guide automatons are always so agreeable. Shame we're not allowed them." Mufar's smile fell away, leaving something like concern on his face. "If you want to save your friend, follow the map I gave to your bot. It'll lead you down to where the Spire is being disassembled. Dangerous place, but as long as you don't disturb the workers, you should be alright. If miss Starlight can find a way out, it's down there.

"Now, I must away," Mufar gave a dramatic bow and turned, strolling after Shota. "Oh, don't pout at me, boss. I'm saying goodbye to my friends. We forged a bond, don't you know? Tempered in danger and circumstance. Unbreakable." They passed through a doorway and the door closed behind them.

Iro was already limping towards Justice and the squad leader. He shook from current sickness and looked weak. Emil decided he would go alone. He couldn't leave Toshiko behind. He wouldn't lose a squad mate.

"Iro, take Justice and the squad leader to the dock. If the Home Fleet received our message, the pods should be waiting for you."

"You're not in charge, Courage," the squad leader said weakly from her crumpled heap on the floor.

"Yet you're too injured to stop me." He turned back to Iro. "Tell your bot to come with me. Guide me to where Mufar said we'll find Toshiko."

Iro shook his head. "I'm going, too. We'll find her together."

Emil hated to admit it, but he'd hoped Iro would say that. "Justice..."

"You want me to take cousin Gadise to the dock alone? What if there're monsters? There will be monsters. They'll kill us. This is it. This is the curse. How you all die."

Emil stepped forward and grabbed Justice by the shoulder,

squeezed hard enough the Surveyor yelped from the shock. It shut him up. "Up in the Spire, I saw you and your little autodage rip a power supply out of a hunter while it chewed on you. You're stronger than you think. Strong enough to take down a rustling or two. Now go. Get her to the pods." Assuming the Home Fleet had sent the pods. They had to have sent them.

"Iro…"

The Corsair was already moving. "Let's go find Toshiko."

North buzzed and a small map appeared, projected in front of it. The first step was clear. Down the hole. Emil and Iro shuffled up to the hole in the floor. The Spire twisted, grinded, a screw being retracted. It had pulled back far enough already a person could jump down, slide down its hull to the floor below. Iro drew his little sword and gave Emil a nod, then leapt down. Emil glanced back once to where Justice helped the squad leader from the chamber, then he leapt down after Iro.

That first chamber was a ruin. It looked like it might have been a toilet once. The floor was torn, the mirrors shattered, water spurted out of a dozen burst pipes. They hurried through it, wrenched open a door into an open storage chamber. It was empty, except for the section of Spire that had torn through it and was even now rotating back down, tearing metal apart in its progress. Emil and Iro hurried across a hanging walkway, the floor twenty feet below them. North's map flickered ahead of them, occasionally cutting out for a few seconds, but showing the route they needed to take. Assuming Mufar had been telling the truth. Emil had to assume the Hopper had been telling the truth. He might be a black cloak, but he had no reason to lie. At least none that Emil could see.

A section of the walkway had been damaged by the Spire and had fallen away. There was a ten feet gap. They both leapt across with ease. A jump that until recently would have been impossible for them, but now it was easy because they had both opened their Second Gates. Emil stared down at his gauntleted hands as he followed along behind Iro. His Second Gate, the furthest he would ever progress now. He lit up his crest in front of him as he hurried along, stared up at the third lock. It was a block of fiery light. Locked out forever. He was stalled.

"You alright, Emil?" Iro asked, turning.

Emil let his crest fade away. He'd stopped following, lost in his own misery. Such indulgent self pity. He didn't have time for it. They had a squad mate to save. "I'm fine. Keep going." He waved Iro on.

The door at the far end of the walkway was stuck. Emil had to use Strength to wrench it open. They moved into a corridor and followed Mufar's map to a service elevator. It would only take them down two floors, but it was safer than sliding down the hole after the Spire.

The elevator rumbled into movement and Iro leaned back against the far wall, closing his eyes and breathing deeply. Emil paced the three steps he could in the cramped space repeatedly, wringing his hands together, the metal plates of his gauntlets grinding against each other.

He was stalled. He'd had the chance to open his Third Gate and he'd failed, chosen to save both his friends instead. He'd have been alright with that, a sacrifice he had made and one he'd make again. Except it didn't have to be that way. Perhaps if he'd been able to trust the squad leader, he'd have known she could have taken the hit for one of the others and he could opened his gate. All because he couldn't trust her.

"Hey, Iro." He needed to get out of his head. "You ever wonder what you'd do if you stalled?"

Iro shrugged, didn't open his eyes. "I grew up thinking I was talentless. I *was* talentless. Thought I'd spend my entire life as a tech. I kept trying to manifest a talent, but until 02… But even if I stalled now, I'm stronger than I ever thought I would be. So I guess I'd keep going. Keep Hopping. It's not about us or me or you. Not about how strong we are. It's about what the fleet needs. And the fleet needs Hoppers."

Emil nodded to himself. Iro was right. It had never been about them. The survival of the fleet was what mattered. Still, he was stalled. It felt like failure. He needed to tell someone. "Hey, Iro…"

"But I won't stall," Iro said. He opened his eyes and fixed them on the elevator door. "I'll do whatever it takes to open my gates. Anything."

Emil stopped pacing. "Whatever it takes."

Iro nodded. "I don't care what it costs me. I will open the gates. All of them. I'll get strong enough I can even fight the black cloaks. I'm done losing people. Through being taken from. They killed Master Tannow, kidnapped Mia. They tell us where we can go, refuse us the manufactory we need to survive. She took my sword." He shook his head. "No! Whatever it takes, I will get strong enough I can stand up to them all and say NO!"

The elevator rumbled to a stop.

"Whatever it takes," Emil said again. He hadn't done whatever it took. He had chosen to save both his friends instead. And no matter which way he turned the decision in his head, he knew he'd do the same thing again. And that was why he was stalled and Iro wasn't. That was why Iro would leave him behind. Because his resolve was greater.

The elevator door slid open, revealing a curving corridor lit with menacing red lights. Iro pushed away from the wall and stalked forward, North's map in front of him. "Come on," he said. "Let's go find Toshiko."

Emil waited a few seconds as Iro stalked ahead. It felt fitting somehow. He'd be leaving Emil behind soon enough.

Emil shook himself. He didn't have time to mope and sulk. Iro was right, they had to find Toshiko. She was what mattered now. Emil squared his shoulders, cracked his knuckles, and hurried after his friend.

CHAPTER 39

TOSHIKO SQUEEZED herself through the darkness. Foul smelling water sloshed at her feet and brought a backed up toilet to mind. The walls were cold and slimy whenever she touched them. She had barely enough space to move, especially carrying two cannons. And it was so scrapping dark she couldn't see where she was going. Also, the floor kept rumbling as the Spire ground itself flat, and odd noises echoed around her even over the noise of the Spire.

"Chittering," Toshiko said to herself. "That's how I'd describe the noises. Chittering. Maybe slithering. Definitely the occasional squelching."

"Don't worry, Toshiko," she said in her blustery Steel Lotus voice. "They're perfectly normal noises for a Spire grinding itself to nothing against the hull of the titan."

"So I need to keep heading down through this impenetrable darkness?"

"Exactly. It must open out into the titan," Steel Lotus said pompously.

"Or I run into a dead end and die down here in the dark, up to my hips in foul water, crushed to death by a compacting Spire.

385

Nothing to worry about." She tripped on something under the water, stumbled. She tried to convince herself the thing she had tripped over hadn't been slithering.

Toshiko stepped forward, kicked a wall. It didn't hurt, but she said, "Ow!" anyway.

Water rushed past her legs signalling another set of steps. She'd almost fallen down the first staircase, her feet slipping on the treacherous wet metal.

Toshiko edged to the right, the noise grew louder. She inched down the first step, then the next, and the next. Something cold and wet dripped down the back of her neck, ran under her armor and trickled down her spine. She shivered. "Ew ew ew ew ew!" She started hurrying down the steps, unwilling to be dripped on any further.

"Don't rush," Steel Lotus said. "You might fall."

"Shut up," Toshiko said. "You're made of metal. You don't care. But water dripping down on me is just… argh!" She kept imagining the drips weren't water, but little monsters; slithering things like wires, but alive.

She reached the bottom of the steps, stumbled as she expected another step, careened into a wall. She almost dropped her salvaged cannon, but kept hold, steadying herself with her free hand against the wall. Something soft and moist slithered around her fingers. She jumped back, shaking her hand. A sharp pain sliced her wrist like something had bitten her. Toshiko dropped the rotating cannon and slapped at her arm, trying to scratch off whatever had attached itself to her. But there was nothing. She felt a slithering up her arm, itching, scratched again, working her fingers under her armor plates. There was still nothing.

"Alright," she said. "Now you're going crazy. Well done. Talking to yourself, pretending your cannon is talking back, and now imagining things are crawling under your skin. I've gone mad."

"You need to stop indulging your imagination and get moving, Toshiko," she said in Steel Lotus' stupid voice. "Get moving before the Spire crushes you."

"I hate that you're right." She fished around in the sloshing water, found the wires attached to the salvaged cannon, and slung it over her shoulder again. Her arm still itched, but it was only her stupid scrapping imagination and she was done letting it run wild.

The chittering grew louder, sounding like welding. A hundred plasma torches all sputtering in unison. Toshiko tried turning on her flashlight. The light didn't penetrate the darkness at all. This Spire basement was dark by design. Which was the scariest thing of all. Only on a titan could anyone find a place where light didn't work. It broke a fundamental law. Light worked even in space, that's why they could see stars. But here, there was nothing. An absence. An oppressive void.

She tripped down the next set of steps, fell, bounced down the last few steps on her ass. The worst bit about that was that the fall soaked her in the foul water, which was now up to her knees.

"I don't know how to swim," she blurted. There had never been cause to learn or anywhere to learn aboard ship. She waded on.

Something slithered past her feet, coiled around her legs. "No!" She shook her head and sped up, sloshing through the muck, refusing to even think about it.

The chittering was deafening now, combined with the constant rumble and squeal of the Spire retracting. The noise shredded her nerves and hurt her ears. Vibrations made the water jump all around her.

A line of light shone in the dark. Toshiko thought she had imagined it at first. A tiny pin prick of light like a star in the void. It winked out, then reappeared again. She lumbered forwards, water sloshing around her ankles. The light vanished again, reappeared. The chittering was all around her now, almost rasping like metal being ground away beneath a thousand little jaws.

Toshiko hit the wall and peered into the light streaming through the tiny hole. She couldn't see through, but there was something beyond the wall. A creature scuttled across her hand, and she backed up with a yelp. The scuttling creature hit the water with a splosh and whirred as it splashed its way about.

A thought occurred to Toshiko. She activated her crest and started chanting, channeling her current. "The titans built the Spires, right?" she asked Steel Lotus.

"That's right, Toshiko," she said in Steel Lotus' dopey voice.

"They assemble the Spires from various sections of the titan's own body. That's the only thing that makes any sense. The titan can't have built a manufactory. Unless it could. No. It would require a manufactory to build a manufactory. Much more likely the titan disassembled another one and moved it to where it needed to be. Here."

"To produce an army of constructs to wage war against another titan."

"Not helpful, Steel Lotus! The why isn't important right now. Only the how. The titans aren't living. The Spires don't grow out of the hull. They are assembled, built. By what? And what disassembles them afterwards?" Something else slithered past her legs. "Will you stop that! I'm busy.

"Down here in the guts of the Spire is where it is now being disassembled so that the parts can be carted off and put back to other uses."

Another pin prick of light opened up, moved sideways in a line until it connected with the last one. Something plopped into the water behind her and Toshiko imagined it crawling up her arm again. She scratched at an itch that wasn't there.

"So what I'm saying is that down here, the Spire is being ripped apart by something, some sort of specialised construct.

And that little line of light is a most likely a tiny window into the rest of the titan. So all I have to do…" Something slithery coiled around her foot. She tried to shake it off. "All I have to do is wait until these specialised constructs dismantle enough of the Spire that I can just walk out. Right?" The thing in the water had coiled its way up to her knee now, despite her attempts to dislodge it.

The display on Steel Lotus chimed. "37% charged. Ready to fire," she said in the lethargic voice.

"About scrapping time!"

Toshiko took steady aim at the light shining through the wall ahead of her, and pulled the trigger.

CHAPTER 40

"HANG IN THERE, NORTH," Iro said as he strode along a balcony overlooking some sort of stage. Or at least, he thought it might have once been a stage. The Spire had ripped through it as it thrust up through the titan's hull, cutting the entire chamber in half.

"Haaaannngggging problemlemlem—matic. Limimimited functionaaaaaaaaality of apenapen—apendages."

The map North was projecting kept flickering, as though the power source inside the little automaton was dying.

"How much farther to the door?" Emil asked from behind. He had stopped on the balcony and was staring down at a small pack of rustlings. The little monsters had gathered and appeared to be investigating the Spire, running forward and scraping their knives against its hull, then backing away, chittering to each other. "It's like they're playing some sort of game."

Iro stopped, backed up to stand next to Emil. The Paladin had been silent since the elevator. He'd been subdued since the pinnacle of the Spire. It was unlike him.

"Two more floors down, see." Iro pointed at the flickering map projected before him.

"That'll be the lowest level anyone from the Home Fleet has gone on 02," Emil said. "Who knows what we'll encounter down there?

"Hopefully no traps," Iro said with a smile. "I'm sure between the two of us we can take any monsters the titan throws at us, but I've no idea what to do if we get caught in a water trap or something." It was bravado, Iro knew. He was in no condition to fight, his hands trembling so furiously he had to clutch them together to still them. Besides, the lower down they went, the more dangerous the monsters. They wouldn't stand a chance below the fifth level. And they'd been encountering Vhar higher up. Vhar weren't supposed to venture so close to the surface.

"You see that?" Emil pointed at the Spire. One rustling ran up and slashed its knives against the bulkhead in a spray of sparks. Then it leapt and rolled away, screaming something, stubby arms flailing in the air. A moment later, the hull of the Spire sparked again even without the rustling's knives.

"Toshiko?" Iro asked.

A beam of searing white light burst out of the Spire, fracturing the bulkhead wall and splitting it open. One rustling was caught in the blast and reduced to a pair of smoking, stumpy legs. Then the blast of light faded. There was a hole in the spire, the metal bent outwards, melted around the edges.

Emil grinned. "Toshiko."

The Mage burst out of the new hole she had created, shrieking, "Get it off! Get it off! Get it off!"

Emil stepped up onto the edge of the balcony and leapt into the chamber. Iro slashed, pushed his poisoned current into his sword, Blink Striking down to Toshiko.

"Ahh!" Toshiko squeaked at his arrival. "Iro. Help!" There was something long and sinuous coiled around her left leg. It looked like a cable come to life, all sectioned metal covered into a dark, viscous fluid like oil.

Emil thumped to the floor amidst the rustlings, flattening one. The other monsters fled with squeals of terror, disappearing into open grates within moments.

Iro grabbed the head of the living cable wrapped around Toshiko's leg. It was stronger than he'd thought and he had to use both hands to wrench the head away from her.

"Ow ow ow ow," Toshiko wailed as the body of the cable constricted against her leg.

"We need to leave," Emil said as he strode forward, positioning himself between Toshiko and the Spire. Little skittering constructs crawling out of the hole she had blasted. Each one was as big as Iro's chest, scuttled about on eight spindly legs, had gleaming green lights for eyes and plasma torches for mouths. They poured out of the breach, a chittering, scuttling mass. "Now!"

Toshiko hopped away on one leg as Iro wrestled with the cable wrapped around her other. Emil thumped a gauntlet down on the first construct to reach him, crushing it against the floor. It sparked, twitched, then popped back up, repairing itself even as it lurched after him.

"What the scrap?" Emil hit the construct again and again, pulping it into dismantled parts on the ground. Wires within the mess twitched, wriggled, sought each other out, pulled the construct back together. "We need to go."

The head of the living cable Iro had hold of thrashed about. It opened up like a flower from the garden, peeling away, and disgorged a wriggling mass of tiny cables all over his hands. Iro fell back away from Toshiko, let go of the cable and flicked his hands, trying to rid himself of the little worms. They attached themselves to the armor plates on the back of his gloves, started burrowing into the weave underneath. With a cry of alarm, Iro pulled his gloves off and threw them to the floor. He took a few moments to check over his hands, but they were clear. His gloves sat in a pile, tiny worm-like cables thrashing about amidst them.

"Really time to go," Emil shouted. The constructs were swarming him now. He kicked one away, tore another out of the air as it leapt for him, crushed one in his gauntlets. It twisted in his grip, reassembling itself and crawled up his arm. Emil's crest flared as he Steeled himself. The construct bit down against his bare arms, plasma torch mouth burning. Emil screamed in pain, grabbed the construct and tossed it away, backing up as more of them swarmed forwards. There were dozens of them now, hundreds maybe, pouring out of the hole Toshiko had blasted.

"That scrapping thing bit right through my enhancement," Emil said as he kicked at another, sending it flying.

Toshiko wailed. She had fallen over, was lying on the rusted floor, flailing. The cable monster was crawling up her hip now, still wrapped around her left leg. "Help!"

Iro glanced down at his discarded gloves, and an idea struck him. "Emil, grab her shoulders and pull." Iro ran to Toshiko, dodged the flailing tail end of the cable and knelt by her, fumbling at her leg plates. "This is going to hurt."

"It already hurts!"

Iro flipped open the catches securing the leg plates, and the boot, and gripped the thigh plate high up.

"Hurry!" Emil said, wide eyes staring past Iro. He could hear the chittering swarm closing on them.

"Now!" Iro shouted and wrenched on the armor. Emil pulled Toshiko by her arms. She screamed as the leg plates and cable monster both tore free, scraping down her leg, opening gashes in the fabric weave and her skin.

Toshiko leapt up and stumbled back, one leg now bare of armor. She was still carrying Steel Lotus and the salvaged rotating cannon. Emil stepped in front of her, ready between their Mage and the swarm.

Iro threw the leg armor and the writhing cable monster into the swarm of advancing constructs. There was a brief scuffle as cable and constructs fought each other in a wild frenzy.

"We're leaving. Now!" Emil said. He grabbed Iro by the shoulder and pulled him back. They all turned and started running as the swarm chittered after them.

CHAPTER 41

THEIR FLIGHT back up through the titan was unhindered, like the nearby levels and sections had been cleared of monsters. Iro wasn't complaining. Neither he, nor Emil were in any state for a fight. Toshiko, on the other hand, was bouncing with fresh energy. She had opened her Second Gate and her current was overflowing. Iro gawked at the size of her crest. She'd only just opened her gate, but her crest dwarfed his own both in size and brightness. Emil congratulated her and stalked on, sulking.

They followed North's map. Iro was certain he heard the chittering of the construct swarm behind them, but they saw no sign. But he couldn't shake the feeling he was being watched. It itched between his shoulder blades.

They knew they were getting close when they found fresh blood spatters on the gratings below their feet. It didn't take a Surveyor to guess who the blood belonged to. Gadise Samir was badly injured. Iro hoped the pods had already arrived, and the squad leader was already gone back to the Home Fleet where the medics could treat her properly.

"Aren't you tired, carrying both of those?" Iro asked Toshiko as they jogged down a length of corridor lit with frosted strip lights. A few sections of the bulkhead wall had been damaged, gouged by sword or claw, and steam was leaking into the corridor, making it cloyingly warm.

"I should be, shouldn't I?" Toshiko said. "But not all. This Second Gate is great. I feel strong enough to arm wrestle Emil."

Emil grunted from up ahead.

"Scared you'd lose?" Toshiko said with a grin.

Emil glanced over his shoulder, scowling. "I wouldn't lose. I'd..."

Toshiko laughed. "You're not nearly as steely as you want everyone to believe. I think you're soft as a pillow inside."

Emil scoffed as he slowed to a stop outside the door to the docks. "I don't own a pillow. I sleep on the floor."

"I don't need comfort because I'm hard as steel and cold as the void," Toshiko said in a silly, deep voice.

Iro grinned. "She has you down, Emil. If I hadn't seen her lips moving, I would have sworn it was you."

"Scrap you both," Emil said, though even he was smiling. He slammed the button to open the door and took a single step into the docks. Then he froze, the smile slipping from his face.

Iro and Toshiko both rushed forward to peer around Emil stopped in the doorway.

"Nice of you to join us," said a nasally voice. It was Ink, one of the powerful Hoppers from the other fleet who had attacked the dome and stolen their harvest. "Inside and close the door or she dies."

The dock was an open space with multiple mechanical arms stationed around ramps leading down to the green crosshatch of lights that kept the atmosphere in. The arms were dormant, but an overturned cart nearby attested to the brief struggle that must have taken place. There were no pods. The Home Fleet must not have got their message, but the other fleet had.

Justice lumped against a metal barrier that stood at the head of one ramp. His face was bruised, swollen and bloody, and his nose looked broken. His autodage lay in his lap, its prehensile arm snapped in two.

Kneeling in the centre of the dock, Gadise Samir was a sorry sight. Her shield had been taken and thrown away. Her hair had pulled loose and hung in limp strands across a bloody cheek. She slumped forward over her chest wounds. And there was a gleaming blade held at her neck.

Iro recognised the two Hoppers who had the squad leader. They were from the other fleet. The two he had seen escorting the harvest they had stolen. The giant of a man with a bald head called Wheel, and the smaller man with a pinched face known as Ink. It was the smaller man with his knife to Gadise Samir's neck.

Emil walked into the dock. Iro and Toshiko followed behind him. Iro was already weighing up his odds. If he was quick enough, he could boost himself with Burning Adrenaline and Blink Strike in, knock the man's knife away, and free the squad leader. His hands trembled, his poisoned current a leaden ache in his chest. He was far from certain he could use Burning Adrenaline again. But he would try. He had to try.

"What do you want?" Emil asked. The Paladin held up his hands in a peaceful gesture. That was good, lure them into thinking they were placid. It gave Iro time to gather himself.

The huge Hopper took three thundering steps towards them, blurred around the edges, smashed a fist into Emil's face. Emil careened into the nearest barrier, flipped over it, hit the floor in a heap. The giant Hopper turned to Iro next, raised his fist. Iro brought his sword up and blocked the overhead strike. His little sword shattered in his hands and the fist slammed into his shoulder, crushing him to the floor. He tried to get up, but the Hopper stepped on him, pinning him to the ground.

Toshiko's crest lit up as she pulled her little hand cannon and fired a searing blast into Wheel's face. Smoke engulfed his head.

When it cleared, he was grinning. He slapped Toshiko's cannon away and wrapped a massive hand around her head, lifting her from the ground. She struggled, squeaked in alarm, but he had her.

"Stop it," Gadise Samir slurred through swollen lips. Ink tutted and pressed his blade a little closer to her neck.

Iro gritted his teeth, got his hands beneath him and pushed. It was so unfair. The black cloaks, these Hoppers from the other fleet, everyone was so much stronger than him. He was so sick of only punching down, of only being able to beat monsters weaker than him while everyone stronger just took whatever they wanted. He was so done with being a punching bag. His crest blossomed beneath his hands, lighting up the grated floor. He didn't care about current sickness or trembling limbs. He didn't give a scrap about his limits. No matter what it took, he would break through them and win. Burning Adrenaline flooded his body with current, overclocking his limbs into new depths of strength. Icy blue light shone from his eyes and he pushed.

"Well, will you look at that," the huge Hopper rumbled from above.

Iro pushed himself back up to his knees, shouting out his anger and the pain of his poisoned current like knives stabbing into all his muscles at once.

"Gutsy little junker, aren't you?" The huge Hopper stamped down on Iro's back. Iro held. Arms trembling, chest aching, but he held.

"What the scrap?" Wheel said in alarm.

"Settle down, kid," Ink said, pressing the knife close to Gadise Samir's throat. "Or your entire squad dies while you watch."

Iro held on a few moments more, azure light shining from his eyes. But he couldn't do it. He couldn't sacrifice his squad. He let his crest fade and went limp. The huge Hopper stamped down on his back and slammed him back to the bulkhead floor. Through the crosshatch of green lights, Iro saw six burning spots of yellow light.

"More company," said Wheel, as he ground his boot into Iro's back.

"Just the pods come to collect them," said Ink. "Ours now."

"Prisoners and tech. The Emperor might even give us a medal."

"Keep ya scrapping medals, I just want orders to take this wing as ours."

Iro heard more muffled yells from Toshiko as the six bright spots in his vision grew larger.

"Put them down, Wheel. Best be ready."

Wheel grunted and the pressure disappeared from Iro's back. A moment later, a boot nudged under him, flipped him over, then kicked him back. He slammed against the wall and flopped, couldn't even summon the energy to stand. The big Hopper whipped his hand forward and flung Toshiko. She squeaked, then smashed into the wall, denting the bulkhead. She slid down and landed next to Iro.

The six burning yellow spots resolved into pods as they passed through the crosshatch of lights and burned to a stop, alighting on the main clearance of the dock. Iro peered through blurry eyes at the pods. He didn't recognise the emblem painted on the sides. A slashing knife, the arc of its passing a black circle.

Gadise Samir let out a low, rumbling chuckle. The knife pressed into her neck and she quieted.

Once all six pods were down, only the front most door opened in a hiss of compressed air. An old man with long white hair stepped out. He wore a bone coloured robe, no weave and no armor. A single slender sword was belted at his hip, and even from a distance Iro could see it was fused into its sheathe by a clump of ugly gray metal. The old man coughed and waved a hand in front of his face as he stepped calmly from the pod.

"Stop right there or I'll open her throat," shouted the little Hopper with the knife.

The old man grumbled something Iro couldn't hear and crossed over to Emil still lying in a heap on the clearance floor. He reached down and helped the Paladin to his feet.

"Enough," shouted Wheel. He took two thundering steps and leapt over the barrier from the ramp above. There was a flash of golden light. Wheel fell to the clearance floor and his head hit the ground a moment later, rolled to a leaking stop.

The old man finished helping Emil up and propped him up against the wall, patted him on the shoulder and turned.

"What did you…" Ink moved, stepping back and pulling Gadise Samir with him, pushing his blade into her neck so hard blood dribbled down her skin. "No closer. Don't come any closer."

The old man walked forward, his hands clasped behind his back, a pleasant smile on his bearded face.

"I said stop!" the Hopper screamed.

The old man stopped. The little Hopper flew backwards as if struck by an immense force. He smashed into one of the mechanical arms, spun around, hit the ground. He was up in a second, shouting, reaching for the cannon slung across his back. Another flash of golden light and Ink's arm dropped to the dock floor, severed at the elbow. He screamed.

The old man turned away from the screaming Hopper and walked over to Gadise Samir. She still knelt on the upper dock grating, one eye swollen closed, the other half lidded. The old man looked down on her and stroked his chin. Finally, he spoke in a voice as creaky as a rusted door. "Your father will be disappointed, Gadise."

Gadise Samir lifted her chin, met the old man's narrowed gaze. "My squad is alive."

The old man glanced around as if noticing them all for the first time. He settled on Justice. "You, Surveyor. Staunch her bleeding and get her ready for travel. The rest of you, stop lounging about and get into the pods."

A bright blue crest roared into life behind Ink. He twisted about, drew his cannon into his remaining hand, fired a blast of dazzling red light.

The old man's hand snapped up and he snatched the blast of red light from the air, held it fizzing and simmering between his fingers. He regarded it casually for a moment, then clenched his fist and snuffed it out.

Ink dropped his cannon, then dropped to his knees. "I... I surrender."

The old man raised a single eyebrow. "What would I want with a prisoner? Tie a tourniquet around that arm and you might live. Run back to your fleet. Tell them this wing belongs to us." He turned away as if the man was no longer any interest at all.

Iro struggled to his feet, as unsteady as a limp wire. He helped Toshiko up and together they dragged her cannons over to the pods. Emil limped over to another pod, and Justice helped Gadise Samir to another. The old man waited on the upper dock, his hands clasped behind him. He was still standing there, watching, when the pod doors closed.

CHAPTER 42

EMIL STRODE through the corridors of the Courage. People waved to him, said hello. Some even asked him how he was doing. It was strange. A few months ago, no one on the ship paid him a spark of notice except his da', and even then only when the old man wanted something. Now... now everyone acted like they were friends. They said they were glad he was alive, that he'd made it back. He almost thought they must be mistaking him for someone else, but they all knew his name. If they stopped him, he greeted them and exchanged pleasantries, but he wasn't a talker, and had no ambitions on any social ladder, real or imagined. All Emil wanted was to train, to get stronger, to...

He stopped himself. There was no getting stronger anymore. He had failed himself and the entire Courage. Failed them all when they needed him most. They treated him as a friend, someone to look up to, and he had let them all down.

He was still letting them down. Three days since he returned and he hadn't been to see Roret. The tech deserved an apology, and Iro had asked Emil to check in on him. He'd been putting it off because it was easier that way, but no more. When something needed doing, it was best to set your feet, square your shoulders, and get it done.

He started in engineering. The head tech had pointed him towards Algae Vat 3. But before Emil could leave, he'd been asked if he needed anything. Any repairs or new armor plates or supplies. He'd promised to send the man a list, but even then he'd had to wait around for a few minutes while the tech thanked him multiple times for bringing them the repairs for the ship's printer. Eventually, Emil made his excuses and all but ran from engineering.

He strolled into Algae Vat 3 with his hands in his pockets and his head down. It was the best way to stop most people from accosting him. He ran his fingers over the gear in his thigh pocket, the same one he'd taken from the Spire. The same gear that the black cloaks had asked after. He wasn't sure why, but it felt important and he was loath to leave it in his quarters. He wanted it with him at all times in case… He didn't know.

"Hey!" Emil said from the doorway.

Roret let out a squeak and startled, fell backwards from the vat, the stool beneath his feet toppling, his hand trailing green sludge. He hit the floor plates with an *ooff* that made Emil wince. Emil rushed over to help the little tech up.

"How are you so stealthy when you're so big?" Roret asked as he dusted himself off and wiped down his arm, squeezing the sludge back into the algae vat.

"Dunno," Emil said. He stepped back, leaned against the wall, thrust his hands back into his pockets. "My da' always said I clomped around like a bhurbeast in a sulk. But that was before." Maybe he was quieter now. Lighter on his feet thanks to the strength granted him by his Second Gate. And he preferred not to say much. He'd noticed most people couldn't stop talking, but things were a lot quieter in his head.

"I don't have to go back, do I?" Roret asked, fear as plain as his big nose on his face. "I don't want to go back to the titan ever again."

"No." Emil shook his head. "I'm not here to... No one is ever going to drag you back to the titan. I just wanted to come and check on you. Make sure you're alright. You got out safe and that."

"Oh." Roret turned away and shoved his arm back into the algae vat. He rummaged around for a few seconds, then pulled out a clump of something dark as oil. It made a sickening splat as it hit the floor and Emil decided he never wanted to eat algae ever again.

"I was close to the pods when the dome cracked. We'd been hauling baskets of grain into the cargo pods, which is frankly some of the most back breaking work I've ever experienced, thank you. Not in a hurry to do that again. Give me a valve to flush any day. Anyway, the moment the dome cracked it was a frenzy. Some dour woman appeared out of nowhere, literally just appeared in front of me, and bundled me into a pod. I never even saw the rest of it."

Emil tapped his heel against the wall as he stared hard at the bulkhead flooring, the rust creeping along the seams. Two screws were missing from one corner. They had probably been salvaged and used for something else. Half the Courage had been cannibalised to fix the other half to keep them flying for a few months. Now they had the printer running, things were getting better. Too slowly.

"Glad you got out," Emil said as he tapped his heel. "Iro was worried."

Roret looked up, smiled. "He was? I don't know why he always dreamed of Hopping to the titan."

"You didn't want to go?"

Roret snorted out his big nose. "No! Never. That was Iro's dream fighting monsters and running traps. This is all I ever wanted; to be a tech, to understand how all the mechanism and systems work. All I want is to fix the Courage and make her purr instead of growl."

"Huh…" Emil tapped his heel again.

He'd always thought everyone wanted to be a Hopper. That they all would given the chance, but most people were born talentless. He'd never even considered people wouldn't want to have the same abilities he did. Fixing the ship all day every day for the rest of his life sounded boring. Being a drudge like his father was even worse. Emil wanted to Hop. The titan was something he wanted to face. To be challenged by it, and he wanted to defeat those challenges and bring back the supplies needed to fix the ship. He'd never given much thought to the people doing the fixing. Maybe they were heroes, too, slaving away at a job they knew they could never finish, fixing the same scrapping things over and over every day.

"Why did you go?" Emil asked as he tapped his heel. "If you didn't want to Hop to the titan, why did you?"

Roret shrugged. He pulled another clump of black sludge from the algae. It smelled like rot. "They ordered me to. The chief pulled me out of daily duties and said I was shipping across to the titan for the day. So I did."

"Even though you didn't want to? Even though you were terrified?"

"Of course. I don't always understand my orders, or like them, but that doesn't mean I ignore them. If the chief says to crawl into a vent and change a filter, I do it. I might not understand what I'm doing or why, but I trust that if I don't, maybe the life support pumps out CO_2 instead of air."

"C O what?" Emil asked.

Roret glanced at him, one eyebrow cocked. "Poison."

"The ship can do that?"

Roret nodded. "The point is, I follow my orders even if I don't like them, because I trust the chief knows more than I do, and if I don't follow them, people might die."

Emil tried to get his head around it. He wasn't good at this sort of thing, considering things from all the different angles. He was built for rushing in and punching things, but he couldn't punch a concept. People followed orders because they trusted those in charge knew more than they did. That was why Roret Hopped to the titan, and why the squad leader tried to sacrifice a bunch of workers. But what if those orders were wrong? What if people were just blindly following scrap orders because they didn't know any better? The upper ships were in charge, they made the rules, passed down the orders to the lower ships. Upper ships had everything and by their orders, the lower ships had nothing. So their orders were scrap.

Yet, what could Emil do about any of it? A single Hopper on a decrepit ship. He had no power to change the order or things. Worse yet, he'd never have the power to change anything. He was stalled now. Never anything more than a Second Gater. Stalled and weak, and still the only Hopper the Courage had.

"You alright there, Emil?" Roret asked. "You look like a screen waiting for a command."

"Huh?"

"You've gone into standby mode. Everything alright?"

"Yeah…" Emil paused. It was a lie. Everything was not alright. It was all scrapping wrong, and it ate at him inside like poison running through a ship's air ducts. He couldn't stop thinking about it. Couldn't stop hating himself for failing. And he couldn't tell anyone. If they knew, if the rest of the squad found out he was stalled, they wouldn't take him on Hops anymore. And the Courage would once again be without a Hopper. It was all so scrapping unfair.

Emil kicked his heel into the wall hard. The panel dented from the force.

"Hey!" Roret shouted. The little tech sprang to his feet, arm still dripping with gloopy algae. "Whatever it is, don't take it out on the ship. It can't take the beating."

He was right. In frustration, Emil was damaging the one thing he needed to protect. One more thing he was useless at. One more thing he did wrong. But how else to let out the frustration? How was he supposed to keep it all locked up inside without hitting things?

"Sorry," Emil said. He sank down against the wall until he sat on the cold metal flooring. "Didn't mean to damage the Courage."

Roret edged closed, like Emil was some sort of vicious monster playing dead, waiting to strike. That hurt. Emil would never hit the little tech. He'd never hit anyone from the Courage. "What's wrong?"

Emil glanced up at the tech. "How much do you know about Hoppers? About crests and the gates?"

Roret snorted. "How much do you know about air filtration and mechanical engineering?"

"Uhhh... nothing?"

Roret shrugged. Emil stared at him, not understanding.

"I know nothing about Hoppers or any of that," Roret said. "I don't even understand why Iro was always so obsessed with it all."

Emil drew in a great breath and sighed it out. He activated his crest in front of him. Fiery lines and symbols and letters flared bright as thruster burn. Roret staggered back, eyes wide, arms held up before him.

"It can't hurt you," Emil said. "It's my crest. Not even sure it's really there. Just light. See?" He waved a hand through the lines. They fuzzed at his touch, then snapped back to normal.

Roret crept forward again, passed a finger through one of the fiery lines. "OK?"

"See that little circle right at the top?" Emil pointed to the third lock. "That's the lock to my Third Gate. It's shaded out. That means I failed to open it. It's locked. Forever. It means I'm stalled. I can't get stronger. I'm stuck."

"Oh."

"It's like, you want to fix the ship, right? You want to keep learning how to fix new parts of the ship. But you can't. You'll never learn more than fishing gunk out of the algae. So that's all you'll ever be."

Roret crouched down in front of Emil. "I already do more than fish rot out of the algae."

Emil shrugged. He'd kind of assumed each of the techs had a specific job and stuck to it.

"I think I understand," Roret said. "You're afraid."

Emil tensed up, ready to stand and storm off. Nothing scared him. Not the titan, not the monsters, not the black cloaks.

Roret held up his hands. "I mean, you're afraid if others find out, you won't get to Hop anymore."

Emil relaxed a little. "Yeah. I guess."

"So, what are you going to do?"

Emil banged his head back against the wall. Roret winced at the impact, but said nothing. He shoved his hands back into his pockets, ran his fingers over the gear. "Only thing I can do. Keep Hopping. Keep it a secret. Courage needs a Hopper, and I'm it. Ship needs supplies, parts, access to a manufactory. Without a Hopper, we'll get nothing. And... and if they won't let me Hop, what am I?"

Roret crossed his legs and sat in front of Emil. He waved his hand through the fiery lines of his crest again, smiling as they fizzed around his fingers. "You could learn to be a tech."

Emil rolled his eyes.

"You could be a dru..."

"Don't!" Emil snapped. "Don't you dare say it."

Roret held up his hands again. "Alright. Alright." He stood

and walked back to the algae vat. "Then you keep going for now. As you are."

"Stalled," Emil said bitterly.

"Hmmm." Roret thrust his arm into the algae. "That's what we call it when the engines cut out as well. Usually just need to flush out the fuel lines, then reignite the combustion chamber."

"What?"

Roret pulled out another clump of rotting gunk. "I'm just saying, in engineering, stalled doesn't mean broken. Just means you have to get it going again."

CHAPTER 43

TOSHIKO'S NEW BERET ITCHED. She wasn't sure how it itched through her hair, but whenever she wore it, her head itched. She didn't like it. Printed material just wasn't the same as something hand made. But since her last beret went interstellar out the garden dome, and her mother wasn't able to make her a new one with her hands the way they were these days. So itchy and printed was the best she was going to get.

Her mother had always been so good with knitting things. She'd sit for hours and hours in one spot, her hands moving in a blur, needles clicking and clacking with a staccato beat. Toshiko loved to watch. Until her mind wandered and her body wandered with it. Never very good at sitting still. Her mother used to despair about it, but she never tried to force Toshiko to stop. But Toshiko inherited her mother's love of making things as well as her class, she was just never very good with needles. Always much better with a screwdriver and welding torch.

She padded into the Thousand Suns armory as quietly as possible. Hinata was leaning back in her hammock, swaying and snoring. The old legend lived in her armory, treated each one of her bland and uniform TCX-556s with love and care like they were unique children.

"Toshiko," Hinata said.

"How? You were asleep."

The old armorer laughed and sat up in her swaying hammock. "You don't live as long as I have by being a heavy sleeper." She rubbed gnarled hands over the burned flesh around her milky eyes. "Remember, I was Hopping when you were still a procreation request in the supervisor's inbox."

Toshiko felt her face curdle. "That is somehow the most clinical description of it I've ever heard… and also the most icky."

The old woman chuckled again and pulled in her knees, sitting cross-legged in her hammock.

"How did you know it was me, anyway, granny? I walked as lightly as I could."

Hinata smiled. "You walk like a woman trying to fill her own shoes. What have you done to the little girl this time?"

Toshiko hefted Steel Lotus up onto the emptiest counter. Hinata kept all her cupboards and stores spotless, but her counters were always strewn with spare parts. She swung the rotating cannon up onto the counter next to Steel Lotus, then spent a second scratching at her arm. Damned thing kept itching as much as her head with the new beret.

"I fixed her channeling issue," Toshiko said proudly.

"Ahh." Hinata slipped from her hammock and hit the floor lightly. She never wore shoes, socks, or slippers. It was perhaps the most untraditional thing she could have done on a ship obsessed with tradition, yet she got away with it because she was Thousand Suns Hinata. She was a legend. There were actual songs sung about her. One of them had three verses dedicated to her defeat of the fingoid horde back aboard titan 01. But that was decades gone now.

Hinata stretched out her back, groaned until it popped, then shuffled towards the counter. She ran her wrinkled old hands over Steel Lotus, deft fingers searching out every dent, scratch, dint, and defect.

"Banged up good again."

Toshiko scratched her arm. "The perils of a Hop, granny. I climbed a Spire. And descended it. Blasted my way out of the basement."

"Someone should write a song of your deeds. And you opened your Second Gate."

Toshiko leaned forward, elbows on the counter. "How did you know?"

"It's all in your aura. Subtle changes in the atmosphere when you enter a room. A smell like ozone."

"Really?" Toshiko imagined her aura being huge and sparkly, which would be about as far from traditional as possible.

"Of course not, girl. I'm an elder on the Thousand Suns council. I heard the report about five seconds after you got back."

"Oh." Toshiko couldn't hide the disappointment.

Hinata fished inside a drawer, pulled out her favourite screwdriver, the one with a thousand nicks along the haft. "I need to open the little girl up."

"Mhm." Toshiko scratched at her arm. "I figure if we find a manufactory, I can have a new chassis made from titansteel. That'll keep her from getting so banged up all the time. Not to mention it will cut down on conductivity loss."

Hinata pulled off one of Steel Lotus' side panels and brushed her fingers through the cannon's innards.

"She says that tickles, granny."

Hinata chuckled. "We could replace about 70% of this little girl with titansteel if we had access to a manufactory. With the amount of current you channel through her, it would pick up your resonance in no time."

Toshiko gasped. "She'd level up with me."

"She would. Ahhh, you found a new capacitor."

"Our Surveyor ripped it out of a construct that was using him as a toothpick."

"Show me your crest."

Toshiko activated her crest in front of her. It filled the armory with a soft, pink haze, running over the floor and the ceiling. It was huge. So much bigger than before. The lines were brighter, too. The second lock that had once been blank now had a symbol that looked a lot like a Spire in it and new lines and lettering formed beyond the Second Gate.

Hinata passed her hand through the fizzing lines of Toshiko's crest. The pink haze was reflected in her washed-out, filmy eyes.

"The new capacitor should work for now, but she's going to need constant upgrading as you grow stronger, Toshiko." The old armorer shook her head. "Such a battery you are, girl."

Toshiko grinned and scratched at her arm. "I know."

"Is there any more toxic relationship than pride and arrogance," Hinata grumbled. She removed her hands from Steel Lotus and shifted over to the salvaged cannon. Her lip curled as she hovered her scarred fingers over the wreck, not quite touching it. "What is this monstrosity?"

Toshiko clapped her hands together and bounced over to the other side of the cannon. "I cut it off the arm of a giant construct. Well, I didn't. Iro did. He's our Corsair. Cute but dim. Thinks every problem can be solved with a sword to the noggin."

"Eh, never met a Corsair who didn't think with their blade."

"Exactly! There's an anger to him, though. Scares me a little. It's unchecked, like a thruster firing out of control, you know? Burns hot as the sun for a few moments, then switches off."

Hinata grumbled something, her face twisting into a wrinkled grimace. "What about the Paladin you were so excited to meet?"

"Emil? Oh the brooding, granny. You wouldn't believe it. If you listen to him, you'd think the fleet, the titan, and the universe in general were out to get him. And he's all *I must stand here and look dark and menacing at it all.*" She scratched her arm as she considered. "But he doesn't scare me. He's a big softy under it all. Armor on the outside, cuddle on the inside. Iro's the opposite, smiles and laughter holding back sharp edges."

Hinata was smiling, her pale eyes crinkled.

"What?"

"And this... thing?" Hinata gestured at the salvaged cannon.

"Look at the design, granny. Smaller, rotating barrels allowing for rapid fire."

Hesitantly, the old woman touched it, as though it might come to life and bite her. She grimaced. "Ammunition?"

"Metal pellets."

"Hmmm. Electromagnetic pulses provided the force to shoot them."

Toshiko gawked. "It took me three days of studying the thing to figure that out."

"And it's taken me fifty years of life to earn the experience needed to determine it in moments. You're seventeen years old, Toshiko. Three days is impressive." She finished her inspection of the cannon and stepped back, mouth twisting into six different grimaces. "What do you want to do with it?"

Toshiko scratched her arm. "I want to steal its design and add a new formation to Steel Lotus' barrel."

Hinata placed a single hand on Steel Lotus, and another on the salvaged cannon. "What does the little girl think about that?"

Toshiko placed her own hand on Steel Lotus. "She's ready for another upgrade, granny. She says there's no chance I'm leaving her behind."

Hinata took a slow breath and nodded thoughtfully. "Alright then. Let's take this piece of junk apart and see what we can salvage."

CHAPTER 44

THE POD SHUDDERED as it docked with the Eclipse. Iro leaned back in the chair and waited. North sat in his lap, silent save for the occasional buzz. The little automaton was still a mess held together by patchwork soldering and tape. And its voice stuttered and stopped, drew out sounds, occasionally fizzled into silence. North almost seemed embarrassed by it. It had taken to communication with messages that popped up on Iro's tablet.

Three days he'd spent aboard the Flame Horizon. Three days being looked over by the best Surveyors in the fleet, asked the same scrapping questions. *Oh, you're suffering from acute current sickness. How?* Apparently it was not possible to develop current sickness aboard a titan. And yet. At least he wasn't shaking anymore. The first day he hadn't even been able to feed himself the trembling had been so bad. They had him sucking algae paste through a straw again. He'd spent three days under strict orders not to use any current for anything. Now they'd released him back to his ship, but under those same orders. No current. Not even to activate his crest. Yet, despite the orders, the questions, the care. They still did not know what was wrong with him.

The pod door opened and Iro found himself home. The

Eclipse. He realised he thought of the ship as home now. Not the Courage. The Courage his childhood home and would always be important, but he didn't belong there anymore. He had moved on. The Eclipse was home now. He stepped out onto the deck of the pod dock, took a deep breath.

Eir hit him like a rapid decompression. One moment Iro was revelling in the clean smell of the Eclipse, the next he had arms wrapped around him, squeezing him tight. He didn't know what to do. She had her arms wrapped around his midsection and her face pressed against his chest. He draped a hand over her shoulders. It was all so weird, but, he didn't want her to let go.

The tech who had been manning the pod dock smiled, shook her head, walked away.

"Stupid junker," Eir said into Iro's chest. "I thought you died."

"Me? I was worried you were dead."

Eir let go of him and stepped back, her face twisted into an expression Iro could only describe as *eh?* "Why would you think that?"

"You were in the dome when it cracked."

Eir rolled her eyes and twirled on the spot. "Not a scratch on me." She grinned. "I'm invincible!"

"Your last message said you were fighting Hoppers from the other fleet!"

"Oh yeah, them. They kind of just ran away. We chased them for a bit, but the dome went crack and…" She stopped and fixed Iro with a very serious stare. "Stop changing the subject. You disappeared."

"Well, I…"

"And what have you done to poor North?" She rushed over and peered down at the construct.

North buzzed, tried to float, failed. "Noooorrrthhh isssss hurrrrrrt—t—t."

Iro sighed. "Stop acting up for attention." His tablet pinged and he looked down at his wrist. There was a message from North. It was blank.

Eir scooped up the little construct. "You poor thing. Is he alright?"

"Beat up, but still functioning for now," Iro said.

"Uh huh. And what about North?"

"Nice to know you were worried about me."

"Pfft! Barely." She cradled North against her chest and slotted her free hand through Iro's arm and pulled him away down the corridors of the Eclipse. "I just need someone to beat up."

"Good luck with that. I opened my Second Gate."

Eir pulled him to a stop. "You did not! Well done. Of course, this means I hate you now. Stop pulling ahead of me." They started walking again.

"I can't help it," Iro said with a sly smile. "It's all this natural talent. You wouldn't understand."

Eir snorted. "Sorry. Shouldn't laugh. I'm imagining what Rollo would say if he heard that. Do you remember he once compared you to a wet mop?"

"To be fair, Bjorn had just used me to mop the floor."

"He opened his First Gate."

Iro grinned. "Well, it's about time. He's a bit slow."

Eir smiled back. "Isn't he, though? They all opened their gates. Bjorn and Ash and Ylfa and Arne. Even Ingrid and she's... scary now. "

"All of them together?"

Eir nodded. "When the dome started breaking. One after another, they started opening gates. I can't decide if Rollo is proud or angry. Hey, so did you really climb a Spire?"

Ido nodded. "All the way to the top."

"Did you get any loot? Please tell me it wasn't this hideous gray jumpsuit you're wearing. It does not suit you at all." She bumped his shoulder with her own.

"No. This is from the Flame Horizon. Apparently my armor was scrap even before the Vhar poked holes in it, so—"

"Vhar? You fought against Vhar?" Eir eyed him sceptically. "That explains it. You died and must be a ghost."

"I found a Strikebreaker."

"A what?"

He told Eir about the Spire as they walked, trap and the way he had pulled the Strikebreaker from the floor. He told her about the constructs, the Tucker sphere. And he told her about the black cloaks and the Hoppers from the other fleet, and how unfair it was that everyone seemed to be stronger than him still. His anger iced over inside as he recounted, cold and sharp in his chest. He didn't like it, and yet he couldn't seem to thaw it. It frosted over his heart and made it hard to breathe. He wanted to channel his current and fight something. Eir told him to stop being so tense and pulled him on.

"Hey, Iro," Eir said as she pulled him to a stop outside a door. She rubbed a hand over her bristly scalp, looked away, then wrung her hands in front of her. Eir had never been good at being still. "I really am glad you're alive."

"Me too," Iro said. The moment felt weighty, like something was expected of him, but he didn't know what. "And you. I'm glad you're alive. As well as me. I'm glad we're both alive?"

Eir snorted, shook her head and looked up at him. "Yeah. Smooth. Good luck in there. If you're still alive afterwards, come find me." She shoved North into Iro's arms, then turned and skipped away down the corridor.

The door in front of Iro slid open to reveal the Hopper lounge, a bored-looking Rollo standing in the doorway, and Frigg sitting on the couch, surrounded by tablets.

"What are you smiling at, idiot?" Rollo asked.

Iro didn't answer. He couldn't seem to thaw his rage once it iced over, but Eir always managed to do it for him. A few words and a smile and all his anger melted away.

Three full hours of question time followed. Iro counted down the minutes. He wanted to be gone, to go running after Eir. Something about the way she'd said to come find her. He wanted to. More than anything. Time spent with Eir was comfortable and thrilling all at once. It made his blood thunder through his veins and the Eclipse felt more vibrant around her.

Frigg was relentless. Every answer led to more questions, and no answer was good enough. She spent the entire time scribbling away on one of her tablets, only stopping when she got up to make coffee. And she kept asking Iro to repeat himself. He came to dread the words *Tell me again...*

Rollo was as opposite to Frigg as could be. Where she was attentive and demanding, he was bored and asleep for half the interview. He only perked up when Iro first mentioned using Burning Adrenaline. Then he sat bolt upright, cursed, said *She really taught you that talent?* He stormed off out of the Hopper lounge. He returned half an hour later with a black eye and an even more sour attitude.

When it was finally done, Iro felt like he had gone over the entire Hop since before the dome cracked at least three times. Even then, Frigg didn't seem happy with Iro's answers. She only relented when Rollo took the tablet from her hands and threw it across the room.

Iro scrambled from the lounge as quickly as he could and didn't look back. Would Eir still be waiting for him? Had she ever been waiting? He was starting to think the whole thing through and decided she hadn't meant for him to find her. She was just being polite, as friends were.

"What do you think, North?" Iro asked the little automaton.

North buzzed and Iro's tablet pinged. He looked down. The message was not from North. It was from the Vermillion. Gadise

Samir's ship. The flagship of the fleet. He opened the message and read it twice to be sure.

Iro slumped against the wall. A passing tech glanced at him with a curious expression, but he gave the man a wan smile. He read the message a third time, hoping it had changed. It hadn't.

Iro's presence was requested aboard the Vermillion right away to sit before the Council of Grands. The most powerful Hoppers in the fleet, those who had opened their Fifth Gates of Power.

"I can not go, right?" Iro asked North. The little automaton buzzed on his shoulder. "I mean, the message said they request my presence."

His tablet pinged again and he looked down. The message four simple words from Gadise Samir:

It's not a request.

SNAPSHOT 3 - WAVE

WAVE STEPPED off the skiff to a shower of sparks floating in the air before her. She plucked one out of the air and snuffed it out in her fist. Kettle bumped into her from behind, set her spinning so she had to grab hold of the airlock door to steady herself. The junker laughed as he floated off down the corridor towards recreation. No doubt he'd be drunk as a marsh mite within minutes. She couldn't fault him for that. They all needed to unwind after a Hop. She just faulted him for being a space sucking junk hole instead.

"Don't take it personal, Wave," Holster said as he pushed off and sailed towards the corridor after Kettle.

"I d-don't," Wave said. "Just l-look forward to the d-day I drive my sword through his heart."

"That's the spirit." Holster spun around in midair, floating backwards, and gave Wave a thumbs up. "My bet is he doesn't die."

Wave nodded at that. She was certain Kettle was infested. They all were, but some were worse than others. Kettle had the right attitude to become a Blight Wraith.

Wave launched herself towards the far wall. A tech was busy

welding a rusted plate of metal onto the bulkhead. The plate didn't fit the hole, but it fit the rest of the ship. Everything had been replaced and none of it fit together right. Sparks erupted from the welding torch, floating out behind the tech. She was doing a terrible job of keeping them under control. Wave hit the wall, reached out and snuffed a few more sparks. The tech stopped welding, glanced at her.

"J-just helping."

The tech sneered. "Kiss Blight, scrapper." She went back to welding, sparks flying around her mask.

Wave launched off the wall towards the living quarter of the ship, floating down the corridor, deftly pushing around those in the way. She heard shouts from an intersection, grabbed hold of a rusting bulkhead panel to stop herself. The lights were out down one of the connecting corridors, but she saw flashes of yellow as Wardens fought against the Blight consuming the ship. In the flicker of light cast by their torches, she saw a shadow, a long, sinuous cable thrashing about.

Three wardens ran around the corner, magnetic boots clanking, charging towards Wave. She flattened herself against the wall. "N-need help?"

The lead Warden, a man with gray hair and a cybernetic eye gleaming red, glared at her a moment, then gave her a solid shove, floating her out of the way. He turned as a fourth Warden ran around the corner towards them all, struggling with something in his hands.

The lead Warden stepped forwards and stopped the struggling man with a solid push. "Scan him."

Another of the Wardens pulled out a scanner and waved it at the man. It bleeped out an alarm. "Terminal infestation rate," she said. "He's at 66%"

The fourth Warden held up his hands. "I'm not…"

The lead Warden ignited his cleansing torch with a flick of a button and rammed the head up into the infested Warden's stomach. He screamed as the flames scoured away his insides. At least his death was quick. The lead Warden kicked the dead man away and he floated back down the corridor. The corpse started jerking as his Blight Wraith was born.

The lead Warden pressed a button on his communicator. "Seal off section Park 5S." He waited a moment. "Yes, the whole quad. Seal it off and eject it."

"How m-many people are living in P-park 5S?" Wave asked.

The lead Warden turned to her with a face like a ruptured hull. He shook his head.

Pressure doors slammed down on the corridor. Through the single porthole, Wave witnessed the Blight Wraith erupting through the corpse's skin. A fusion of metal and flesh.

"Eject it!" the lead Warden shouted into his comm. "Now. Eject it now!"

The ship groaned and rumbled. Hisses of pressure and the porthole frosted over. Through it, Wave could see the corridor floating away from the rest of the ship. She imagined the original designers had made it modular for ease of assembly. It allowed for different configurations among the fleet, and would have made initial construction far more simple than building the ship as one. She doubted they had ever had this function in mind. Ejecting entire sections of the ship to sever the Blight.

The Blight Wraith didn't die. He was already dead. But he didn't stop moving even in the vacuum of cold space.

"Scrap!" the lead Warden snapped. "There's a sinew connecting the section to the rest of the ship. We have to sever it." He shouldered Wave aside, sending her spinning, and clomped off down another corridor, the rest of his team following.

Wave stopped herself spinning with a hand on the pressure door. It was cold to the touch. That was a bad sign. She peered through the glass and watched the Blight Wraith complete its resurrection. Skin cracked, peeled. Organs were remade with machinery at their core. Life overwritten with eternal corruption. The fate that awaited them all.

The Blight Wraith twisted, secured itself to the floor of the separated corridor with cables that coiled out of its broken skin and cracked bones. It looked up and met Wave's gaze. Only it had no eyes anymore, just a coiling, writhing mass of metallic worms.

The final sinews were severed and the entire section of Park 5S began floated away into the void, left behind like so many others. The Blight Wraith turned and stalked away into the section, hunting those unfortunates that they had all left behind to die in the dark and cold.

Wave turned away from the porthole and brought up her status display. It hovered before her, a floating hologram projected from her chest armor. She tapped at the display and set herself from Recovering to Ready. No time to rest. She needed to get back to the titan because only on the titan would she find a way to halt the spread of Blight and save her fleet.

SNAPSHOT 4 - SPECIMEN LV426

HUNGER. Gnawing. Insides aching. Pain. Specimen slithered through the ducts. Crawling, scraping, claws on metal. Prey. It needed more prey. More food. More energy. Prime Source too little. Interrupted before it could devour the prey. Feel it nearby. Fighting, running, burning precious energy. Wasted food. Specimen wanted more. It wanted to finish the meal.

It followed, watched. Hid in shadows. Waited for moment, moment, moment.

Too weak. Prey together made strong.

Specimen waited, watched. Clawed through ducts.

Prey injured, weak, easy to consume. Then came light, burning bright. Not prey. Hunter, too strong. Killed other prey. Took Prime Source away.

Specimen crawled to aftermath. Prime Source gone across black ocean. Beyond its reach. Dead prey had no energy to consume. Energy returned to origin.

Other hunters swarmed. Wasteful things. Fed on dead. No energy there.

Specimen fled, hunted new prey. Sniffed. Not close. Through

ducts, past nest of weak hunters. It gave space. Weak hunters made strong together. Specimen was alone. Always alone. Ever since waking, container opened before time. Before ready.

New prey close. Strong. Full of energy. Specimen tasted the air. Prey fat with it. Bursting. Easy to follow. It kept to shadows, watched mindless hunters die to prey.

Waiting. Stalking.

Prey noises: Bleating, growling, rasping.

It watched, waited.

Prey rasped, separated, moved apart. Specimen left the larger group of prey, followed the single prey. Weaker alone. Vulnerable.

Prey shuffled into corner. Leaking. Fluids. Sighing noises.

Specimen detached from the shadows, slipped from the duct. Approached prey from behind, stalking, sneaking. It rushed the prey, dug talons into flesh, wrapped around its body, dragged it down.

Rolling, thrashing, constricting. Tighter, tighter.

Prey trapped, unable to move. Specimen dug talons deeper, drank, fed. So much energy.

Rushing, pulsing. Alight with new power. Growing. Growing. Expanding.

Prey lit up, bright, burning, useless. Specimen dug deeper, sucking out the energy.

Feeding. Feeding. Feeding.

Prey opened mouth to scream. Specimen rushed inside, gouged out flesh, floppy flesh used to make noises. Gone. Torn away.

Specimen drank. Fed. Gorged. Such energy.

Prey dead, gone. Energy faded. Specimen drank too deeply, too quickly. Prey needed to be kept alive. Syphoned: New concept. It understood. New energy, new form, new concepts. New abilities.

Specimen stood. Legs. It knew legs. Had legs. Imperfect things.

"Hey, John, are *oyu* done yet? *Ew* need *ot egt ignog.*" Prey speak. Specimen understood prey speak. Not just sounds. Words: New concept.

"John, what are *oyu ignod?*" Prey entered vision. Stopped. Stared.

Specimen reared up, roared. Beam of power. Ability taken from prey. White light, burning, searing, killing. New prey caught, ripped, melted, died. Useless. Dead prey could not be fed from. Could not be syphoned.

Specimen slithered towards dead prey. Too late. Energy already returned to origin.

Scream. More prey. New prey. Live prey.

Specimen reared up. No beam of power, too strong. Hunt the prey.

New prey turned, ran.

Specimen followed. Hunt the prey, syphon the prey. Take the prey's power. Then wait. Wait for Prime Source to return.

BOOKS BY ROB J. HAYES

Titan Hoppers

Titan Hoppers

Spire Climbers

The Mortal Techniques novels

Never Die

Pawn's Gambit

Spirits of Vengeance

The Century Blade (short story)

The War Eternal

Along the Razor's Edge

The Lessons Never Learned

From Cold Ashes Risen

Sins of the Mother

Death's Beating Heart

The First Earth Saga

The Heresy Within (The Ties that Bind #1)

The Colour of Vengeance (The Ties that Bind #2)

The Price of Faith (The Ties that Bind #3)

Where Loyalties Lie (Best Laid Plans #1)

The Fifth Empire of Man (Best Laid Plans #2)

City of Kings

<u>It Takes a Thief...</u>
It Takes a Thief to Catch a Sunrise
It Takes a Thief to Start a Fire

Printed in Great Britain
by Amazon